LAST OF THE
ANNAMESE

LAST OF THE
ANNAMESE

A NOVEL BY TOM GLENN

NAVAL INSTITUTE PRESS
ANNAPOLIS, MARYLAND

This book has been brought to publication with the generous assistance of Marguerite and Gerry Lenfest.

Naval Institute Press
291 Wood Road
Annapolis, MD 21402

Library of Congress Cataloging-in-Publication Data is available.
ISBN: 978-1-68247-093-0 (hardcover)
ISBN: 978-1-68247-094-7 (eBook)

♾ Print editions meet the requirements of ANSI/NISO z39.48-1992 (Permanence of Paper).
Printed in the United States of America.

25 24 23 22 21 20 19 18 17   9 8 7 6 5 4 3 2 1
First printing

This book is dedicated to those who suffered through Vietnam,
were jeered and spat upon when they returned to the world,
and have yet to be thanked for their service.
May our country awaken,
recognize your sacrifice,
and honor you.

CONTENTS

THE BURNING CHILD   1

THE BUDDY   3

NO WAR BUT THIS   65

HEAVEN WEEPS   109

THE TOMB AND TET   143

THE HIGHLANDS   171

GALAXY   207

COMMUNICATIONS DECEPTION   253

OPERATION FREQUENT WIND   287

Author's Note   317

Glossary of Acronyms and Slang   319

The Burning Child

DA NANG, 1967

When Chuck and Ike, still in their jungle utilities, had finished distributing Christmas gifts to the orphans, they turned to their guide. She was a young Vietnamese, barely more than a child herself, in the floor-length gray-violet smock of a laywoman caregiver. She led them across the orphanage courtyard, shaded from the midday sun by ancient banyan trees. They entered a shoulder-width passage between the gray stone walls of what had been adjacent villas during the days of the French domination. At the rear of the walled compound, the young woman in gray stopped at a doorway and pulled aside a worn muslin curtain. Chuck and Ike went in.

The air was putrid. The only light came from a small window in the wall opposite the door. A dozen children lay on the dirt floor, some covered with rags.

"We have only these few still in infirmary," the guide said. "As children improve, we move them to Cité Paul-Marie in Saigon. Too crowded here."

One little boy was sobbing, his voice rising to a screech, then fading to a moan.

"What's wrong with him?" Chuck whispered.

"He got phosphorus in his skin." The woman uncovered the boy. Chuck flinched at the stench of his body. A wisp of smoke curled from the boy's upper arm.

"That the phosphorus," the woman said. "It still burning in his skin. Mother Monique say they try to cut it out. No can do. He dying now."

"Surely any surgeon—"

"We have no doctor."

"*Jesus . . .*"

Eyes locked on the child, Chuck backed away, whirled, and made for the door. He dashed to his jeep parked outside the courtyard, dragging Ike behind him. With a spray of dust from the spinning wheels they were gone. Less than an hour later they were back. The jeep skidded to a stop by the gate. Mother Monique and their guide met them.

"I've brought a doctor." Chuck hooked his thumb toward a third officer in the jeep.

Monique turned and trudged through the gate, hands in her billowing skirt.

Chuck pushed past the lay caregiver. "What the hell's the matter with her?"

"No, you wait," the caregiver called after him.

He sprinted into the compound and burst into the infirmary, Ike and the doctor behind him, and ran to the child. A tattered sheet was over the child's face. Chuck yanked it off. Traces of smoke scattered. The child lay twisted, not moving. Not breathing.

"I try to tell you," the young woman cried behind him. "Mother Monique, she is getting ready to bury him. You leave now. Okay?"

The doctor knelt by the child, felt his neck, and pulled the sheet over his face.

Chuck swallowed hard, pivoted, nearly lost his balance, and stumbled out of the infirmary. In the narrow passage he leaned his forehead against the stone wall. Tears forced themselves from his shut eyelids, ran down his face, and dripped from his chin.

"Let's go, Chuck." Ike rested a hand on his shoulder.

Chuck mopped his face with both hands. Ike led him to the jeep. The doctor followed. They headed into the city streets, not speaking.

The Buddy

SAIGON, NOVEMBER 1974

CHAPTER 1

The Chinese maid had dry-cleaned and pressed Chuck's tuxedo, starched his formal dress shirt, and buffed his patent leather shoes. All he had to do was bathe and dress. One housemate, Sparky, was going early to help with the setup. The other, Ike, was invited to the Ambassador's pre-ball cocktail party at the Caravelle Hotel, probably because he was a member of the Marine contingent at the embassy. Maybe the Ambassador, a southern gentleman, hadn't personally reviewed the guest list or hadn't remembered Ike was black. Whatever. Chuck would go alone to the palace.

Given the formality of the gathering he went by military cab, a sedan. It turned through the gate into the Gia Long Palace's curving drive, drove past the Vietnamese and American Marine guards and white-uniformed police—Americans privately referred to them as "white mice"—and deposited him at the foot of the steps that led through the neoclassic portico. He marched past more guards into the entrance hall, but as he approached the staircase leading down into the ballroom he balked.

A forbidden memory skittered past his line of defense. Those miniature bulbs, thousands of them, in the chandeliers, the wall sconces, even the brass floor lamps, sparkled against the beige marble. Ben had loved little lights like those. "See how the snow reflects them?" he'd said at six. Chuck's chest hurt.

"Happy birthday," a voice said behind him—Ike looking out of place in Marine officer's Evening Dress blues, his captain's bars polished to a mirror shine, his black skin shining as if wet.

"Happy birthday." Chuck tried to shake off Ben's memory. *Act normal. Get the cynicism working.* In the ballroom below, white-uniformed

5

Army officers, Marines in blue, tuxedoed civilians—all retired military or foreign service officers—and gowned women glided through light diffused by the polished marble.

"Happy birthday, gen'men." Colonel Thanh came from the entrance toward them. His grin looked sincere, even merry, despite the disfiguring scars that licked up from his neck like flames and pushed one eye out of place. Thanh in dress blues—the effect was eerie.

"Mister Griffin, Captain Saunders." Thanh shook their hands. "Mister Griffin, you do good work at Cité Paul-Marie. The sisters, they tell me. I thank you very much. And now, you forgive me, I don't stay long. I explain to Colonel Mac the war don't wait for nothing, not even Marine Birthday, I must go to JGS, you understand?" He patted their hands and hurried down the stairs into the marbled elegance.

"Doesn't look like the Tiger of Phat Hoa tonight, does he?" Ike said under his breath.

Chuck shook his head and let his eyes roam over the crowd in the ballroom. "Who's the oldest Marine?" Chuck said.

"Colonel Macintosh."

"The youngest?"

"Sure as hell ain't me."

Chuck checked his watch. "What time's the cake cutting?"

"We set it for 2100 so's we could clear out by curfew."

They fell in step as they followed Thanh down the stairs. The sound of voices and music echoed as if in a cathedral.

Chuck hung back while Ike paid his respects to Colonel Macintosh and Thanh worked the room, greeting all with his rapturous grin. He and Macintosh conferred briefly, then Thanh marched to a side alcove obscured by a folding screen and disappeared. A moment later he emerged and hurried up the stairs.

Chuck forced himself to mingle. As he spoke with Colonel Macintosh, he knew he was coming across as edgy. His smile was false, his manner distracted. He greeted his boss, Army colonel Troiano, as etiquette demanded, and moved away to be alone long enough for his defenses to kick in. When the orchestra took a break, he retreated to the bar in an arched niche that looked like a baroque church's side-chapel and dawdled over a gin and tonic. He was tired to his core. Maybe the alcohol would brace him.

Ike was beside him. "Get your fuckin' act together. You ain't shell-shocked." He nodded at the bartender, "Schlitz," and glared at Chuck. "You're actin' like Colonel Macintosh smells bad."

"Get bent."

Ike huffed. "What brought this on? Snap out of it."

"Go fuck yourself."

"It's Ben, isn't it? Jesus, Chuck, it's been seven years." Ike slapped the bar. "Do what you have to do. Whatever it takes."

Chuck tightened his jaw. Ike was right. "I'll go sit with Molly. Where is she?"

"At a table by the orchestra."

Chuck headed into the ballroom. He spotted Molly Hansen's blond mop under a tiara. "Okay if I join you?"

"Why? Am I coming apart?" She gathered her full skirt to make room for him. "How's it hangin', Chuckie?"

"You look great all dolled up." He tried to smile.

She nibbled chocolate between sips of champagne. "Black is flatter-ing to the full-figured woman."

"Ike likes your figure."

"Hush. Nurse Molly doesn't fraternize in public." She tossed down the rest of her drink. "Like Ike says, 'Th'Ambassador don't 'prove of no mixed-race shack jobs.' I wouldn't have even been invited if they weren't short of women." She snagged two champagnes from a pass-ing waiter. "Shouldn't have worn the tiara. Adds to my Dragon Lady image. And my height. That's why I stick with Ike. He's the only man in Saigon bigger than me." She fluttered her lashes. "'Cept you, of course."

The orchestra struck up the Emperor Waltz. Sherry's favorite. She'd smiled up at him during that waltz at more Marine balls than he could count.

"What?" Molly said.

Chuck shook his head. He didn't even know where Sherry was. She'd moved to California after Ben's death. He'd meant to keep in touch.

Molly rested a hand on his arm. "Having a rough time of it tonight, huh?"

He tightened his chest muscles and sucked in his belly. Everywhere he looked he saw the miniature lights. All he could hear was the waltz. He made himself sit straight. He willed his body to relax.

A waiter handed him a note. He opened it and read, "Would you care to join us?" The waiter nodded toward the alcove Thanh had stopped in before he left.

"Who's that from?" Molly said.

"Thanh's people, I guess."

He pulled in air until his lungs could hold no more, then let his breath seep away. "Protocol is protocol. Catch you later." Skirting the dance floor, he headed for the alcove. Behind the screen, seated at a table, were two Vietnamese women. Both looked very young, but he knew better. Vietnamese women looked like girls or grandmothers— nothing in between. One was chunky, in a full-length orange sheath. The other made his heart thump.

Her dress of white silk left her shoulders bare, and her blue-black hair, threaded with rhinestones, was pulled back from her face. Diamonds at each ear and around her neck caught the light. Her prominent cheekbones pushed up the outer corners of her eyes, creating the look of a pixie that belied her straight-backed dignity.

"Good evening, Mister Griffin," she said in careful English. "I am honored that you joined us. Please to sit."

"It is I who am honored, Miss—"

"Tuyet."

"Twet."

Her laugh sparkled. "No, you must say it up, as if a question."

"Twet?"

"That is quite good. The tone is right and the pronunciation, it will follow. My name, Tuyet, it means 'snow.' You are Charles Griffin?"

"I go by Chuck."

"Chuck?" She laughed again. "Your name means 'certain' in Vietnamese. You are at the Intelligence Branch of the Defense Attaché Office, the DAO. You know my uncle, Pham Ngoc Thanh."

Chuck didn't recognize the name.

"He knows all DAO people," she said. "He knows your Colonel Mac."

"Macintosh? He's not at DAO. He's here TAD."

Her brows wrinkled.

"Temporary additional duty," he said. "Just visiting."

"Ya, I know. Thanh met him when they trained together in the States."

"Is your uncle military?"

"Marine co-lo-nel—no, you say 'kernal,' no? I speak French before English so sometimes I get mixed up."

"The only colonel I know is Thanh."

"No, no, pronounce it right. Not 'Tahn.' Say 'dying,' and squeeze it all together and put T at the beginning."

"Ty-ing?"

"Very good."

"He pronounces it 'Tahn,'" Chuck said.

"He is from Hue. His family, they are peasant people." Her smile faltered. "He married my mother's sister. My family is Nguyen, same as Bao Dai, the emperor of Vietnam."

Chuck blanked.

"You know who he is," she said. "The Communists, they forced him to abdicate." She nodded toward the thickset woman. "This is my sister, Lan. You forgive her. She speaks no English." She turned. "*Ông này là Ông Go-rì-phân.*"

Lan grinned until her cheeks crinkled. "*Mist-tah Go-rì-phân.*"

"You are in Vietnam before," Tuyet said.

"In 1967. I was a Marine officer then. Posted to Da Nang."

"Thanh told me. Why you came back?"

The question startled him. It was not something he talked about.

"I apologize," she said. "I am impolite."

He gave her an embarrassed smile and shrugged.

"Thanh wants to invite you to the midday meal one day," she said. "He says you do good work at DAO and at the orphanage, Cité Paul-Marie. You will come?"

Chuck lowered his eyes.

She put her hand on his. "Please say you will come."

Lan touched Tuyet's shoulder, glanced toward the ballroom, and murmured. Tuyet withdrew her hand, but the sense of her touch lingered.

Diplomatic courtesy demanded that he accept. "Of course," he said. "I'm honored by the invitation."

Her smile caressed him. Over her shoulder he saw Ike coming around the screen.

"Pardon the interruption, ma'am," Ike said. "Chuck, it's time to cut the cake."

Chuck got to his feet. "If you'll excuse me—" The orchestra sounded a fanfare. "I'll bring you cake."

Chuck trailed after Ike to the center of the ballroom. Ike joined the active duty officers at the front, but Chuck stood at the rear with Sparky and the other retired Marines as Order Number 47, proclaiming the Marine Corps Birthday, to be celebrated 10 November 1974, was read. Next came the commandant's message. Finally, the commanding officer, Ike's boss, who oversaw the contingent of embassy guards—the only Marines left in-country—cut the cake with his ceremonial sword. He presented the first piece to Colonel Macintosh, who gave the second to a black corporal, the youngest Marine present, along with some words of guidance Chuck couldn't hear. The orchestra played the Marine Corps Hymn, and pieces of cake were offered to active and retired Marines. Chuck took three pieces and headed for Tuyet's alcove. He passed the screen and stopped short.

The table was deserted.

Chuck woke early. No need for an alarm. By 0600 he was bathed and dressed. He sat at the teak dining room table ignoring the geckos slithering across the walls and ceiling. The coffee he poured from the carafe was so strong it tasted like gravel, the only kind Chi Nam knew how to brew. Across from him Sparky, reddish-blond hair unkempt as usual, squinted into the most recent *Stars and Stripes*, flown in from Japan and only four days old. The pocket-sized portable radio Sparky carried everywhere lay on the table. He'd tuned it to American Radio Service—ARS—now reduced to a single broadcast station in Saigon. It was playing John Denver's "Annie's Song."

Neither Sparky nor Chuck was expected at the office; Marines, active duty and retired, were supposed to use the Veterans Day holiday to recover from the birthday celebration. But Sparky had major rumblings in I Corps to keep track of, hangover or no hangover, and Chuck had drunk little. The military taxi had left Ike and Molly at the Cercle Hippique for the post-ball bash and returned Chuck to the villa before the midnight curfew. Years ago, he'd caroused with the best of them. Sherry'd always nursed him through the hangover. "Only once a year," she had said.

He put down his cup. *Do all memories have to hurt?* He'd go to the office, bury himself in captured documents, after-action reports, signals intelligence data. He'd post unit movements on the maps, sort facts for the daily briefing, draft the weekly summary. Most important, he'd let his consciousness rove over patterns and trends and the flow of events until he knew what was going to happen next. Then he'd write his estimate. His skill as a forecaster made him Troiano's most cherished asset. He'd rather be in the field fighting the war, but his body was too old now, and with last year's cease-fire the American troops were gone. Still, his mind was intact, and intelligence had been his specialty. He'd do everything he could to win this war.

He had to win it. For Ben's sake. If he won the war, Ben hadn't died in vain. And yet . . . Ben would still be dead. *How much of it was my doing?*

Ben had been Chuck's reason for living, the man-child who gave immortality to the father. He was Chuck's little Tuffy, blessed with Chuck's Nordic good looks, destined to surpass his father in manhood. When Ben was six, the family celebrated Christmas in the Vermont village of Bascomb at a bed-and-breakfast famous for its Christmas fare. Tiny white lights sparkled everywhere throughout the Victorian house, but what enchanted Ben was the array of hundreds of lights wound through the snow-lined limbs of the leafless weeping cherry tree by the front door. Ben stood before the tree, gazing up, his mouth open.

"Come on, Tuffy," Chuck had said. "It's getting dark. And icy."

Ben stood fast, eyes moving from light to light.

Chuck took him by the shoulder. "They're just little electric bulbs."

"See how the snow reflects them?" Ben asked.

That year, Chuck took Ben hunting for the first time. The next spring he taught Ben to swim. As Ben grew, Chuck coached him in how to defend himself in a fistfight, bought him a bicycle, and helped him learn to ride it. From the time Ben was thirteen, father and son were regulars at the gym, spotting for each other, hoisting barbells and dumbbells until the sweat poured, then racing home on bikes. At sixteen Ben was already an inch taller than his six-foot-two father. At seventeen he could do more pushups and sit-ups than Chuck. But unlike Chuck, who excelled at football, Ben liked basketball. So they played together evenings and weekends. As a senior Ben was the leading scorer on his high school team.

Chuck showed Ben how to knot a tie, taught him to shave, and explained the facts of life. He trained Ben in the proper manners a young woman deserved from a gentleman—seating her at table, opening doors for her, even walking on the curb side of the sidewalk. And if Ben's school grades were no better than Chuck's had been, they were good enough to get him into college. Maybe even into the Naval Academy. Chuck researched whom he could approach to nominate Ben.

Whether it was the Academy or someplace else, there was no question that Ben, like his father and grandfather, would go to college and join the Marines, become an officer. Maybe he'd be the first Griffin

Marine general. Chuck kept Ben's hair in a burr cut, never more than an inch long across the top. He prepared Ben to take "jarhead," "gyrene," "leatherneck," "devil dog," and "snuff" as compliments. "Semper Fi" became their common motto for honor and pride. The Corps was the sacred society that awaited Ben in manhood. Marines called it "the Crotch," Chuck told Ben, but the term was affectionate as well as earthy. The eagle, globe, and anchor, in faux burnished copper, hung over Ben's bed.

Then Anita came along. Ben and she were lab partners in junior-year chemistry. They dated, went together to the prom. Chuck found himself lifting weights and dribbling the basketball alone because Ben was out with Anita. After the senior ball, Ben, still in his tuxedo, told Chuck and Sherry that he had proposed to Anita and she had accepted. He'd decided not to go to college. "But you'll be drafted," Sherry cried. No, he explained, he'd avoid that by enlisting. He'd join the Army, get out after four years, and get a job. Not the Marine Corps. He'd had enough of that.

At first, Chuck was stunned into silence. His eyes moistened and his hands trembled. "Give up everything we've trained for?" His rage spiked. "Throw your life way?" He lunged for Ben, but Sherry screamed, leapt between them. Chuck threw her aside. Heaving, he glared at Ben. *"You make me ashamed!"*

Ben paled, then set his jaw and his face reddened. Without a word he stomped from the room.

At his graduation a week later Ben refused to shake Chuck's hand. The next day he disappeared. Three days later an envelope addressed in Ben's hand arrived for Chuck. It held copies of Ben's enlistment papers. He was a private in the U.S. Army.

Chuck and Ben exchanged no letters during Ben's basic and advanced infantry training at Fort Ord. Sherry forwarded to Chuck, now deployed to Da Nang, Ben's occasional notes. The first one told him Ben and Anita had married and shared a one-day honeymoon before Ben was inducted. The following February 1967, Ben's letters showed an APO return address—he was in Bien Hoa.

The official notification of Ben's death came in late May. Back in the States on compassionate leave for the funeral, Chuck dug into the official files until he found out what had happened. Ben had burned to death in a gasoline fire set off by enemy fire. Chuck slowly taught himself how to numb his feelings. He never told Sherry the cause of their son's death, but the loss still leached the spirit out of her. The separation was gentle. She insisted it wasn't Chuck's fault. She packed and left without a word. For days, Chuck rattled around the empty house. More than once he checked before going to bed to be sure the door to Ben's bedroom was open so he could hear him if he called out during the night.

Sparky swallowed the last bit of bacon and slid a toothpick into one corner of his mouth. "You ready to hit the road?"

"You go on," Chuck said. "I need to work on the Thanksgiving guest list."

Sparky got to his feet. "Okay. See you at the salt mine." He trudged toward the side door to the driveway. Within seconds he was back. "Oops. Forgot my lunch." He snatched the paper bag from the table and was gone.

"Breakfast, sir?" Chi Nam stood in the kitchen doorway, a long white apron over her *áo dài*.

"Not today," Chuck said.

Food, like sex and the company of human beings, had lost its charm. His weight was going down again. He was backsliding. He'd work harder, practice numbing himself, keep an eye out for downturns.

After he retired, VA counselors reassured him that he was suffering from depression, which they termed an injury, like a wound or broken bone. "You'll never get over Ben's death or forget it, but you need to come to terms with it." He had to *want* to confront his grieving. Keep busy, they said. Take up weightlifting again. Find a regular job. Do volunteer work. Go back to school and get a graduate degree. He'd done all that. He'd scraped by. Word went out that they were looking for civilian professionals to man the Intelligence Branch of the Defense Attaché Office in Saigon, which replaced the military following the cease-fire in 1973. Chuck applied, and here he was. In spite of his chronic weariness, he drove himself. He was in the office six, sometimes seven days a week and worked out each day at the Cercle Sportif. Every Thursday, and often other days, too, he helped with the orphans at Cité Paul-Marie. The only time he was free from his own troubles was when he was with the misshapen, urine-scented toddlers whose need eclipsed his.

Before him was the blank paper on which he, as the senior member of the household, was supposed to be writing the Thanksgiving guest list. Because he and his housemates had been in-country long enough to earn billeting in a villa rented by the U.S. government plus unrestricted use of a jeep—two of the benefits used to entice qualified civilians to sign up for hazardous duty—they had to host holiday meals. Macintosh would still be in town, so Ike would invite him as well as the skipper of the embassy Marines. That meant Thanh, Macintosh's Vietnamese Marine counterpart, would have to be invited. Was it insensitive to Vietnamese custom to invite Thanh's wife? He'd ask Macintosh. Should the two nieces be invited? He pictured Tuyet. The touch of a woman. No. The time to slake that need was past. He would be alone from here on out. Then why didn't his body and his soul accept that? *Enough.*

Maybe he should include the British and Australian attachés. Molly would be here. So would Sparky's friends. Chi Nam knew how to cook a turkey American style. She'd proven that last year. He'd get the bird from the commissary, and Sparky would buy the booze at the PX. Champagne? He'd ask Ike to check with protocol at the embassy.

Was Ike here or at Molly's? Oanh, the Chinese maid, always left the bedroom doors open after she cleaned, but Ike's was shut tight. Yeah, they'd probably crashed here at four in the morning. Maybe by tonight they'd be sober enough to help him with the list, but he couldn't wait much longer. The invitations had to go out this week.

With the bag lunch Chi Nam had packed him in one hand and his car keys in the other, he went out to the shaded driveway. The jeep was gone. Sparky had taken it. Oanh, in her usual shiny black peasant pajamas, trotted from the servants' quarters in the rear. She swung open the gate to the street and slammed it after him. He flagged a tiny blue-and-white Renault taxi to carry him out of the city proper to Tan Son Nhat.

The cab headed north on Cong Ly, the main drag out of the city, then angled off onto Cach Mang. Above the confusion of one- and two-story shanties lining the street, overhead electrical wires ran through banyans and palms choking in the exhaust-filled air. Women in conical hats, men in ragged shorts, and endless children wearing next to nothing mobbed the roadsides, indifferent to the blur of traffic inches away. Above, discolored by the dirty air, orange-and-white propaganda banners swayed over the chaos.

He heard the sirens before he saw the blood. The cab skidded to an angled stop behind a jumble of bicycles and cyclos halted by white-uniformed police. Other cars and taxis shuddered to a standstill until the street was a maze of seething vehicles. Just ahead, the shell of a burning sedan belched black smoke. Two bodies in South Vietnamese army uniforms lay on the pavement. A third, still in flames, sat at the wheel of the destroyed car. The stench of burning flesh overrode the smell of flaming gasoline. High-pitched cries of the policemen ordered people away. The crowd struggled to turn their taxis and pedicabs and bikes, but the backup barred their way.

Chuck eased from the cab into the tangle and spoke to the closest policeman. "Viet Cong," the policeman said. "VC. Use grenade, you know? You go, you go." He pointed to the cab.

The traffic snarl wouldn't be moving anytime soon. Chuck paid the cabbie and set out on foot. As he edged through the traffic labyrinth he glanced up at the orange banner stretched across the intersection. Rising hot air distorted the Vietnamese words written in the Western alphabet with zany diacritical marks, dots, little question marks, and tildes over and under the letters. Chuck studied the indecipherable collection of symbols. He didn't know what the words said, only that they were propaganda urging the populace to support the Republic of Vietnam and defeat the Communists.

Just before reaching the gate into the military side of Tan Son Nhat, where the DAO was situated, he passed the Republic of Vietnam Armed Forces Joint General Staff—the JGS. The only building in the compound he'd ever been inside was Thanh's humble office toward the back, a decaying single-story villa left over from the French colonial era, more unkempt now than elegant. The generals probably gave it to Thanh as a reward for his savage victory at Phat Hoa in 1972. As a colonel, he didn't rate much grandeur in those flag-rank surroundings. Besides, the Vietnamese military hierarchy did not hold him in high esteem. The generals kept him there as an "advisor" with no real duties. Perhaps they didn't trust him? Maybe it was his rustic background, or maybe he was too much of a grunt for the aristocratic senior officers. Chuck sensed it was something else. Despite his self-effacing manner and giggling good humor, Thanh didn't suffer fools. He had a habit of telling the truth as he saw it. That was why his bosses kept him invisible when the American brass were around.

At the Tan Son Nhat U.S. military compound Chuck flashed his base pass to the Vietnamese guard and trotted up the road to the DAO enclosure. At the gate he showed his picture ID to the Marine guard and walked across the parking lot to the mammoth vanilla DAO building, the so-called Pentagon East. Sparky had parked the house jeep in the assigned spot by the tennis courts. The crowded parking lot and the lively foot traffic in the long corridors inside made it clear no one but the Marines was observing the holiday. Chuck poked the requisite six-digit code on the cipher lock keypad and entered the Intelligence Branch. He walked past the comms center, where a dozen invisible guys received and sent messages twenty-four hours a day, then past Troiano's office to the windowless bay everybody called "the tank." Here every wall was covered with sliding map boards, the deck crowded with twenty-odd gray government-issue desks, all dust-free and orderly per orders from Troiano. The regulars, middle-aged intelligence analysts, were at their desks or posting at the maps. Most, like Chuck, were retired military—the cease-fire stipulated that no more than fifty U.S. active duty military personnel could be in-country at any given time. Sparky, toothpick still hanging from his lower lip, was recording reported clashes at wall-sized maps of the provinces in II Corps.

"Since we're not supposed to be here anyway," Chuck said, "I'll be leaving early. I want to go to Cité Paul-Marie, then to the Cercle Sportif for a workout. Okay if I take the jeep?"

Sparky slid the wall board to get to the map behind it. "Going to consult with the midget manglemorphs?"

Chuck frowned.

"The orphans," Sparky said.

"Cut it, Sparky."

"Sorry. You got a strong stomach. Sure. I can snag a blue-and-white."

Chuck reviewed the developments he'd posted yesterday on the III Corps maps. At his desk he rifled through everything that had arrived during the last twelve hours—incoming cables, signals intelligence wrap-ups, translations of prisoner interrogations, aerial photo readouts, and after-action reports. Nothing out of the ordinary. And yet . . .

He turned in his chair to study the maps of I Corps and II Corps in the northern half of the country. Something was up. Big stuff was going on just south of the DMZ, the demilitarized zone that separated North and South Vietnam, and in the highlands along the Laotian and Cambodian borders. North Vietnamese divisions moving in. Infiltration of men and matériel from North Vietnam way up. Some major clashes. He couldn't discern a pattern in the south—III Corps and IV Corps, his area of responsibility—but transcripts of propaganda broadcasts from the North Vietnamese–backed Liberation Radio had taken on a tone of triumphant arrogance. Enemy probes looked aimless, unrelated. But that wasn't how the North Vietnamese operated. He felt the tingle at the base of his spine that had always been the signal to be wary, the mindless uneasiness that had saved his ass so many times in combat.

He studied the map of Phuoc Long, the northernmost province in III Corps. Nothing major there, just oddities. Last week a prisoner stated that he was from the North Vietnamese 3rd Division, newly formed in Phuoc Long. The 7th Division was alleged to be nearby, and villagers reported hearing tanks moving by night, but reconnaissance teams found nothing. Skirmishes around Phuoc Binh, the capital, looked random, too random, as if the North Vietnamese were testing friendly defenses while preparing for a major attack.

Sparky came to Chuck's desk with a yellow teletype sheet. "That incident you got caught in this morning? It was a VC grenade, all right. Probably tossed in an open window from a bicycle or motorized cyclo. The sedan was filled with cans of gasoline. Looks like some mid-rank officers chose the wrong time to filch from the JGS motor pool. Must have scared the hell out of the VC."

Chuck worked until 1500, combing through reports and cables, trying to isolate parameters that might suggest an organized campaign. Nothing stood out. With a grunt, he cleared and locked his desk and filing cabinet and headed to the parking lot.

Chuck rang the bell at the gate set into the whitewashed walls of Cité Paul-Marie, where both the sisters and the orphans were Vietnamese but spoke French. Sœur Annette-Marie, in her bleached wimple and habit, admitted him to the courtyard with her usual greeting, *"Bon jour, bon ami."* As she led him down the walkway toward the center of the compound, a one-legged girl hobbled by on a crutch. The sister spoke sharply to her. The child responded with a raspy, *"Oui, ma Sœur."*

Behind the chapel they entered the children's play yard. Here, in the spot farthest from the street and a possible grenade attack, were more than a dozen children, most Amerasian—fathered by American GIs with Vietnamese women. All had been brought here from the main orphanage in Gia Dinh, northeast of the city, or from Da Nang, where the orphan population was outgrowing the facilities. He could no more judge the children's ages than he could those of the Vietnamese sisters. The Viets were the tiniest people he'd come across, and these kids, like the ones he'd seen in Da Nang seven years ago, had been malnourished to boot. Most were mutilated or crippled, their faces pinched, their limbs twisted. He looked from child to wiry child until his gaze settled on Philippe, the smallest of the boys, dressed in sunsuit and zoris and squatting in the shade of the chapel wall.

Chuck hunkered down and lifted the miniature brown chin. "Hi, Pipsqueak."

Philippe raised his scarred face, lacking one cheekbone, eyes out of alignment, and offered Chuck a disfigured smile. "Hi, Pee-kwee." He reached for Chuck.

Chuck lifted him into the sunshine. "I missed you." He folded Philippe into his arms. Ben was this size when he was a year old, but he weighed more than Philippe, whose arms were barely thicker than Chuck's thumb. The sisters didn't know how old Philippe was. They didn't know his real name. They said nothing about how he came to be in the orphanage.

As usual, a sister carried a folding chair into the yard and opened it for Chuck. Philippe nestled in Chuck's embrace, pressed his head into the curve of Chuck's neck, and grasped Chuck's shirt in a tight fist.

Chuck rocked him. "You all right, Pipsqueak?"

"Pee-kwee?" the boy said in perfect imitation of Chuck's intonation.

"You want me to sing to you today?"

"Seen too yoo?"

"Okay." Chuck started "Froggy Went a' Courtin'" in a quiet, deep voice. He'd read, back when Ben was a baby, that children responded more to the vibrations of the male voice than to the sound, and sure enough, Philippe contoured himself against Chuck's chest. One by one, the other children crouched close to Chuck's feet. He sang three verses and stopped. The wolfish, meager faces watched him.

"Can't you smile?" Chuck asked them.

They went on staring.

"Smile." He opened his eyes wide and used two fingers of one hand to push his own lips into a grin.

The little girl closest to him covered her mouth and giggled. A boy laughed out loud. Soon they were all laughing, even Philippe. A passing sister shushed them but kept going.

"You want another song?" Chuck said.

"Song?" Philippe said, nearly inaudible.

Chuck sang as much as he could remember of "She'll Be Comin' 'round the Mountain." At the end, the children screeched with laughter.

"You should clap," Chuck said with a grin.

"Ka," Philippe said.

"I—" Chuck pointed at himself, then performed a charade of singing. "You—" Holding Philippe in the crook of one arm, he pointed at them and clapped.

Again he pointed at himself, sang a few notes, pointed at them. The girl at his feet clapped three times silently.

"Yes," Chuck said with a big smile. He repeated the pointing and singing. Half the children clapped hesitantly. "Good for you. Again." This time they all clapped.

The singing and clapping went on until the last of the sunlight had moved beyond the courtyard. Chuck told them that was all, and they moaned in unison. He stood and carried the weightless Philippe back to his spot by the chapel wall. "I'll come see you again soon," Chuck said.

"Soon," Philippe repeated.

On his way out, Chuck left the customary twenty in U.S. green in the empty saucer inside the compound gate. Time to work out. He headed to the Cercle Sportif. The autumn air dulled the stink of the city, but most of its population, numbered in the millions, was out and about. Endless waves of bicycles swamped the smoke-clogged streets and slowed the jeep's progress. At every intersection cars, trucks, and motorized cyclos played chicken with the rolling throngs of pedestrians.

If the North Vietnamese took South Vietnam, what would become of the Cité Paul-Marie kids—half-American, French speaking, Catholic? Things were iffy, but Saigon was in no imminent danger. Not as far as he could tell from prisoner interrogations, aerial photography, agent reports, and intercepted messages. Still . . . the North Vietnamese were up to something in the provinces just north of the capital. Nothing he could pin down, but it was enough to make him uneasy. That was fine. He needed to focus on his work to keep his mind off Ben. *There you go again.* He'd let himself remember. He concentrated on the image of Philippe's mutilated face and felt his memories go quiet.

———————

Muscles still quivering from his workout, Chuck stepped into the tepid water of the Cercle Sportif's showers and slipped into his bathing suit for the requisite ten laps in the pool. The tropical sunset was turning the palms into lazy shadow puppets when he dove into the water. The usual Vietnamese aristocrats, mostly women in bikinis, along with a handful of French expats sipped vermouth and Citroën at the tables on the shaded deck or played desultory tennis in adjacent courts. He caught sight of one dark Indian in a turban, almost certainly a merchandiser, but he saw not one American face in the crowd. Voices murmured, saying nothing in every language but English. That's why he came here instead of going to the DAO gym and pool. No need for hail-fellow-well-met bullshit. The regulars here ignored him, except for an occasional curious glance, and he pretended they were invisible.

Breathing more heavily than he liked, he finished the tenth lap, hoisted himself over the edge of the pool, and snatched his waiting towel. Drying himself as he walked, he headed up the stairs, past the covered deck. He'd have to hurry. Chi Nam didn't approve of late diners, although she had to put up with plenty during increasingly common crises.

"Chuck?" A woman's voice.

At a bistro table on the deck were two women, both in bikinis. Chuck narrowed his eyes. Thanh's nieces, Tuyet and Lan. Lan's bathing suit was a sickroom green that emphasized her stocky build and olive skin. Tuyet's was white; it revealed no hint of a tan line on her pale body. Her face, framed in the black of her loosened hair, was an oval narrowing to her chin. Her cheeks were concave, her mouth full. Once again his heart thumped.

"You come have a drink with us?" Tuyet called.

Trapped. Diplomatic etiquette required him to join them. In Saigon, sipping intoxicating refreshments wearing nothing but boxer trunks at a minuscule table with two almost naked women was acceptable, even admirable behavior. He eased into the free chair and finished toweling off. A waiter, in white to his high-throated collar, appeared and planted a stemmed glass on the table. Chuck tasted it. "Martini?" he said in surprise, looking after the waiter.

Tuyet scanned the pool. "Thanh tells me Americans like them. I instructed the waiter on how to make it. It is all right?"

He sipped again. "It's different."

Her smile faded. "You don't like it?" Her face hardened, and she called to the waiter. "*Boy!*"

"It's fine." Chuck waved the waiter away. "What're you two doing here?"

"We like to swim. We come here often."

Lan was smiling at him with more eagerness than he liked. When he glanced at her, she turned her face away. He avoided looking at Tuyet but couldn't ignore her perfectly shaped, all-but-bare breasts. A flicker of desire startled him.

"Is Thanh here?" he asked.

"He flew to Kontum this morning. Much fighting in the highlands."

He started to agree but stopped himself. Best to avoid subjects he held classified information about. "You disappeared from the ball before I could bring you cake."

"It is not proper for women to attend a gathering like that one. Thanh made an exception for the Marine Corps Ball. But we could not remain without a male protector. Thanh left, so we, too, must leave."

"But you come here alone, dressed—" Chuck stopped himself.

Tuyet laughed. "Here we follow modern customs. Ways we learned from the French."

Lan spoke briefly to Tuyet.

"You want to swim?" Tuyet said to Chuck.

The prospect of frolicking in the water with Tuyet in a bikini awoke something deep and carnal within him.

"Lan would like to swim again," Tuyet said. "I can wait for you here."

"Thanks, but—" He tossed down the last of his drink. "I need to be getting home." He got to his feet.

"We, too." Tuyet murmured to Lan. "Thanh does not like us to be out after sunset. Cabs are difficult, and cowboys are about."

"Cowboys? As in the Wild West?"

She blushed. "We borrow your word 'cowboy' to describe hooligans. When we first hear the American word, it makes us laugh. *Cao bôi* in Vietnamese, it means 'erect penis.'"

Chuck stifled a smile. "Maybe I should drive you home?"

"You are most kind." She stood. "We meet you in the front garden when we are dressed."

They left the table. Tuyet moved with fragile grace, but she carried herself straight, with dignity.

Back in his regulation Saigon civilian work clothes—short-sleeve dress shirt and slacks—he waited for them inside the broad pedestrian gate, among the hibiscus and trimmed bougainvillea. The Cercle, like Saigon itself, had seen better days. The ochre pillars at the façade were peeling, and white pockmarks, probably from stray bullets, disfigured the tall yellow compound walls. Everywhere the air was tinged with smoke. But the garden retained its defiant manicured splendor, indifferent to the anarchy of its surroundings.

As he breathed in the scent of frangipani, Tuyet and Lan came down the stairs into the garden. Both carried parasols and wore *áo dài*—long-sleeved surcoats, open in the front and extending to the thighs, over white satin underdresses that covered them from neck to toe.

"My jeep's in the side lot," he said.

He hoped Tuyet would sit next to him during the drive, but both women got into the backseat.

"We are at 108 Tu Xuong," Tuyet said over his shoulder. "I give you directions."

He angled toward the automobile gate. "Thought you lived out by Tan Son Nhat."

The parking lot guard, a Nung by the look of his massive shoulders and grizzled hair, lifted the metal bar and opened the gate.

"We stay right now in the villa of my cousin," Tuyet said. "He is in France on business."

Tu Xuong was a one-way alley barely wide enough for one car. It was lined with majestic villas hidden by high walls topped with barbed wire, spikes, or broken glass.

"Close by here," Tuyet said.

Chuck stopped in front of a gate large enough to drive a car through. Set into the wall was a blue tile with white numbers 108. He hopped from the jeep and helped Tuyet to the street. Lan climbed from the jeep on the other side and rang the bell. Dogs barked inside, a slot in the gate opened, and a pair of dark eyes peered out. Next came the sound of locks, latches, and bolts. The gate creaked open, and a large, middle-aged woman in a brown *áo dài* bowed. Lan chattered to Tuyet.

"Thanh," Tuyet said, "would like to invite you to the midday meal a week from Saturday. You work only half-day Saturday, yes? You come here, not Tan Son Nhat, okay?"

No escape. He had to say yes. "I would be honored."

The women nodded to him and passed through the gate. The servant swung the gate closed. It vibrated like a gong. A metal bolt clanged, two latches slammed into place, and the lock clicked.

Chuck disliked briefing the Ambassador, but it was part of his job. The second Thursday of each month, after the morning briefing at DAO, he rode into town in Troiano's black sedan, waited in the outer office until the Ambassador summoned him, then sat next to the great mahogany desk with charts he had prepared that morning. The Ambassador preferred that Chuck brief him with no one else present. "Reduces the influence of politics," he'd said back in '73 when Troiano first suggested that, as he put it, his best forecaster spend time once a month with the most powerful American in Saigon. The Ambassador rarely said much, and Chuck suspected that he was more annoyed than enlightened by their tête-à-têtes.

So, four days after the Marine Ball, which the Ambassador had declined to attend, Chuck eased himself into the chair at the Ambassador's side and opened his locked briefcase. "Infiltration of men and matériel from North Vietnam has spiked." Chuck spread his charts on the desktop. "And communist activity in all four corps looks more and more like long-term offensive preparations. The classic indicators have yet to appear, but the pattern is clear. Enemy activity in Phuoc Long Province, sixty miles north of us, has yet to congeal into major attacks, but communist units there are on the move."

The Ambassador sipped coffee and gazed out the window.

Chuck went through the specifics that put him on edge—infiltration numbers, the probing and withdrawing, the evidence, yet to be confirmed, that division-sized units were lurking in Phuoc Long.

"In short," the Ambassador interrupted him, "you have nothing concrete."

"It's the pattern, sir, the movements that reflect planning for attacks rather than actual preparations. If I'm correct, offensive precursors will appear shortly."

The Ambassador flipped through papers on his desk. "When they do, come back and see me. Until then—"

"Sir, if the Communists launch a major offensive on the scale of the 1968 Tet offensive or the 1972 Easter offensive, the results would be disastrous. Without U.S. air power and with the congressional cut in aid to the Republic of Vietnam—"

"And what makes you think that the Communists *want* to attack? By signing the Paris peace accords, which they have so far honored for the most part—"

"Forgive me, sir," Chuck interrupted, "but my evidence shows they have not abided by the accords. Infiltration alone, not to mention stepped-up attacks in the last month all over the country—"

The Ambassador gave him a forgiving smile. "Son, I have sources, channels of information of which you know nothing. Until you have facts, leave the estimating to me."

Chuck felt as though he had been slapped. "Yes, sir."

"Good morning." The Ambassador opened a file on his desk. The briefing was over.

All the way back to Tan Son Nhat, Chuck went back over the Ambassador's words. What sources of information could he have? Chuck was cleared for all intelligence relevant to Vietnam. The only thing he was not privy to was diplomatic exchanges. What could possibly show up there that would contradict evidence on the ground?

CHAPTER 2

Just after dawn, Mai, Tuyet's personal servant, slipped from the Tu Xuong villa and flagged down a cyclo to take Tuyet to Cité Paul-Marie. Covering her head with a dark mantilla as she entered the chapel, Tuyet knelt in one of the pews installed for the Americans. The sisters and older orphans filed silently into the open space nearest the altar. As the sun sent horizontal beams through the tracery in the walls, the city roused. First came the hiss of traffic with horn calls and human cries. Next were the exhaust fumes that grayed the sunlight. The priest came to the altar. Tuyet stood, knelt, and followed in her missal as the sisters and orphans mumbled responses in their ghastly French. She came to this church because the Mass was in French, but why must they desecrate it? Their enunciation was almost as bad as that of the Americans, who would not deign to learn a single word of Vietnamese and polluted French with their twangs.

During the Gradual, Epistle, and Gospel, her mind wandered. She forced herself to pray along with the priest during the Offertory. Returning to the pew after Communion, she knew she'd come here to store up holiness before she sinned. She was going to be unfaithful to Thanh, her husband, whom she'd married under canon law. She was going to sleep with a man who had moved her before she ever met Thanh. She had not forgotten him in the seven years since. She didn't want to sin. She didn't want to hurt Thanh more than she already had. But this war required sin. This man, a man of power, could save her son.

The Mass over, she dropped a few piastres in the plate by the gate and rode back to the villa in a creaking, open cyclo. The driver's gnarled legs pumped in the rhythm of a dirge while she remembered sitting at poolside next to Chuck Griffin. She knew his name now. For seven years his gingery smell, the piercing blue eyes, the deep rumble of his voice, so unlike the high pitch of Vietnamese voices, had lingered in her memory. He had leaned against the orphanage wall in Da Nang, tears falling from his chin. His eyes were lined now, as if from too much grieving. He was thinner. His cheeks had sunk. His yellow hair had taken on a sheen of silver. He was more of a man now, a man honed by sorrow.

He hadn't remembered her. She must look very different. She'd been a modest slip of a thing then, barely eighteen, already betrothed to Thanh, whom she'd never met. The birth of Thu less than a year after the marriage had filled out her form and matured her into a woman. Chuck had looked into her face without the slightest trace of recognition. *Peu d'importe.* She'd succeeded in attracting him. The next step would be the midday meal a week from Saturday.

At the villa, she slid from the cyclo. Mai, waiting outside the gate, paid the driver without looking at him, then pushed the gate. It wavered open with a groan.

"Breakfast in the garden," Tuyet said.

"*Oui, Madame.*"

"Is Lan up?"

"Miss Lan is already eat and is dressing herself."

Tuyet froze her face muscles to avoid wincing at Mai's French. After more than twenty-five years, one would think . . . She cut across the circular driveway and past the fountain, climbed the three steps from the courtyard to the double glass doors, now taped in case of a grenade attack, and let herself in. Dropping her mantilla and missal in the vestibule where Mai would find them, she passed through the sitting room to the garden. Here in the cool of the morning, shaded by banyans and bamboo, she would not be interrupted. She settled into a padded wrought-iron chair by the oval pool and pulled off her gloves.

Thanh would, of course, know sooner or later. She'd long since gotten past her surprise at the way he divined things without being told. She made no pretense of understanding him. Maybe suffering under the Viet Minh had made him clairvoyant. Or maybe it was the

years he spent as a monk and what he called his "practices," the meditations he performed every morning and evening. His spirit, his soul, as
the Catholics would say, radiated from his deformed body. That luminescence frightened her. His ugliness repelled her. His courage awed
her. He was a mystery, and she loathed mysteries.

As she knew now, he'd seen her long before she'd seen him and had
loved her from afar. She'd first laid eyes on him—a broad-chested hulk
of a man made hideous by burn scars, one eye pushed higher than the
other—at their betrothal. He'd caught the revulsion in her eyes. She'd
seen the hurt in his.

She folded her gloves and laid them on a spare chair for Mai. The
men in her life had effectively enslaved her as they prepared her for life
as a cultured, submissive mate to a prince. The emperor, Bao Dai, had
insisted that she study in France. Her father had directed her training
in the etiquette of a royal court that no longer existed. She'd married
Thanh because her father commanded it; family ties to a rising star
of the new regime in the south would strengthen what little power
the royal family still had. In that first year, her respect for Thanh had
grown into wonder. Sure that he was a great man, she tried to love him
but couldn't. Unable to master her fear of him, she masked it with
condescension.

He would know, and he'd be hurt. Not so much, though. She'd
inflicted the great wound when she demanded her own bedroom after
Thu's birth. She had done it as gently as she could, but the pain in his
face was unmistakable.

Maybe she could keep the affair from him for a while. The servants
were too frightened of her to say anything, and if Lan found out, Tuyet
could intimidate her into silence. She despised hurting Thanh, but her
future was as gray as the polluted sky over Saigon. A marriage without
love and life in a shabby, undersized villa on the fringes of the airport
at Tan Son Nhat. She tightened her fists. She could endure that life,
just as she'd lived through the fall of the Nguyen dynasty and her flight
from the north, but she couldn't accept imprisonment, torture, and
execution for herself and Thu at the hands of the North Vietnamese.

She'd never have found herself *dans cette galère* if Ho Chi Minh hadn't rallied the Vietnamese or if the French hadn't been so corrupt and inept. She'd have married an aristocrat—another member of the royal family, perhaps one of her cousins—and lived the life she was born to or sought exile on the Riviera, like the emperor himself. Instead, she'd had to accept a dirt farmer as husband for the good of her family. She'd had to learn Vietnamese so that she could speak it with him, then studied English to be a proper helpmate in his dealings with the Americans. Her personal fortune, so ample in the north when the French were still in power, was all but gone. She could no longer afford to dress in keeping with her station or dine on French delicacies at Cercle Nautique, and she was behind in paying dues to the Cercle Hippique. Even her jewels were paste. A trip abroad was out of the question.

She first met Chuck Griffin by chance. Thanh, a senior officer in the Vietnamese Marine Corps, had let it be known that it would please him if his betrothed worked as a volunteer in the orphanage that his counterparts, the American Marines, had adopted. Overcoming her distaste for the filthy, maimed children, she'd obediently enrolled for training as a nurse, then clad herself in the floor-length gray-violet smock of a laywoman caregiver and presented herself to help the sisters and translate for the U.S. Marines at the asylum in the poorer section of Da Nang.

On Christmas Day 1967 a jeep rumbled to a stop outside the courtyard gate. It was driven by a huge black American Marine second lieutenant. Next to him was an equally enormous blond, blue-eyed major. They were bringing gifts for the children. In the infirmary, the last stop of their visit, the major spotted a boy dying of phosphorus burns. He rushed away and came back less than an hour later with a Marine officer who was a doctor. It was too late. The boy had died. The major shuffled out. Tuyet found him outside the infirmary door, face against the wall, crying.

She couldn't fathom how this man, blessed with strength and beauty, a warrior from the most powerful country in the world, could grieve over the death of a nameless peasant boy of no consequence. He saw in these diseased children something she could not. She yearned to know who he was but had no way of finding out. She'd never seen him again until last month, when Lan had pestered her into joining the Cercle Sportif and she saw him swimming laps. A few discreet inquiries, sweetened with piastres, and she learned his name, his job, and when he swam at the Cercle. In a deliberately offhand way, she told Thanh in passing that she'd seen Chuck Griffin at the Cercle. Did Thanh remember him? Thanh had filled in a few details, including that he and Griffin had fought side by side at Tra An. Griffin had retired from the Marine Corps and was now working at the DAO Intelligence Branch. He regularly visited the orphans at Cité Paul-Marie. He'd never mentioned a wife. Hints that Lan, Thanh's niece, was of marriageable age and that an American husband would be ideal were enough to persuade Thanh to arrange for Lan, his deceased sister's child, to be invited to the U.S. Marine Corps Ball with Tuyet as her chaperone.

As she anticipated, Tuyet had attracted Chuck's attention. She'd seen the lust in his eyes at the Cercle. And he was a man moved by children. She would let her son, Thu, captivate him. Thu's striking resemblance to his father would be lost on Chuck, as it was on all Americans, who saw no family resemblances among the Vietnamese. Attracting Chuck to her bed after Thu had charmed him would be easier. Once Chuck was her lover, he'd overcome all obstacles to ensure escape for Thu and her.

Mai materialized with *cà-phê philtre* and croissants. Chuck was a Marine, a man of honor. Tuyet knew he would never allow himself to desire the wife of another Marine. So she had deceived him into believing that she was Thanh's niece and Lan's sister. She and Lan were obviously not related. Lan was stubby and graceless, like Thanh, peasant stock. Tuyet had the fine bones and spare body of the royal Nguyens. Oblivious to the obvious difference between the two women, Chuck had taken her at her word. And he had responded to her. Her pulse quickened as she remembered his eyes on her body at the bistro table.

She shook her head as if waking from a reverie. What was she doing? Could she, a Nguyen princess, stoop to such devious and sinful behavior—to cuckold Thanh and deceive Chuck? It shamed her that her lies to Chuck, first at the ball, then at the Cercle, had been so facile. But Thu's life was in the balance. She must degrade herself, even to the point of risking her immortal soul.

"Good morning, older sister."

Lan had seated herself. Mai brought her tea. Tuyet quelled the doubts fluttering in her belly. Time to put the next part of the plan into action. "Younger sister," Tuyet said in Vietnamese, using the same polite form of direct address Lan had used, "I've been thinking about the midday meal with Mister Griffin a week from Saturday."

Lan blushed.

"You must try to appear more shy and demure," Tuyet continued. "American men, more than others, like to feel powerful and in charge. You must let Mister Griffin make the first move." She sipped her coffee and looked through the foliage. "Even when he expresses himself attracted to you, you must be modest and distant. That will whet his appetite and make you a challenge. Men like that." She patted Lan's arm. "We can practice, to be sure you convey the proper reserve."

Lan turned away and folded her arms.

"You'd do best," Tuyet said, letting her voice cool, "to listen to the advice of a woman older and wiser than you. You know I have only your best interest at heart."

Lan looked close to tears.

"You're a pretty young woman," Tuyet lied, "but you are nearly nineteen with no prospects. Perhaps we should speak to Thanh about betrothal to a suitable Vietnamese officer—"

"Mister Griffin pleases me," Lan said in the voice of a petulant child.

"He's really too old for you."

"Uncle Thanh is much older than you," Lan pointed out.

Tuyet ignored her rudeness, gave her a sweet smile, and took her hand. "And ours was an arranged marriage, probably the best kind in these uncertain days."

"The first time I saw Mister Griffin at the Cercle Sportif," Lan said, "he pleased me very much."

"I suspect you are seduced by his size and fair coloring. You barely know him."

"He displayed excellent manners at the ball and at the Cercle."

Tuyet raised her eyebrows and suppressed a sigh. "Very well. Let us see what we can do, but—"

Alarm crossed Lan's face again.

"But," Tuyet continued, "it would be prudent to proceed slowly. For example, I think it would be advisable for you to join us only briefly at the Saturday midday meal, then retire."

Lan's eyes narrowed but she drank her tea, waiting.

"We shall leave the next move to Mister Griffin. After several weeks if we haven't heard from him, we can arrange an apparently coincidental meeting, perhaps at the pool."

Lan looked as though she were about to object.

"Don't contradict your older sister," Tuyet said, resuming the formal tone. "Leave it in my hands." She finished her coffee.

Thanh would fly home from the north on Thursday. So Wednesday morning Tuyet sent Mai to Tan Son Nhat with a message to have the driver at the Tu Xuong villa that afternoon. When the gate bell rang announcing the car's arrival, all three were ready. After the gardener had secured the dogs, Mai admitted the black 1968 Chevrolet Impala.

Tuyet loathed the ride through the stink of the city, but Lan watched the traffic with excitement. En route they passed under half a dozen orange-and-white banners hung over the streets to reassure the populace that all was going well with the war.

"Don't open the window," Tuyet said sharply as Lan reached for the crank. "Grenades."

Lan sighed.

Thanh's villa, given to him by virtue of his position as the Special Advisor at JGS, left no doubt of his status in the eyes of the Vietnamese government. It had been hastily built only a year ago in the swamps on the outskirts of the official military housing, paid for by the Americans. It had only seven rooms, all on one level—only two of them, hers and Thu's, with glassed-in windows and air conditioning—and the roof leaked during the monsoon. Beyond its high courtyard walls topped with barbed wire lay the cardboard-and-plastic huts of cyclo drivers and laborers scattered through the overgrown marshes.

The car passed through the gate, eased around Thanh's jeep, and stopped at the steps to the porch. Tuyet and Lan proceeded into the sitting room leaving Mai and the driver to manage the bags. In the door to the dining room stood a smiling Chi Hai, Thu's amah.

"Welcome home, Madame."

Thu peeked from behind her. His face was a childlike incarnation of Thanh's without the lines and scars. Tuyet dropped to her knees and spread her arms. He threw himself into her embrace. "My little idol, are you well?"

"Very well, *Maman*."

"Have you obeyed Chi Hai?"

"*Oui, Maman*."

Tuyet held him at arm's length and studied him. "Tonight we'll work on your lessons and I shall read to you from the *Chanson de Roland* and put you to bed myself. Next week, on Saturday, you will come with me to the Tu Xuong villa. We won't need to return until Monday. Does that please you?"

"May I swim in the pool?"

"Of course—but only so long as one of us is with you."

Thu hugged her.

She got to her feet and bent to take both his hands. "You have not greeted your cousin. Impoliteness does not become a member of Nguyen family."

Thu faced Lan, clasped his hands in front of him, and inclined his head, a subtle demonstration of his superior station, just as Tuyet had taught him. "Hello, cousin," he said in northern dialect Vietnamese. "I render to my cousin my apologies."

"No regrets, little one," Lan said.

Tuyet peeled off her gloves. "Chi Hai, tell Chi Ba we will take tea in the sitting room. The master will be home late tomorrow morning. Everything must be ready. We will have a full midday meal and then the master will need to rest undisturbed until late in the day. And now, little hero," she said to Thu, "you can tell me all that has happened since I left."

Thanh, dirty and exhausted, arrived on schedule. Chi Tu and Chi Ba served the midday meal in the dining room. Thanh ate his *pho* without first bathing or changing from his stained uniform. Lan shared the noodle soup with him, but Tuyet and Thu had cutlets and lightly steamed green beans prepared by Mai. Only Tuyet drank the Algerian red wine. After the meal, Chi Hai put Thu to bed for the siesta and the women retired to their rooms to rest.

Tuyet had undressed and switched on the air conditioner when she heard a light tap at the door.

"Madame," Chi Ba's voice said, "Monsieur wishes to speak with you."

Tuyet buttoned her kimono to the throat, so that she was completely covered, and padded barefoot to Thanh's room. It was empty. He must be bathing. She steeled herself and went to the serving room at the rear of the villa. Cooking and eating accouterments had been cleared away, and the wooden tub had been moved to the center of the tile floor. In it, Thanh sat in steaming froth. Suppressing the mix of awe and repugnance he evoked in her, Tuyet averted her eyes and stood waiting for him to speak.

"Pull up a bench and sit," Thanh said.

Tuyet obeyed.

"The American Marine colonel Mac is required to leave the country by mid-December—cease-fire rules. I have invited him for the midday meal Saturday of next week. I'd like you and Thu to be here."

Tuyet shot a quick glance at him and again lowered her eyes. "Forgive me, but I have made other arrangements for that day. Surely you could tell Mac that Vietnamese women do not attend affairs like this one."

"Mac will be our salvation when the end comes," Thanh said. "He can arrange for you and Thu to leave the country."

"Mac will be far away. How will he—"

"The Americans can do anything they choose to do, and Mac is a powerful American."

"How can you be so certain the ending will be disastrous?" Tuyet said. "The Americans—"

"The Americans have abandoned Vietnam."

Tuyet shook her head. Better to have Thanh believe her ignorant. "I don't believe that."

"Nor do most others—publicly. The JGS generals profess that the patriotic forces of the Republic of Vietnam will triumph, but they all have quietly arranged ways to leave the country when the end comes."

"You are too harsh. The Republic's army is strong, its leaders competent. Even the Americans say so."

Thanh scrubbed one shoulder with a large sponge. "Corruption and lies thrive in the stench of defeat. Had our leaders spent less energy on their villas and bank accounts, had they worked to help the people, the ending might have been different. Now it is too late. I travel to prepare my troops to be bold and brave, because I know the ending will be painful. Many, many will die. I do not tell them, as my superiors do, that victory is only months away."

"Do not allow defeatism to destroy us."

Thanh laughed. "You have been reading the banners stretched across the streets of Saigon. 'Be bold and stamp out the vermin Viet Cong.' 'Glory to the Republic.'"

Tuyet took a deep breath. "You know that I have profound respect for you. You know that I have great admiration for your courage and leadership. You know that I have never disobeyed you. I beg you not to put me in a position of displeasing you. Do not require me to be here for the American Marine colonel."

"Tuyet, time is slipping away. Don't waste it in subterfuge. As the monks taught me, so I teach you: adversity is a gift to those who wish to grow. Make the most of it. And prepare yourself. The ending will be brutal." He got to his feet.

Tuyet gazed at his mammoth chest and muscular legs snaked with burn scars. This man was power. She turned away.

"Chi Ba," he called.

The servant hurried forward with towels.

Tuyet retired to her room. Thanh underestimated her. Of course the country would fall. She was not blind to the omens. Of course the generals had made escape plans. Thanh had not. He was going to stay with his troops. He expected her to depend on Colonel Mac to evacuate herself and Thu. Poor Thanh. So ready to believe that the Americans were magicians, able to do whatever they wished with no effort. Mac would not even be in the country. And was he to be more trusted than President Nixon, who had promised that America would rescue Vietnam? Put her fate in the hands of a lying American official who was far away and cared only about avoiding entanglements? She laughed aloud. No, she needed an American here, with American power at his command, yet subject to her. Her only hope was to make Chuck Griffin her lover.

At seven on the appointed Saturday morning, Tuyet, Lan, and Thu departed Tan Son Nhat for Tu Xuong in the Impala. Once inside the villa, Tuyet set to work. She counseled Lan to bathe and dress in her *áo dài* with the Chinese red surcoat. "Reds and oranges are flattering to a woman with an ample body." Lan was to appear when Tuyet signaled, share an aperitif with Griffin, and then withdraw to the dining room for her midday meal of *pho* while Tuyet and Chuck remained alone in the garden. "I shall subtly ascertain the level of Mister Griffin's interest." She instructed Chi Hai to dress Thu in a pure white sunsuit, but only after he'd taken his midday meal, and to have him ready to come to table when Tuyet called. Mai was to serve martinis and a light meal of *bifteck* with béarnaise sauce, peas, and baby potatoes. A small pastry would follow the meal. Last of all, she checked the gardener's work and gathered flowers for her bedside tables.

By midmorning she was alone in the master bedroom. Mai had made the bed with sheets of moonlight blue. Fresh flowers stood in vases on both tables. Tuyet turned back the bed and checked the bathroom. She flipped on the water heater so that a hot shower would not be delayed and switched on the air conditioner. There was nothing she could do about the geckos. Americans despised them. Would they distract him? Not likely. He'd been too long in Vietnam.

Lastly she gave full attention to herself. She removed her wedding ring and opened her wardrobe. The white silk underdress with a pale blue surcoat and blue star sapphire earrings, yes. But not the sapphire pendant. Better to be simple and pure. After showering in lukewarm water she applied a hint of Parisian lilac perfume and pinned her hair so that it would tumble to her shoulders when she slid the combs free. Before the mirror at the vanity she applied makeup, only the lightest touches so he would not see it. She laid out a bathing suit, a modest one-piece style in midnight blue. From the armoire she retrieved a pair of men's trunks and held them out before her. Probably the right size. She carried them to the second bedroom and placed them on the bed where he could find them easily.

She didn't expect Chuck until 1300, but by noon everything was ready. She'd inspected the house and each person (she ordered Chi Hai to change from the black pajamas to an *áo dài*). Now each of them waited upstairs for the command to appear.

Just before 1300 the bell sounded and she heard a taxi pulling away. The gardener secured the dogs and swung the gate open as Tuyet watched from behind the glass doors. Chuck, carrying a bottle of wine, paused inside the walls and admired the fountain. Her heart raced. In her machinations she had forgotten his looks—tall and blond, with a face etched by sorrow. Tuyet counted slowly to five, then swept open the doors and moved across the tiles and down the steps to the gravel. He handed her the wine.

"Chateauneuf-du-Pape!" she cried. "Where did you buy it?"

"At the American PX. They get French wine sometimes."

"We cannot get it here. We must drink Australian or Algerian. A formidable gift. Thank you." She held the wine behind her. "Forgive me. I forget my manners." She bowed from the waist. "I am honored that you are here." Leading him through the sitting room and into the garden, she gestured toward chairs at the table, and they sat. *"Nous sommes prêtes,"* she said without raising her voice. Silence. "Mai . . ."

"*Oui, Madame,*" a voice said from close to the house.

"What did you say?" Chuck asked.

"I called the servant. She is Mai Xuan. It is the name the empress gave her when she entered the royal service. It means 'tomorrow is spring.' She is my personal servant, not part of the serving staff."

Mai came from the shadows, took the wine, and stood waiting.

Chuck looked toward the house. "Thanh will join us later?"

"Please to accept Thanh's apology. He is detained. Your Colonel Mac is visiting him today."

"Captain Saunders told me. I thought perhaps the gathering was here."

She shook her head. "At Tan Son Nhat."

"So it will just be the two of us?" Chuck said.

"And Lan. And someone I want you to meet. We start with cocktails."

Mai bowed and moved away.

"A secluded garden in the middle of the prettiest part of Saigon," Chuck said. "Everything shaded and cool. The birds singing in the trees."

"Many trees here. The birds love this place."

"Your cousin is a very lucky man."

She smiled. "And the little pool is for swimming in the heat of the day."

Mai came forward with a tray. She placed two stemmed cocktail glasses before them and set a vase of white chrysanthemums in the middle of the table.

"Martinis," Tuyet said. "I shall try one, too." She watched him sip, lifted her glass to her lips. Immediately her throat burned—as she expected. She set the glass down and coughed.

"You all right?" he asked, half standing.

She cleared her throat. "I do not drink alcohol. You pardon me?" She slid her glass in front of him. "For you."

"No pardon needed," he said. "But you drink wine—"

"Wine is not the same. They tell me you do not have frangipani plants in the States. Or do you say CONUS?"

"For 'Continental United States.'"

"No frangipani in France either. You like it?" She tilted her head toward the tree beside the pool. As he turned to look, she gestured, without taking her eyes from Chuck, to Mai, who stood in the shade by the door.

Chuck sipped. "The scent—I've always associated it with Vietnam."

Lan came into the garden and waited by the table, eyes downcast. Chuck stood.

"Please to remain seated," Tuyet said.

Lan and Chuck both sat.

"Very good so far," Tuyet said to Lan in Vietnamese. "He is interested. Continue to maintain your modest attitude."

Mai brought tea for Lan, who was smiling dreamily at Chuck. Tuyet cleared her throat. Lan lowered her eyes.

"Miss Lan, do you go to school?" Chuck said.

Tuyet translated, Lan answered.

"She says," Tuyet said, "that she finished school in Da Nang before we moved to Saigon."

"When was that?"

"Last year, when her uncle was transferred to JGS."

"You mean Thanh?"

"Yes. She is Thanh's sister's daughter. The Viet Cong kill her family."

Chuck cocked his head. "Her family?"

"Our family," she said quickly. "We eat now." She nodded to Mai. Lan mumbled something and stood.

"Lan will take the midday meal indoors," Tuyet said. "Unmarried Vietnamese girls are careful to avoid the sun. It darkens the skin. You would be so kind as to excuse her?"

Chuck stood. "Of course."

With a bow, Lan went into the house. As Chuck started on the second martini, Mai emerged with the food on salad-sized dishes, diminutive flatware, and napkins, and carried away the empty martini glass and teacup. Tuyet picked up her fork. Chuck followed suit.

"You said unmarried girls," Chuck said. "Does that mean you are married?"

Merde. She must be more careful with her words. "I mean to say young girls, you know?"

"And Lan is not your sister?"

"In Vietnam we say 'sister.' It is a form of address. Lan is my cousin. Thanh married my mother's sister. We will have the wine."

Mai came forward with two glasses and the bottle wrapped in white linen. She poured and withdrew.

"I have not had Chateauneuf-du-Pape since my student days in Paris," Tuyet said.

Chuck tasted. "So Thanh's family is from Hue. What about yours?'

"We are from the north, Nam Dinh. The French allowed the royal family to continue nominal rule. The Communists, though, they kill us. My father brought us south in 1953." She brushed her napkin over her lips. "We lived for a long time in Da Nang."

"I was posted there. That's where I met Thanh and Ike Saunders—he's with the Marine guards at the embassy now. He was a mustang second lieutenant. We helped out at the orphanage Thanh told us about."

Mai removed their dishes and put down three miniature forks and fresh napkins and small plates with pastry.

"Lan is joining us for dessert?" Chuck said.

"No. I want you to meet someone."

The door opened and Thu ran to the table, followed by Chi Hai.

"My son, Thu," Tuyet said. "And this is Chi Hai, his amah."

Chuck blinked, stood. "How do you do, Mister Thu?"

The child frowned at Tuyet, who translated, then answered, *"Très bien, merci."*

"Can you say 'fine'?" Chuck said to Thu, bending toward him. Tuyet translated. Thu observed Chuck gravely.

"Come on, you can do it," Chuck said.

"Phánh?" Thu said imitating Chuck's intonation exactly.

Chuck laughed. "Very good."

Tuyet took Thu's hand and told him that the gentleman was Mr. Griffin, a friend of his father's.

Thu smiled for the first time. *"Bon jour Monsieur Griffin."*

"Can he call me Chuck?"

Thu giggled.

"What's funny?" Chuck said.

"Your name," Tuyet answered. "I tell you before. In Vietnamese your name means 'certain.'"

On impulse, without thinking, Chuck reached out to the child, tousled his hair. Thu drew back.

"Don't be afraid." Chuck knelt so that his head was lower than Thu's. "Can I be your buddy?"

Thu glanced at Tuyet. She translated.

"No," Chuck said. "Tell him to say 'buddy.'"

"Bo-dì," Thu said.

Chuck grinned and shook Thu's hand. "Very good. You're my buddy. I'm your buddy."

Thu laughed and grasped Chuck's hand with both of his. *"Bo-dì."*

Tuyet smiled. This was going very well. "Please to sit and enjoy the sweet." She gave the barest of nods to Chi Hai, who bowed and went into the house. Tuyet, Thu, and Chuck sat at the table and ate in silence.

"So Vietnamese names all mean something." Chuck said. "What does the amah's name mean?"

"'Chi' means 'miss.' Chi Hai is 'Miss Number Two.' Servants know their place. They do not expect their masters to remember their names. At the Tan Son Nhat villa we also have Chi Ba and Chi Tu— Miss Number Three and Miss Number Four."

"So many servants."

She waved his words away. "In Vietnam, the number of one's servants defines one's status. They also benefit. We provide them food and a place to live."

Thu chattered and giggled.

"Thu is your son?" Chuck asked.

Tuyet nodded.

Chuck faltered. "Forgive me for asking. Are you married?"

"I am estranged."

"Divorced?"

"In Vietnam we do not divorce."

Chuck straightened in surprise.

"I am Catholic," Tuyet explained.

"Not Buddhist? Thanh—"

"He is Buddhist but also worships the ancient Vietnamese deities, like the Mother Goddess and the Holy Fool. In Vietnam, religion is *syncrétique*—you say syncretic? All symbols of divinity and virtue are accepted. As I explained before, Thanh is my uncle by marriage."

Thu scraped the last morsel of pastry from his plate and wiped his mouth with his napkin. "Can I swim now?" he asked Tuyet.

"Not unless an adult goes into the water with you. Would you like Chuck to swim with you?"

"*Oui!*" Thu looked at Chuck.

"Thu wishes to know if you would go into the pool with him," Tuyet said to Chuck. "He is not allowed to go in alone."

"I don't have trunks."

"Perhaps I could lend you," Tuyet said. "Thu can show you where to change." Thu bounced from the chair and waited.

Chuck laughed and stood. "Sure. Lead on, Tuffy."

Thu ran ahead of him, glancing over his shoulder. Tuyet sat until they were out of sight then hurried after them. Inside, she waited at the foot of the stairs until she heard two doors close before proceeding to the master bedroom on the second floor. She put on her bathing suit, careful to tie the neck strap in a bow so that a single tug would loosen it. By the time she returned to the garden with towels, Chuck and Thu were swatting water at one another from the middle of the pool. She sat on the edge and dangled her feet.

Chuck lifted Thu from the water and held him high, then lowered him with a splash. Thu exploded with laughter. Chuck did it again and waited, looking intently at Thu.

"You want me to do it again?" he said to Thu.

Tuyet translated.

"Let him say it," Chuck said. "Again."

Thu bit his lip. Tuyet told him to repeat Chuck's word.

"*À ghên,*" Thu said.

Chuck catapulted Thu into the air, caught him, and brought him down with a smack to the surface of the water. Thu squealed with laughter.

"*À ghên!*"

This time Chuck let Thu fall into the water. Thu bobbed to the surface wide-eyed.

"Again?" Chuck said.

Thu took a deep breath. "*À ghên.*"

Within a few minutes Chuck was tossing Thu into the air repeatedly and catching him just before he hit the water, and Thu couldn't stop giggling.

"*Cela suffit,*" Tuyet said.

"*Ah, Maman*—" Thu began, but a raised eyebrow from Tuyet was enough to make him climb from the pool. When she had dried him thoroughly, she told him to go to Chi Hai, who was waiting by the door. Chuck swung himself over the side of the pool and accepted the towel she offered. His body was spare and solid, but now she'd glimpsed something beyond his flesh—he was a man of gentleness.

He yanked up his trunks. They were too large. Tuyet silently scolded herself.

He spread the towel on his chair and sat. "Thu's a charmer."

She sat close to him. "What you call him? Tough-something?"

"Tuffy. Sorry. A pet name in my family. I used to call—" He closed his eyes.

"Forgive me if I am rude. You have children?"

Chuck folded and refolded the towel. "I had a son once."

So that was the sadness that darkened his aura. "I apologize." She bowed her head.

He brushed the towel across his face. "It's okay. It's the martinis. I shouldn't have . . ."

She put her hand on his arm. "I am very sorry, Chuck."

He mopped his face. "I should go."

"No, please," she said, then caught herself. "Have another martini."

He attempted a laugh and dabbed at his eyes. "No more martinis."

"Coffee, then."

"I need to get home."

"Very well, but you will need to shower."

"I'll just get dressed."

"It is unhealthy." Surely he knew that the only water to be trusted in Saigon was that which had been filtered or boiled.

He hesitated. "Okay, if it's not too much trouble."

"Of course not. Come."

She led him to the master bedroom. "The bathroom, it is here." She went ahead of him to the shower stall and turned on the water. "Already hot."

"My clothes," he said.

"The servants will bring them."

He scratched his shoulder and gave her a weak smile.

"Is something wrong?" she said.

He shrugged. "Waiting for you to leave, that's all."

"No need."

He rocked from foot to foot as if deciding what to do, then, holding up his loose trunks with one hand, he reached past her, adjusted the water temperature, and stepped under the hot jets. She followed him into the shower stall. He opened his mouth in surprise.

"What is it?" she asked.

"Well, you know, it's not proper—"

"You are silly. We Vietnamese are not shy like you Americans," she lied. "It costs too much to heat the water. We cannot waste it. Wash."

They washed in silence.

"I wash your back," she said.

"I don't—"

She turned him around and began to scrub. "You Americans are so funny. There. My turn."

She handed him the soap, pivoted, untied her neck strap, and let the bodice fall. As if sleeking back her wet hair, she lifted the comb, and her tresses fell about her shoulders. For a long moment she felt nothing. At last his hands tentatively spread soap on her shoulders and slowly worked down her spine. She quivered and held her breath.

"Rinse," he said, his voice ragged.

She faced him, put her arms around his neck, and kissed him. He stood inert. She pushed closer and kissed him again, flipping her tongue across his lips. His arms went around her. Eyes closed, she inhaled his breath and moved her hands to his hips to push down his trunks. They had already fallen and lay tangled around his ankles.

CHAPTER 3

Thanh completed his morning meditation before sunrise and went to the dining room in the bathrobe Mac had given him at the luncheon Saturday. Mac acted as though the gift were a joke, recalling the time at Camp Pendleton when Thanh had dressed completely before going to the dining room for his morning tea in the bachelor officer quarters suite he shared with Mac; he had nothing to wear but his uniform. The robe was a man's kimono, forest green silk with a honey-colored border that Mac had bought in Japan. Thanh knew Tuyet would appreciate its quality.

He sat at the head of the table. The sun was about to breach the horizon; the glow of the sky reflected through the high glass-free windows latticed against grenades. Chi Ba, in her black pajamas, scurried across the tiled floor with his tea.

"Is the mistress up yet?" Thanh said.

"Yes, sir. The mistress and young master did not return last night."

The servants' habit of showing respect by responding to all questions in the affirmative before giving the factual answer saddened him. He had tried to break them of it. One more thing to be resigned to.

Tuyet was still at her cousin's villa on Tu Xuong. Her way of escaping him. Early in the marriage her royalty had intimidated him. He was of the lowest peasant class and could not keep her in the style to which she was born. His only income was his paltry military salary. He would not stoop, as other officers did, to bribes, the black market, or siphoning his men's pay, and he had no living family he could turn to for cash. But now his humble origins no longer mattered. He'd long since given up on kindling love in Tuyet. Their marriage, maintained only for appearances, was over.

And yet, he was disappointed that she was not here. Her mere presence warmed him. Her body, barely half the size of his, was blessed with a tiny waist and breasts like plump star apples. Her eyes reminded him of the holy sprites in old scrolls, but she moved with the grace of a swan. And her haughtiness, in one so petite, amused him. Granted, her pretense of superiority diminished her, but that was youthful foolishness. After all, she was only twenty-four. She was far too bright to continue clinging to the ways of a spoiled princess from a royal house effectively dethroned a century ago, a family long since co-opted by the French. He prayed to the Mother Goddess that Tuyet would mature before the coming debacle tested her mettle.

He'd accepted that the marriage was dead, but he hadn't counted on the gradual alienation of Thu. The war left Thanh little time to spend with his son. He'd planned an outing at the zoo on Sunday, but Tuyet had taken Thu to Tu Xuong. To prevent him access to Thu? Tuyet was raising Thu to be a pampered young prince rather than a man of strength. Nearly six years old, Thu treated both Thanh and Lan with the genteel disdain he'd learned from Tuyet. Must Thanh be resigned to losing his son, too?

He'd lost so much. As a youth, he'd presented himself as a novice at the Thanh Loi Pagoda in Hue, where he learned to read, studied ancient texts, and became a teacher for the laity. During his twelve years as a monk, celibacy chastened him and meditation freed his soul. All of that ended when the pagoda was gutted during a battle between the French and the Viet Minh. The Communists captured and tortured him, murdered his family. They aroused in him a savagery he'd not known he possessed. To fight them, he joined the fiercest branch of the South Vietnamese military, the Marines. Commissioned on the battlefield for his heroism, he rose quickly through the ranks, but the flag-rank officers' distaste for his peasant ways prevented him from earning a general's star. In 1966 the Americans mistakenly targeted his position. The napalm nearly killed him and left him scarred and grotesque. Now his failed marriage and his inability to instill integrity in his superiors had bled away his fervor. As the future darkened, he devoted himself to preparing his men for the end and to finding a way for Thu and Tuyet to flee the country. He had lost them, yes, but he could still save their lives.

The luncheon with Mac had been a failure. The JGS sent along Major Nghiem, assigned to Mac ostensibly for protocol, and Thanh could not speak openly. What Mac did not see was that Nghiem was Mac's keeper, instructed to ensure that he heard only what the JGS wanted him to hear, saw only what it wanted him to see. Thanh had been gracious and talked over old times with Mac, reminiscing about their training together in the States. Neither Mac nor Nghiem saw Thanh's desperation.

Unable to sit any longer, he left his tea on the table and went to his room to dress. A warrior first and a bureaucrat second, he swung himself into his jeep and drove to JGS in his utilities, the combat uniform. The preferred attire was the more elegant class A uniform. The flag-rank officers also didn't approve of Thanh driving himself, and they frowned at his central Vietnam accent. General Tri had once told him, in a rare moment of candor, to carry himself like a gentleman rather than a muck farmer. Thanh allowed himself a bitter chuckle. General Tri was like the nobleman in the ancient myth who didn't care how much he lost at gambling as long as he did it with grace; he ended up the most graceful of the kingdom's beggars.

Corporal Vien opened the gate for him. When Thanh had parked in the unpaved courtyard and plodded past the dusty palms to the porch, Vien was waiting to hold the door open.

"Bring me the translations of all last week's DAO Intelligence Branch daily briefings," Thanh said.

"Does the Colonel wish the J2 JGS briefings as well, sir?" Vien said.

"Only the American ones." Thanh stopped himself before expressing his contempt for the official JGS documents. "And open the shutters. Too dark in here."

Vien laid the documents on the corner of Thanh's desk and went outside to swing open the shutters. Thanh lit the tea stove. At his desk, he flipped open the folder. Across the top of the first page beneath the Tôi Mât—Top Secret—classification was emblazoned "DAO." Ironic. Thanh harrumphed. The Americans were oblivious to the meaning of Ðao in Vietnamese, a term the Buddhists used to mean the right way, the path of virtuous conduct.

The report was dated last Wednesday. More recent ones had yet to be translated; or, more likely, the JGS front office simply hadn't sent them to him. The pattern he'd watched since the beginning of the month was becoming more pronounced—unit movements, testing probes, rumors that North Vietnamese units of division size were slipping across the border. They were planning an offensive. He was sure of that now.

"Vien, fetch me the last Minh report."

Thanh poured the heated water into the teapot. The agent codenamed Minh had disappeared. The Viet Cong had almost certainly unmasked him. Probably compromised by sloppy security practices. The generals were too arrogant to follow rules made by low-ranking security specialists. Time after time, some flag rank blabbed on the telephone and a source vanished. They never learned. Thanh opened the folder.

The rereading brought nothing new to light. Minh reported that the North Vietnamese Politburo had decided in October that the time was ripe to launch a full-scale invasion of the south in the coming year, 1975. The signal event had been the U.S. Congress' decision in August 1974 to cut off most of the aid for the South Vietnamese military. Despite the solemn promise from President Nixon, deposed last summer, that the Americans would intervene if North Vietnam attacked, the Americans' actions told a different story. Now only time stood between the corrupt southern regime and its destruction at the hands of the ruthless North.

Thanh slapped the file shut. "Vien."

"Yes, sir."

"Find out when General Tri will be returning to II Corps. If he is to be here today, get an appointment for me."

The Saigon-bound generals might play deaf to the American intelligence reports, but Tri's forces were up against the North Vietnamese divisions in the highlands. Any military man wanted to know everything he could about the enemy he was facing.

Vien was back. "General Tri will be in Saigon until tomorrow. The only time he has open is fifteen minutes at 0830 hours."

Less than half an hour from now. A gentleman's way of saying he didn't want to see a petitioner of a lower rank and different service.

Thanh stood. "Tell his staff I will be there."

General Tri's office was on the bottom floor of one of the new two-story buildings built by the Americans. Square and flat, they looked like the offspring of the gargantuan DAO building across the barrier to the left, the same vanilla color, the same steel-and-vinyl construction.

Vien pulled the jeep up at the foot of the broad steps, and Thanh jumped to the pavement. "Be back in twenty minutes." He headed up the stairs. In Tri's outer office, six officers dressed in class A uniform sat in chairs along the wall. An army colonel Thanh's height but half his girth stood at parade rest behind the aide-de-camp's desk. He was gazing up at the three-dimensional relief map of the highlands, lit by a floodlight from below, that was more decoration than tool.

"Liem?" Thanh said. "The General brought his G2 to Saigon with him?"

The colonel turned. "Thanh! We wanted to see if the Americans can confirm reports we've been receiving. We spent Sunday with Colonel Troiano."

"Did he verify—"

"And how are your lovely wife and fine son?" Liem interrupted smoothly.

The aide rose from his desk. "Gentlemen, the general will see you."

Liem followed Thanh through the door to the inner office. The others trailed silently behind in rank order. Cigarette smoke blurred the furnishings in the room, but Thanh could make out a carpet that once might have been maroon. Cushioned wicker chairs arranged in a semicircle faced the large window. Behind a polished desk with his back to the window was General Tri. He went on reading, his lips forming the characteristic sardonic Tri smile.

Thanh locked his throat. His eyes smarted from the smoke, which now was forming into rolling balls. Tri made a single sound. Liem answered him with the customary honorific glottal stop and all sat. Immediately, an adjutant served tea.

On the rug in front of the general's desk, a cigarette lay burning. Three more, now dead, were nearby. Tri flicked the Bastos he had been smoking into the air without looking up, lit another. He raised his eyes. "Thanh."

Thanh stood, looking down respectfully.

"Saigon is no safer than Dragon Mountain," Tri said, eyes half closed, the same smile on his lips. "A fortnight ago, three officers assigned to this office were killed three kilometers from here. VC, probably on a bicycle, dropped a grenade into the window of their sedan."

"Sir, word has been sent out to all in the capital region to keep windows closed, especially on sedans. The VC—"

"My men were carrying cans of gasoline to my villa. The fumes probably overcame their better judgment."

Thanh said nothing. He'd heard the reports of gasoline disappearing from the motor pool. The black market was well supplied, and no one mentioned it to the Americans.

"You wished to see me?" Tri said.

"I am honored the General took the time from his schedule to talk to me. Reports from the Americans have caused me great concern, sir. Several North Vietnamese divisions have moved down the Ho Chi Minh Trail in Laos and crossed the border into Kontum and Pleiku. The II Corps forces have captured three soldiers who, under interrogation, have said they are from North Vietnamese units—"

"Liars," Tri interrupted. "My men have been working with them. Two have admitted they are members of the local guerrilla forces. The third will come around."

"General, the battle at Plei Mlang on 3 November showed the presence of more than one enemy division—"

"Thanh, you must not believe the first reports from the field. They are always subject to grievous error. We now know we encountered regional forces at Plei Mlang."

"Sir, the casualties—"

"Greatly exaggerated. The result of panicky low-level personnel reporting half-truths and fears rather than facts. The data have been corrected."

Thanh knew better. More than thirty of his own Marines had been lost. On his trip to the north he'd spoken with the survivors. "Early last week, American aerial reconnaissance spotted large troop movements and trucks west of the Chu Pao Pass."

Tri scowled. Liem moved quickly to the large map on the wall and pointed. Tri walked to the map and studied it.

"In short, sir," Thanh said, "every indication suggests an offensive of the size not seen since Tet of 1968. We have radio intercepts and agent reports—"

"A disinformation campaign," Tri snapped. "Communications deception and propaganda disseminated by the communist Politburo. Designed to undermine our morale. Only a fool would give credence to such gibberish." Tri walked to his desk. "Or a traitor."

The room reverberated from the silent gasp. Tri resumed his seat. The interview was over.

"Forgive my boldness, sir," Thanh said as the others stood, "but why would the Communists wish to spread such rumors? Would they not fear the return of the Americans?"

"The Americans will never return." Tri picked up the paper on his desk and began to read. "They have no more stomach for protracted war than the French."

The other officers were heading toward the door. Liem tugged Thanh's sleeve.

Tri raised his head. "Thanh, I will be going on leave after the Tet new year celebration to see about my French Riviera property in

Saint-Tropez. Perhaps you would care to accompany me and look into something for yourself?"

Liem followed the others from the office.

"My funds," Thanh said, "would not permit it, sir. Besides, my troops—"

"Perhaps I can assist you." Tri returned to his reading. "We will speak further of it the next time I'm in Saigon."

Thanh stood at attention and saluted. "Very good, sir."

He executed an about-face and marched from the room in quick-step. First a threat, then a bribe. Tri wanted to silence him.

It was well past dark when Thanh pulled the jeep into the courtyard of his villa and parked by the newly trimmed bamboo. From the dining room came the bubbling laughter of women. The sound vanished when he entered. Chi Ba and Chi Hai, kneeling on the floor beside the table, bowed deeply. Mai, standing by the barred windows, hands folded, inclined her head. At the table, Tuyet, Thu, and Lan lowered their eyes respectfully. They were just finishing the last course—mango and papaya for Lan, pastries for Tuyet and Thu.

Thanh tried a smile. "Please continue. Chi Ba, *pho* for me." He sat at the place awaiting him at the head of the table. Tuyet, Lan, and Thu resumed eating in silence. Thanh understood. Formality and the pretense of respect insulated Tuyet. Thu imitated her. Even Lan's affection for him had chilled in the ambience of ritual deference Tuyet had enforced since Thu's birth. Chi Ba served him and knelt, her bare feet soundless.

"Son," Thanh said. His voice shattered the quiet. Tuyet flinched. "What did you do today?"

Thu raised his eyes. "*Dans la matinée*—"

"In Vietnamese," Thanh said.

"Yes, sir. This morning, *Maman* sent me—"

"Vietnamese, son." Thanh swallowed his irritation.

"Yes, sir. Mother sent me home from Tu Xuong in a cyclo with Chi Hai. *Maman* and Cousin Lan went to the Cercle Sportif, then came home in the Impala."

"Did you swim in the pool at Tu Xuong?"

Thu brightened. "Yes, sir. I had an especially good time on Saturday with—"

"With the lovely weather," Tuyet interrupted. "Perhaps we should try to get to Nha Trang while it is still cool, perhaps next month?"

Thanh cocked his head. "You know it is no longer safe to drive outside the city."

Tuyet paused as if considering. "Yes, of course . . . we could go by plane."

"The prices, Tuyet—"

"Your plane."

"It is not my plane. It belongs to the government."

"Other officers—"

"You know I never do that," Thanh said. "What made you suggest it?"

Tuyet shook her head briefly and returned to her pastry.

"And you, Lan," Thanh said with a smile, "did you meet any charming young men at the Cercle?"

He awaited her blush and giggle, but instead she sat glaring at her plate.

Thanh patted her hand. "Forgive my joking."

Lan said nothing.

"Have I offended you?" Thanh said.

"Please, Thanh," Tuyet said, "Lan is not at her best."

Thanh understood the phrase, words Tuyet always used to tell him discreetly that a woman was menstruating. He turned again to Thu. "I must travel for a week or so, but afterward, I would enjoy taking you to the zoo."

"Thank you, sir." Thu said it with the courtly condescension he used when he did not wish to be impolite.

"You don't want to go to the zoo?" Thanh said.

"*Maman* took me last month."

"There is much to see there. One visit isn't enough."

Thu finished his pastry. It was clear he didn't want to go. Had he seen it all; or was he, too, avoiding Thanh?

How different this family was from the boisterous flock he'd grown up with. His parents, grandmother, and three siblings assumed that what was worth saying was worth shouting. No feeling, however faint, went unexpressed. He remembered lying on his pallet next to his brothers and sister and grandmother in their one-room hut listening in the dark to his parents' groans of passion. When food was scarce, especially during the war against the French, when drought and flood took turns oppressing them, when work started before dawn and ended after dark, his father and mother turned to each other for the only pleasure in their lives.

"Will the master take fruit for dessert?" Chi Ba was at his shoulder.

"Only coffee, thank you, Chi Ba."

"Time for your bath," Tuyet said to Thu. "Then I'll read you to sleep."

The women and Thu asked permission to leave the table. Chi Hai and Mai followed them from the room. Chi Ba placed a cup before Thanh, put the metal filter with ground coffee over the cup, poured boiling water, and moved away without a sound. Even her black pajamas didn't rustle. So Vietnamese. His people understood the ecstasy of silence. Little wonder the VC were so good at eluding the Americans.

Chi Tu locked and bolted the front gate, switched off all but the security lights, latched all the doors and shutters, and followed the other servants to the bungalow in the rear of the house with the key to the back door in her hand. Thanh lay awake. His meditation hadn't gone well. He tried in vain to immerse himself in the exquisite quiet imposed by the curfew, but his own breathing, the whisper of his movements, and the beating of his heart polluted the stillness. Worse was his brain swarming with thoughts he could not lull into the stupor of sleep. He rose, covered his nakedness with the robe Mac had given him, and left his room. Feeling his way with bare feet through the hall, he found by touch the deadbolt key in the lacquer box on the credenza and opened the front door. In the reflected glow from the security lights atop the walls, he walked past his parked jeep and the dark of the bamboo grove and found the ceramic seat in the side garden. He searched the sky, remembering tales his grandmother had told him as they lay on the path near their hut peering into the heavens. The star of Princess Thuy, who lived in the kingdom by the sea, hung low in the southern sky. She sacrificed her life to save Prince Nguyen, son of the king of the forest realm, so that evil could be defeated and the harmony beloved of Heaven could be restored. And when Prince Nguyen wept over Thuy's death, the Mother Goddess said to him,

> *What is there in your life, little swallow,*
> *That tears should ever darken those eyes?*

What indeed? Thanh was homesick for his village, long since destroyed in the war, and his family, all dead now. He'd tried to entertain Thu by reciting Thuy's tale, but Thu, already enchanted with Roland and Charlemagne and confused by the archaic Vietnamese, endured Thanh's poetry with barely concealed boredom. Vietnamese, after all, was not Thu's first language, and he spoke it, albeit imperfectly, in his mother's aristocratic northern dialect. More than once he had come close to correcting Thanh's pronunciation.

Thu needed to learn, to accept, and to celebrate his roots, as Thanh had when the old monks taught him the true history of his country. The northern dialect, which Tuyet insisted on with such rigor, was a corruption of the original language, tainted by its proximity to the hated Cantonese. The true dialect, the original one, came from native speakers in the central and southern parts of the country, driven there by the Chinese incursions over the millennia. He, Thanh, born in the central heartland, came from the ancient stock, the people who called their country An Nam, "peace in the south," centuries before the

Chinese slur Viet Nam, "troublemakers in the south," was forced upon them. Tuyet's legacy to Thu was the blood of the Nguyen dynasty, corrupted by the French. Thanh's legacy was the bedrock of the country.

And yet . . . Thanh sucked in the night air. None of it was Thu's fault. He was the spawn of a mismatch. Thanh never should have married a princess, but he had initiated the betrothal because links with the aristocracy would enhance his standing within the military hierarchy. Not that it mattered. He had loved Tuyet from the moment he glimpsed her in her father's garden in Da Nang the day he visited to pay his respects to the elder dignitary. A dutiful daughter, she had accepted his proposal without ever seeing him. She was a passionate woman, as he had discovered to his joy, yet she always reserved a part of herself. She had never loved him, but at least in the beginning she honored him. Even now, along with the rigid decorum she demanded, he sensed her involuntary awe for him as the ascetic turned warrior.

He could force her—she was in his power—but a submissive, frightened Tuyet would be a hollow victory. He wanted her as she was, and all the power of heaven and earth could not make her want him. Easier to alter the seasons than to change a woman's heart.

In the old days he could have returned her to her father's house and declared her an unfit wife. He would never have done that. She was too lovely and too sensuous. Someday she would take a lover. If they survived the war. He would know when it happened. Or maybe he would not allow himself to know. Or maybe he would be dead by then. He prayed that the man who took her would be a man of sinew and subtlety who cherished silence and knew that gentleness was as manly as strength.

When the North Vietnamese conquered the south, Thanh would be tortured for information and then executed. Tuyet didn't yet realize that Mac was her salvation—without his help, she and Thu, as members of the royal family, were doomed. Thanh would see to it that, with Mac's help, they escaped before the collapse. It was his responsibility, conferred on him by the same Heaven that gave him one happy year with her in the beginning.

The last, feeble hope of avoiding defeat lay with the Americans. Perhaps they didn't realize what was about to happen. Maybe, like the Vietnamese, they believed their own propaganda rather than their intelligence. If only he could talk to Mac, make him understand, make him see that catastrophe was at the gates. But protocol would never permit them to be alone.

Protocol *would* allow Thanh to fraternize unattended with some of Mac's associates, but the only two U.S. Marine officers left in-country were at the embassy. The commander was all spit-and-polish, good at his job but without nuance. His subordinate, Captain Isaac Saunders, the one they called Ike, was not a man of great subtlety. Could he be trusted to serve as a go-between without tipping his hand to the JGS generals? Thanh looked to the skies, to the Mother Goddess, and found no answer.

The next morning, bleary from lack of sleep, Thanh sat in his JGS office and read after-action reports. More of the same. Small victories and small defeats in the highlands and south of the DMZ. What were the North Vietnamese up to? They baited traps, struck unsuspecting units, and withdrew. They were biding their time. Farther south, in Phuoc Long Province, north of Saigon, more reports of sightings of large formations, more hamlets and villages slipping into the grasp of the VC. This was new. Were the North Vietnamese going to engage in large-scale battles close to Saigon and do nothing in the north? How and when would the enemy reveal himself?

Vien at the door interrupted his speculations. "Sir, General Tri has departed for Pleiku."

"Thank you, Corporal."

Tri had left Saigon. The general was a stranger to wisdom; he was corrupt and self-serving. But he was no fool; he got what he had come for, some real intelligence from the Americans. He might not be able to look into the future as Thanh did, but he could not help seeing the present. And he was preparing his property in Saint-Tropez.

Vien again. "Sir, this just arrived by courier from DAO." He handed Thanh a large, square manila envelope.

Thanh opened it. A formal handwritten invitation: "The honor of the presence of Colonel Pham Ngoc Thanh, Marine Corps, RVNAF, and family is requested for Thanksgiving dinner, Thursday, 28 November 1974, fourteen hundred hours. 475 Yen Do, Saigon. RSVP." It was signed Charles E. Griffin, Intelligence Branch, DAO.

Odd. Why would Griffin be inviting him to dinner? "And family"? Griffin knew better. Vietnamese officials never attended functions with their families. Thanh had made an exception for the U.S. Marine Ball, but only because Tuyet had pestered him, insisting that Lan needed to meet American men. The women had remained out of sight in a nook by the dance floor where they could see but not be seen. How Lan was supposed to be introduced to American men under those circumstances was lost on Thanh, but he'd given Tuyet her way, as usual.

He turned the invitation over, looked inside the envelope for something further, read it again. Griffin kept to himself. Thanh had seen him only a half-dozen times in the last year, and then only on business. Yet each time they met, the bond between them was as strong as ever. Thanh remembered. March 1967.

The joint task force made up of American and Vietnamese Marines struck the enemy by helicopter at Tra An, west of Da Nang, just before sunrise. Griffin's chopper was hit, and Thanh, now on foot, led his troops into the firefight surrounding the downed aircraft. Working together, the American and Vietnamese Marines had driven back the North Vietnamese long enough for Thanh to drag Griffin from the wreckage. As they retreated toward their own lines, a communist platoon ambushed them. When Thanh fell, stunned by a head wound, Griffin manned the M60 machine gun and drove them back. Finally, together, the only survivors, Thanh and Griffin limped to safety, each supporting the other lest they fall and be overtaken.

Griffin was a fine Marine, Thanh's brother in blood. He was younger than Thanh by perhaps fifteen years. Unobtrusive. Bright. Sardonic but respectful. A man, like Thanh, intimate with death. He'd been at the Marine Birthday Ball with Saunders. Clearly they were friends.

The pieces came together. Marine Corps. Colonel Mac. He'd still be in-country on Thanksgiving. Saunders, as one of the few Marines in Vietnam, would, of course, invite Mac to dinner. That meant inviting Mac's Vietnamese counterpart, Thanh. Mac didn't hold with the Vietnamese custom of keeping women and children out of sight, so Thanh's family was included in the invitation. But why did *Griffin* sign the invitation? He must be the host, outranking Saunders.

"Vien."

The corporal came in at once.

Thanh handed him the invitation. "Check the JGS files for a CV on Mister Griffin."

Vien returned almost immediately. He offered Thanh a single page. It confirmed that Griffin was a retired Marine. He'd lost a son in combat in Bien Hoa in 1967 and was divorced. He'd served as an active duty Marine in Da Nang through 1968. Of course. He'd served under Mac's command. He probably knew Mac better than anyone else in his household. Older, more mature than Saunders—a man like Thanh who had seen enough of the brutal side of life to be alert to the impending tragedy. Could Thanh exploit the blood bond between them? Would Griffin be willing to serve as a circumspect intermediary between Thanh and Mac?

"Vien, put through a telephone call to Colonel Mac."

Thanh knew that his phone was monitored by JGS Communications Security, and almost certainly by the VC as well. He'd have to speak carefully. He picked up the receiver. After a moment, he heard Mac come on the line.

"I have received an invitation," Thanh said, "to the Thanksgiving dinner that you will be attending, but I won't be able to come. Please to accept my regrets."

"Sorry to hear that. I was really looking forward to meeting your family. I'll accept your apology only if you promise that before I leave I'll have the pleasure of making the acquaintance of your lovely wife, your son, and your niece."

"I promise to arrange it. Perhaps a reception at my home." He paused for emphasis. "I'll depend on Mister Charles Griffin to act as my liaison to make the arrangements."

Mac was silent, then said, "I see. I didn't realize . . . Have you spoken to Griffin?"

"Not yet. In fact I hope you will talk to him."

Another pause. "Sure, if that's how you want to handle it."

"Mister Griffin," Thanh said, "knows how to contact you, now and later?"

"Of course."

Thanh hung up. The private link with Mac was established. If any of the Americans would listen, Mac would. Now Thanh would have to wait for Griffin to initiate the contact.

No War but This

THANKSGIVING 1974

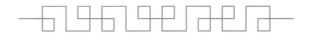

CHAPTER 4

Tuyet slept in Chuck's arms. He lay still, trying to control his rapid heartbeat. This was only the third time he'd laid eyes on Tuyet—first at the ball less than two weeks ago, then at the Cercle, then today at lunch—and here he was in her bed. It never should have happened. The force of his lust astonished him. The two martinis had weakened his defenses. The child in the pool had awakened old memories. And this amazingly beautiful woman . . .

She snuggled closer and opened her eyes. "Hold me."

He slid until his back was against the headboard.

"You are frightened." She leaned her head on his chest. "The Buddhists speak of living in the moment. Only the unenlightened brood about the future."

"You're Catholic."

"I'm Vietnamese."

"What if you get pregnant?"

She scooted to a sitting position beside him. "I take a pill. My cousin sent ten from Paris. I asked for more, but he is suspicious. He assumes that I am estranged from my husband."

His muscles tensed. *If she has pills, maybe she does this all the time.* "So I'm one of many?"

"You are the only one."

"You've known me only two weeks."

She shook her head. "We met seven years ago."

"Seven years ago I was in Da Nang."

"You don't remember. Christmas Day, 1967."

Christmas. He searched his memory. "Couldn't have happened. Ike and I were at an orphanage."

"The boy," she said, "with phosphorus in his skin."

He pulled away. "How do you know this?"

"I was the nurse. I acted as interpreter."

"No," he said, "the nurse was a child in a long gray dress." His mouth opened.

"You are a *dàn ông My*. That means 'American man.' But *my* also means 'beautiful.' You are a beautiful man. When you saw the dead child, when you wept . . ."

He was still.

She rubbed against him. "I found you again one month ago at the Cercle Sportif. You looked through me, didn't see me. I decided we must meet. And so, at the ball . . ."

He took a deep breath. So she'd planned to seduce him. Why? Was he being set up?

"You were sad even before the child died," she said. "Now I know why. Your son."

He shut his eyes.

She rested her head on his shoulder. "That is why you came back to Vietnam, yes?"

"If you don't mind—"

"Please tell me. I want to understand."

"I came back because I don't want him to have died for nothing."

"You loved him very much, I think, more than you have ever loved anyone, more than life." Her voice broke. "I, too, have a son. I am always so frightened he will be harmed. I know the love you have. I know the hurt."

He wrenched away. "I should go." He wiped his face.

"When will I see you again?"

"I don't know. I haven't thought this through. The war—"

"No war but this," she said. "It is our war."

"I don't understand."

"No matter. If we let ourselves love each other, the future will write itself for us." She put her hand on his arm. "You come back Thursday morning? It is your Thanksgiving. You don't have to work."

"We're having a big dinner. I have to be there."

"See me first. Early in the morning. Promise me." She kissed his ear. "Now, you make love with me again?"

Chuck kept his promise to Tuyet. Thanksgiving morning, carrying winter roses from Dalat, he arrived at the Tu Xuong villa shortly after 0600 when curfew ended. Mai admitted him with her unwavering gravity. Tuyet met him on the circular driveway, took the bouquet from him. Once inside the door she handed Mai the flowers, kissed him, took his hand, and led him upstairs.

It was close to noon by the time the blue-and-white dropped him at his own villa on Yen Do.

Ike, looking all wrong in a suit, his blue tie hanging around his open collar, met him at the door. "Where the fuck have you been? Guests'll be here in two hours—"

"I'll hop in the shower and be right down."

Chuck's suit, made by a tailor in Hong Kong during a rest-and-recuperation weekend, was the same navy blue as Ike's, so he wore a red tie. As he hurried down the stairs, Chi Nam's voice came from the kitchen: "You out my kitchen, you go, you go!" Sparky, licking his fingers, came through the door.

"Looks like you got caught," Chuck said.

"With my hand in the cookie jar. In the stuffing bowl, actually." Sparky wiped his hands with his handkerchief.

"How'd you get your hair to lie down?"

"Wildroot Cream Oil."

Chuck grinned. "They still make that stuff? You buy it at the PX?"

"My wife sends it to me."

"Probably the only thing that can keep that peach fuzz under control. Speaking of the PX, what wine did you get?"

"They were out of the good California red, so I had to settle for the French stuff."

Chuck glanced over the table set for fourteen. "Champagne?"

"Oops." He gave Chuck a sheepish smile. "Forgot the bubbly. I'll get some from my cache. Australia's finest. I did restock the hooch cabinet. You guys owe me a bundle."

"You know what? We shouldn't be calling you Sparky. With a memory like yours, we should call you Oopsie. Be sure you remember to get ice out just before people start arriving. Colonel Macintosh likes his martinis very cold."

"Already put the gin and the martini glass in the freezer. Vermouth's in the fridge."

Chuck gave the main floor and the veranda at the back of the villa a walk-through inspection. In the living room, the tile floor was mopped, the rattan rugs swept, and the cane chairs and sofas and the glass coffee table supported by ceramic elephants were freshly dusted. The credenza, the end tables, the Chinese screen—all polished. When he switched on the ceiling fan, no dust blew from the corners. He must remember to compliment Oanh.

As he reentered the front hall, Molly was coming down the stairs.

"Wait—don't move," Chuck said. "You look like . . . can't remember the name of it. *Lewd Descending Staircase*. Great dress. Blue's your color. It reflects your eyes. Never saw your hair like that."

"It's called a French twist. Took me hours."

"Where's Ike?"

"Trying to get his tie right." She glanced at her watch. "Almost an hour before the crowd crashes in. I'll take these off." She stepped out of her heels and stooped to pick them up. "Buy me a drink?"

"Scotch on the rocks?"

"How sweet. You remember. I'll imbibe in the salon." She turned toward the living room.

In the kitchen, careful to steer clear of the harried Chi Nam, Chuck dropped two ice cubes into a squat tumbler then went to the living room. From the liquor cabinet he took his bottle of Chivas, covered the ice, and handed the drink to Molly.

"What're you having?" she said as he sat opposite her.

"Too early for me. You're wearing heels today?"

"I like to look down on people." She gave him a closer look. "You're all grins. You get some this morning?"

Chuck wiped his mouth with the back of his hand.

"Seriously, buddy." She leaned forward with a smile. "You're more thawed than I've ever seen you. Who is she?"

He shrugged.

"Never mind." She sipped. "You're fixed up with someone. Sparky's married. Everybody but me's got someone."

"You're with Ike, right?"

"He's got a wife and kids back in the world, remember? Not what a woman wants, but like Ike says, you do what you have to do. Whatever it takes. I just wish . . ." She rubbed her glass against her upper lip. "Ever work in an embassy dispensary? Lots of life-threatening stuff like hemorrhoids and sunburn and the trots. For this I starved myself through grad school to get an MS in nursing? I wanted to end up as a nurse practitioner, doing important work; you know, helping people."

"Things are rough all over. Bet you cry all the way to the bank."

She tossed down her Scotch and handed him the glass. "Don't be so stingy this time. Yeah, we're all paid more than we're worth. That's what happens when you bribe civilians to do the military's job." She took the drink from him. "Before this job I worked with oncology patients. This one lady said to me, 'The onliest thing worth a damn is what you do for someone else. When the end comes, I want to be able to look back at my life and say, "Nice goin', Sadie. You done good."' I was with her when she died a week later, completely at peace. She done good. What good have I ever done for anyone?"

"Jesus, Molly, you're surrounded by people who need what you have to offer. Have you been out in the streets lately?"

She shook her head. "I can't just stop people and pop pills at them."

"Ever been to Cité Paul-Marie? There's an orphanage there. Some of the saddest kids I've ever seen."

"They need a nurse?"

"They need people to visit the kids and play with them and sing to them and make them feel human. Tell you what. I'll take you. I'll introduce you to my little guy named Philippe—"

Ike strode in, all fluster and sweat. "Did anybody check on the hors d'oeuvres?"

"They're not horse ovaries." Molly stood. "Say after me. *Oar durves.*"

Ike headed for the kitchen.

Colonel Macintosh was the first to show up, at 1400 on the dot. All three housemates greeted him in the hall.

"Would the Colonel care for champagne?" Ike said.

"Dry martini. Truly dry. To get it right, send a twix to Washington with the word 'vermouth' in it, but tell them not to read it aloud."

Colonel Troiano and his wife were at the door next. By 1500 all the guests, even the Australian military attaché, were sipping champagne and sampling the appetizers Oanh offered on a tray. Sparky announced that dinner was served, and the group migrated to the big dining room table.

"Colonel Thanh sent his regrets, sir," Chuck said to Macintosh while Ike was destroying the turkey with a carving knife. "Had to be with his troops."

Macintosh's face lost its good humor. "I talked to him, but he . . ."

Chuck hesitated. "Could the Colonel spare me a moment after dinner? There's a matter I'd like to discuss."

Macintosh's eyebrows shot up. "Did Thanh talk to you?"

"No, sir."

"Mashed potatoes, sir?" Sparky held a bowl out to Macintosh.

After dinner the guests adjourned to the living room for brandy. Molly sat next to the colonel, munched chocolates served by Oanh, and asked for an ice cube in her snifter. Chuck gave her one without comment, but Macintosh laughed.

"Sorry," she said to the colonel, "but if it's worth snorting, it's worth snorting on the rocks."

Macintosh eyed the ceramic elephants—one green, one purple—supporting the glass top of the cocktail table. "I see a lot of these. Are they a Saigon special?"

"We call them bufes—big ugly fucking elephants." Molly ignored Ike's wince. "Yeah, you can pick them up on Tu Do for a few thousand pee." She held her glass to Chuck. "Would you?"

Chuck turned his refill duties over to Sparky. "Would the Colonel care to take a look at our garden?"

"A pleasure, Griffin." Macintosh followed Chuck through the French doors to the rear veranda. "Let's stroll." He led the way down the steps to the stone path through the sculpted shrubs and crape myrtle. Far enough from the house that they couldn't be heard, he fixed Chuck in his gaze. "Thanh talked to me. He wants you to be a liaison between him and me. He didn't say much, but I get the idea he wants to convey something confidential. He wants you to contact him."

Chuck waited.

"I'll talk to Troiano and set up a private comms channel between you and me," Macintosh said. "We'll use Special Security Office—SSO—channels so we can send code word material. We'll mark the messages EYES ONLY NOFORN."

Macintosh paced along the walk. "Something's not passing the sniff test, Griffin. The Jolly General Staff crowd are a little too merry. Their upbeat briefings are all giggles and grins. They give me facts and figures that don't match Troiano's. I asked for a session with Thanh and didn't get it. Every time I see him socially, that goddamned major is there. You got any feel for what's going on?"

"Maybe, sir," Chuck said. "It's getting hairy in I and II Corps, and Thanh knows it. Yet nobody here seems to be noticing. The Viets gloss over it, and the U.S. policy types seem to be ignoring it. I can't talk classified detail here, but I think the highlands could be overwhelmed. And big stuff's afoot by the western end of the DMZ near Khe Sanh."

Macintosh held up his hand. "Roger that."

"Sir, if we don't want Vietnam to fall, we need to intervene—"

"You got to understand, Griffin. The U.S. is sick of this war. We want out. We don't even care about losing face anymore. I tried to tell them way back when I was a lieutenant colonel that we were fighting the war all wrong—worrying about major battles and body counts when we should have been in the villages and hamlets helping the people, gaining their support. I've been telling them ever since. Why do you think they don't let me talk to the press? Why do you think I never earned a star?"

"But, sir, if the U.S. would send forces back in—"

Macintosh laughed. "That'll happen when Jane Fonda gets drafted. You don't get it. It's over. From here on it's fucking damage control. We quit last year when we signed the cease-fire, stopped air support, and cut funds to the South Vietnamese government. That way when it all goes to hell, and it will, we can act surprised and blame the North Vietnamese for violating the terms of the agreement. Wasn't *our* fault. In short, we lie. If we're going to lie effectively, we have to live the lie."

Chuck worked to control his breathing. "Colonel Macintosh, too many have died—"

"Don't tell me how many have died." Color rose in Macintosh's scalp. "The Corps is my family. Fifteen thousand of my Marines have died here." He straightened as if coming to attention. "Wait a couple of days, so it won't look like I put you up to it, then get in touch with Thanh. Arrange a visit with him. Tell him it's to set you up as a protocol intermediary between him and me. Be sure no one else is present. Find out what's up." He leaned forward and whispered. "And *always* keep your back to the wall."

Fully dressed and finished with Chi Nam's elaborate Sunday breakfast, Chuck was ready to head out for the Cercle Sportif, Cité Paul-Marie, and, later, for the midday meal at Tu Xuong. He had to talk to Ike first, but Ike and Sparky hadn't stirred yet. He went down the hall to Ike's room and tapped. Silence. He tapped again. A man growled and a woman coughed. Muffled thumps and groans, then the door opened four inches. Ike's naked body blocked the view.

"What?"

"Sorry," Chuck said. "It's after nine. Need to talk to you."

"Wait."

The door closed. Muted voices and footfalls. The door opened.

"Come on in," Ike said, "you clueless bastard."

"You know what time it is?" Molly sat on the tousled bed, her feet bare, her hair wild, her plentiful body in oversized hospital scrubs.

"I bet *you* don't," Chuck said. "I didn't know you were here."

"It doesn't pay to advertise." She snatched her purse and headed out to the hall. "Don't say anything important while I'm in the head." She closed the door behind her.

Ike dug through the flotsam in the bottom of his armoire and found a pair of shorts. "Okay, what's happening?"

"I'm seeing someone."

"God damn." Ike scratched his crotch. "You woke us up to tell me that? Okay. My advice: watch your ass."

"She's on the up-and-up," Chuck said. "She says she's in love with me."

"Any whore in Dakao'll tell you that."

"I need a favor."

"Here it comes." Ike retrieved a T-shirt and flip-flops.

"I need pills for her."

"You come to the wrong guy. I don't do drugs."

"Contraceptives. She only has a few left. I have no way to get any. I was hoping I could get you to ask Molly. She uses them, doesn't she? Gets them through the dispensary some way?"

"Why don't you ask her?" Ike said.

Chuck grimaced. "Kind of embarrassing."

"Come on, Chuck. Molly's as down and dirty as any jarhead." Ike wiggled. "Wish she'd hurry up. I need to take a leak."

The door opened and Molly marched in. Her hair was pulled back from her face and her makeup was in place.

"Be right back." Ike hurried down the hall.

Molly closed the door. "To what emergency do we owe this coitus interruptus?"

"Don't give me that," Chuck said. "You were both asleep."

"Right, and now you've spoiled the mood."

"Sorry 'bout that. Maybe some coffee and chocolate would sweeten the pot?"

"Matter of fact." She fluffed her hair before the mirror on the armoire door. "But that won't get the mood back." She thrust in two combs to hold her hair behind her ears.

"What, no tiara?" Chuck said with a smile.

"Don't change the subject. What's going on?"

"I asked Ike to ask you for a little favor, that's all."

"You going to tell me what it is?"

Chuck bit his lip.

Molly snorted. "It's written all over you. Men. You're all transparent. Female trouble, right?"

"She needs birth control pills."

"Who is she?"

Chuck shuffled in place. "I'd rather not say."

"No talkee, no laundry."

"All right. It's Colonel Thanh's niece, Tuyet."

"Tu . . . Never mind. I'll just call her Tooey. A good Irish name."

"Tuyet," Chuck said. "Come on, you can say it right."

"Tuyet."

"You got it. I'm proud of you. But, seriously, keep it quiet. If security finds out I could lose my clearance."

"For boinking a Viet?"

"The Intel Branch security chief is a hardline bastard. He's the Ambassador's man, and the Ambassador is an old-line southern gentleman. Doesn't approve of boinking, least of all with a foreign national."

Ike came into the room at a quick march. "We need coffee."

"Chuck volunteered to get us some," Molly said. "Before he heads out to see his honey. I wormed it out of him."

"You going to do it?" Ike said.

"I'll go get coffee." Chuck cocked his head at Molly. "And chocolate." He slipped into the hall.

ᒋᄂ᤽ᒋᄂ᤽

As Chuck did his Sunday laps at the Cercle, Macintosh's words ran through his brain like a tune he'd rather forget. At the Cité, holding Philippe on his knee, he wondered how the child's life would go if South Vietnam capitulated. Maybe the North Vietnamese would make him one of those drones who worked themselves to death in the service of the Fatherland. Maybe they'd kill him outright as too damaged to be of any use to the party. Or execute him publicly as an Amerasian bastard.

Late in the afternoon, as he lay with Tuyet in his arms, the memory of Macintosh's face haunted him. *You don't get it. It's over.* He pushed the thought away, slid up in bed, and rested his back against the headboard. "If security finds out we're seeing each other, I could be fired. I'd better come clean with them before they—"

"No one will find out. Thu told Thanh you are often here. Thanh assumed you are interested in seeing Lan. I said nothing. That is all very proper. Security won't care. Remember, I am an estranged married woman. It is improper for me to be with a man. Not Lan, so long as she is chaperoned. Thanh sees me as the chaperone."

"He's your uncle. He should know about us. When I see him—"

"Say nothing," she said. "He would not approve."

He straightened. "I don't like sneaking around."

"If you tell him, I will not be able to see you again."

Now what had he gotten himself into? "No. Thanh is a fellow Marine. We've fought side by side. He saved my life. You don't try to put one over on a blood brother."

With slow deliberation, she moved from the bed and put on her panties and bra. She took her white underdress by the skirt and pulled it over her head. When her face emerged, he saw the tears. As she reached for her surcoat, he rose from the bed and caught her in his arms. She tried to wrestle free.

"Please," Chuck said.

She eased from his grasp, put on the surcoat, and stepped into her shoes. Before the mirror, she swept back her hair.

"Talk to me," he said.

She dried her eyes with tissues. "I believed you cared more about me. If you tell Thanh, we will not meet again. I will be punished."

"My God. What will he do?"

"If I believed you cared about me, I would tell you. You do not. You need not know."

He took her by the shoulders from behind and pressed against her back. "I care very much about you."

"Say nothing."

"That would be a lie."

"Then tell him and forget me." She slipped away from him and left the room.

He threw on his clothes and hurried after her. "Tuyet, wait." She was not in the corridor. "Tuyet?" He darted down the stairs. Not in the sitting room, nor the vestibule. He threw open the French doors and dashed to the garden. Lan sat alone at the table by the pool, clutching a spray of blood-red hibiscus.

"Tuyet?" he said.

Lan gave him a look of pure hatred and averted her gaze.

He returned to the house. With a sigh of frustration he went through the vestibule to the front court. Mai, stone faced, opened the gate to the street for him and closed it behind him. The bolt boomed into place.

At the daily briefing Monday morning, Chuck ignored the gathering evidence of the North Vietnamese troop buildup in the highlands,

Laos, and I Corps. The maps before him, littered with unit symbols and arrows, faded behind flashes of memory—Macintosh's frown, Philippe's wistful eyes, and Tuyet's tears.

He was jarred to attention when one of the comms guys hurried to the lectern, whispered to the briefer, and handed him a sheet of yellow copy paper straight from the teletype. The briefer read it silently, then told the audience that the III Corps commander had reported increasing action and enemy troop movement in Tay Ninh and Phuoc Long Provinces, less than a hundred miles north of the capital. New evidence, so far unconfirmed, indicated that at least two North Vietnamese infantry divisions supplemented by armor were preparing for the conquest of Saigon.

It tormented Chuck to realize that a whole chorus of the muzzled, like him, knew the threat and strained against the silence dictated by politicians and commanders who didn't want to know they might lose the war. Saigon could fall if they didn't act. Then Ben would have died for nothing.

Back at his desk after the briefing, he shoved aside the pile of reports and reached into the bottom drawer of his desk for the Ben file, unopened for almost a year. Inside he found the message dated 29 May 1967, the official condolence, the letter from Ben's commander in Bien Hoa, the old pictures. One showed Ben on a basketball court, shining with sweat. Chuck studied Ben's smiling face. Even in this snapshot, taken only months before his death, Ben, the rebel who turned against his father, had a kind of glow that only innocence can give. Sherry was never the innocent type. God knows Chuck wasn't. Maybe Ben's purity of heart came from God. Handsome boy. Had all the looks in the family. To think how he died in flames . . . *I told him I was ashamed of him.* He forced back his tears.

He returned the pictures to their envelope. A message, two letters, and a handful of snapshots. All that was left. Killed in action. That's all he ever knew. He'd written to Ben's commander, a major, to find out what happened, but the major never answered. Chuck hadn't had the stomach to pursue it. That was wrong. He had to face what happened to

Ben. He picked up the letter. James H. Carver, Major, U.S. Army. The intel business was better than most at tracking people down. Troiano was Army. Maybe if Chuck asked him . . .

He walked to the desk of Troiano's secretary. "Hey, Cindy, how about seeing if you can get me a minute with the colonel?"

Waiting for a summons from Troiano's office, he put the Ben file away. What the hell was he doing? Stirring up old pains when, in the last couple of weeks, he'd finally started to feel better. That was Tuyet's doing. He'd forgotten the comfort of a woman's touch. She gave him something he'd lost long ago, made him want to put his shield aside. The intensity of his feelings for her frightened him. Macintosh's words rumbled again through his memory. *Always keep your back to the wall.*

She'd weakened him; she'd given him hope.

He yearned to see her again, but he couldn't be underhanded with Thanh. He'd have to get *her* to tell Thanh they were seeing each other, but he didn't know how to contact her. In all likelihood, neither the Tu Xuong villa nor the Tan Son Nhat villa had a telephone; even the villa at Yen Do didn't have one. Send a note to the Tan Son Nhat villa? Maybe not. If Tuyet was right and Thanh wouldn't approve, the wrong way to tell him the truth was to have a servant show him an intercepted lover's note. Maybe he could send a brief letter to her at the Tu Xuong villa. He took a blank paper from his drawer and drafted a quick note. "I'm sorry about our disagreement. When can I see you? Send a note back with the person who brought you this."

Next he typed a note to Thanh:

Dear Colonel Thanh,

Colonel Macintosh has requested that I contact the Colonel to arrange a meeting. Colonel Macintosh suggests that the Colonel wishes me to act as a protocol intermediary. I await the Colonel's pleasure.

Charles E. Griffin
Intelligence Branch, DAO

His intercom sounded. "Chuck?" Troiano's secretary. "He'll see you now."

Troiano got to his feet and shook Chuck's hand.

"Sorry to bother the Colonel with something personal, sir," Chuck said. "Can the Colonel help me track down this man?" Chuck handed him Carver's letter. "He was a major in 1967, so he's probably still on active duty."

Troiano read the letter.

"I want to ask him what happened," Chuck said.

"You sure you want to do this? Might be better to let healed wounds alone."

Chuck took a deep breath. "I came back to Vietnam to help win this war so that my son's death wasn't for nothing. I have to have the guts to find out how he died."

Troiano returned to his desk and copied Carver's full name and rank. "I'll see what I can do."

"Thank you, sir." Chuck turned to go.

"But, Chuck—"

Chuck faced him.

"Don't put too much stock in victory. I suspect the United States is about to learn what it feels like to lose a war."

That evening, Chuck sent Oanh via cyclo first to the Tu Xuong villa with his letter to Tuyet—instructing Oanh to bring the letter back if Tuyet wasn't there—then to Thanh's villa at Tan Son Nhat with the note he had typed at the office. Oanh returned after dark, gave him back his letter to Tuyet, and told him that she was not at the Tu Xuong villa. And Thanh was still away and wouldn't be returning until the next day. She'd left the note to Thanh with the gardener.

Tuesday evening the bell gate rang. Oanh answered and brought Chuck two envelopes. The first contained a note in Thanh's broad hand inviting Chuck to visit him at 1715 on Wednesday evening,

4 December—the next night—in Thanh's office in the JGS compound. The second was an invitation to Captain Isaac Saunders, USMC, and his associates to attend a formal reception in honor of Colonel Macintosh on Monday, 16 December, the night before Macintosh's departure, at Thanh's villa at Tan Son Nhat.

Wednesday, Chuck secured his workspace early and left the DAO enclosure. He went on foot to the gate out of the Tan Son Nhat military base. As the sun slanted through the rambling shacks on the far side of Vo Tanh Boulevard, he walked past the fortified fence that separated the U.S. base from the JGS and presented his ID to the gate sentry, who logged him in. Once inside the JGS walls, he moved past the gleaming headquarters building and the more recent additions, in vanilla and olive drab, toward the rear wall of the compound where a few odd remnants of the French era still survived. Here ragged banyans, palms, and tall grasses were already gathering dust even though the dry season was less than half over.

Chuck didn't like any part of this. Sneaking around grated, but that was the mission Macintosh had given him. Jaw set, he entered the gate to the small enclosure. In the center stood Thanh's office, a sagging single-story building, probably a lackey's residence during the French occupation. Thanh's jeep was parked by the front door. No one was in the hall that now served as an anteroom. At the entrance to the main office Chuck hesitated, then tapped. The door, not latched, swung open.

The only light in the office was the last of the sun's glow through the wide window across from Thanh's desk. The lit tea stove beside the desk gave off the raw aroma of burning Sterno. Thanh sat behind the desk, his eyes on the luminescent sky. Chuck stood in the doorway, waiting for Thanh to acknowledge him. Finally he spoke. "Sir?"

Thanh turned. "Mister Griffin." He closed the folder on his desk, rose to meet Chuck, and shook his hand. "Tea?"

"Thank you, sir."

Thanh poured. "Only here, in the south, do we have skies like this one." He nodded toward the startling sunset blazing red behind the irregular horizon of silhouetted palms and roofs. Thanh waved toward a small table and chairs by the window. "Colonel Mac talked to you, yes? It is very important, you understand, that we meet quietly and no one know. I will tell you things for you to tell Mac. You must tell no one else. You understand?"

"Yes, sir."

Thanh inhaled deeply, as if to pull in all the darkening air of the evening. "New divisions from North Vietnam are now in I Corps and the highlands. They are ready to attack. In the south, only a hundred kilometers from us, the enemy's 7th and 3rd Divisions and the M-26 Armor Command have moved into Tay Ninh and Phuoc Long. The North Vietnamese will strike close to Saigon first to see if the Americans will react. If the Americans do nothing, the highlands will be next. Our forces are stretched too thin."

Thanh straightened in his chair and looked sidelong at the floor. "Many of our commanders and politicians are corrupt. They are already planning their escape. At the end, they will abandon their troops." Uncharacteristically, he fixed Chuck in his gaze. "I have written all this in a letter to Mac." He lifted a paper from the table. "You read."

Chuck unfolded the paper. In the deepening dusk he could barely make out Thanh's bold handwriting. He was starting on the final paragraph when Thanh spoke.

"You tell Mac for me. If the Americans do not come back, we fall. You understand. We fall."

Chuck refolded the letter and thrust it into his breast pocket. "I will tell Colonel Macintosh all the Colonel has said."

Thanh resumed Vietnamese courtesy by averting his eyes. "You wish more tea?"

"No, thank you, sir."

Thanh nodded. "You meet me here in two weeks, 18 December at 1930 hours? I do not like sending notes—too insecure—and the telephones are monitored. My superiors must not know."

"I understand, sir. I will be here."

"One more matter." Thanh handed him an envelope. "An invitation for Mac to a reception at my house. I told Mac you would convey it to him—my excuse for setting you up as our intermediary." Tension tightened Thanh's shoulders. "In wartime a man worries about his family. I must ensure that they are safe." He turned his eyes toward the failing light. "I will have a message for Mac about that later."

"Has the Colonel arranged for them to leave the country if—"

"No." Thanh stood and tilted his face upward as if to get more breath. "It is too soon to speak of these things. One step at a time. In Vietnam we say, 'The second step will never come if the first is not taken.'" He walked to his desk. "You forgive me now?"

It took Chuck a moment to realize that the interview was over. He got to his feet. "I thank the Colonel for his time. Good night, sir."

"May the Mother Goddess sing as you sleep," Thanh said with a sad smile.

At the obligatory deskside briefing for the Ambassador the following week, Chuck repeated the growing evidence of a forthcoming offensive sixty miles north of Saigon. "If the North Vietnamese want to take Phuoc Long, the Republic of Vietnam, with no U.S. air support and without financial aid, won't be able to stop them. It will be a gross violation of the cease-fire. If the U.S. does nothing, the highlands will be next." The Ambassador sighed his impatience, thanked him, and sent him on his way.

CHAPTER 5

Tuyet stayed hidden in the upstairs guest bedroom and listened at the door as Chuck left the master bedroom and clattered down the stairs to the sitting room calling her name. She heard him open the French doors to the garden. Nothing for a moment, then his footsteps went through the house to the vestibule, out the front door, down the steps to the front courtyard. She hurried to the barred window and watched as he exited onto Tu Xuong Street and Mai slammed the gate behind him. Mai was coming into the sitting room as Tuyet descended the steps.

"He's gone?" Tuyet asked.

"*Oui, Madame.* He searched for you, spoke to Miss Lan in the garden."

Tuyet proceeded through the doors to the garden. Shredded crimson hibiscus petals trailed from Lan's fingers to her lap.

"What did he say to you?" Tuyet said.

Lan lowered her head.

Tuyet seized her arm. Flower fragments scattered. "Speak to me."

"He asked for you then went back into the house."

Tuyet pondered. Would Chuck tell Thanh? Not likely. She'd rattled him with her tears. Still—

"What you do with that man is immoral," Lan said. "You cannot expect me to remain silent."

"What takes place between me and Mister Griffin is not your concern."

"You're using me. Uncle Thanh believes Mister Griffin comes here to court me. I'll tell him what you're doing."

"And make me your enemy? That would be unwise."

"You are already my enemy. You are exploiting me."

Tuyet sat, extended her hand, and examined her fingernails. "You know, of course, that one word from me and Thanh would turn you out of the house. We've both had enough of your parasitic dependence."

Lan paled.

"A woman with no means," Tuyet said, "on her own in a war-torn city. What can she do? Only one answer, Lan." She raised her eyes to the spreading branches of the frangipani. "Your body is not beautiful, but men would pay to use it for their pleasure." She ignored the gasp from Lan. "You will remain silent. Go inside. Tell Mai I am ready for the midday meal."

Trembling, Lan darted into the house.

Tuyet closed her eyes. Revulsion for what she was doing pumped through her veins. She commanded her body to calm itself. She would do whatever she had to do to save Thu. Lan would say nothing. And Chuck? An honorable man. Not given to dissembling. How could she be sure he wouldn't talk to Thanh? The key to Thu's salvation was to get Chuck back in her arms.

She relaxed and let her flesh remember him. What had started as pretense of passion had turned real. His face and body left her breathless. And his hands! She had never known so great a pleasure as his touch evoked in her. Her triumph was his orgasm—quaking, his voice breaking, his grasp tightening. And yet, it was his gentleness that moved her, the rapt attention he gave her. Not because he was afraid of her or wanted to exploit her power, like most of the men in her life, but because he cared about her. He treated her with respect, awe even. In their lovemaking, her pleasure was paramount to him. The only other man who was genuinely concerned about her was Thanh. But she couldn't love Thanh. She'd tried.

She called back her memory of Chuck's face as he tossed and caught Thu. Chuck was a man of compassion. He saw people's needs, their suffering, their privations—all that she had been trained to ignore. She ached to understand, to feel what he felt. She didn't know how.

All that was beside the point. Chuck's kindness and his love of children would move him to save Thu. She couldn't lose herself in her passion. She must marshal her strength to control events. Over time he'd forgive her deceit, understand that it had been necessary.

If Thanh knew she had taken a lover, not much would change, but if Chuck found out she was Thanh's wife before she could prepare him . . . *That* must be prevented.

Thanh was arranging a reception for the American colonel on the sixteenth, more than two weeks hence. He'd insist that she and Thu be present. She would have to find a way to ensure that Chuck wasn't invited. How? Ah. Lan. She'd tell Thanh that Lan no longer wanted to see Mr. Griffin, that she was annoyed with him, or that he'd tried to kiss her, or that she was furious over some slight. After the reception, she'd tell Thanh the lovers had reconciled.

Mai served the midday meal.

"Go to Tan Son Nhat at once and send the sedan," Tuyet said. "We'll be returning this afternoon. Tell Chi Hai to prepare Thu for the trip."

After the evening meal Tuyet tapped lightly at the door to Thanh's bedroom.

"Yes?"

She opened the door. "Forgive the interruption."

Dressed in fresh utilities, he was at his desk, papers spread before him. "You are always welcome."

She entered, closed the door behind her, and tugged it to be sure it was latched. Hands at her waist, and her eyes lowered, she spoke low in her voice. "It's Lan."

He turned to face her. "Something is amiss?"

"She's angry with Mister Griffin. I don't know why."

He nodded. "That's why she's so morose? Has he offended her?"

"She hasn't said. I simply wanted to warn you, in case you were thinking of inviting him here to further their liaison. Or . . . ," she hesitated for emphasis, "for Colonel Mac's reception."

"Their tiff was serious enough to bar him from the celebration for Mac?"

"Respect Lan's dignity. Do not invite that man here."

"Mister Griffin is a good man, Tuyet. I should be proud if he asks for Lan's hand."

She steadied herself. "Has he approached you?"

"I have not heard from him, but he and I have some business. We will meet soon."

"May I be permitted to ask what business?"

"Tuyet, the less you know about my work, the better. When the end comes, if you have not escaped, ignorance could spell survival. Very well, I will not invite Mister Griffin to Mac's reception. Is there anything else?"

"No."

"I will be leaving momentarily for the airport. I am flying to Hue for a meeting tomorrow morning with the commanding general of I Corps. I'll be home tomorrow before evening." He turned to his work.

Back in her room, Tuyet paced. She had to get to Chuck before he saw Thanh. She could send him a note. Better to talk to him face-to-face, arrange a reconciliation. Where could she find him? The Cercle Sportif? Too public. She could wait for him outside DAO, intercept him on his way home. That wouldn't do; others would see her. What other place did he frequent? Of course. Cité Paul-Marie. Chuck went to the orphanage on Thursday evenings. She'd be sure to arrive before him. She commanded Mai to go to Tu Xuong Thursday afternoon and prepare the villa and the evening meal for two.

Thursday afternoon Tuyet removed her outer clothes and rested, but she couldn't sleep. At midafternoon she bathed for the second time that day and prepared herself. Her clothing must be simple, suggesting grief at the separation. A plain, deep blue *áo dài* over her white underdress would reflect the state of her mind. She'd let her hair, pulled back from her face, flow about her shoulders. No jewelry.

A novice met her at the gate to Cité Paul-Marie and accompanied her to the visitor's room. Mother Monique appeared a moment later, bowed, and fixed her eyes on the floor, her hands thrust into the large sleeves of her habit.

"What is Madame's pleasure?" she asked in French.

"I wish to be conducted to the place that Mister Griffin usually visits. It is important that I have a private meeting with him. My presence here is confidential. Please tell no one. I am on a mission for the government."

"*Oui, Madame.*" Monique led her to the play yard. "The children assemble here for their recreation before the evening meal. This is where Mister Griffin visits them. I will send a chair for Madame." She bowed and left.

Tuyet looked about the enclosure. Under the chapel's outswept eaves, the wall was pierced with decorative openings large enough to allow air and light but too small for a grenade. It bounded the play space on one side; whitewashed plaster surrounded the rest. The floor was concrete. Bits of grass grew through cracks. No furniture.

A young sister approached with a folding chair. She opened it for Tuyet, bowed, and left. Tuyet was no sooner seated in the corner of the yard, out of the line of sight from the entrance, when a flock of children, fewer than twenty, all smaller than Thu, flowed silently into the yard, herded by two sisters who scolded them and departed. The children turned and saw her, pulled away, and clumped against the walls. One mixed-race boy had only one leg. Another with a mutilated face walked with a bizarre limp that resembled the movements of a crab. A tiny girl rubbed her forehead with a fingerless hand. Tuyet turned away, wishing she, like Chuck, could put aside her revulsion and minister to these *petits misérables*. She wrinkled her nose against the odor of urine.

As the last of the sunshine bathed the wall opposite her, Chuck came through the entrance followed by a sister with another folding chair. He went to the limping boy. "Hi, Pipsqueak." The boy didn't respond but went on staring at Tuyet. Chuck turned. His mouth dropped open.

She rose, went to him. "My dearest Chuck."

He started to embrace her, but she stepped back. "Not here," she said. "You forgive me?"

The hideous little boy tugged at Chuck's pants leg. "Hi, Pee-kwee, hi, Pee-kwee."

"Excuse me." Chuck picked up the child. "This is Philippe."

"*Bon jour*," Tuyet said to the child.

He gaped at her.

"Sit with me and the children for a little while," Chuck said to Tuyet. "Then we can talk." Chuck sat in the chair the sister had opened for him. Tuyet pulled hers next to his. The children gathered round.

Chuck talked to them, made faces, sang to them. All his sadness vanished. The children clapped and giggled. Then, when the sky darkened, he bade the children good-bye and rose.

"We can talk in the chapel," he said. "No one will see us there."

They left the play yard and wound through the walkways to the chapel entrance. Inside, they sat in a pew. Massed votive candles gave the only light.

Tuyet glanced about to be sure they were unobserved, took his hand. "Don't make me to lose you."

"I want to be with you," he said.

"You have not spoken to Thanh about us?"

"When we met, our business was serious. I didn't mention you. I want *you* to—"

"You have met with him?"

"Last night."

She suppressed her shock. "I understand how you feel about deceiving Thanh. Even so, do not tell him right away. Wait a week. Let us have time to be happy together first. Once you tell him, I will not be able to see you again."

"Tuyet, I think he'll understand. He won't separate us or punish you." He hesitated. "I think it would be best if *you* told him."

"Me?" She ducked her head to hide her relief. Why hadn't she thought of that? "Yes, of course. Far better for him to learn of it from me." She tightened her grasp on his hand. "Come to Tu Xuong with me tonight. Mai is preparing a dinner for two. Stay the night. You can catch a cab home at six in the morning when the curfew ends."

He caught her in his arms and kissed her.

She pulled away. "I will leave first. Wait five minutes before you depart."

It was dark by the time they got to Tu Xuong. By candlelight, Mai served Chuck a martini in the garden and, for the first time, smiled at him. After a brief frolic in the pool, he and Tuyet ate the evening meal in their swim clothes. Mai placed a tray with brandy and snifters at poolside. Tuyet dismissed her for the evening, turned to Chuck, and gestured toward the pool. Once in the water Tuyet tugged off Chuck's too-large trunks and shed her bathing suit. He kissed her with the same tenderness he'd shown the orphans. As desire awakened in her, he pulled her from the pool, dried her, and led her to the upstairs bedroom. They slept little that night. Or Friday or Saturday night.

He was magic, this sad American. Her own passion amazed her. Sunday morning they found dried blood on the sheets from the wounds her fingernails had left on his back. She allowed herself, briefly, just at moments, to love him. She lay naked in his arms and wept.

Sunday morning, he sat against the headboard. "I have to go home and clean up. I promised Philippe I'd visit him today."

"And you must go to the Cercle. You have missed several days of exercise."

He laughed. "I've had plenty of exercise."

"And I must go to Mass. It is December 8, the Feast of the Immaculate Conception. Later I return to Tan Son Nhat."

"When can we be together again?"

"Perhaps Tuesday. But next week my cousin returns from France to close out his business dealings and sell this villa. He believes it is no longer safe in Vietnam. We won't be able to meet here after that."

He considered. "You could come to my place. No one would say anything."

"People might see me come and go."

"We could be careful."

⎯⎯ 6⏀9⏀9 ⎯⎯

Thanh returned from Phuoc Long before evening and ordered Chi Tu to ready his bath. Tuyet changed for the evening meal. As she came into the dining room he glanced at her, straightened, and studied her.

"What is it?" she said.

"You. What has happened?"

"Nothing. What do you mean?"

"You're blushing."

She laughed. "A virus must have attacked you in Phuoc Long. You're hallucinating."

He went on watching her as Lan and Thu sat down.

"I didn't think it would happen so soon," he said more to himself than to her.

When the meal was finished, Tuyet retired to her room, undressed, and lay on the bed. She remembered the flicking touch of Chuck's tongue, the power of his thrust. She yearned to be in his arms again. How wonderful, she thought, that there was no conflict between her enjoyment of Chuck and the salvation of Thu. The one begot the other.

A knock at the door snapped her back to reality.

"*Madame*," Chi Tu's voice said. "The master would like a word with you."

Tuyet covered herself with the kimono that cloaked her from head to toe and went to Thanh's room. She stood before him, hands clasped, eyes lowered.

"Close the door," he said. "Please sit down."

She sat in the chair farthest from him.

"You have taken a lover," he said.

Only rigid self-control prevented her from jolting to her feet.

"I don't need to know who it is." He watched her steadily, his eyes sad. "I will find out sooner or later. Not that it matters. I ask only that you behave with discretion. Scandal will not help me in my work, and it will be an impediment to your safety when the country collapses. Promise me that you will do everything in your power to keep this matter private."

She couldn't speak.

"Do you promise?"

Her voice refused to function.

"Tuyet?"

"Yes," she whispered.

"Thank you." He turned back to his work. "Good night."

CHAPTER 6

Ike tried not to complain, but Molly's maid, Huong, was a pain in the ass. She had her own key and came at 0630 every morning to Molly's apartment, even on days when he had stayed over and was still in the rack with Molly. Huong cleaned up from the previous night's dinner, did any laundry Molly had left in the hall, and, after checking the bedroom to be sure Molly was there, made coffee. Molly told Ike that Huong would be happy to shine his shoes—her previous employers had taught her how to spit shine—and polish his captain's bars and the brass buckle on his belt. *Fuck that.* No way was he going to let a person who wasn't military, wasn't an American, wasn't even a man, get her hands on his military gear.

One Sunday morning in mid-December, still half asleep, he wandered into the kitchen in his skivvies. Huong, unperturbed, smiled brightly, poured him coffee, and said, "Sir, yes, sir. You up and at 'em, *sir*."

He grunted. Back in the bedroom, he rummaged for clothes. "Huong speaks English like a drill sergeant."

"Before the cease-fire she worked in a villa rented by U.S. Special Forces guys," Molly said. "She's a quick study."

"Couldn't you ask her not to come the mornings I'm here?"

"Why? She's comfortable with you."

He scratched.

Molly grinned. "You don't like strange women seeing you naked?"

"I don't traipse around naked."

"Those boxer shorts don't hide much. Would you rather I fixed you breakfast?"

"You don't cook."

Her smile turned triumphant. "I rest my case. Besides, she's Chinese. Doesn't give a damn. Saves me oodles by shopping for me. I would have paid five times as much for the Christmas tree."

"You call that a Christmas tree? And the ornaments . . ." He shook his head.

"Quit your bitchin'. We're in the tropics, remember?"

"And since when are you hard up for money?"

Molly shrugged. "That's not the problem. It's Huong who needs money—five kids and her husband in the army up north somewhere. She won't let me pay her for time when she isn't here. So if I give her time off, she loses money. And just between you and me, she takes an unacknowledged commission for the stuff she buys for me, and I pretend not to notice."

"She isn't here most of the day. She must have other employers."

"Maybe a dozen, most of them in this building."

Ike sighed. "Okay." He glanced at his watch. "What time you due at Peter-Paul-and-Mary?"

"Cité Paul-Marie. I told Chuck we'd meet him at 1400." She kissed him. "You're coming, right?" Her smile vanished. "I'm scared."

"Of a bunch of orphans and nuns?"

"I never did anything like this before."

"Chuck'll be there."

"Chuck's not my bunkmate." She got to her feet. "I'll shower first, okay?"

After lunch, Ike dawdled over coffee while Molly primped. "Almost 1330," he called to the bedroom.

Molly came down the hall in an A-line skirt and black high-top boots with three-inch heels.

"We're not going to the Caravelle," Ike said.

Molly waggled her fingers through her hair. "I want to look *respectable*. Got your keys? I'm taking my little purse."

They flagged a blue-and-white at the corner of Nguyen Hue and Le Loi. The effort of stuffing themselves into the backseat left Molly breathless. Ike squelched his amusement—she was sensitive about her size. The cab scooted through tangles of bikes and cars, under the ever-present propaganda banners, past the cathedral and the presidential palace. Six blocks later, on a narrow lane deprived of sunlight by the villas on both sides, they pried themselves from the cab and paid the driver. Chuck was waiting in front of a wrought-iron gate set into the eight-foot-high wall topped with shards of glass.

Molly pulled her skirt down to its intended position, just above the knee. "Hi, Chuckie."

"Ready to meet Philippe?" Chuck said.

Molly didn't move. Ike hooked her arm in his and pulled her through the gateway.

They followed the cracked cement walk between whitewashed buildings to the visitor's room, where Chuck introduced Molly and Ike to Reverend Mother Monique. Severe in her white wimple and scapular, she gravely asked in French-tainted English what they desired.

"Maybe I can help," Molly said, eyes downcast. "I'm a nurse."

"And you, sir?" Monique said to Ike.

Ike gave her an embarrassed smile. "I'm with her."

"Very well," the Reverend Mother said. "You may begin by accompanying Mister Griffin to the play yard. Then we see, yes?"

She led them to the open space behind the chapel where nearly twenty children drew back silently as the adults came in. A mutilated Amerasian kid spotted Chuck and shouted joyously, "Hi, Pee-kwee."

Mother Monique reprimanded him in French. His smile vanished and he lowered his eyes. Chuck scooped him up.

"Philippe, I introduce you," Chuck said, stressing each syllable. "This is Ike."

"*Ách*," Philippe said.

"And Miss Molly."

"*En mià Ma-lì*," Philippe repeated.

Molly narrowed her eyes. "What happened to him?"

"They've never told me," Chuck said. "Might have been napalm." He handed Philippe to Molly.

"Poor little guy." Molly's eyes misted.

Philippe recoiled. "Pee-kwee, Pee-kwee." His arms reached for Chuck.

"He's not used to you." Chuck took Philippe into his arms. "It's okay, Pipsqueak. Nobody's going to hurt you."

Philippe cringed against Chuck's chest.

Molly's eyes ranged over the children clotted together against the walls. "They're afraid of us."

Ike laughed nervously. "Probably ain't never seen no splib dude up close before."

Molly cocked her head at him.

"A black Marine brother," Ike said.

"Ike," Chuck said, "a lot of them are half black."

"Ain't never seen their fathers neither, I'm guessin'," Ike said.

Molly stepped toward one group in the corner of the yard. They shifted away from her. She knelt within reach of them and put out her hand, as if to a strange dog. A little girl, her eyes stretched with terror, wept and babbled in French. All Ike could make out was "*ma Sœur.*"

Mother Monique spoke, and the child was silent.

"Please don't be afraid," Molly said so softly that Ike could barely hear her. "Here, touch me. Go ahead. It won't hurt."

The girl pushed against the wall and put her arms over her head as if to ward off a blow.

Philippe squirmed in Chuck's arms and pointed down. Chuck lowered him to the pavement. He crab-limped to the girl, put his hand on her back, and spoke to her. Tentatively, he grasped her hand and moved it away from her head toward Molly's outstretched hand. With a smile made garish by his mangled face, he hurried back to Chuck and raised his arms. Chuck lifted him into his embrace.

Molly and the girl were still. The child watched Philippe in Chuck's arms, then turned her head toward Molly. With a tenderness Ike had never seen before, Molly stroked the palm of the girl's hand. Mother

Monique spoke again. With painful slowness, the girl moved an inch from the wall. Molly bent toward her and took her hand. Philippe called to her. The girl shot him a frightened look.

Molly cocked her head. "Will you let me hold you?" She slipped her fingers under the girl's arms and picked her up. The child gasped. Still on her knees, Molly held her in one arm and smoothed her hair. "See? You don't need to be afraid."

"Her name, it is Angélique," Mother Monique said.

Molly caressed the child's ear with her fingertips. "Beautiful name. I need an angel. Will you be my angel?"

That night, as the three housemates were finishing dinner, Ike turned to Chuck. "Got something for you, but it'll cost."

Sparky laughed. "The captain is turning mercenary. Too bad they don't pay the military better."

"Molly says he's worth every penny," Chuck said with a smile.

Sparky did a double-take. "Is this the Ghost of Christmas Past being cheerful?"

Chuck offered them an apologetic smile. "Guess I've been kind of gloomy."

"Don't worry your pretty head about it," Sparky said. "You've just been in a bad mood for a couple of years. We all have our down times."

"Suck out, Sparky." Ike turned to Chuck. "Just pretend he ain't there and he'll go away."

"What do you have for me?" Chuck said.

Ike grinned. "What's it worth to you?"

"Would a glass of Courvoisier make you generous?"

"Try me."

Chuck and Ike moved to the living room, and Chuck poured two snifters of cognac. He gave one to Ike and they eased into chairs.

Ike handed Chuck a small box. "Birth control pills. From Molly. Last thing you need is a mixed-race bastard."

"I don't know. Maybe later."

"You talk like this is a permanent shack job. Gettin' a little is one thing, but—Chuck, she's Vietnamese. You thought this through?"

"Meeting Tuyet has changed things. I might quit DAO and take her back to the world."

Ike clenched his jaw. This was serious. He took a deep breath and leaned forward. "You and I been tight for what, eight years? We've kicked ass together, looked out for each other. I seen you through times when you were so down you couldn't get out of the bunk in the morning. I always knew getting bred would do wonders for your shitty outlook, and I tried to fix you up. But you wouldn't go for it, right? Now look at you. In all those years, this is the first time I ever seen you smile like you mean it. But, man, you know . . . Look, buddy, no question a little nooky is good for a man, but don't get carried away."

"Maybe I want to." Chuck sat straight. "It's not the sex. It's . . . I feel like I'm alive again. I'm pretty sure Tuyet really loves me, and I'm pretty sure I—"

"Give me a break." Ike slammed down his glass. "Love? Chuck, think about it. What's in it for her? What does she want from you? Money? A way to get to the States? U.S. papers?"

"She hasn't asked for anything but having me near her."

Ike sighed and sat back. "Okay. I tried. You watch. One of these days she'll turn up pregnant, never mind the pills. *Then* she'll quit frontin' and tell you what she really wants."

"Maybe." Chuck studied his folded hands.

"Talk to her, Chuck. I did that with Molly before we ever screwed. She knows we're not permanent. When my tour's over, I kiss her goodbye, give her one last slap on the fanny, and I'm out of here. She accepts that. We both know where we stand."

Chuck gave him a knowing smile. "When you leave, Molly'll go into mourning."

"Only until the next guy comes along. That's what I like about her. Cold-blooded and real. Like a guy."

"That's not the woman I saw at Cité Paul-Marie."

"Women are always up to their eyeballs in emotion, Chuck, but when the shit hits the fan, they know how to get what they want."

Chuck laughed. "You're a cynical son of a bitch."

"And you're a love-sick puppy. Let's see who comes out of this with the fewest scars."

б Ꙑ б Ꙑ

Ike left the embassy early so that he could prepare properly for the reception at Thanh's Tan Son Nhat villa. This time he'd wear his brown suit—the invitation specified mufti. When he wasn't in uniform he had to spend more time than he liked getting his clothes right so that he wouldn't feel like he was in disguise. He'd gotten his hair cut that morning, and he'd spit-shined his shoes. He shaved with more than usual care, showered, and dressed, but his tie wouldn't cooperate.

He went down the hall to Chuck's room. "Help me with this fuckin' thing," he said in the doorway.

Chuck, still in his underwear, retied the tie and pulled it tight. "How come you're dressed so early? The reception isn't until 2000 hours.

"Colonel Macintosh's sedan is picking me up at 1915. I'll go to the Caravelle and escort him to the party. You guys taking the jeep? I'll ride home with you."

"Does Thanh know Sparky and I are coming?"

"The invitation said 'and associates.' Who else would that be?" Ike went on fiddling with his tie. "Why'd you go to the Caravelle last week? What's up between you and Macintosh?"

"Leave your tie alone. Nothing I can talk about. I had to deliver a message to him."

"From who?"

"If you were authorized to know, I'd have told you, jarhead."

"The recruit stands corrected, sir." Ike executed a stiff salute.

Back in his own room, Ike studied himself in the mirror. He looked ridiculous. With a sigh, he put a fresh handkerchief in his pocket, took his wallet and keys, and set out for the street, where a chauffeured black Ford Crown Victoria waited.

At Lam Son Circle the sedan idled by the curb in front of the Caravelle while Ike met Macintosh, also in a suit and tie, at the bar and accompanied him to the car. As they headed out Cong Ly toward Tan Son Nhat, Ike tried to chatter amiably without much success.

"I insisted on helping Thanh defray the cost of this shindig," Macintosh said. "He's embarrassed about his lack of money, but he'd never admit it. Be sure to praise him for the spread."

"Of course, sir."

Both sides of the dirt road that ended at Thanh's villa were already crowded; half a dozen sedans and jeeps were jumbled among the mangroves and undergrowth. An array of security lights sprouted above the barbed wire atop the villa compound walls. Below, chauffeurs, some in military uniform, played dice games in the dirt while nervous white-clad policemen, who really did look like white mice and outnumbered the drivers, paced and conversed quietly. Macintosh's sedan stopped in front of the gate. He and Ike passed through the courtyard and into the villa. Thanh, merrier than usual, shook Macintosh's hand and greeted Ike with an ecstatic smile. He led them through the crowded sitting room, which was lit by strings of bulbs in a sparsely decorated fake Christmas tree. Ike was sure it had come from the American PX.

Macintosh eyed one of the Viets. "Major Nghiem."

Nghiem gave Macintosh a phony grin and bowed.

Just past the tree, Macintosh halted to gaze at a pearl gray porcelain elephant two and a half feet high. The animal wore a golden halter and head covering with multicolored tassels, and over its back lay a blanket of pale orange decorated with a raised filigree in blue, green, and red. Its luminous skin was glazed and reflected the candles in the room, but its eyes, toenails, and adornments were opaque. Macintosh bent and touched the blanket.

"That's not cloth," he said. "That's ceramic, too."

"It is from Hue," Thanh said. "The monks at the Thanh Loi Pagoda gave it to me as a thank-you gift when we drove the VC from Hue in

1968." He brushed his fingers along the embroidery on the elephant's headpiece. "They do the finest work in Vietnam."

Macintosh smiled. "Talk about craftsmanship."

"It is dear to me," Thanh said, "because of the monks."

Thanh escorted them to the dining room and waved his open palm over the table spread with trays of cut vegetables, tiny egg rolls, petite sausages, and cubes of glutinous rice, backed by half a dozen bowls of condiments. "Please to try some Vietnamese delicacies."

The guests around the table moved back to make room for them.

"Quite a spread, Colonel," Ike said. "You sure know how to do it up."

Thanh grinned. "Martini?" he said to Macintosh.

"Dry," Macintosh said, "truly dry."

Thanh spoke to an aide behind the improvised bar who took a stemmed cocktail glass from the freezing compartment of a small refrigerator (undoubtedly from the PX) and put a drop of vermouth into it. He covered it with a second frosted glass, shook it, and dumped the vermouth. Spearing an olive with a toothpick, he eased it into the glass. Next he poured two jiggers of gin into a silver cocktail shaker filled to the brim with shaved ice, swirled it, and poured the gin into the glass.

Macintosh's grin was just short of a laugh. "You remember," he said to Thanh. "And you were able to teach this fine troop the technique." He took the glass. "Thank you, my man." He tasted the martini, smacked his lips. "This young warrior has a great future ahead of him."

"My family awaits us in the garden," Thanh said.

He led them through a large room with tiled walls, then outdoors to a stoop three steps above the ground. Tiki torches flamed throughout the garden, their light overpowered by the security spotlights. Beyond the small lawn, at the edge of a natural stone patio, the family waited as if posed for a group photo—a woman in blue sat in a garden chair; a heavier woman in yellow stood next to her, her arm resting across the back of the chair; and a boy, all in white, sat cross-legged at her feet.

As Thanh, Macintosh, Ike, and Major Nghiem walked across the patio, the woman and child stood.

Thanh positioned himself beside them and extended his arm over them, as he had over the food table. "My family. This is my niece, Lan." The woman in yellow bowed.

The face—yes, Ike recognized her—one of the women at the ball, behind the screen in an alcove.

"My son, Thu," Thanh went on. The boy tented his fingers and touched them to his lips. "And my wife, Tuyet. Mrs. Thanh."

Ike blinked. Thanh's wife? She was Thanh's niece, wasn't she? Isn't that what Chuck told him?

"My niece's name, Lan, means 'orchid,'" Thanh said with his characteristic blissful smile. "My son's name, Thu, it means 'autumn,' our favorite time of year. And my wife's name, Tuyet," he put his arm around her, "her name means 'snow,' something rare and precious here in the south."

Ike coughed. The woman named Tuyet *was* his wife.

"We are honored to make your acquaintance," Macintosh said. "Thanh, you have a lovely family."

Ike focused on Thanh's wife. She had to be the woman he'd seen at the ball; but no, it couldn't be the same person. *There must be another Tuyet.* He cleared his throat. "With the Colonel's permission, I seem to recall that the Colonel has *two* nieces."

Thanh's wife's eyes signaled alarm. Macintosh scowled. Ike was suddenly acutely aware that his question, if not actually unmannerly, was slightly disrespectful.

Thanh's joviality was undiminished. "I wish I had more like Lan, Captain, but I do not. Sadly, only one is still living, but she is a jewel that shines enough for two."

Footfalls behind Ike. Sparky and Chuck, in suit and tie, were coming down the steps into the garden.

Chuck hurried ahead to Macintosh. "Colonel, my apologies. Grenade incident on Hai Ba Trung. Traffic rerouted." He faced Thanh. "Colonel, forgive our tardiness."

Thanh took both of Chuck's hands in his. "It is nothing." Beaming, he extended his arm toward his family. "You are acquainted with my niece, my son, and my wife."

Chuck was watching Tuyet, a smile lighting his face. Tuyet, pale, raised her head. Lan squared her shoulders in triumph.

"It is a pleasure to see you again," Chuck said. "Miss Lan, Miss Tuyet, and Mister Thu."

Thanh laughed. "It is *Mrs.* Tuyet." He took Tuyet's hand. "No, we don't say that in English. Mrs. Thanh."

Chuck froze. His eyebrows knitted. Tuyet nodded almost imperceptibly.

"You are—" Chuck stammered.

Tuyet took a deep breath and straightened. "Mrs. Thanh."

Chuck's mouth opened.

Thanh's eyes flitted from Chuck to Tuyet. "Mister Griffin, Mister Groton," he said in a low voice, "you have no drink. Come. We go to the bar."

"Stay with your family, sir." Ike hooked Chuck's arm in his. "I'll show him where the drinks are." He guided Chuck toward the house.

Sparky trailed along. "What's the matter?"

Ike shushed him. At the bar, the three of them got beers. Chuck grasped the bottle rigidly, his face a frozen mask.

"Easy," Ike whispered. "It'll be okay."

"She's his wife," Chuck said.

"Would someone please tell me what's going on?" Sparky said.

"Sparky," Ike said, "you stay with him. Make it look like everything's all right. I'm going back to talk to Colonel Macintosh like the situation's normal. Wait 'til Chuck calms down, then bring him out to the garden to socialize-like. Got it?"

Sparky nodded doubtfully. Ike headed out the door to the patio. When he rejoined the group, Macintosh was questioning Thu with Thanh as interpreter. Lan was beaming, but Tuyet stood with her eyes lowered. Ike smiled and laughed and chatted and occasionally glanced toward the door to the house.

After a very long twenty minutes, Sparky and Chuck came down the steps into the patio and rejoined the family. Ike watched Chuck out of the corner of his eye. Chuck's hands were fists, his mouth clamped shut. When Macintosh addressed him directly, he forced a smile. He and Tuyet never once looked at one another. Thanh watched it all.

"You forgive, yes?" Thanh said. "My family will retire."

Tuyet, Lan, and Thu bowed and went into the house. Thanh suggested that he and his guests return to the bar. "Mac can have another Vietnamese martini."

⎯⏑⎍⎍⏑⎍⎯

As soon as the first guest departed, the three housemates courteously bid Macintosh good night, thanked Thanh for a lovely evening, and made for the door. At the gate, Chuck bolted. Ike took off after him up the dirt road through the gaggle of drivers and police. He caught up with Chuck beside the jeep just as Chuck was drawing back his arm until the elbow jutted behind him. He slammed his fist into the windshield. Ike seized Chuck's arms, forced them behind his back. Chuck bucked, but Ike held on. Chauffeurs and policemen scattered like pigeons after a thunderclap. Ike and Chuck lost their footing and fell into the road, where they rolled, snarling and panting. Ike flung Chuck onto his back, clumped his knees on Chuck's chest, and held Chuck's wrists in the dirt on either side of his head. He bent until his face was inches from Chuck's.

Chuck thrashed and flopped his head from side to side. "Get off me, you son of a bitch."

"Not 'til you stop this."

Chuck's face twisted, and a growl choked past his locked teeth. The tension seeped from his body. He lay still. Ike released his wrists and stood.

"Come on, buddy," Ike said. "We'll take you home."

Sparky hovered beside the jeep. "What's gotten into you guys?"

"Help me get him in," Ike said.

They put Chuck into the jeep's passenger seat and snapped his seat-belt into place. Sparky, bug-eyed, climbed into the back.

Ike drove in silence. Chuck sat quietly, chin on his chest, hands in his lap. At the Yen Do villa, Oanh opened the gate for them. Without a word Chuck started upstairs.

Ike grasped his shoulder. "Let me see that fucking hand." He took Chuck's wrist and lifted the hand into the light. "Damn." The flesh along the four knuckles was lacerated. Blood darkened Chuck's suit jacket and trousers. "Let's get you to the dispensary. The after-hours guys—"

"No."

"You could of broke some bones," Sparky said.

"No."

Ike huffed. "You stubborn bastard. Do what you have to do. What-ever it takes. Okay. Let me bandage it. Regular dispensary hours start at 0800. I'll drive you. Sparky, go on to bed. I'll handle him." He led Chuck to the upstairs head. "You're all grubby. Take a shower. And wash that hand *clean.*"

By the time Ike heard the shower shut off, he'd gotten into shorts and dumped his muddy suit in the garbage. He opened the bathroom door as Chuck was toweling off. "Let me see that hand." He doused the torn flesh with peroxide, applied germicidal ointment, and wrapped it in gauze. "I'm going to tape this tight. If it comes off in the night, you call me."

Long after Chuck was in his room with the door shut, Ike sat in the darkened living room with a Schlitz. Maybe if he'd lost a child and then a wife he'd be a freakin' basket case, too. Chuck's problem was that he'd been hurt too bad and had locked up his need so's he could go on being a man. Then a chippie comes along and opens the floodgates, and Chuck's heart flows right out of him. Ike hacked and spat into his empty beer can. Damned good thing Ike had found Molly. She knew the score. He pictured her in her scrubs, breasts pushing out, nipples forming little tents in the fabric. He smiled. Good woman. He remembered her face as she held Angélique. Better than good. He spat again. When his tour was up, he'd miss her.

Heaven Weeps

DECEMBER 1974

CHAPTER 7

Chuck's hand throbbed. She'd stood before him, slender and lithe in her blue *áo dài*. His heart had leapt at the sight of her. Then Thanh corrected him. "Mrs. Thanh." The pain in his chest was worse than anything he felt in his hand.

He clicked on the bedside lamp and looked at the clock. Past four. He'd get to his feet, into shorts. *Go down the hall to the head. Shave, bathe, and dress and drive the jeep to DAO.* He'd use work to keep going. And Tuyet? God willing, he'd never see her again.

The brightly lit corridors of DAO were empty and, as always, antiseptically clean. Once inside the Intelligence Branch, he stopped by the comms center to alert the midnight shift that he was going to be in the tank working and took the incoming mail. Troiano's office was dark, with an artificial white Christmas tree on one side of the door across from the secretary's desk. When he flipped on the lights in the tank, the tawdry seasonal tree, larger, more ornate, more tasteless than Troiano's, sucked attention away from the maps covering the four walls, where the story of imminent destruction hung bleeding. At his desk, he unlocked the drawers and his safe, sorted the mail—intel wrap-ups from stateside agencies, signals intelligence reports, prisoner interrogations, translations of Liberation News Agency dispatches, and State Department cables—and started through the III Corps and IV Corps after-action reports.

At seven he prepared his notes for the 0800 briefing. Major General Homer Smith, the defense attaché himself, and senior U.S. intelligence personnel from the embassy and the four corps would be attending. Heavy fighting in Tay Ninh Province sixty miles northwest of Saigon. Farther east, in Phuoc Long Province, Bunard had fallen and Don Luan was under heavy bombardment. Two North Vietnamese divisions and a tank battalion plus local forces were preparing an assault on the provincial capital, Phuoc Binh. The North Vietnamese had interdicted the roads. If they took Phuoc Binh airfield, resupply would be impossible. If the province *and* its capital fell, it would be the first time in the Vietnam War the Communists took and held an entire province.

As the lights came up after the briefing and Chuck was filing out with the crowd, Troiano hooked him by the arm and pulled him aside. "You look like shit," Troiano said in an undertone. "You hitting the bottle? What happened to your hand?"

"An accident," Chuck said. "Had a beer last night is all. Got a case of the trots. Kept me up all night."

Troiano smiled. "Thought you'd spent so much time in-country your bowels had acclimated."

"So did I, sir. Guess I got into some bad *nuoc mam*."

Troiano blenched. "That stuff's made from rotting fish. Stay away from local food. That's an order. Can't lose my best forecaster."

The next night, Wednesday, 18 December, Chuck left DAO at 1900 and headed for Thanh's office on foot. As before, the office door eased open when he knocked. Thanh sat, not at his desk but at the small table by the window. A dim desk lamp on one side and the flicker of the tea stove on the other illuminated his figure.

"Mister Griffin," he said. "Please to sit. Tea?"

Chuck sat facing him. "Thank you, sir."

"You have recovered from your illness?"

"Sir?"

"Your illness at my reception," Thanh said. "And your hand is bandaged?"

"Not serious."

"Very well. I am weary, and when we have completed our talk I must go to the airstrip for a flight to Phuoc Binh. I meet with the Phuoc Long Province chief, a fine man and good soldier. I must prepare him . . ." Thanh waved his hand. "You delivered my letter to Colonel Mac?"

"Yes, sir."

"And Colonel Mac write back?"

"Colonel Macintosh said there was no need to write anything."

"He is a wise man."

"He asked me to explain that the United States is a nation tired of war. It wishes peace."

"He told you to tell me," Thanh said, "that your country will not come to Vietnam's aid."

Chuck's throat muscles tightened.

Thanh nodded. "*Được rôi.*"

Chuck waited. Thanh sat immobile.

"Does the Colonel wish to send another message to Colonel Macintosh?"

Thanh said nothing, lost in his own thoughts.

"Colonel?" Chuck said.

"Tell Colonel Mac to watch Phuoc Binh. When Phuoc Binh falls, Vietnam falls."

The tea stove sputtered.

Thanh stood. "Give Colonel Mac my best wishes. Tell him I cherish his friendship. Convey to him that I will ask his help for one more thing. Not now. Later. I will humbly beg of him to evacuate my wife and son."

Chuck rose. "Colonel Macintosh left Vietnam yesterday." He hoped Thanh would understand.

"Yes. I saw him off. No matter. He can save my family."

Chuck forced himself to speak evenly. "Perhaps the Colonel should send Mrs. Thanh and his son out of the country now. They can return if—"

Thanh raised his eyes and looked directly at Chuck. "I have no money to send them."

"A friend might be able to lend money to the Colonel."

"To beg Mac to save my family shames me. Taking money to send them away shames me more. I will do that if all else fails. Not until then. You forgive me now?"

"Of course, sir."

"We will meet again in the new year," Thanh said. "I will inform you."

Chuck walked as quietly as he could from the room, through the courtyard, into the dusty Saigon night. At the street, he flagged a cyclo to carry him to Yen Do. As it creaked through the quieting streets, Chuck knew that Thanh's despair, like that of the Cité Paul-Marie orphans, was far greater than his.

⎯ 1969 ⎯

Less than a week until Christmas. Time for the annual maintenance on the jeep—always scheduled for Christmas because the Vietnamese mechanics didn't celebrate and the Communists usually backed off, just as they did during the Vietnamese New Year's celebration at Tet. The lull usually lasted until the Western New Year. Sparky wouldn't need the jeep for anything personal. He and Ike and Chuck's DAO colleagues had long since finished holiday shopping and mailing to family in the States. Chuck had no one to send to.

On Christmas Eve Chuck put in his usual ten hours in the tank and did his workout at the Cercle. Rankled that he should have to forgo what was good for him solely to evade Tuyet, he swam his laps but avoided looking at the terrace. As he was leaving the pool, he couldn't resist canvassing the poolside deck. She wasn't there.

At 0700 Christmas morning, Chuck was at his desk in the tank. Since he was the first in the office that morning, he hoisted the fifty-five-cup stainless steel coffeemaker from its table next to the refrigerator onto a cart. In the head, he filled its reservoir, wheeled it back to the tank, loaded the basket with ground coffee, and plugged it in. While he waited for it to brew, he worked his way through the growing pile of reports and cables from Phuoc Long. No holiday lull this year. Artillery bombardment of key locations was more intense every day. President Thieu had ignored pleas for reinforcements, but he ordered resupply by land and air. "Don Luan cannot hold out much longer," Chuck wrote in his notes for the briefer, "and Phuoc Binh will be next."

Midafternoon, Troiano's secretary buzzed Chuck. "The colonel wants to see you."

Troiano's workspace was cleared and his safe was secured. He wore not his usual starched khakis but a tweed sport coat and red tie. "On my way to the Ambassador's residence for the annual Christmas reception, but I wanted to talk to you first. James H. Carver, Major, U.S. Army. You wanted to find him? He's a colonel now, working at the J3 Staff in the Pentagon. He remembers your son." Troiano tightened his tie. "He might be in-country on a fact-finding visit after the beginning of the year. Told me he'd be glad to sit down with you and go over everything he knows. But—" He rubbed his forehead. "I did a little checking on this guy. He's RA all the way, old school officer. My buddies at JCS tell me he's a Marine hater. You might want to keep your military background to yourself."

Troiano's secretary was in the doorway. "Car's waiting, sir."

He clapped Chuck on the shoulder. "Merry Christmas."

After the distribution of gifts to the orphans at Cité Paul-Marie, the embassy sedan took Chuck, Ike, and Molly to Yen Do. Sparky, already slurring his words, met them at the door with a hearty "Merry Christmas" and glasses of eggnog. "Jingle Bell Rock" boomed from the living room stereo, and the aroma of roasting turkey filled the hall.

Chuck excused himself from cocktails and slipped upstairs, aware that Ike was watching. He lay on his rack, hands behind his head.

Admit it. You're hooked. What was it about Tuyet? She exuded a mix of arrogance and vulnerability that charmed him. She was brighter than he was, and where he was slow she was quick. Her body, so small that he could carry her with one arm, brimmed with strength and passion. But it was more than that. She gave him what he had denied needing—the love of a woman. And she was married to Thanh. What a fuckup.

A tap at the door. "Can I talk to you?" Molly's voice. The last thing he needed right now. The door opened a few inches and her face peered in. "Hey, baby." She stepped in, glass in hand, and shut the door. "What's the problem?"

"Did Ike send you?"

She sat on the bed. "Nurse Molly spotted a laceration and decided to treat it. It's Tuyet, isn't it?"

"Let me handle it."

"You're not handling it."

"Let me leave it alone, then."

"Spoken like a true sniveler," she said. "Come on, Chuckie. Buck up. It's not the end of the world."

"Only the end of the Republic of Vietnam. Listen to the news from Phuoc Long. If it falls, get ready to pack out."

"I thought this was about Tuyet."

He slid to a sitting position against the headboard. "Try this on for size. The woman I got mixed up with is from the royal family. Her husband is a staunch enemy of the Communists. When the country falls, the Communists will torture and execute both of them. And their little boy."

"Who says the country's falling? Come on—"

"The North Vietnamese will take Phuoc Long. The U.S. won't do anything. Once that's clear, the North Vietnamese will be balls-to-the-wall to march on Saigon."

"Jesus." Her eyes wandered to the window. "I signed up for hazardous duty, not combat." She tossed down what was left of her drink. "I think I'll get drunk."

"Do it quick so you'll have time to get over the hangover before the evacuation begins."

"That's not funny."

"It wasn't meant to be."

"Screw it." She stood and looked at him with narrowed eyes. "Very well, Professor Moriarty." She clumped to the door. "You've won this round, but you haven't seen the last of the Dragon Lady and her faithful sidekick, Joy Stick." She strutted from the room and slammed the door behind her.

Chuck leaned his head back, closed his eyes, and breathed the tropical Saigon air. He was getting better. Nasty was a step up from moping.

The party went on downstairs. Perry Como's "A Christmas Dream" was punctuated by boozy laughter that stopped abruptly when the gate bell sounded. The gate scraped open. Then nothing.

"Mister Chuck, sir." Oanh's voice outside his door. "A people want see you."

Chuck rose and headed downstairs. His housemates and Molly were in the hall at the foot of the steps, gawking at him. Ike waved his hand back and forth like a warning semaphore. At the bottom of the staircase, Chuck turned toward the front door. A cloaked and veiled figure waited behind Oanh.

"You wanted to see me?" Chuck asked.

"We can talk privately, yes?"

Tuyet. He found his voice. "No."

She lifted the veil. "I have come to plead with you to save my son." She stood before him hands folded at her waist, eyes down.

Her son. Thu. The kid in the pool. His stomach tightened. "In the garden."

Chuck pushed his way past Molly and the housemates. Tuyet followed. They moved through the living room, past the tree and the stereo now blaring a rock version of "I Saw Mommy Kissing Santa Claus," and out the French doors. He followed the walkway until they reached the small patio screened from the house by bamboo.

She took off the veil. Her hair lapped over her shoulders.

"How melodramatic," he said sarcastically. "Dark night of the soul?"

"It is important that no one recognize me."

"Afraid Thanh might see you?"

"Thanh is at Phuoc Binh. He knows I have a lover and asked me to avoid scandal. He does not know it is you, but he will. He senses things."

"And the punishment?"

She shook her head. "I lied to you. He will not punish me. He accepts me as he knows I am."

"So many lies."

"That is why I come see you. I have wronged you. I beg your forgiveness."

"You have it," Chuck said.

"I want to explain you. Perhaps you hate me less."

"I really don't care about extenuating circumstances—"

"Please, you listen me, okay?"

"Your English is going to hell."

She tightened her clasped hands. "I do not lie to you about everything. My marriage to Thanh was arranged for political gain. I never loved him. I saw you before I ever met Thanh. I tell you I am estranged. It is the truth. Thanh and I are not husband and wife. We have not slept in the same bed for more than six years. I am Catholic, a member of the royal family, and cannot divorce. We have to live in the same house to avoid scandal, but we have separate bedrooms. I know the North Vietnamese will kill me when the end comes. I hoped you would fall in love with me and arrange for Thu and me to be evacuated. I lied about Thanh. I hoped you would love me and forgive me. Then, the more we were together, the more I cared for you."

She stopped talking and tensed, as if trying to regain control. "You know that I am telling the truth," she said. "You have held me naked in your arms and felt my tears on your skin. You have given me a great gift. For a little while, for the first time, I was very happy."

When he started to speak, no sound came. He cleared his throat and tried again. "You should go. The curfew—"

"One thing more; the reason I come here. Thu. The North Vietnamese will kill him, or worse, turn him into an object of hate before the people. Thanh believes that Mac can somehow evacuate him when the end is at hand, but Mac is far away. You are here." She bit her lip. "Will you save Thu?"

"I don't have any authority to do that." He sighed. "All right. I'll do what I can, but you must promise to escape with Thu."

"If I can."

"Not good enough. You must assure me you'll get out of the country with Thu if I can arrange it."

She sighed deeply, as though relieved that her work was finished. "I remain in your debt. Now I must go." She gathered her cloak, veiled her face, and turned toward the house. In the living room, Ike slumped on the sofa, Molly and Sparky beside him. They watched in silence as Chuck followed Tuyet to the front of the house where Oanh stood in the doorway.

"The lady," Oanh said to Chuck, "not can go. No cyclo now. No cabs. Curfew begin in fifteen minutes."

"I've got a curfew pass," Chuck said. "I'll drive you home."

"The jeep's in the shop, numb-nuts," Sparky said from the living room.

"The lady stay here tonight," Oanh said.

Chuck shook his head. "We have no spare rooms."

Tuyet nodded toward the living room. "I wait for dawn in there."

"There's a party going on. Won't end soon."

"Please. The police will arrest me."

She stood humbled before him. If her bond to Thanh was really no more than a marriage of convenience that was now over . . . no. He couldn't do it. Sleeping with Thanh's wife was too great a betrayal. It would dishonor both Thanh and him. He remembered her tears on his chest. She raised her eyes to his.

He took her hand and led her up the stairs.

CHAPTER 8

olly had signed up to take off the Thursday, Friday, and Saturday after Christmas, so she'd have five full days away from the dispensary. She was spared doling out salt tablets to those who'd been in-country less than a year and still suffered from excessive sweating, liquid cement (Kaopectate) and a stern lecture about the dangers of dysentery to employees who'd insisted on eating snacks hawked by street vendors, and plague vaccinations to diplomats who had failed to get them before coming to Southeast Asia. She relished the occasional crisis—a genuine case of malaria, a dengue attack, emergency treatment after a grenade incident, cutting shrapnel fragments from the leg of a man who'd held an outdoor party in defiance of security regulations. Granted, she only got to render what amounted to first aid before the victim was medevacked to the hospital at Clark in the Philippines, but at least it was exciting until the patient was hauled off to an ambulance for the trip to the airport.

Ike worked reduced hours that week, and Molly exulted in the extra time in bed with him. He knew by instinct what would excite her and never failed to surprise her, one time kissing her behind her ear, the next burying his face in her belly and licking her navel. But it wasn't really the sex. It was the man Ike was—a warrior dedicated to his cause, courageous to the nines, dripping with self-confidence but devoid of arrogance. It was the way he tilted his head and grinned, his discomfort with civilians and their ways, and his inability to tie a tie. He was natural and earthy with no pretensions whatever, and more precious to her than all the emeralds of Burma.

The day after Christmas she threw on blue hospital scrubs and went to the kitchen to ask Chi Nam for coffee—rich and thick and bitter, like the French roast at the Continental Hotel. She carried it to the living room where she read the week-old *Stars and Stripes* and wiggled her bottom while she listened to George McCrae's "Rock Your Baby" on ARS.

That evening she met Chuck at Cité Paul-Marie and sang to the children every Christmas carol she could remember. Angélique was willing to sit on her lap for a few minutes.

As they were leaving, Mother Monique touched Molly's arm. "You have a beautiful voice."

Molly laughed. "Get out of here."

"Sundays at ten, the American monsignor, Father Sullivan, says Mass in English in the chapel for the Americans. He has started a folk group to furnish music for the celebration. He is seeking more singers. Perhaps—"

"Me?"

"Be kind enough to consider it." Mother Monique bowed.

What was it about this woman, always in immaculate white, her face always serene? The only other Mother-anything Molly had ever heard of was Mother Teresa. Maybe you had to be a saint before they let you be called "Mother" in the Catholic Church.

Late Friday afternoon, after running some errands, Molly returned to the Yen Do villa by blue-and-white in time to see Tuyet, heavily veiled, going in the gate. As Molly came into the hall, Tuyet rounded the landing on the stairs and disappeared. Molly shook her head and mixed martinis, then climbed the stairs. The door to Chuck's room was closed. She sighed, went to Ike's room, and changed into purple scrubs. As she was coming down the stairs, Ike banged in.

"Martinis on the veranda," she said. "Lose the uniform. Tuyet's here, by the way."

He bounded up the stairs. Molly was waiting at the wicker table on the veranda when he came through the door in shorts and a tank top.

Sparky, already in shorts and T-shirt, came from the kitchen. "Reliable sources report the sighting of martinis in the vicinity."

"You forgot to bring a glass," Ike said.

"Oops." Sparky wheeled and headed to the kitchen.

"Where's Chuck?" Ike said when Sparky returned.

Sparky slurped. "Bollixed up with visitors—Representative Ryan's staff. Then he has to see about how to get names added to the evac list."

"Representative who?" Molly asked.

"The congressman." Sparky helped himself to a refill. "We might have to work Sunday."

After dinner Molly instructed Chi Nam to prepare another plate and carried it, along with a glass of wine, up the stairs. She knocked at Chuck's door. "Tuyet? I brought you food."

After a long silence, the door cracked an inch. Tuyet peered at Molly. "I apologize."

Molly pushed in. "Nothing to be sorry about. You must be hungry." She set the plate and glass on the desk.

Tuyet had shed her cloak and veil. "You are very kind, Miss—"

"I'm Molly, a friend of Captain Saunders. I saw you Christmas night. We didn't actually meet, but I know who you are. Please eat something."

Tuyet sat at the desk. "Chuck will be home soon?"

Molly perched on the edge of the bed. "He'll be late. Visiting VIPs." At Tuyet's questioning look, Molly laughed. "Very important people. From Washington."

Tuyet ate silently. Molly watched. "I do not need to detain you further," Tuyet said.

"That's all right. Got nothing to do anyway."

Tuyet went on eating. *Pretty little thing.* Probably half Molly's size, maybe a third her weight. How could a man as big as Chuck make love to anything that tiny?

"So, you're staying the night?" Molly said. "It's okay. I'm staying, too."

"You don't live here?"

"Nope. Got my own place. Apartment building at the corner of Tu Do and Ngo Duc Ke. Just across from the Catinat Hotel."

"So you are Captain Saunders' . . ."

"Girlfriend. Lover. Mistress. Take your pick. Sometimes we stay here, sometimes at my place."

Tuyet turned away.

"Sorry," Molly said. "Delicacy ain't my strong suit."

"Not to distress yourself."

"And you're Chuck's whatever, right?"

"Please." Tuyet put down her fork.

Molly leaned forward and rested her hand on Tuyet's arm. "Listen, sweetie, we women have to stick together. Avoiding the issue don't help. You're in a tough spot."

Tuyet shrank from her touch.

"Want to talk to me about it?" Molly said. "Maybe I can help."

Tuyet didn't look at her.

Molly smacked her lips. "You know what? You could use my place. If someone saw you downtown, it wouldn't be any big deal. Not like here, the residential district. And . . . I don't know how to say this exactly, but those pills Chuck gave you? They came from me."

Tuyet straightened.

"He thought I use them," Molly said. "If you fuck up and forget to take them, I know where you can get it taken care of. It's all hush-hush, the embassy looks the other way."

Tuyet stood. "No. I could never—"

"I did." Molly looked away. "That's why I can't have children. The guy was a lot older, married. My father would have killed me. We women are used to sacrificing. You do what you have to do—"

The door swung open and Chuck strode in.

Molly stood. "Think about it, honey. I'll be here if you need me."

Sunday morning Molly stepped from a cab at the Cité Paul-Marie gate and joined a stream of other Americans heading through the walkways to the chapel. Once inside she sat in the pew closest to the rear door. As the church filled—it probably didn't hold more than two hundred— her eyes were drawn to a group of five on one side of the altar, two holding guitars.

The apparent leader, a plump man close to Molly's age, was speaking in a low voice to the other group members while he tuned his guitar. He checked the tuning of the second guitar and turned to the congregation. "You'll find the words to today's songs in the pews," he said. "Please sing along with us. We'll greet Monsignor Sullivan with 'The Spirit Is a-Movin'. Let's run through it once to warm up."

Molly found the mimeographed sheet. The two guitars played an introduction, and all five group members sailed into the song. Molly had never heard country-western music in church. She tapped her toe to the rhythm and by the third verse was singing along.

The Mass began. Molly had been in a Catholic church maybe half a dozen times in her life, always for funerals or weddings, and she had no idea what was going on. But the music speeded her heartbeat, especially what the group leader called a meditation hymn after Communion, a song called "Hear, O Lord." Its melody soared, and its harmonies put a lump in her throat. After two verses, the group divided. While three members began the third verse, the leader and a woman sang a counter melody, which turned out to be "Where Have All the Flowers Gone?" Molly's eyes teared up.

After the recessional, "They'll Know We Are Christians by Our Love," Molly waited until the chapel was nearly empty, then ventured to the altar rail. The folk-group members were folding music stands, packing guitars in cases, and stowing sheet music in a briefcase.

"Excuse me . . ."

The group leader, on one knee beside his guitar case, smiled. "Hello." He came to the altar rail.

Molly felt her skin burning. "Do you have to be Catholic to sing at Mass? Mother Monique told me you were looking for singers. I can't read music, but I love to sing."

"Can you come to rehearsal here Friday at 1800? We'll see."

Molly grinned. "I'll be here."

Weary of housemates and constrained by the curfew, Molly and Ike decided to have a cookout on the balcony of her apartment on New Year's Eve. Ike bought booze at the PX while Molly shopped for Porterhouse steaks at the commissary. When she returned home that evening, she heard a wet mop slapping the tile floor. On the far side of the counter dividing the dining area from the kitchen, Huong, in her usual black pajamas, was scrubbing away.

"Huong," Molly said.

Huong jumped, saw Molly, and smiled. "Miss Molly, ma'am, yes *ma'am*. Home from work so soon?"

"The dispensary closed early—it's New Year's Eve. Mister Captain and I will be grilling steaks. Um . . . why are you here?"

"I come back because I want talk to Mister Captain just a tad. I wait him, it is okay?"

"Oh, sure. He'll be here any minute." Molly mixed a pitcher of martinis, poured a glass for Ike, and added two olives. As soon as she heard the click of his key in the door, she swooped, martini in hand, to the hall. When the door opened, all she could see in the dim light was his smile and his eyes. "Hey, hunky," she said.

"Hey yourself, sexy." He wrapped her in his arms, kissed her, and thrust his hips against her. His hands were on her buttocks when Huong spoke.

"Mister Captain, *sir*." She bowed.

Ike started, peered over Molly's shoulder.

"You excuse, okay?" Huong said. "I come back because I want chew the fat with you, you know?"

With a growl, Ike took the martini and dropped into a chair. "What you need, Huong?"

"My husband is soldier," Huong said. "He in Pleiku now long time."

Molly eased into the kitchen, poured herself a drink, and arranged smoked oysters and crackers on a tray.

"He not write to me now it is two months," Huong said. "I very freak out, you know?"

Molly carried the drink and tray to the living room and sat next to Ike. Huong stood kneading her hands, eyes lowered, face distressed.

"What unit is he in?" Ike said.

"Ranger Group 25," Huong said.

"Where is it operating?"

"The highlands, *sir.*"

"Pleiku?"

"I not know, sir."

Ike was dubious. "What do you want me to do?"

"You find him for me, sir. You tell me he is okay, not snafu."

Molly stifled a grunt. Why did the Vietnamese—and apparently the Chinese, too—persist in believing that Americans were wizards who could do anything at the mere snap of the fingers? How the hell could Ike find some army enlisted man somewhere in the wilds of the highlands?

Ike shook his head. "I don't know. All right. Write down his name, rank, and unit, and where his unit was located that last time you knew. I'll see what I can do."

Huong scampered to the kitchen for paper and pen and wrote, biting her lip. She hurried back and handed Ike the paper. "I thank you so much, sir."

"Don't get your hopes up," Ike said.

"You find him," Huong said. "I know you find him. Now, Miss Molly, you forgive and I go way. I come in the morning, clean up, fix breakfast."

"Come late," Molly said. "We'll be sleeping in."

Huong picked up the wooden-handled canvas bag she always carried and, with one more smile, left.

"Why'd you tell her it was okay to come back in the morning?" Ike said. "It's New Year's. I thought we'd go to the Caravelle for brunch."

"She'd be here no matter what I said. I'll tell her to fix a Sunday breakfast. Why'd you tell her you'd hunt for her husband? How're you going to do that?"

"I couldn't say no. I'll ask Chuck."

Molly left the dispensary early on Friday and went straight to the folk-group rehearsal at Cité Paul-Marie. She learned two of the songs well enough to fake her way through them and mouthed the rest.

Sunday, butterflies in the belly notwithstanding, she got through the Mass without any major screw-ups. She helped the group pack up, then squeezed into a blue-and-white for the ride downtown to La Pagode, the open-air patisserie, to meet Chuck and Ike for coffee—hot chocolate for Molly—and pomegranate muffins.

"Visitors still running you ragged?" Ike asked Chuck.

Chuck shook his head. "They left. It's the war that's driving me nonlinear."

"That place you told me about," Molly said, "sounds like Long Fuck?"

"Phuoc Long Province. Things are looking dicey. Don Luan fell the day after Christmas, and Phuoc Binh, the capital, is overwhelmed with refugees. It's been under heavy artillery attack."

Molly's cheerfulness drained away. "You said if that place falls—"

"It's going to fall, Molly."

"So what?" Ike said. "The South Vietnamese will take it back again."

"Why's Phuoc Long such a big deal?" Molly asked.

"It's a test," Chuck said. "It's close to Saigon. If the North Vietnamese seize it and the U.S. does nothing, they know they're good to go."

"Meaning?"

"They can conquer South Vietnam and the U.S. won't interfere."

Molly studied Chuck's face. It had that dead look she'd seen when he told her to be prepared to evacuate.

CHAPTER 9

When Chuck sat down for breakfast Monday morning, Sparky had ARS playing on his portable as he wolfed down Chi Nam's sausage and eggs. Chuck ate beside him, trying to read an article in the four-day-old 2 January 1975 *Stars and Stripes*. After Judy Collins' rendition of "Send in the Clowns," the newscaster reported that *The Godfather II* and *Chinatown* were running neck-and-neck for the Oscars. Then, "in local news, North Vietnamese forces have penetrated Phuoc Binh. After tank bombardment and heavy mortar fire, the North Vietnamese are fighting a pitched battle against South Vietnamese troops in the streets of the provincial capital."

Chuck dropped his fork. "They're fighting in the streets?"

Sparky pushed his plate away. "You ready to hit the road?"

As they exited the house, Sparky stopped. "Oops. Forgot my keys." He went back inside.

Chuck waited by the jeep. The sky looked in an ugly mood.

"Rain?" Sparky came down the steps into the driveway and squinted at the black clouds.

"Never rains in January," Chuck said. "Dry season." A drop of water hit Chuck's head and ran down his cheek. They stretched the canvas top over the jeep's roll bars, snapped the door skins in place, and headed out into the thicket of bicycles and cyclos. By the time they reached Cach Mang Boulevard, fat drops were splattering across the windshield. The orange-and-white propaganda banners overhead were wilting.

At his desk in the tank, Chuck worked through stacks of reports about the siege of Phuoc Binh. The South Vietnamese air force had tried to resupply the beleaguered troops ten times, but the enemy seized all the bundles. Artillery surrounded the town, which was choked with refugees. Enemy tanks were rolling in the streets. Liberation Radio gloated over the VC triumphs: "The courageous liberation forces have reduced the so-called Republic of Vietnam Army to chaos as it frantically tries to defend Phuoc Binh. The puppet army has collapsed in panic at the approach of our gallant soldiers, and patriots within the city have begun an insurrection against the cowardly military commanders."

"Phuoc Binh," Chuck wrote in his text for the daily briefing, "will fall before dark."

At midafternoon Chuck received the yellow teletype paper he'd expected. The Phuoc Binh province chief, wounded, had fled the city with what remained of his men. Fewer than a tenth of the friendly forces had escaped. Chuck trudged across the room to Sparky's desk.

"I need to go to JGS to check on Thanh. If I'm not back before closing time, take the jeep home."

By the time he reached Thanh's office inside the JGS compound, the rain had turned the dry-season dust to thin, soupy mud. Thanh's jeep was not inside the walls. A Vietnamese corporal met Chuck at the door.

"Co-lo-nel," the aide said, "he not here. He spend the night here. Now he go home to rest."

It cost Chuck fifteen minutes to flag down a cab in the downpour. The ride through the mash of traffic took another fifteen minutes. At Thanh's villa, a maid cowering under a vinyl poncho nodded, smiled, chattered, and motioned him through the house to the back steps. Chuck descended into the garden, now blurred gray in the rain, and waded through the flooded grass.

He found Thanh alone, sitting on a Chinese garden seat at the rear of the compound in a grove of bamboo. He was in utilities but hatless, wet to the skin, his sparse hair plastered to his head. Chuck sat next to him. Together they watched the rain.

At last Thanh turned to him and spoke. "Phuoc Binh fall."

"Yes, sir."

"You tell Mac for me, yes?"

"Yes, sir."

Thanh's face turned upward again. His eyelids quivered as rain-drops splashed down his forehead. "The Heaven." He pointed upward. "The Heaven weeps. An Nam no more. An Nam was. You listen to her weep now."

Chuck listened to the rain. He heard the weeping. Thanh was no longer the Tiger of Phat Hoa, Thanh the fierce, Thanh the incorrupt-ible. He was just a little man sitting in the rain, a man grown suddenly old. *Thanh is a dead man.*

"You go now, please," Thanh said.

By evening the rains had vanished. The dry season was with them again. At dinner, Ike laid a crumpled paper on the table in front of Chuck. "Any way you can check on this guy? He's Molly's maid's husband."

Chuck smoothed the paper and read, "Corporal Giuong Minh Phuc, Ranger Group 25, Pleiku." He shook his head. "I don't see how—wait a minute. Thanh goes north all the time to work with the troops. Maybe . . ."

"Do what you can," Ike said. "That little gal is something else."

A new congressional party invaded the next day, this time the staff peo-ple of Senator Sam Nunn, who was himself due to appear on the thir-teenth. Chuck and Sparky buried themselves in fact sheets, briefings, and question-and-answer sessions, but Chuck stole a few moments to write a note to Thanh asking if he would be so kind as to try to locate Corporal Phuc, perhaps during a visit to the highlands. Next he drafted a brief cable to Macintosh, Secret Noforn Eyes Only, recounting his visit to Thanh the day before.

Thursday morning, it being the second Thursday of January, Chuck trundled to the embassy for his monthly session with the Ambassador. He reported that the North Vietnamese now controlled Phuoc Long Province and its capital, Phuoc Binh. "It's the first time in the war that the North Vietnamese have taken and held an entire province." He was about to talk about the imminent threat to the highlands when the Ambassador interrupted him, saying he had to cut the briefing short. He mumbled something about other priorities and had Chuck shown out.

By Saturday, more of Senator Nunn's people were on the scene. One of them explained to Chuck that the Ford administration was preparing to request funds to keep the Republic of Vietnam afloat, and the senator needed data. Working late in the evening and through the weekend to assemble fact books that the senator could carry back to Washington, Chuck and Sparky nevertheless returned to the Yen Do villa before curfew each night and welcomed Molly's martinis—she made it a point to be there to look after them.

Chuck was low enough in rank that he escaped most of the official parties the embassy and DAO staged to honor the visitors, but since he had personally briefed Senator Nunn after his arrival on Monday, the thirteenth, he was required to attend the embassy cocktail party for the senator that night. Ike was invited, too, as was Molly—to ensure that enough women were on hand to impress the senator with the orderliness of official life in Saigon.

At 1800 hours an embassy sedan ferried Chuck and Ike, in Bangkok-tailored suits and ties, to the Ambassador's residence at the corner of Phung Khac Hoan and Phan Thanh Gian Streets, two blocks from the embassy. Both streets teemed with white mice and U.S. Marine guards, oddly surreal in the white dazzle of security lights.

The two U.S. Marines on each side of the gate saluted as Chuck and Ike passed through. Straight ahead of them was the house Chuck remembered as the Personal Protective Unit building, manned by fourteen Vietnamese Special Police. Three of these thugs, armed to the teeth, now glowered as the two Americans headed left through another gate into the formal garden fronting the residence. There, a middle-aged American hostess in an iridescent Thai silk cocktail dress smiled them up the porch steps and into the formal French colonial vestibule, redolent with the scent of gladiolas and jasmine. A male version of the hostess, swathed in morning coat and silver tie, waved them to the right through a tiled hallway, down a flight of steps, and into a patio awash with bougainvillea and orchids. Cocktail tables with tea lights dotted the grounds.

"It's going to be outdoors?" Chuck said in an undertone.

"It's safe here," Ike whispered. "Deep inside the compound with its own walls. No grenade could reach us."

Besides two waiters offering drinks and hors d'oeuvres, the only other people present were a sinister-looking bald gentleman with a lecherous smile and Molly, in her black dress and tiara. Chuck started toward her, but Ike held him back.

"Molly and me don't hang out together in public," he said quietly. "The Ambassador's a southern gentleman, son of a preacher. He don't hardly 'preciate no miscegenation."

Molly's eyes fluttered from the gentleman to Chuck and back again.

"Who's the guy?" Chuck asked.

"Christians in Action honcho."

"CIA chief of station? I didn't recognize him."

"You never seen him on the make before." Ike snatched champagnes from a waiter, handed Chuck one. "Not supposed to be a large gathering. It's just for the ass out working class. That's why there's no reception line. And why it's called a party, not a reception. There'll be a state dinner later. All the bigwigs will show up there." Ike snorted. "But since the senator's gonna be here, they'll be here, too."

The Ambassador, tall, elegant, and withered, came down the steps into the patio with two aides. As he surveyed the arrangements, his eyes fell on Ike and he frowned. He muttered something to the aides and strode across the enclosure to Molly and her leering admirer. The defense attaché, General Smith, came next. Then other guests were ushered in; all proceeded to the Ambassador to offer obeisance. Chuck recognized most of them as DAO and embassy intel and logistics specialists. More waiters hurried about with trays of drinks and appetizers. As the space filled, Chuck wished he could sit down.

Thanh, in class A uniform, looking as unnatural as he had at the Marine Corps Birthday Ball, hurried down the steps with Major Nghiem right behind him. This was the old Thanh, merry to a fault, bestowing his grin as he moved through the crowd. He approached the Ambassador with shoulders hunched, eyes on the floor, head bowed. For a moment, it looked like Thanh was going to genuflect and kiss the Ambassador's ring, but instead he turned to the other gentleman and was introduced to Molly.

Next to come down the stairs into the garden was a man Chuck didn't recognize. He moved with the easy self-confidence of someone who expected deference. The Ambassador moved through the crowd to greet him. With formal smiles, the two shook hands.

"Who's that?" Chuck said to Ike in an undertone.

"He must be the Hungarian member of the International Commission of Control and Supervision, the ICCS."

"How do you know?"

Ike smirked. "Snuck a look at the guest list."

"What's a Commie doing at a party for Senator Nunn?"

"Hey," Ike said, "I just work here. Don't ask me to explain the ins and outs of diplomacy." He leaned toward Chuck's ear and whispered. "Scuttlebutt is he's a go-between linking the Ambassador and the North Vietnamese."

Senator Nunn, balding, affable, peering though horn-rimmed glasses, emerged at the top of the steps with three of his staff, then, smiling, descended to the patio. The Ambassador and the senator met in the middle of the compound and shook hands as their minions arranged themselves into a picturesque circle around them. The formalities over, the guests relaxed. Chuck and Ike shared a table.

Thanh worked the room as he always did and finally found his way to Chuck. "I must travel to the front soon," Thanh said to Chuck, "to Long Khanh and Binh Tuy, but next month I will visit I Corps.

Then in March I go to the highlands. I would be honored if you would accompany me on both trips."

"It is I who would be honored," Chuck said.

"It will be rough travel. Not like this." He waved a hand over the assembly. "But you know that life. I will discuss with your Colonel Troiano and issue an invitation."

Chuck inclined his head. "I will await it impatiently."

Thanh nodded and moved across the patio to Troiano's table.

Chuck and Ike had been back at the Yen Do villa long enough to shed their suits and get into shorts and tank tops before Molly arrived by cab, still in her party finery. Before going upstairs to change, she prepared martinis, snitched some chocolates from her private stash, and told Chi Nam she'd be staying for the later-than-usual dinner. When she came down in scrubs, she joined the three housemates on the rear veranda.

Sparky, the perpetual toothpick at one corner of his mouth, stood and bowed. "All those years of medical training paid off, Molly. You mix the best drinks this side of CONUS."

"Molly," Chuck said. "I did you and Ike a favor—gave the name of your maid's husband to Thanh. He'll try to track him down. Now it's payback time."

"Uh-oh," she said. "Here it comes."

"I want to use your place for a couple of nights after the congressional types clear out. Friday through Monday. You told Tuyet we might stay at your apartment sometimes. Thanh will be out of town."

"You could stay here," Sparky said. "What happens here stays here."

"She doesn't like to come to this neighborhood," Molly said. "She's afraid someone will recognize her and wonder what she's doing here. But if an acquaintance spotted her downtown, near my place, they'd assume she was shopping."

Chuck cocked his head. "How'd you know that?"

"Women share secrets." She waggled her tongue in the martini. "Anyway, it's okay with me if Joy Stick agrees to have me here all that time."

"Joy . . ." Chuck said. "You mean Ike?"

Ike rolled his eyes.

"Sorry," she said. "Just slipped out."

"Uh-huh." Ike turned to Chuck and Sparky. "Only three things this lady cares about—chocolate, booze, and *big* men, if you know what I'm saying."

"*Ike!*" she cried.

"Sorry," Ike said. "Just slipped out."

"Right." She slugged his bicep and turned to Chuck. "I have extra keys. I'll give you two, one for each of you."

By the time the senator and his staff were airborne on Tuesday, Chuck was so tired his eyelids were scraping. At midafternoon Troiano told him and the other analysts to knock off early—by tomorrow follow-up questions would be flowing in from Washington. As soon as he got to Yen Do, he sent Oanh with a note and a key for Molly's apartment, both to be delivered personally to Tuyet. Since Thanh was flying north, the note said, would she spend the weekend, Friday night through Monday morning, with him at Molly's apartment? He gave the address, a building on Ngo Duc Ke a block from the river. He would expect her at dinnertime. By sundown Oanh was back.

"The lady say she not write nothing, you know. She say I tell you yes, she be there."

Wednesday morning, Molly and Ike were already at the table for breakfast when Chuck took his chair.

Sparky plunked down but immediately stood again. "Oops. Forgot my radio." He took the stairs two at a time and was back with his portable. "You guys are up awfully early."

"The dispensary has extended its hours." Molly helped herself to coffee from the carafe. "The embassy's expecting an upswing in terrorist incidents. I go in at seven from now on."

While Sparky's radio whined the news from ARS, Chi Nam served ham and eggs. Ike rattled through the most recent *Stars and Stripes*, and Molly checked her eye makeup in her compact mirror.

"And in Washington," ARS droned, "Secretary of Defense James Schlesinger told Congress that the United States is not keeping its promise to South Vietnam of severe retaliatory action for North Vietnam's violation of the Paris peace accords."

"Good." Molly fluttered her eyelashes in the mirror. "Now the U.S. will get its ass in gear and go after those bastards."

Chuck laughed, and Sparky harrumphed.

"What?" she said.

"Honey," Chuck said, "I don't know how to break this to you, but it's all over."

"Jesus," she said. "Your cynicism is showing. Go put some clothes on."

"You really think we'd come back to Vietnam?" Chuck said.

Molly put away her compact. "Maybe we wouldn't have to. A CIA guy came into the dispensary yesterday—bad case of the trots. He told me on the sly that the Ambassador thinks the North Vietnamese don't want to conquer South Vietnam. They're waiting for President Thieu to resign, then they'll negotiate for the formation of a coalition government including representation from the National Front for the Liberation of South Vietnam."

Sparky pushed his plate away. "The NFL is a front organization for the North Vietnamese."

"So what?" she said. "So we get a government with Communists in it."

"Molly," Chuck said, "you really think the North Vietnamese want to negotiate when they're about to win the war?"

"I've never met such a bunch of naysayers." Molly stood. "I'm planning on finishing my tour. Did I tell you I'm going to redecorate my apartment? In May I'll spend a weekend in Bangkok and see what they have in green and yellow Thai silk."

Chuck shook his head. "Do anything you like, as long as you have an overnight bag packed with enough clothes to keep you going for a week."

⊢ 다 다 다 ⊣

After getting Troiano's blessing for a couple of days off, Chuck left work at 1700 on Friday, swung by the commissary for steaks and the PX for wine, and went by blue-and-white to Nguyen Hue, the street of flowers. He sought out the flower stall that sold roses. The flower seller, the young boy Chuck remembered, had winter roses from Dalat but charged three times the usual price. "All costs go up now, you know?" the boy said. "It is the war."

Flowers under one arm, bags with food and wine in the other, and his overnight bag hanging from his shoulder, Chuck cantered down Nguyen Hue toward the river, hooked a left into Ngo Duc Ke, crossed Tu Do, and found Molly's address. The entrance to the luxury apartment building was, typical of Saigon, an enclosed alleyway, dark and foul smelling, lined with bags of trash, scattered refuse, and tin basins used by the maids for laundry. The passageway ended at a door to a murky hall with a stairwell and an open elevator that looked like an animal cage. He doubted it would carry him and his parcels. He climbed the stairs to the sixth floor but discovered that all the apartments numbered in the five hundreds. Of course: in Vietnam, as in France, the first floor was the one above the street floor. Up one more flight of steps, he found the right number, tried the key, and went in.

Molly's apartment was small—intended for one person—and she had turned it into a bludgeon of color. Her teak furniture, probably from Indonesia, was decorated with upholstered cushions of Thai cotton in a fiery orange print, and the drapes in front of the glass doors leading to her balcony were neon yellow. On both sides of the sofa were her bufes—ceramic elephants so roughly crafted they looked mass-produced—one each in orange and green. In the bedroom, all but suffocated in nacreous green and blue Thai silk, Chuck turned back the single white blanket. Pink sheets.

In the kitchen, he thrust the roses into a vase, opened the wine, and improvised a salad from Molly's bantam refrigerator. On the balcony, a ten-foot-wide ledge cut into the side of the building seven stories above Ngo Duc Ke, he filled the grill with charcoal from a plastic box and lit it, then set the glass-topped bistro table and put the roses on the serving pedestal next to it. Satisfied that everything was ready, he showered and put on a T-shirt, shorts, and rubber sandals.

He was settled on the sofa with a glass of wine when a key turned in the lock. The door swung open, and a squat Asian woman bustled in carrying a canvas bag with wooden handles and a laundry basket filled with folded clothes. Chuck stood.

Startled, the woman dropped the bag and basket. "Oh. You are Mister Griffin?" she said, recovering.

"Yes. You are—"

She smiled broadly. "I Huong, *sir*. Miss Molly's maid. I bring back her clean clothes and I make dinner for you. No big deal."

"Thank you, but there's no need. I have steaks ready to grill."

"I know to grill." She squared her shoulders. "Miss Molly and Mister Captain, they teach me. I grill number one steak."

"Thanks, but I'd like to do it—"

"No, no. I cook you, you know? You fagged out. You take it easy."

She hurried into the kitchen, dropped her bag, and carried the basket to the bedroom. Chuck blew the air from his cheeks. This wasn't quite what he'd had in mind. Now Huong was back, puttering in the kitchen.

"You have steak and salad, yes? I fix you potato, some nice sauce, yes?"

Without waiting for an answer, she lit the oven.

A key sounded in the lock and Tuyet stepped in, followed by Mai carrying bundles.

"You are already here." Tuyet hurried to him, and he took her in his arms.

Mai started toward the kitchen, saw Huong, and stopped dead. Huong stood her ground.

"Who is this woman?" Tuyet said.

"Huong. Molly's maid. She insisted on cooking for us."

"I brought food. Mai will cook for us."

"Huong already has potatoes in the oven," he said. "Maybe—"

"Better that Mai cook."

Mai and Huong faced each other with hands on hips as if ready to draw. Tuyet spoke in Vietnamese, her voice laced with quiet authority.

Huong turned to her and bowed. "*Da. Vang. A.*" She took her bag, pushed past Mai, and left. Mai, nose wrinkled in disdain, proceeded into the kitchen.

⊔⅂⅄⊔⅄

When their meal was finished, Mai washed dishes, bade them a respectful good night, and left. Chuck and Tuyet pulled their chairs side by side and lingered on the balcony lit only by the candles.

"Why didn't Huong and Mai get along?" he asked.

"Huong resented Mai as an intruder. And Mai—she has spent her life serving the Nguyen dynasty. She gave up her family, never married. She has no tolerance for lower-class people. Thinks they are too crude to serve royalty. Besides, Huong is Chinese."

"How do you know?" Chuck said.

"She *looks* Chinese." Tuyet wrinkled her nose. "The way she dresses. Her accent. Her name is Chinese. But Mai has changed her feelings about *you*. She has decided you are my consort. She honors you as she honors me."

"Your consort. Quaint."

Tuyet fingered the flowers. "You buy me roses." She pulled a bloom from the vase and held it to her nose. "No war but this. Our war."

"What's wrong?"

Tuyet took a deep breath and placed her hand over his. "I need to tell you but do not want to. I believe I am . . . I don't know the American word. *Enceinte. Tôi lại có mang.* I will have a baby."

Chuck jumped. "You're pregnant?"

"I do not bleed for more than a month now."

"But you're on the pill . . ."

She shook her head. "I run out of pills before you gave me more."

"But you said—"

"I lied. I was afraid you would not stay with me."

He yanked his hand away. "Another lie. How many more lies are there?"

"None." She folded her hands in her lap and stared at them. "I was sure it wouldn't happen." She glanced at him. "But I am a woman. My royal blood does not change that."

He rose, walked to the railing, and looked down. The glow from the thoroughfare below turned the buildings across the street sinister. Exhaust tainted the air. Pregnant. Through her own doing. He laughed to himself. Ike had told him this would happen. A way for her to get him by the balls.

With deliberation he turned, grasped the vase with roses, and slammed it into the bistro tabletop. Fragments of glass flew across the balcony and caught in Tuyet's hair. "How could you do this?"

Trembling, she brushed broken glass away. "My sins against you are too great. You will leave me now."

Leave her carrying his child? Let her stay in Vietnam when the North Vietnamese took over? Would she live long enough to bear the child? If the child were born, an Amerasian bastard, what future would it have? He tightened his fists around the railing. "Let's go in."

He put out the candles and led her through the glass door. Their shoes crunched the broken glass. She sat on Molly's sofa in the dark. The hiss of the air conditioner masked the clatter from the street below.

He stood with his back to her. *Carrying my child.* She had him by the short hairs for sure, just as Ike had said. The child in her womb, his child, was blameless. If the North Vietnamese got to it . . . He sat beside her. "Monday, we'll go to the embassy and apply for visas for you and Thu. Tomorrow I'll go to the Pan Am office and buy tickets for the first flight to San Francisco. My cousin lives there. I'll wire her to meet you. I'll ask Molly for the name of a good doctor."

Still shaking, she nodded without looking up. *No war but this. Our war.*

At the Pan Am office on Tu Do Street, Chuck asked for two tickets on the earliest available flight to San Francisco. Everything was sold out for the next week, so he settled for the flight departing at 0900 on Sunday, 26 January. He used his American Express card and was charged in U.S. dollars at an exorbitant exchange rate. Next he went by cab to Yen Do and asked Molly to recommend an obstetrician. She gave him two names, an obstetrician and "someone who takes care of mistakes." With the names in his pocket next to the tickets, he returned to the apartment by cab.

Breathless from the stairs, he handed Tuyet the airplane tickets. "For you and Thu to depart a week from tomorrow, the earliest flight I could get. And I have the names and addresses of an obstetrician and somebody else Molly recommended. They'd be closed today. So is the embassy. But Monday, we'll get your visa and go see the doctor."

She took the slips of paper Molly had given him. "Doctor Cuong. I know him. Thanh knows him. No. I cannot see him. Huong must know good Chinese doctors. They never have contact with Vietnamese. I must conceal this, you understand? I'll talk to Huong."

"What about this other guy? Address in Cholon—"

She shook her head. "No." She tore up the second slip.

The Tomb and Tet

JANUARY 1975

CHAPTER 10

Thanh boarded his aging C-47 for the flight from Binh Tuy Province back to Saigon. As the aircraft whined upward, its two engines shuddering, he looked down on the wandering La Nga River, the war-scarred town of Hoai Duc, and the mountains northeast, soaking up the January sunshine. It was only a matter of time before Hoai Duc and its sister towns of Tanh Linh and Vo Xu fell to the North Vietnamese. Three North Vietnamese regiments and a newly formed division were on the move. He'd talked to the anxious soldiers, urged them to pray and seek serenity, and, although he didn't use those words, to prepare for defeat and death. The young faces looking up as he spoke, the frightened eyes pleading for hope, had depleted his reserves. He must not allow himself to sink into despondence as he had the day Phuoc Binh was lost. Too much work left to do. Too many hearts to unburden. Too many souls to comfort.

He longed to go home and replenish his spirit, but he had no home. The villa near Tan Son Nhat was a shell devoid of love. Did the Mother Goddess deliberately burden the strong more than the weak? She had weighed him down, but he knew—and she apparently did, too—that he had reserves as yet untapped. He would need every droplet of vitality in him to make it through to the end. That he was suffering was irrelevant.

When the plane landed on the military side of Tan Son Nhat International, Corporal Vien was waiting on the tarmac in the jeep. His smile warmed Thanh. He, too, was a man of sinew, and he was devoted to his master. Thanh reminded himself to be especially generous with gifts for Vien's eight children come Tet, the lunar new year, now less than a month away. All men should feast at Tet, the time of newness and fresh beginnings, and all men's children should have enough to eat. Vien stepped from the jeep and saluted. Thanh returned the salute, slid behind the wheel, and drove off the runway.

On the way home, Thanh let his memory slide back to new year's festivals in the past. His grandmother had always scraped together enough money to buy the ingredients for *cha gio*, vegetables and bits of fish rolled in rice paper and deep fried. Each person got only one. The family would sit in a circle on the ground outside the hut eating in nibbles, making the delicacy last as long as possible, while Grandmother recounted the myths of the Mother Goddess and the twelve spirits who oversaw life on earth. Her voice would rise and fall, her eyes bright, her hands creating dragons and deities.

At later celebrations, in Hue, Thanh had refused to eat *pâté chaud* because it was French. Instead, he and his fellow monks solemnized the day by sharing gifts of grilled fish in lemon sauce and *nuoc mam* and by drinking green tea. Those were his peaceful years, purified by continence and nurtured by a joy of the soul he had now all but forgotten. As a young monk he had studied the techniques of meditation with the masters. Within a year he had progressed from giving full attention to his breathing to relying on visualization and mantras. Before the war against the French had driven him from the temple, he had learned, at least at moments, to still his being and abide in divine silence.

Perhaps the force to carry him through the terrible times ahead would come from the inner quiet he had learned then. Now, as then, he was celibate, but though he still meditated twice a day, he rarely used the techniques from his monastic days—they were difficult and time consuming. Yet he needed to brace his flagging spirit and find transcendence. He would return to the old practices. He would proceed step by step, mastering the methods one at a time, until he reached the zenith—total freedom from thought and feeling, the abnegation of the self. He raised his eyes to the Mother Goddess and thanked her for the inspiration.

At the villa, the gardener opened the gate for him with the usual obsequity. Chi Tu welcomed him with a deep bow and went to prepare his bath. Tuyet, Lan, and Thu met him in the sitting room. Their manner, as he had expected, was distant. After tea and his bath, he told the servants he was not to be disturbed. In his own room, wrapped in his silk robe, he lowered himself onto his meditation rug, crossed his legs in the lotus position, and gave himself over to inward contemplation.

The next day, after another meditation, he drove to JGS. A five-day backlog of reading awaited him. Fighting had picked up in all four corps. Each time JGS redeployed forces to meet new threats the vacated areas came under attack. He skimmed through after-action messages from each corps and studied reports of fighting in Binh Tuy. He shook his head. Even the Holy Fool who sat at the Mother Goddess' feet could see that capitulation was less than six months away.

Late in the day, Vien carried in the afternoon bulletins. On top of the stack was an account of a press conference President Ford had given. He had told reporters that the United States was unwilling to reenter the war in Vietnam. Thanh turned the report facedown. The last days were coming sooner than he expected. No time to work his way methodically through the steps of meditation. He must move quickly to the highest level, selflessness. Nor could he afford to grieve. That would come later. If he survived.

Tuyet and Thu. It was time to ask Macintosh to get them out of the country. He lifted the receiver and dialed Intelligence Branch, DAO. A young woman answered. Thanh asked for Charles Griffin. She put him on hold, then Griffin's voice came on the line.

"Mister Griffin, this is Colonel Thanh at JGS. I have a gift I will ask you to send to Colonel Mac for me. A token of my respect. Would you be kind enough to stop by my office tomorrow evening at 1930 and fetch it? And may I impose on you to ship it for me?"

"Of course, sir. It would be an honor."

"Very good, Mister Griffin. Bring your jeep. The package, it is large. I thank you very much."

Thanh hung up. Innocuous enough. Major Nghiem, listening on the wiretap, wouldn't consider the matter worthy of his presence. That evening Thanh ordered the gardener to take the porcelain elephant from the sitting room first thing in the morning, have it carefully crated for shipment to the United States, and deliver it to Thanh's office. After Chi Hai took Thu to his mother for bedtime stories, Thanh readied himself for the evening meditation. He must open his soul to the soundless, imageless, timeless messages from eternity. From now on he would spend his evenings learning how to live in this state so that no earthly turbulence could shake his quietude.

<hr/>

Thanh remained late at the office the following evening. Just before 1930 he called to Vien. "You are dismissed for the evening."

Vien, at the door, saluted. "With the Colonel's permission, I have come across a bit of information."

"Yes?"

"Forgive my impertinence, sir, but is the Colonel meeting Mister Griffin this evening?"

"That is none of your affair, Vien."

"Of course, sir, but an aide to Major Nghiem visited me today to ask why Mister Griffin is coming to see the Colonel, always in the evening, after the close of the regular business day. The aide told me Mister Griffin has been here several times. The guard at the gate is required to log the name and identification number of all visitors to JGS. Major Nghiem's office monitors the guard's log."

So Nghiem was tracking Griffin's visits.

Vien stood at attention, his eyes downcast. "I thought the Colonel should know."

"Well done, Vien." Thanh rose, smiling. "You are not only devoted but watchful. I thank you."

Vien colored. "I am privileged to serve the Colonel." He turned smartly and left.

Thanh lit the fire for tea and darkened the office. At precisely the appointed moment, Griffin tapped at the door.

"Please to come in, Mister Griffin," Thanh called.

The door opened and Griffin, dressed as always in a white short-sleeve dress shirt and slacks, walked to the table by the window where Thanh awaited him. Thanh remembered Griffin in suit and tie, Griffin going pale at the words "Mrs. Thanh." Was this man Tuyet's lover? Yes, almost certainly so. Perhaps it was Griffin who would be called upon to save Thu and Tuyet when Thanh no longer could. If any man were to be Tuyet's lover, who better than Thanh's blood brother? A spirit not unlike Thanh himself, an irony worthy of the Holy Fool.

Thanh added the boiling water to the loose tea leaves in the pot. "Please to sit down, Mister Griffin. Will you take tea?"

"Thank you, sir."

Griffin had learned the Vietnamese manner of avoiding eye contact with a superior. Most Americans, when they practiced Asian politeness, hinted at insolence or irreverence when doing so, as though the etiquette was slightly comical. Not Griffin. His respect was genuine. Thanh took his hand. Griffin looked up, surprised.

"My gratitude to you is deep," Thanh said. "You are a man of virtue."

Griffin opened his mouth to speak but stopped and lowered his eyes.

Thanh withdrew his hand. "You have been following the progress of the war, Mister Griffin?"

Griffin nodded.

"And the U.S. government's response?" Thanh said. "So you know the real reason I asked you here. I do have a gift for Colonel Mac, but it is an excuse to be able to speak with you. Let us carry the gift to your jeep, then we talk."

Together they hauled the crate to Griffin's jeep and secured it with canvas straps. Back in the office, Thanh poured tea.

"Does the Colonel wish me to forward a message to Colonel Macintosh about the war?"

"About my wife and child."

Griffin's eyes flashed alarm.

"Colonel Mac," Thanh said, "can save them. The end is coming soon. I must ask him to act quickly to take them out of Vietnam. That is the message I ask you to convey to him."

"Forgive my impudence, sir, but Colonel Macintosh is far away. Perhaps the Colonel would consider entrusting the safety of his family to someone close at hand."

Thanh smiled. "You have read my thoughts. I wish you to suggest to Colonel Mac that he assign *you* the responsibility of ensuring the escape of Tuyet and Thu. Dare I impose this burden on you?"

Griffin hesitated, took a deep breath. "Yes, sir. I will convey the Colonel's message to Colonel Macintosh, and I pledge to do my utmost to get the Colonel's wife and son out of the country. In fact, sir," Griffin swallowed, "I have already begun. I beg the Colonel's permission to send them out right away."

"Of course. We have no way to know when the end will come. They must not be here when that happens. If they are still in Saigon when the North Vietnamese march in the streets . . ." He shook his head.

Griffin leaned forward and placed his hands, palm down, on the table. "Pardon me if I am impolite, sir, but what will the Colonel do if the North Vietnamese take Saigon before he and his family escape?"

"We cannot live under the Communists."

"Perhaps—" Griffin began.

Thanh shook his head. "No. I fight until they kill me."

"But if you and your family were captured—"

"They will not capture us. If the Republic falls and capture is at hand, I will shoot my son, I will shoot my wife, and I will shoot myself." Thanh stood. "Thank you, Mister Griffin. You forgive me now?"

Griffin stumbled to his feet. "I will tell Colonel Macintosh all that the Colonel has said." He started toward the door, turned back. "With the Colonel's permission, I will ensure that the evacuation plans also include the Colonel."

"No, Mister Griffin. Ask only that Tuyet and Thu be evacuated. Leave my future to the Mother Goddess. She will watch over me."

Griffin closed his eyes and lowered his head. Reluctantly, he raised his eyes. "Good night, sir."

"Good night, Mister Griffin. May the Mother Goddess watch over you, too."

⊢⊢⊢

The evening meal had ended by the time Thanh reached the villa. Chi Ba served Thanh fish and rice garnished with *nuoc mam*. The familiar flavors took him back to his childhood. The Fatherland he loved and fought for would soon be lost. Tuyet and Thu would be far away, in the United States. Thu would never know his heritage, An Nam. If only Thanh could take Thu to Hue, the ancient capital, to see the royal palace, the temples, the Thanh Loi Pagoda. Too dangerous now.

But Saigon was not bereft of history. Thu had seen the zoological garden and the museum, but he had never visited the tomb of Le van Duyet. Thanh himself hadn't been there in years. A perfect outing for father and son. Thu couldn't avoid being impressed by the magnificent tomb, its temple, its gardens. Thanh would speak to Tuyet first, but he wouldn't allow her to stop him.

"Chi Ba, ask Madame to join me in the garden."

"Yes, sir. Madame is already in the garden with Miss Lan and Thu."

Thanh descended the steps to the grass. Tuyet, Lan, and Thu were sitting under the banyan tree while Tuyet read to them by candlelight. In French, of course. Thanh set his jaw. Time to insist that Thu was Vietnamese. As Thanh crossed the patio, they stood respectfully and fell silent.

"Thu, my son," Thanh said, "the last days of winter are here. Before the heat and monsoons return, I wish to take you to the tomb of Le van Duyet, the great general who put down the Tay Son rebellion and united Vietnam."

Thu said nothing, eyes lowered.

"One of your ancestors," Thanh said, "the emperor Gia Long, the founder of the Nguyen dynasty, raised Le van Duyet to the rank of marshal. He is part of your history."

Tuyet, submissive to perfection, folded her hands and kept her eyes trained on the ground. "Thu has not yet studied Vietnamese history. Perhaps we should wait."

"We will go tomorrow morning," Thanh said.

All three raised their eyes. Thanh smiled.

"Sir," Thu said, using his mother's northern dialect, "*Maman* has promised to take me to the Cercle Sportif tomorrow. With your permission—"

"No," Thanh said, "we cannot wait. I will be traveling soon and we will have no time. Your mother and your cousin Lan are invited to come with us." Thanh reentered the house.

Thanh slept soundly, as he always did when meditations were going well. In the morning he rose early, dressed in his Japanese robe, and spent thirty minutes freed from time and space in selfless contemplation. Then, dressed in clean utilities, he ordered the gardener to hail two cyclos immediately after breakfast. As he escorted Tuyet, Thu, and Lan down the steps to the front courtyard, Tuyet faltered.

"The Impala—"

"Today we go by cyclo," Thanh said, "not in an American car given us as a sop."

"But the time it will take, the dirt of the city—" Tuyet began.

"Our lives are too insulated. We need to feel, to hear, to see the peoples of ancient An Nam."

The gardener helped Tuyet and Lan into the first cyclo while Thanh climbed into the second and lifted Thu in. The women opened their parasols, and the pedicabs groaned up the dirt road and into the mass of bicycles, cyclos, tiny cabs, jeeps, trucks, and pedestrians. Thu sat silently next to Thanh and squinted from the exhaust fumes. The two drivers pedaled serenely in the right lane of each street and called to one another to be sure they stayed together. After thirty minutes they eased to a stop at the curb.

Before them was the tomb. Encircled by pale yellow walls pierced by two ceremonial gates, one for entering and one for exiting, it occupied a city block. It had once stood alone in its majesty, the centerpiece of a vast park. Now drooping power lines, crumbling sidewalks, and the garbage in the streets encroached from all sides. Thanh gazed at the exterior walls, scarred with holes where the plaster had fallen away revealing the rubble beneath. The holy edifice was discolored by exhaust fumes and profaned by placards and graffiti. This was not what he remembered, not what he wanted to show his son. War, poverty, political corruption—all had left their mark here.

He took Thu's hand and walked up the slight rise. Tuyet and Lan, parasols open, followed. A swarm of beggars hurried from nowhere and pawed at them. The most hideous, a woman without teeth and only one eye, shoved a child with no legs toward them. Thu jerked away from them and sought Tuyet's arms.

Thanh shooed the beggars away. "Leave us in peace." He herded the family toward the tomb. "They mutilate themselves and their children to move us to give them money. Pity them."

Inside, in the tomb's outer court, the solemnity Thanh remembered was gone. Knots of middle-aged women chattered, their hair piled on their heads, some with turban-like cloth wrapped through it, their teeth blackened by betel nut or glinting with gold, accompanied by young children who rollicked undeterred by the solemnity of death. Thanh hurried Thu, Lan, and Tuyet past them through a second gate to the oblong inner courtyard. Here an oversized altar under a tiled roof with upswept eaves left little maneuvering room. Above them cones of coiled incense hung from the rafters. Half a dozen women chanted to themselves, shook joss sticks and cast them, and added more incense to the cloud that half-hid the altar in blue smoke.

A third gate led to the tomb itself, a mass of mortar and stone, once decorated with oversized lotus blossoms, now reduced to time-worn nubs. More women knelt here, chanted, tossed sticks. One, her streaked hair loose over her shoulders, raised her arms to Heaven, fell prostrate, rose again, shaking her head from side to side. She twisted, saw Thu, and seized his hand.

"You worship with me, worship with me." She fell forward.

Thu, with a cry, wrenched free and fled to Tuyet.

Thanh's stomach turned cold. Failure. His son would remember this experience with revulsion. Nothing had been gained. Much had been lost.

So the Mother Goddess demanded this of him, too? So be it. She had given Thanh strength. Now she required him to sacrifice. She had shown him that he was fierce enough to endure the coming immolation. He lowered his head. *I surrender to you, only you, and you will fortify my spirit and grant me peace.*

He gathered his family around him and urged them through the exit gate. The web of bicycles in the street included no cyclos. Perhaps they could flag a cab at the traffic circle, where six streets met. They edged along the sidewalk under the orange banners, sidestepping beggars and refuse, until they reached the intersection. A policeman in white uniform and helmet directed traffic from the hub. His eyes found Thanh. He smiled, saluted, and bowed. As he did, a motorized cyclo in the innermost lane slowed. The passenger rose, aimed a pistol at the policeman, and fired. The policeman's helmet flew off. His fists clenched, his head flew back. Blood splattered from his face. The assassin whipped his pistol toward Thanh and fired again. The slug slammed into Thanh's shoulder and nearly toppled him. The flow of vehicles around the circle congealed. Thanh shouted to Tuyet to run, stumbled through the lurching bicycles, and knelt by the fallen policeman. A cylinder tumbled across the road and bounced toward them. A grenade.

Thanh threw himself on the grenade. His last seconds of life. He called to the Mother Goddess. Peace flowed over him. His serenity was at last complete. Seconds passed. No explosion. More seconds. Nothing. The grenade was a dud. He rolled away from it. "Don't touch it," he cried at the crowd in the circle. "It could still detonate."

He staggered back to the policeman, cradled him in his lap. "Hush now. Just wait. It will be over soon. Don't struggle. You are a strong man. Let it come. Rest now." He pulled the twitching man close. The quivers stopped. The death rattle darkened the silence.

Thanh let the air slip from his body as though he himself were dying. Stillness all around him. He raised his eyes to the faces of those crouching nearby. One figure stood tall. Tuyet. She was immobile, her gaze focused on Thanh.

"Thu?" he said.

"Lan took him away."

When the reports were filed and all the questions of the police and security forces were answered, an ambulance carried Thanh, faint from loss of blood, to the Seventh Day Adventist Hospital. A doctor extracted the bullet from his shoulder, gave him a transfusion, and put his arm in a sling. Thanh insisted on going home afterward. At the villa, despite Tuyet's protests, he ordered Chi Tu to prepare his bath. He doffed his bloody utilities, told her to bring him fresh ones, and submerged all but his bandaged shoulder in the sudsy water. Cleansed, he dried himself, put on a clean uniform, and, boots under his arm, headed to his bedroom. He refused to shuffle, but the pain was getting the better of him. He closed the door behind him, locked it, and sank into the lotus position. Reciting the healing mantra in his mind, he banished all thought, all images, all memories until his consciousness was blank. Sometime later—he had no idea how long—he allowed awareness of the present to return. His pain now compartmented, he went to the dining room and took his belated midday meal alone.

Tuyet interrupted his solitude.

"You are in pain."

"It is nothing."

She eyed the sling. "You should have stayed in the hospital."

"I have important work."

She frowned. "You're going to JGS?"

"Of course."

"Stay here. Let me care for you."
He didn't answer.

⌐ᒣᑐᒣᑐ⌐

As he drove to JGS, his wound, hidden by the sling and his fatigue jacket over it, thrummed again with pain while his mind retraced the events of the morning. Thu would always cringe when he remembered this day. Lan was probably close to hysteria. Tuyet was deeply troubled. But she hadn't fled. He knew very well that she didn't love him. What had possessed her to stay and risk her own life?

At the office, poring over the latest reports of death and destruction, he relived the moments when he embraced the grenade. He'd felt transcendence, as though he'd fulfilled his purpose in life. Was this peace a gift from the Mother Goddess? No, it was the fruit of his own work and study. And yet, he experienced it as if it originated outside of him. Perhaps, as an old monk had taught him, divinity is within us, and we are within divinity. In short, he didn't have to rely on the Mother Goddess. He could depend on himself and the divinity in his own soul. Did that mean she didn't exist? He had no idea. Nor was it important. The divine existed. The Mother Goddess was one way to think about the godhead. *We believe what we can believe, what we choose to believe, not what logic and evidence show us.* He would go on believing in her, but he saw that his conception of divinity was humanly imperfect—he could never grasp the breadth and width of the divine.

His thoughts were cut short by a tap. Corporal Vien stood in the doorway.

"I apologize to the Colonel for the disturbance. Major Nghiem is here. He wishes to speak with the Colonel."

Thanh wavered. He needed to shed his meditative state and prepare for mental dueling. No. He'd learned better. Let him greet his enemy with peace. He nodded. A moment later Vien escorted Nghiem into the office and left.

Nghiem stood before the desk and saluted, his eyes on the sling. His form was correct, but his substance was sovereign contempt. His lips sneered faintly, his eyes looked down on Thanh, who, as the superior, did not stand. "The Colonel was wounded?" Nghiem, always punctilious to etiquette, addressed Thanh in the third person, as was proper for a subordinate, but he spoke in the purest northern dialect—although, as Thanh knew, he was a native of the Mekong Delta in the far south. "I trust the Colonel is not suffering."

"I am well enough, thank you. And you?" Thanh let his peasant central dialect permeate his words. He used the familiar form of address, as one does with an inferior.

"Strong and fit," Nghiem said. "My superiors have learned that the Colonel recently sent a gift to the American Marine colonel Macintosh by way of a Mister Griffin—a functionary at Intelligence Branch, DAO, who has visited the Colonel several times after hours. Protocol dictates that all gifts be approved. We have no record that the Colonel cleared the gift with the foreign relations staff. I am mandated to warn the Colonel that infractions of the rules of diplomacy cannot be tolerated."

Thanh's internal quiet was undisturbed. "I am chastised. I have committed an error and beg pardon."

"Very good, sir. The staff would appreciate knowing what the gift was."

"A porcelain elephant crafted many years ago by the monks at the Thanh Loi Pagoda in Hue."

Nghiem's face darkened. "A gift in doubtful taste. The Americans use crude and degrading names for our ceramic elephants."

Thanh ignored the insult and gave Nghiem a forgiving smile. "I am aware of the vulgar practice, but this piece is a work of art, deserving of the highest respect."

"Then perhaps it ought not to have been put into the hands of a foreigner. We must preserve our heritage."

"I am doubly contrite, but the American colonel Mac has sacrificed much to help Vietnam. He deserves a worthy tribute."

"Yes, sir." Nghiem was momentarily off balance. "I will report your words to my superiors." He continued, contempt again curling his lip, "An honorable gift of such value should properly have come from the JGS or at least one of the ranking flag officers."

"Indeed, but when the JGS and its generals failed to act, I took the initiative."

The subtle insult was not lost on Nghiem. "I will carry that message to the generals." He saluted, pivoted toward the door, and marched out.

Sniveling ninny. Thanh deepened his breathing to regain his mystical quiet. That the staff had sent a subaltern to castigate him was a calculated snub. Trivial men with trivial agendas seeking a superior moral justification for selfishness and cowardice. With the end at hand, they were powerless to hobble him. Odd that he had not foreseen that they would take umbrage at his gift to Mac. He laughed. He'd always lacked political instincts, was always surprised by the antics of the weak.

He'd been a fool to use the telephone to arrange to see Griffin. Henceforth he would depend on notes hand-carried only by the most trusted of servants. He must warn Griffin not to telephone. He drafted a brief note asking Griffin to come to his office the next night, then tore it up. The gate guard logged each visit by Griffin. He started over, suggesting that Griffin stop by Thanh's villa at 2100 hours the following evening. As soon as he reached home, he'd send the gardener to Griffin's villa with the note.

The next night, at the dinner table, Thanh broke the silence. "I am expecting a visitor at 2100. We will talk in the garden. It is of utmost importance that we have complete privacy and not be disturbed." He turned to Tuyet and Lan. "I'll ask you to have Thu in bed"—he bestowed a loving smile on his son—"and to remain in your rooms until the visitor has left."

Tuyet stared at the table. "May I ask who the visitor is?"

"It is not for you to know," Thanh said.

"As you wish. May I make bold to suggest that you might do well to dress? The robe Mac gave you—"

"The robe is the finest garment I own."

By 2045, the common rooms of the house were empty. Thanh sat alone on a garden seat surrounded by tall bamboo that filtered the glow from the security lights. Next to him were another seat and a small wrought-iron table lit by a single votive candle. The gate bell sounded. A moment later the gardener led a figure from the back door of the villa through the dark to the table. Thanh stood. "Mister Griffin. I am again in your debt. Please to be seated."

"I am flattered the Colonel asked me," Griffin said.

The gardener bowed and scurried away. Chi Tu came forward with tea, served them, and dissolved into the darkness. Thanh waited a moment before speaking to be sure she was out of earshot.

Griffin spoke first. "I am told that the Colonel was shot yesterday." His eyes strayed to the sling. "Perhaps the Colonel would permit me to arrange for an American doctor—"

Thanh shook his head. "It is nothing. You have sent a message to Colonel Mac? You have told him about the gift I sent him?"

Griffin nodded.

"And," Thanh said, "my suggestion that you act for him in arranging for the evacuation of my wife and child?"

"Yes, sir, but so far no answer. It's possible that Colonel Macintosh is abroad."

Thanh suppressed a sigh. "One must be patient. There is yet time."

"I have made discreet inquiries," Griffin said. "I am assured that the Colonel is on the list of high-priority evacuees should the country fall."

"You are kind, but do not trouble yourself about me."

Griffin's eyes winced, but his face remained immobile.

"There is another matter," Thanh said, "the reason I wanted to speak with you. The JGS has become aware of our meetings. We must not speak again by phone. Our rendezvous must be away from the office. We will depend on notes carried by loyal servants."

Griffin inclined his head. "As the Colonel wishes, sir."

"And now, if you will forgive me . . ."

Griffin was on his feet.

"I will see you out," Thanh said.

"No need, sir."

Thanh waved away the objection.

They crossed the patio and the grass and climbed the steps to the rear door leading to the serving room. As Thanh pulled open the door, Tuyet jumped back into the house, startled.

"My apologies," Tuyet said. "I wanted to see if you needed more tea."

She was lying. She'd been spying on them. She raised her face toward Griffin, her lower lip trembling. Griffin gazed at her, blushed. This was indeed the man Tuyet had taken to her bed. Thanh's heart bowed in compliance to the Mother Goddess. He lifted his head. "You remember Mister Griffin." His voice was detached.

Tuyet clasped her hands and nodded.

"Good to see you again, Mrs. . . . Thanh." Griffin's voice had lost its lower octave.

Thanh narrowed his eyes. Griffin had enunciated his name with the northern pronunciation and the correct tone—as used by northerners. He must have spent considerable time with Tuyet.

"You will forgive us?" Thanh said to Tuyet. "Mister Griffin was just leaving."

"Of course." She stepped back.

Thanh accompanied Griffin through the house to the front steps and watched as he climbed into his jeep and started the engine. The gardener swung open the gate. Thanh waved as Griffin drove out.

He headed back into the house. Tuyet had vanished. He walked through the hall to her room and opened the door. She spun, startled. "I will not countenance eavesdropping," he said. "You will never do such a thing again."

"You are hiding things from me." She sounded like a peevish child.

"I am protecting you. When the North Vietnamese are victorious, what you know could condemn you."

Her shoulders sagged. "Forgive me."

"I have nothing to forgive. You have hurt yourself, not me. You diminish yourself by resorting to stealth. Tuyet, terrible times are coming. Enrich your moral power, don't weaken it."

She sat on the bed and massaged her hands. "You are a great man come too late."

"I am a humble servant."

She nodded. "And in that, you are great."

"Why didn't you run away from the grenade attack?"

"I wanted . . ." She swallowed. "I was afraid for you."

"Why? You don't love me."

Confusion skittered across her face. "I don't understand. You were ready to sacrifice your life to save a handful of dirty street people. You helped a man meet death." She looked into his eyes. "I have never seen that before." She studied her clasped hands.

She sat before him humiliated, hurt, shorn of her pride. She belonged to another man now. "I'm glad you are with Griffin," he said. "He is a strong and honorable man. He can save you and Thu."

She started as if he had slapped her.

"Go with him," he said, "both of you. Go soon. The end could come without warning."

She avoided his eyes, squirmed. Knowing he would never again touch her after tonight, he took her, inert, in his arms and kissed her. She neither responded nor resisted. He turned, walked out the door, and closed it behind him.

CHAPTER 11

As the door clicked closed behind Thanh, Tuyet wrapped her arms around her torso and shivered, out of control. He knew. He saw in a way that was more than seeing. She was defenseless against him. He could watch her soul. She crumpled onto the bed. She'd lied to herself—and to him. She hadn't stayed by his side because she was afraid for him. She'd wanted to be with him, to keep him in her sight. She'd been blind but only now was starting to see. He lived at a level far beyond her understanding. That was why he could see what others could not. That was why the generals feared him and the common people loved him. And that, now that she could see it, was the beacon that drew her: this man was transcendent. If Thanh was to die, she had, in that moment in the street, wanted to die with him.

She pulled herself to her feet and teetered to the vanity. The face in her mirror was drawn and bloodless. A few days hence she would load the Impala with their baggage and ride with Thu to the airport, where Chuck would meet them and see them off on the flight to San Francisco. Salvation was in her grasp. The happiness she'd dreamt of with Chuck was hers. Escape was only two days away.

And she'd never see Thanh again.

The next day, queasy, she kept to her room. The mere thought of food sent twinges through her belly. Before the evening meal, Thanh sent Chi Ba to ask Tuyet to join him in the front courtyard while he inspected the gardener's work. She found him fingering the hibiscus.

He gave her a gentle smile. "I didn't have a chance to tell you. I have asked Mister Griffin, as Colonel Mac's representative, to arrange for you and Thu to leave the country."

"Are you commanding me to depart?"

"I have never commanded you." He paused at the foot of a palm and looked up into its fronds. "Chi Ba tells me you are sometimes nauseated. Are you with child?"

She swallowed her surprise.

"I see," he said. "Does Lan know?"

She shook her head.

"Lan took advantage of your absence at the midday meal to tell me that you are carrying on an affair with Mister Griffin. She was shocked that I already knew. She badgered me about punishing you." He wandered to the first of the frangipani. "Lan must care a great deal for Mister Griffin—she reminded me that before the French came an unfaithful wife could be put to death."

Tuyet felt the blood rush to her face.

"Have no fear," he said. "I will not punish you for following your heart, but you should know how much Lan hates you."

"She has reason. I misused her."

"Tuyet, it is time for us to put aside the things that fetter the spirit. We need all our resilience." He assessed the cloudless sky. "Cataclysm comes closer. You can smell it in the air. One day soon the birds will abandon Saigon. When they do, the end is at hand." He turned toward the house. "Time for the evening meal. Let us savor the simple joys while we still have them."

The next morning, Tuyet asked Lan to come to her room after breakfast. She despised what she had to do. It was humiliating, degrading, but she knew Thanh was right. She needed all her strength.

Lan tapped at the door, came in, and sat opposite Tuyet. She refused to raise her eyes to meet Tuyet's gaze.

Tuyet breathed deeply to fortify herself. "Thanh told me that you informed him of my affair with Mister Griffin. You pointed out that in the old days, an unfaithful wife could be killed."

Lan tensed.

"He wanted," Tuyet went on, "to be sure I understood how much you hate me. I believe I do understand. You are correct to feel as you do. I abused you without pity. I am grievously sorry for what I did. Can you pardon me?"

Lan raised her head. Her mouth dropped open.

"I promise you," Tuyet said, "that I will do everything I can to make amends. Troubled times are ahead. I will do my utmost to help you."

"You exploited me," Lan whispered. "You used me to hide your sinful lust. You threatened to turn me out of the house to lead a shameful life on the streets. You seduced the man I was in love with."

"I confess to all of that and worse. I am guilty and deserve punishment."

"I will never forgive you for what you have done to me," Lan hissed. "You deserve damnation."

Tuyet nodded. "I hurt many people. I am being punished as we speak. As the end of the nation draws closer, I'm carrying Mister Griffin's child."

A shudder rippled through Lan.

"I said I would help you," Tuyet said. "I have two Pan Am tickets for the United States. You can leave the country before it falls."

"I will not travel at your side. You sicken me."

"The tickets will be for you and Thu. You can take him to safety."

Lan glared. "The Republic will soon defeat the North Vietnamese. All the street banners say so. You pretend that disaster is close at hand so that you can rid yourself of me and your son. We hinder your illicit relationship with Griffin."

"Lan, time is short. The North Vietnamese move ever closer to Saigon."

"No. I will not fall into your trap."

"There is no one else I can ask to take Thu away from here," Tuyet said.

Lan shook her head. "May the Mother Goddess and all her spirits have mercy on you and forgive you, because *I never will*." She stalked from the room.

Tuyet sat in a cyclo en route to the Pan Am office to change the departure date. She must allow time for Thanh to heal. She shook her head. Why lie to herself? Thanh would heal whether she was here or not. The truth was she was loath to leave his side. She couldn't turn away from her beacon, the Thanh she could now see clearly. Not just yet.

But Thu's survival was at stake. And she carried Chuck's child. She opened her mouth to tell the cyclo driver to turn around, then closed it again. She was not risking their lives by staying a little longer. She rode on.

The agent told her he could not change the departure date. All scheduled flights were sold out with waiting lists. She could either leave on the assigned date or turn the tickets in for a refund. But he could not give her dollars—she would have to take piastres at the official exchange rate and pay a penalty for returning the tickets. She left the office with her purse stuffed with piastres worth less than half what Chuck had paid for the tickets. At Lam Son Circle she hired a cyclo to take her to Yen Do. The Chinese maid admitted her and told her that Mr. Griffin would be home shortly; it was Saturday and he worked only a half-day.

"I will wait for him," Tuyet said.

The woman led her into the sitting room and switched on the ceiling fan.

The breeze from the fan was too cool. She was shivering. No, it wasn't the cold. It was her terror that made her shake. What had she done? She'd given up the one certain way she had of saving herself, Thu, and her unborn child. But she was incapable of leaving Thanh. She'd be able to later. She'd find a way. Chuck would find a way. He'd have to find a way.

The gate bell rang. She heard a jeep drive into the courtyard, two men talking. The man with reddish-blond hair who lived here, the one Chuck called Sparky, came in the front door followed by Chuck. The maid pointed toward the sitting room. Tuyet stood.

Chuck's face radiated a smile. "Tuyet!" He hurried to her.

She turned her face away from his kiss.

"What's the matter?" Chuck said. "Sparky knows about us."

The man and the servant stood in the entrance hall watching, as if they already knew something was wrong.

Chuck took her hand. "Tuyet, why are you here?"

"I cannot go." She opened her purse and withdrew the stack of piastres. "I returned the tickets. The agent wouldn't give me dollars. Here."

She pushed the wads of piastres into his hand and closed his fingers over them. Bills fluttered to the floor and danced across the room in the breeze from the fan. The look on his face changed from shock to fury as she watched.

"Why?" he growled.

She reached for him to explain.

"No." He stepped back. "Tell me why."

How could she make him see? "I cannot leave Thanh right now."

"Are you telling me you love him after all?" Chuck said.

"*No*. He is wounded with no one to care for him. I . . . I don't know how to explain. I go home now." She drew a shuddering breath and started for the door.

Chuck caught her hand. "Not until you explain what you have done."

He lowered his head, clenched his jaw. Then he shuddered and relaxed. "All right. I'm calm now. Come with me. We'll talk."

He put his arm around her as one would comfort a weeping child and urged her toward the veranda doors. Outside he settled her at the wicker table and sat across from her. "Okay. Tell me."

Without looking at him she recounted her conversation with Thanh. "He knows you are my lover."

Chuck gasped.

"He told me to go with you," she said. "He thinks you can save Thu and me."

"He's right. If you'll let me. I don't understand why you won't leave. Thanh is keeping you here somehow?"

She shook her head. "It is I, not him."

"You said you don't love him."

"I love *you,* but I cannot bring myself to desert him. He is hurt now. When he is better, maybe . . . You will be patient with me?"

"We won't be able to get airplane tickets."

"Your government must have evacuation plans."

He shook his head. "We should at least send Thu out of the country."

"He is too young to travel alone."

"You know anyone leaving?"

"No."

He rubbed his cheekbones with both hands. "I went to Thanh's office Wednesday night. He asked me to act in Colonel Macintosh's stead and get you and Thu out of the country. I asked him what would happen if you didn't escape before the North Vietnamese took over. He said he would shoot you and Thu and himself."

Panic shimmered in her belly. Of course that is what Thanh would do. Better to die at his hand than suffer torture and execution.

"And you still want to stay with him?" Chuck said.

"I will leave Thanh as soon as I can."

With Tet now less than three weeks away, Tuyet set the servants to work cleaning. The gardener had long since been pruning the flowering bushes and plants to ensure maximum bloom on 11 February, the day of Tet itself and the peak of the new year celebration. The weather warmed and the vegetation thrived. It would be a Tet full of flowers.

Ignoring Tuyet's pleas, Thanh renewed his travels despite his wound. Chuck bought Tuyet a shortwave radio at the PX so that she could listen to the BBC, ARS, and the French and Vietnamese broadcasts of Voice of America. For the first time she paid close attention to the news of the war. She learned that Republic of Vietnam forces were making headway in the north and, to a lesser degree, in the highlands, but south of Saigon fighting had been fierce with heavy casualties. On 28 January President Ford requested an additional appropriation of three hundred million dollars from Congress. Congressional delegations would be visiting Vietnam to see firsthand how the war was going. That meant Chuck would be spending long hours at the office. He told Tuyet that his boss, Colonel Troiano, had refused an invitation for Chuck to accompany Thanh to I Corps during February—Chuck had to be in Saigon to brief the visiting congressional delegations. He didn't know if he'd be able to accompany Thanh on the trip to the highlands in March. Meanwhile, during the current Congressional delegations' visit, he'd have no time to spend with her.

Thanh would be away at Tet. He planned to observe the holiday with his troops on the front lines and perhaps seek out his few living relatives near Hue. Even in his absence, custom required that Tuyet be at Thanh's villa during the new year. She would exchange gifts, eat the sanctioned foods, and participate in rituals at the villa with Lan, Thu, and the servants.

She and the servants finished the preparations before sunset the Sunday before Tet. Night closed in on the villa, and the gardener flipped on the security lights. The evening meal was dreary. Lan, as usual, sat in belligerent silence while Thu prattled in French and the servants came and went like shadows, soundless and all but invisible. Long after the pastry, while Chi Hai bathed Thu, Tuyet fondled her wine glass and listened to the fading sounds of the city in the distance. Tet was the day after tomorrow. She'd go through the tedious rites with Lan, Thu, and the servants. While Thanh was in the middle of the war preparing his troops for the end. While Chuck worked at his office and visited the orphans. Hers was a useless, meaningless existence. What had Thanh said? *Terrible times are coming. Enrich your moral power.* He was right. She needed to fortify her spirit.

If only she could be like Chuck, doing good for someone. Even Molly was working with the orphans. She'd been consulting with Sister Évangéline to improve the children's diet. . . . Tuyet cocked her head. Maybe she could be just a little like Chuck and Molly. Bring a little joy to the orphans. Chuck and Molly had visited Cité Paul-Marie on Christmas, brought presents, celebrated with the children. She could do the same at Tet—take them gifts and food. She remembered the mutilated little bodies, the scent of urine. Better that than the claustrophobia of this villa. She'd do it. Tomorrow she'd go to Cholon in the sedan and buy gifts, and on Tuesday, the peak of the holiday, she'd drive to the main orphanage in Gia Dinh and spend the day with the orphans.

The Highlands

MARCH 1975

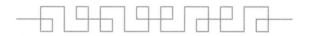

CHAPTER 12

At 0500 Chuck was on the tarmac. Weariness dogged him. After working until midnight in the tank, here he was, dressed in camouflage utilities, ruck on his back, boarding pass and orders in his hand. Odd to be in utilities again. Felt right, though. He found himself talking to Ben in his mind. *We're not going to win this one, son. You gave your life for it, and I'm giving it all I've got. Maybe that's the best we can do.* That wasn't what he longed to say to his son. *As God is my witness, I was never ashamed of you.*

It hurt to remember. Ben standing before him, Sherry between them holding Chuck back. Hurt and fury. "You make me ashamed." Ben's face going pale, and a moment later crimson with rage. He stalked out. Ten months later he was dead.

"He died with honor." That's what his commanding officer had written. Sounded so dignified, so orderly. Evoked pictures of young heroes standing tall in beams of sunlight with the flag unfurled next to them while the strains of martial music swelled. Chuck could feel good about it, proud even, as long as he didn't have to smell the burning flesh, didn't have to hear the screams, didn't have to see the dismembered bodies and guts spattered across the battlefield. He shook his head. *The lies we tell ourselves.*

The sky hinted at dawn. He moved under a runway light and looked at his invitational orders, issued by Troiano, authorizing him to travel to Pleiku, Kontum, and Ban Me Thuot beginning 6 March 1975 and returning not later than 13 March. "Find out everything you can about the North Vietnamese offensive in the highlands," Troiano had said. "Talk to intel officers everywhere you go, but away from their operational commanders." Chuck already knew the routine. Intel types were open with others of the same ilk, especially if politics wasn't involved. The higher you got in the chain of command, the more personal agendas colored the facts. Trouble was, he was traveling with Thanh and would be more of an observer than an investigator. Besides, it would all be in Vietnamese except when Thanh translated for him.

Two jeeps sped across the apron and squealed to a halt. Thanh, still wearing the sling, eased from the first vehicle and introduced the five junior officers, all captains and majors, who spilled out behind him. The seven of them boarded a rickety C-47, a two-engine World War II–vintage aircraft designed to carry twenty-odd soldiers. The plane cranked up and taxied to takeoff position as they strapped themselves in. It roared down the runway; the engines groaned and the cabin vibrated. Chuck tightened his grasp on his armrest until the plane was high in the air, catching the first glimmer of the sun. Only then did the engines settle into a healthy hum.

Chuck was roused from a dream-driven sleep when the engines resumed their unhappy groaning. A look out the tiny window told him they were descending. The countryside stood out raw in the overcast glare. Far to the west were craggy mountains, hostile and bare of vegetation. The plane turned south to make its landing approach, and he looked to the east. There the mountains gave way to hills and, far beyond, flatlands. Everywhere the earth was red, the twisting terrain interrupted only by a lone tree or clump of grass. Gray buildings and olive drab tents clustered in the foothills above the airstrip. As they approached the ground, the broken pavement of the runway glistened from recent rain. Of course. The monsoons in the highlands hadn't ended yet. They wouldn't begin in the lowlands around Saigon until they finished up here.

As soon as the plane rolled to a stop, the enlisted man threw open the door and lowered the small staircase. Thanh, now minus the sling, left the plane first, followed by Chuck, who was apparently the guest of honor. The officers followed in rank order. Waiting for them in the murky gray light were three jeeps, engines running, their drivers at attention. Thanh mounted the first jeep alone. Chuck climbed into the second with two of the Vietnamese officers. The remaining officers clambered on board the last. Chuck's vehicle leaped away, close behind Thanh's.

The jeeps bounced along pockmarked roads into a valley. Montagnard women, chickens, and an occasional soldier dispersed before them. They pulled up smartly before the least modest of a series of structures, a two-story building made of stripped logs built at the highest point on the valley floor. In front was a flagpole, as tall as the building, flying the orange-and-gold flag of the Republic of Vietnam. A sign over the door, painted in the same colors, proclaimed something in Vietnamese ending with "II." Guards saluted as the party went through the entrance. The visitors went up a flight of steps and into an anteroom. A colonel stood by the window looking down at their jeeps. He turned to Thanh, and Chuck read the name LIEM stitched above his right fatigue pocket.

Thanh and Liem smiled, saluted, and shook hands. The adjutant interrupted their conversation and gestured toward the door to the inner office. Thanh glanced behind him as if to ensure that his entourage, including Chuck, was with him and entered the office.

Smoke blurred the features of the room. Cigarettes, two of them still burning, littered the deck. The snakelike man behind the desk, a lit cigarette in his hand, gave no indication that he knew eight people were standing before him. He went on reading, smiling at the document in his hands. Without looking up he made a single sound, and the officers sat in a row of chairs facing the desk. Chuck hurriedly joined them. The adjutant served tea.

Chuck squinted through the smoke at the man reading. His fatigues' nametag read TRI, and his shoulders bore the two stars of a major general. The slant of his egg-shaped bald head drew the eye to his mouth, the lips closed, the corners turned up. Something about his smile activated the tingle low in Chuck's spine. It was a sardonic smile, a sneer.

Tri raised his eyes and said, "Thanh." Thanh stood at attention, his eyes downcast, and spoke several sentences. Then he turned to Chuck. "Mister Griffin, I introduce you to General Tri." Chuck jumped to his feet.

Tri fixed Chuck in his gaze. "I am honored to meet you, Mister Griffin."

Chuck started to answer, but Tri shifted back to Thanh and went on speaking. He gestured to Chuck to sit, tossed away his cigarette, and lit another.

Throughout the exchange, the smile never left Tri's face. Maybe it was less an expression than a facial feature. His eyes remained half closed, as though in disdain for the colonel in front of him. His speech, marked by viperous hisses, cut through the smoke.

Chuck's weariness, aggravated by the smarting of his eyes, lulled him. The singsong chatter worked like a drug. Nodding off in Tri's presence would constitute a calculated insult. He tightened his muscles, arched his back, fluttered his eyelids, but the smoke he inhaled weakened his will.

A bark from Tri jarred him awake. The general was glaring at Thanh. Liem stood and spoke quietly, his eyes averted. Thanh's voice, pitched low, repeated Liem's words. He looked directly into Tri's eyes, his gestures calm, and pointed to the large II Corps map on the wall. Liem moved to it and waved circles around Ban Me Thuot, in Darlac Province, directly south of Pleiku. The smile left Tri's face for the first time. He directed half a dozen sentences at Thanh with undisguised hostility. The interview was over.

They exited the office as they had entered, in rank order, Thanh leading. In the hall Thanh turned to Chuck. "Please wait for me one minute at the jeep. I talk to Liem."

Outside, Chuck leaned his weight on the fender of the lead jeep. He wished he had a cup of coffee. To fight off his sleepiness he paced. He breathed in air much cooler than that of Saigon. The sun was out now, casting black shadows as it moved up from behind the western mountains. Even here in the valley the elevation was several thousand feet above Saigon. No swamps. Just sterile rocks and red dirt. Rough terrain. A brutal place to fight a war.

Thanh bolted from the building, his retinue scuffling behind. "We go Ban Me Thuot," he said to Chuck. The caravan lurched back to the road. The C-47 was already warming up, the passenger door open, the steps in place. Thanh waved everyone on board. Before Chuck could snap his seatbelt in place the aircraft was moving.

After the plane had attained cruising altitude, Thanh moved to the seat next to Chuck's. "You forgive the hurry, okay? We must be at Ban Me Thuot before sundown so we can land safely, you understand?"

"Excuse me, sir, but I thought we were to stay overnight in Pleiku, then go to Kontum before the trip to Ban Me Thuot."

Thanh gave him a serene smile. "The war, it changes." He leaned back in the seat. "I tried to explain to General Tri. The North Vietnamese 316th Division prepares an attack on Ban Me Thuot. Liem told him the same. He does not believe us. 'Ban Me Thuot is nothing,' he says. 'Pleiku will be the target. II Corps headquarters is at Pleiku. *I* am at Pleiku.' Afterward, Liem showed me most recent troop sightings. Attack will begin at Ban Me Thuot very soon. So we go to Ban Me Thuot. You understand?"

Chuck hesitated. "No, sir. If they are going to attack Ban Me Thuot, why do you want to go there?"

Thanh laughed, his eyes liquid. "My people need me now. I go to give them strength and courage, so they can endure the end." He looked past Chuck, out the window. "Liem knows that the end is here, but Tri would punish him if he spoke it." He grew quiet. "I tell you before. First Phuoc Binh. The Americans did nothing. Now the highlands—Ban Me Thuot, then Pleiku. Then comes I Corps, then Saigon."

Cold enveloped Chuck's stomach. He looked down, then raised his head. "And your wound, sir?"

Thanh cocked his head as though he were remembering something that had slipped his mind. "Mister Griffin, An Nam is dying. My wound is nothing."

Once again the groan and shudder jolted Chuck awake. They were going for a steep descent to evade small arms fire. Through the slanting rays of the sun beneath the clouds he scanned the terrain, which was much like that of Pleiku, and spotted the muddy airstrip on a ridge between valleys. The plane dived toward it and abruptly leveled. The touchdown was rough.

Thanh handled the commanding officer's protocol ritual with peremptory brevity and began rounds of talking to the troops. Chuck and the five officers followed him through the ragged hills from squad to squad. Haggard young faces, grim from combat, looked up at Thanh from every angle, eyes glistening in the failing light. After sunset the visitors, who'd had no food since morning, ate the evening meal sitting cross-legged in the dust with enlisted men, rice bowls and chopsticks clattering while Thanh spoke. The smell of *nuoc mam* and rice covered the scent of the damp earth.

With the onset of darkness, Thanh dismissed the junior officers but signaled Chuck to follow him. "We go to the infirmary tent."

A woman stood outside the entrance lamenting, her voice rising to a shriek. Thanh questioned three other women standing nearby, took the woman in his arms. As the woman's cries subsided, Chuck heard another sound, a steady scream halted from time to time by an intake of breath. The voice was shattered, broken by constant use but forced to operate in spite of itself, like a machine driven to ruin. Chuck followed Thanh into the tent.

Inside was an overflow of human wreckage—battered, dismembered men, alive only because death hadn't gotten to them yet. Chuck held his breath to ward off the stench and locked his throat to keep from vomiting. But he couldn't block out the screaming.

The source was a man at the far end. His skin was charred and bloody, his body a mangled parody of human form. His eyes, with no eyelids to protect them, started from his skull. His mouth was forced open to its limit. His teeth were broken and blackened.

Thanh knelt beside him. He gathered the burned body in his arms and spoke in a singsong, almost a lullaby. The screaming stopped. The body ceased moving. Thanh straightened. He pulled a stained sheet over the man's face. Without getting to his feet he turned to the next mat and spoke to the soldier lying on it.

Chuck watched from the narrow aisle between mats. Thanh moved through the tent and talked to each man. Before Thanh had finished, Chuck, feeling as though he was witnessing death rituals too intimate for a stranger's eyes, walked from the tent.

He slept fitfully that night in a cleft of the mountain, a spot marginally protected from shelling. The highlands air chilled him, and his neck ached from the struggle to use his canvas ruck as a pillow. Small arms fire woke him twice. When mortars jarred him awake before dawn, he rose, stripped, shaved, and washed with cold water from his canteen. Dressed in clean socks and underwear and his spare set of utilities, he set off looking for the rest of the party. He found Thanh and a group of ragamuffin followers, a mix of military and civilians, gathered around a small fire boiling their morning portion of rice.

By sunup he and Thanh were off by jeep to visit outlying emplacements and makeshift villages of soldiers and their families. They found hovels pieced together from cardboard, tin, canvas, and burlap housing young soldiers and their wives, their unfinished faces aged by war, their children dirty, underfed, and shriveled. Thanh stopped at each hamlet and outpost, talked, listened, sometimes wept with the spindly inhabitants, and moved on. At midday they ate with six Montagnard families consisting only of women, children, and old men. Thanh had brought rice with him to share with these silent, resentful folk, who added acrid vegetables to the bowls they handed Chuck and Thanh.

In the afternoon they returned to the garrison, washed, and met with the unit's command staff. A young officer armed with charts and maps briefed them. Standing at rigid attention, his voice chanted and trilled, rose and dipped. A mortar attack dispelled them to sandbagged trenches. Twenty minutes later they resumed their talk as if nothing had happened.

Thanh, Chuck, and the junior officers had dinner with the unit commander and his lieutenants. The formalities over, Thanh ignored the displeasure of the officers and resumed his talks with the enlisted troops. Chuck understood. Thanh was the good mandarin, teaching and explaining to disciples who sat in the dust at his feet. Toward midnight they retired. Chuck zipped his field jacket to his chin against the mountain wind.

Over the breakfast rice, Thanh told Chuck that a major attack would begin that day. They would take off at once for Saigon. Chuck's chopsticks stopped in midair.

"You are surprised?" Thanh laughed. "You think we stay and face attack?"

"Yes, sir. That's what I thought the Colonel intended."

"And you stay if I say so?"

"Yes, sir."

Thanh smiled. "You are a *fine* Marine."

"Not any more, sir."

"You never mind." Thanh patted Chuck's shoulder. "*Fine* Marine." He paused, looked away. "No, I must go to Saigon. If I stay here, maybe I am killed or captured. Not now. Still much work to do. You understand?"

Breakfast finished, Chuck packed. His dirty clothes had been washed, dried, and carefully folded. The utilities were immaculate, as were his olive drab boot socks. But his underwear was baby pink, a souvenir of the red highlands clay that colored everything, even the unfiltered water.

As the sun rose among gathering monsoon clouds, Thanh, Chuck, and the five officers went by jeep to the ridge airstrip where the troops were assembled for an honorific farewell. The soldiers stood at attention in eight silent rows, motionless and silent except for the rustling of their clothes in the wind. Chuck waited to one side while Thanh and his entourage went through the motions of an inspection, attended by the commander and his adjutant. At its completion, the first sergeant called parade rest in a kind of scream that startled Chuck. Clouds hid the sun. Rain fell in a delicate patter. Thanh wandered between the columns. He spoke in high-pitched bursts punctuated by long silences as his eyes searched the soldier's faces.

Small arms fire erupted far below in the valley to their west. Chuck could see tiny flashes and puffs of smoke followed by a chattering of muzzle reports. The soldiers stood stock still, their backs to the valley, seeing nothing.

Thanh continued his speech. He moved among the troops, his hands behind his back. Tension in the ranks stiffened the soldiers. Still Thanh spoke on. Strain darkened the lined young faces as the sound of battle grew louder. At last Thanh became silent. He walked the full length of the rows, reading the faces. Now close to the plane, he called out a single short sentence three times. His voice gone soft and tired, he said something low. The sergeant screamed them to attention and issued an order. They scattered on the run.

The rain pounded. The C-47 started its engines. Thanh, Chuck, and the junior officers dashed to it. All around them soldiers hurried to their battle stations. They saluted and waved at Thanh as they ran by.

A pepper of small arms fire raised plumes of mud at their feet. The airstrip was under attack. They scrambled on board the plane, which rushed down the runway before the door was closed. Once aloft, it strained into a steep ascent. Chuck held on. He hoped the bellowing engines wouldn't fly apart. Finally the plane righted itself above the clouds and the engines purred as if in relief.

Thanh sat long at the window looking back, saying nothing.

At Tan Son Nhat the plane taxied to the military terminal. Through the window Chuck spotted Thanh's two jeeps waiting. The passengers exited the aircraft once again in rank order, and as the officers piled into the second jeep, Thanh pulled Chuck aside.

"My friend Colonel Liem, he checked on the Chinese corporal, Giuong Minh Phuc, like you asked. Corporal Phuc is now a sergeant, promoted. That is very good for a Chinese, you know? He is in good health. He has not been able to send mail to his wife because his unit has been in the field for many weeks, but he gave Liem a letter and money to be carried to his wife." He handed Chuck an envelope. "Phuc's wife, her name is Huong, yes? You will be so kind as to convey this to her?"

Chuck took the envelope. "Mrs. Phuc is honored by the Colonel's help and will send her thanks."

Thanh looked up into Chuck's face. "Mister Griffin, I salute you. You are a brave man."

"I thank the Colonel. It was my honor to accompany him."

Thanh studied him. "You stay in Ban Me Thuot if I ask. You knew the danger, but you were prepared to fight by my side one more time." He smiled. "Thu will be your son. Raise him to be a brave man, like you. Instruct him in goodness and the sanctity of silence, and teach him that nurturing and wisdom are the traits of a strong man." The smile lingered. "I entrust my son to you, Mister Griffin. Love him well."

Thanh walked to the jeep, climbed in, and turned to wave at Chuck. The two jeeps sped away.

CHAPTER 13

Ike swore under his breath. The bad news from the front was making Molly lousy in bed. He couldn't blame her, but he was disgusted that women let outside events get in the way of good sex. Sparky and Chuck made it worse. Fucking walking corpses mouthing bullshit about death and destruction. Oopsie, more forgetful than ever, was sleeping at the office half the time. He told them the North Vietnamese had launched a major offensive in the highlands, something called Campaign 275. They had interdicted Routes 19 and 21, destroyed bridges, and launched attacks in Kontum and Pleiku Provinces. The only resupply was by air, but the U.S. Congress hadn't authorized funds for fuel to fly the planes. Thanh and Chuck had cut short their trip and flown home two days early. This morning, Monday, ARS had reported that the North Vietnamese 316th Division had penetrated Ban Me Thuot. When Chuck and Sparky limped in that night as Ike and Molly were heading to bed, they said that Ban Me Thuot was in enemy hands.

"God, those guys look bad." Molly stepped out of her panties and climbed into the rack beside Ike. "They'll get sick if they keep this up. Did you notice Chuck's hair is turning white at the temples?"

"You do what you have to do," Ike said. "Whatever it takes."

Molly snuggled next to him. "I've been pinch-hitting with Philippe. He cuddles up to me and looks up with those battered eyes and says, 'Pee-kwee? Pee-kwee?' That's what he calls Chuck. The nuns have started bringing in more orphans from Gia Dinh. Things are getting hairy out there. You should go with me next time I visit. Tuyet goes out there, too."

"How come? She ain't no nurse."

"Matter of fact, she is. More important, she's a woman and a mother and she knows how to love a child."

Ike wondered. Tuyet had never seemed very motherly to him. More like an empress.

"Huong asked me to thank you for the info on her husband," Molly said. "The money, too. Turns out what he sent is less than I pay her in a week. She's the breadwinner."

"Too bad her husband is in the highlands. The North Vietnamese are cleaning our clocks up there."

Molly cringed. "You know what? I don't want to hear any more. I'm up to here with the war."

A low rumble shook the floor.

"Thunder?" Molly said. "Monsoon's not due 'til late April or May. Besides, who ever heard of thunder in the tropics?"

"That wasn't thunder, Molly."

It came again. She tensed.

"Rockets, maybe." He lifted his head and listened. "No. Artillery. Never heard it that close before."

"Them or us?"

He gave full attention to his ears. "Them."

The soft whish of the air conditioner. A gecko's scuttle. Their breathing. Nothing more.

On Friday, 14 March, ARS reported that Congress had voted not to appropriate funds for Vietnam. The war was over. Somehow nobody in Saigon had been notified, and the North Vietnamese were ignoring the fact as they seized more territory. Ike's country had forgotten that he was here and faced daily threats to his life.

Riding to and from the embassy as the days warmed toward the lowland monsoon season, Ike watched the city change. The good-natured clatter of bikes and hurrying pedestrians was gone. In its place was a city much quieter and wound ever tighter. Faces on the streets showed worry. Refugees were everywhere.

The embassy, always marked by the lilt of southern hospitality, developed an uneasy edge. Ike's men felt the change. The boyish horse-play faded. The snuffs kept their weapons cleaned and oiled, never more than an arm's reach away. They asked Ike what was happening. He shrugged. The Ambassador, a gentleman under all circumstances, continued to preside over the embassy with grace and good breeding.

In dinner-table talk Sparky and Chuck reported daily disasters. On Saturday the Saigon police apparently panicked and shot to death a French journalist. Sunday night, shaken, Chuck said that President Thieu had ordered the evacuation of the highlands. The North Vietnamese had blocked National Route 19, the direct road to the coast, so more than twenty infantry battalions and ranger groups, three arty battalions, a tank battalion, an engineer group, and a support group had all started down Interprovincial Route 7B, not much more than a trail. It was overgrown with brush, and its fords and bridges were impassable. By Monday night panicking civilians, a hundred thousand of them, swamped Route 7B, bogging down the troops, while the North Vietnamese attacked from all sides. Already people were calling it "the trail of blood and tears." Meanwhile, cities were falling in the northern provinces south of the DMZ, and the royal city of Hue was under siege, its citadel struck by artillery.

Molly showed up at the villa the following Saturday night with a suitcase. "It's my getaway bag," she told Ike, "in case I'm here when the end comes. Got another bag at the dispensary and one at the apartment." In her other hand she carried a clothes hanger with a full-length purple dress. "That's the color of the priest's vestments during Lent. Tomorrow's Palm Sunday, and I want to fit in—you know, look properly dismal."

She rousted him out of bed at seven the next morning—she had to be at Cité Paul-Marie before nine for the pre-Mass folk group rehearsal. Downstairs, Chi Nam's face was grave as she put the carafe on the table.

"What's the matter?" Ike asked her.

She put mugs in front of them. "Quang Tri, the city of my family, the Viet Cong, they take it. My people flee south. I hear on the radio that Route 1 south from Hue is blocked. Too many refugee, you know? People are hurt, they have no food." She escaped to the kitchen.

They went to church by cab. While Molly was rehearsing with the group, Ike ventured out into the streets. Nice neighborhood, nicer than Yen Do. Lots of money here. Narrow lanes with high walls topped by spikes or barbed wire. Pastel villas rising above with graceful balconies now enclosed in mesh to ward off grenades and broad windows taped against shattering from explosions. Odd that no one was on the streets. The mongers with their noisemakers and high-pitched calls had disappeared. No women in *áo dài* carrying parasols hailing cabs. It was too quiet.

By 0945 he was in the chapel. There was Molly to the side of the altar in her somber purple, bigger and louder than anyone else in the folk group. They were still practicing as worshippers drifted in. They sang something discordant about death, ending with the refrain, "My God, my God, why have you forsaken me?" Sunlight streamed through the perforated walls. Uncomfortably warm. The stink of the city, strongest in the spring heat before the monsoons washed away the accumulated sludge of the dry season, rolled through the church. Ike loosened his collar, mopped his forehead.

As Monsignor Sullivan came up the aisle toward the altar, the group sang the folk hymn "Watch One Hour with Me." Ike recognized the words from long hours in the Baptist congregations of his childhood as a paraphrase of Jesus' words in Gethsemane asking his disciples to stay with him as he died. Was the church aping daily life?

The Gospel recounted the crucifixion. The text was brief, blunt, and direct.

As perspiration rolled down Ike's back, the Mass finally ended. Monsignor Sullivan and his troop of mixed-race altar boys came down the aisle toward the entrance while the folk group intoned yet another desolate hymn. Ike blocked out the words. He'd had enough.

In the brilliant sunshine outside the gate, Molly, palm leaf in hand, looked about. "Let's eat breakfast out. How about the Arc-en-Ciel in Cholon?"

"They don't serve breakfast."

"I want a big Chinese meal. It's past eleven. We'll call it brunch."

The cab dropped them on Tran Hung Dao Avenue before the multistoried Chinese restaurant, probably the biggest eatery in Saigon. They sat side by side at a table on the third floor, surrounded by noisy Chinese—no Vietnamese—in a room bigger than the whole of the Yen Do villa. The illustrated menu was in Chinese with brief Vietnamese translations, but Molly ordered using a combination of pidgin Vietnamese and sign language and pointed at pictures of the dishes.

When the five entrees and a tureen of rice arrived, Ike grimaced. "You ordered sautéed chicken feet?"

"Sorry 'bout that." She dished out bowls of rice and ate Chinese style, holding her rice bowl in one hand and brandishing her chopsticks over the assortment of delicacies with the other.

"What's this?" He pointed to a plate of browned meat in gravy. "Hope we don't get dysentery."

He picked at his food. She scarfed up serving after serving.

"When we're done," she said, "let's go back to the apartment. I don't think I can stand another doom-and-gloom evening with your housemates. Let's belt a few, then get in some quality time in bed."

"Thought you'd never ask." He grinned. "You're in a good mood, right?"

"Yeah." She pushed away her empty rice bowl and plumped her stomach. "Big transformation ahead for yours truly. I've made up my mind. I'm going to convert."

Ike dropped his chopsticks.

"Yeah," she said. "Thought it through. Sex, booze, and chocolate don't cut it anymore. Been watching the nuns and orphans and such. They got it and I don't. So I'm going to get it."

"When?"

"Not sure. Monsignor Sullivan says they can double-time the instruction. Might be able to do it in a couple of weeks. For sure I want to get it done before Saigon falls and I have to clear out."

He coughed. "What about us?"

Her smile vanished. "That's been the hardest part. I've gotten so I don't want to do without my Joy Stick. But we'll still see each other. We just have to stay out of bed when we're together."

"Okay, so we stay out of bed. We can screw on the sofa."

"Come on, Ike. You know what I mean. We have to make it, you know, platonic."

He folded his arms. "First you're never in the mood because of the war. Now you want to become a virgin."

She took his hand. "Hey, babe, help me with this. Have a heart."

The way she was looking at him, her eyes moist, that half-smile, he knew she'd made her decision. He swallowed hard, looked down, nodded.

"It won't be so bad." She stroked the back of his hand. "We won't be able to be together after we're evacuated anyway. You'll be back with your wife. And I, . . ." she blinked, "I'll find my own way."

He watched her. "I don't get it."

"I don't either. All I know is, I'm doing what I have to do."

"Whatever it takes." He filled his lungs and let the air filter away.

"I had a one-on-one with Chuck." She folded her hands on the table. "I made him promise to tell me when we're at the end. He figures we've got a month, maybe six weeks. I'll put off the baptism until the last minute. Until then, we're good to go."

Back in the apartment they made love. Molly was her old horny self. As always, he dropped into deep sleep afterward. Consciousness returned slowly late in the afternoon. He could hear the whoosh of the air conditioner and Molly's regular breathing. Then came a clunk. He opened his eyes. A chair scraped. *Huong.* He groaned out of the rack, found his clothes, and went to the head. Huong waved, all smiles, from the kitchen. He splashed his face with cold water and headed down the hall. A glance out the window told him it was dusk.

"Hello Mister Captain, *sir,*" Huong chirped. "You have good hanky panky?"

"You fix us something to eat, okay?"

"You bet. Toot sweet." She scurried to the kitchen. "I whump up some vittles. You eat Dinty Moore stew? Some noodle soup? All in can. Easy does it."

"Wait 'til Miss Molly comes out."

"Hold my horses. I go do laundry, then check it out."

She took the laundry basket and left.

Molly came from the bedroom in scrubs. "Let's turn on ARS, see what's going on back in the world."

Ike switched on the stereo while Molly clinked ice into the cocktail shaker.

" . . . unable to reach Tuy Hoa on the coast," the announcer said. "Both military units and refugees are stymied east of Cheo Reo. With bridges out and fords impassable, evacuees detoured onto Route 436, but the temporary bridge built by engineers collapsed and enemy forces attacked again. Elsewhere, Tam Ky and Hue are both under assault. Farther south—"

"*Turn it off!*" Molly cried. "Everywhere I turn—*Stars and Stripes,* your goddamn housemates, ARS."

Ike took her in his arms. "Easy, babe."

She pulled free, sloshed gin over the cracked ice, added a drop of vermouth, and stirred. "No time to chill these. No time to relax and let my hair down. No time to love." She slopped the mixture into the waiting glasses. "I didn't ask for this war. I can't stop it. I can't do anything."

"You *are* doing something. The orphans—"

She heaved a shaky sigh and took her martini to the sofa. "I've got to find a way to get Angélique and Philippe and all the rest out of here.

Some guy at USAID has been yakking about getting a plane in here, one of those big-ass jobbies, to evacuate the nuns and the kids. I'm trying to find out if it's for real."

He sat next to her. "I'll ask at the embassy." He took her hand. "Babe, don't take it so hard. I'm . . ." The words didn't come easy. "I'm here for you."

She snuffled. "Even after I convert?"

He nodded. She put her arms around him and pulled him close.

Huong burst in, empty laundry basket in hand. "I fix food now, okay?"

"Please," Molly said.

They sat on the sofa while they drank a second martini and ate their canned dinner.

"I want us to sleep here for a while," Molly said. "I want to get away from the bad news bores."

"Sure," Ike said. "I did hear 'us,' didn't I?"

"Yeah. Salvation can wait a few weeks."

"Mister Captain, *sir?*" Huong stood in front of them, taking off her apron. "You talk me a little, just a tad, okay?"

Ike fortified himself with a swig of martini.

"Mister Captain . . ." Huong wrung her apron in her hands. "I need ask a favor. People say that our troops, they flee Pleiku, you know? You can tell me, this is true?"

Ike bit his lip. "It's true, Huong."

"And Ranger Group 25, my husband's unit, it flee, too?"

"If it was in Pleiku, it's relocated."

"Where they go, Mister Captain, sir?"

What could he tell her? "The headquarters and the troops are heading to Tuy Hoa on the coast."

Relief fluttered across Huong's face. "So they be okay?"

"We don't know yet."

"So, when we know?"

"We'll know when they get to Tuy Hoa."

Huong twisted her apron. "Pleiku to Tuy Hoa. One, two day, yes? When they leave Pleiku?"

"A week ago."

Huong stopped moving. "But they not yet come to Tuy Hoa?"

"No." Ike couldn't look her in the eye.

"So they stop somewhere?"

Ike sighed. "They been fighting the North Vietnamese all along the way. Bridges were out, fords torn up."

"So nobody get to Tuy Hoa yet." It was a statement, not a question. Huong stood silently, unmoving, her eyes downcast. "Mister Captain, sir, you able find my husband before. You bring me letter, money. You find him again, okay? And you tell me."

"I'll do what I can."

Huong bowed. "Thank you, Mister Captain. You very good to Huong."

She scooped up their plates and glasses, went to the kitchen, and began washing. Molly put her hand over Ike's.

CHAPTER 14

Chuck was kneeling on the deck in the tank posting the latest attacks at Oanh Mit, Tay Ninh, and Tri Tam on the sliding map boards when he saw Sparky's feet. Sparky held out a yellow page straight from the printer in the comms center. Chuck took it and read. After a three-day siege, the Republic of Vietnam Armed Forces had abandoned Hue. The civilian population was fleeing to the coast, hoping for escape by sea. The North Vietnamese could now take the royal capital unopposed. Chuck sat on his heels. Two of the three ancient Vietnamese capitals were now in communist hands—Hanoi in the north and Hue in the center. Only Saigon remained.

"What else?" Chuck said.

"Chu Lai is being evacuated. Da Nang's in chaos. More than two million people are in the streets trying to find a way out. Police desertion is on the rise. Armed soldiers are looting. And Liberation Radio has gone gross, getting its jollies by reporting the bloodletting in gory detail."

Chuck picked up his unit symbol decals and marking pen and fell into his chair. His eyes closed. He folded his arms on the desk and rested his forehead on his wrists. *Come on, Chuck, get a grip.*

A hand on his shoulder brought him upright. Sparky dropped a stack of eight-by-ten black-and-white photos on his desk.

The first four pictures, shot from a low-flying aircraft with a hand-held camera, showed a road mobbed with people. Off to the sides were wrecked military vehicles, some of them smoking; hundreds of bodies littered the ground.

"Where were these taken?"

"Highlands. Route 7B, east of Cheo Reo, a week ago."

"Jesus. Just like I told the Ambassador when I briefed him." Chuck slid the glossies to the bottom of the stack. The next set, also taken from the air, showed the coast. Piers extending into the sea were alive with people overflowing into the water. Two barges were covered with massed humanity.

"Chu Lai," Sparky said. "This morning."

Chuck flipped through the remaining photos. They showed Route 1 south of Hue, the port at Tan My, the streets and airfield of Da Nang. People, hundreds of thousands of them, swarmed like disoriented insects.

He handed them to Sparky. "Where'd these come from?"

"Troiano collected them to show to General Weyand."

"The Army chief of staff?"

"Oops." Sparky grinned. "Forgot to tell you. He'll be here tomorrow. No time off for us in the foreseeable future."

"What's this all about?"

"Weyand's been tasked by President Ford to make a personal assessment. He'll meet with the Ambassador, General Smith, Troiano, and the Viet leadership." Sparky's grin turned edgy. "Guess who'll have to write Troiano's presentation."

"Us?"

"You. Troiano thinks you can see the future." Sparky headed back to his desk.

Yes, he could see the future. Death and destruction. And Tuyet was still in-country. She wouldn't let go of Thanh. He rubbed his eyes. Maybe the way to get her to leave was to lure her, using Thanh as bait. If the U.S. government officially invited Thanh to come to the States, the Vietnamese hierarchy would be unable to refuse and Thanh would be required to make the trip.

He rolled a message form into his typewriter, typed SECRET EYES ONLY NOFORN, and addressed it to Colonel Macintosh: "As I am sure the Colonel is aware, the prognosis for the Republic of Vietnam is poor. Colonel Thanh has made no provision for escape if the country is defeated. Suggest the Colonel issue an official invitation to Colonel Thanh to visit the United States for consultations as soon as possible."

Chuck's eyes roved over the wall maps. *An Nam is dying. My wound is nothing.* The trip to II Corps had been Thanh's test of Chuck's worthiness, and Thanh had judged him to be the proper father for Thu. In the highlands Chuck had seen the force of Thanh unleashed. Like the Vietnamese and Montagnards, Chuck honored Thanh with a kind of fierceness he had never felt before. No, more like worshipped. Tuyet, at last, saw Thanh's fire, too. Now she was drawn to him in a way Chuck couldn't rival. A humorless giggle bubbled from his throat. Bested by the man he had cuckolded.

Sparky catnapped in the tank that night, spelling other I Corps and II Corps analysts, but Chuck drove the jeep to Yen Do before the midnight curfew. He was coming unglued. If he didn't get a few hours' rest, he wouldn't be able to think.

He was back in the tank by 0630 the following morning. III Corps and IV Corps, his responsibility, were heating up. No more time to help Sparky and the I Corps and II Corps crowd. Besides, he had to draft Troiano's presentation for Weyand. Before 0730 he'd finished his text for the morning briefing—the raging battle at Truong Mit, less than one hundred miles northeast of Saigon, could go either way. Losses heavy on both sides.

At his desk after the briefing, it came to him for the first time that the presentation to Weyand offered one last chance to make the case for U.S. reentry into the war, one final shot at justifying Ben's death. He shook his head. Crazy idea. He'd do it anyway. He turned to his typewriter.

> The northern half of South Vietnam is lost. The southern half could survive temporarily under three conditions:

1. The government is able to extract its forces from the north intact;
2. The North Vietnamese do not increase their forces in the south; and
3. The United States immediately resumes the air war and delivers essential ammunition, equipment, and supplies.

As this is written, it is clear that none of these conditions will be met. Casualties in the north have been overwhelming, and the remaining troops are in a rout. Meanwhile, the North Vietnamese are infiltrating the southern provinces at an unprecedented rate. And the United States has ceased its matériel and air support. In short, what is left of South Vietnam will fall within weeks.

In the long term, the only option available to avoid capitulation is the reintroduction of U.S. forces—ground, naval, and air. President Nixon promised to bring U.S. military strength to bear if North Vietnam violated the Paris Agreement. Gross violations by North Vietnam are now legion. Failure to rescue Vietnam will be recognized worldwide as evidence of bad faith.

He looked up. Troiano's secretary was standing by his desk.

"Two Vietnamese ladies at the door. They want to talk to you."

Chuck pulled the paper from the typewriter. "How about giving this to the colonel right away? It's for the Weyand presentation."

He went to the front door. In the corridor were Tuyet and Mai, each with hands clasped at her midsection, eyes down.

"Forgive the interruption," Tuyet said.

Chuck stepped into the hall and closed the door behind him. "How did you get into the compound?"

"JGS identification papers. From Thanh."

"What's wrong?"

"Mai insisted," Tuyet said, "on talking to you, the princess' consort, before she leaves."

He swallowed his surprise. "Where's she going?"

"She is returning to the royal family."

"I don't understand."

"Mai came to us when she was very young," Tuyet said, "before I was born. She was sent by Empress Tu Cung, mother of Bao Dai. It is the custom that the emperor or empress may give a servant, but in time of need the servant must return to the imperial court. Mai is going back to serve Tu Cung."

"The empress is still living?"

"She is the queen mother now."

"I'm glad Mai's going," Chuck said. "She'll be safe. Is the queen mother in Paris? Or maybe Nice?"

Tuyet hesitated. "You don't understand. Tu Cung is in Hue."

"But surely she can leave Hue. The North Vietnamese would let her go—"

"No. She's very old now. Hue is the royal capital. She refuses to leave."

He caught his breath. "Tuyet, don't let Mai go. The roads are mobbed with refugees and deserting soldiers. The military is routed, the civilians in panic. People are starving, dying of exposure. Even if Mai makes it to Hue, the Communists will—"

"I cannot stop her. Her sworn duty to the Nguyen dynasty must be fulfilled." Tuyet faltered, straightened. "It is better this way than waiting here for the North Vietnamese to take her."

Mai stepped toward him, rigid and unbending. Eyes lowered, she spoke to him in throaty Vietnamese, punctuated with honorific glottal stops, then moved back, clasped her hands, and stood immobile.

Tuyet translated. "She says she thanks you for your kindness. The time has come when she can no longer watch over the princess. She consigns little sister Tuyet to your protection. She charges you to take care of Tuyet. She will pray for us."

Chuck cleared his throat. "When is she leaving?"

"Tomorrow morning, first light."

"God bless you and keep you, Mai," he said.

＊＊＊

General Weyand arrived on schedule Thursday and immediately began consultations with the Ambassador, General Smith, President Thieu, and the commanding Vietnamese generals. On Friday word arrived that the constant shelling of Da Nang was pushing the city into hysteria. Saturday, according to a JGS bulletin, Thanh managed to take off from Da Nang and was returning to Saigon. Later that day two World Airways 747s flew to Da Nang to rescue women and children, but in the disorder at the airport only one landed, and it was mobbed by soldiers.

After lunch on Saturday Chuck made a food run to the snack bar. Halfway there he spotted a nurse in a white uniform carrying a briefcase, blond hair piled under her cap. Molly. "What are you doing here?"

"Orphan business." She glanced around to be sure they were not heard. "It's OPERATION BABYLIFT. President Ford overruled the Ambassador and authorized the use of U.S. transport aircraft to evacuate four thousand orphans from places like Cité Paul-Marie and the Gia Dinh orphan asylum. A lot of them are half-American, fathered by GIs. The North Vietnamese would be brutal to them. We gotta get them out of here. But it's all hush-hush. Don't want to let it be known we're evacuating people. The Ambassador's afraid it might cause a panic."

"I don't get it. You're embassy personnel. Why are you involved?"

"I'm a volunteer. Lots of charities are in on it. I'm the Catholic charities rep for Cité Paul-Marie and the Gia Dinh asylum. But don't let on, okay?"

"Wow." He grinned. "Nice goin', Molly. You done good."

Her mouth opened in surprise. "You think so?" Her smile was soft. "You know what else?" She darted looks up and down the corridor, continued in a whisper. "Monsignor Sullivan's been giving me instructions. I'm getting baptized next week."

"I'll be damned."

"Maybe I won't. That's the idea, anyway. Right after the baptism I make my First Holy Communion. But keep it to yourself. Nobody knows—except the people in the folk group. Had to tell them. Speaking of that, tomorrow's Easter. Come to the ten o'clock Mass at Cité Paul-Marie. I'm singing my last Mass as a heathen."

"I don't know," he said. "Things are kind of freaky."

"That explains why you look like you should go to the nearest old folks' home and turn yourself in." She stood straight. "The Dragon Lady will brook no defiance. Do as you are commanded." She let her shoulders droop. "Come on, Chuckie. Do this for me. Oh, and don't say anything to Joy Stick about the baptism. Haven't told him that I'm actually going through with it. We'll have to start abstaining."

"Molly celibate? Next you'll be telling me you're giving up chocolate."

She shook her head. "Naw. I'm getting baptized, not canonized." She looked at her watch. "Gotta go. See you at Mass."

He wagged his head. "Maybe."

"Be there, gyrene. And that's an order." She trotted down the corridor.

⎯⎰⎱⎰⎱⎯

As Chuck was sorting the late afternoon take from the comms center, Troiano's secretary came to his desk. "The colonel wants to see you."

Troiano, in his standard class A uniform, sat at his desk. Standing close by was an Army officer in starched, hand-tailored fatigues and boots buffed until they glowed.

"Chuck Griffin," Troiano said, "this is Colonel James Carver, from the operations staff, JCS. He's here with General Weyand's party."

Carver. Ben's commanding officer. The scent of the man was at odds with the spit-shine image—stale cigarettes and the woody smell of rye whiskey.

Chuck extended his hand. "A pleasure."

"All mine," Carver said. "I wanted to meet you while I was in the building. I'm off to JGS but thought maybe we could get together at the DAO mess Monday after close of business. Only time I have open. My PCOD is Thursday."

Chuck blinked.

Carver grinned. "Pussy cutoff date. DEROS. I'll be taking off for the world Thursday. Let's make it 1700 hours. That'll put us there during happy hour."

Chuck returned to the tank and worked through the night. Too much information from the battlefield was flooding them. When Troiano got in at 0600 Sunday morning, Chuck asked permission to take time off to go to church. It was Easter.

"And Chuck," Troiano said as Chuck headed out the door, "after church, go home and go to bed. I need you able to function."

Chuck climbed out of the blue-and-white by the wrought-iron gate to Cité Paul-Marie just before 1000. The crowd flowing into the compound for Mass was mostly Americans. They were quieter than usual, less gracious, more fidgety. He merged with them and sat in a pew toward the middle of the church. He spotted Ike several rows in front of him. Molly was at the side of the altar in a full-length spring yellow frock, dominating the group by sheer girth. The guitars thumped and the group sang, "I am the resurrection and the life—he who believes in me shall never die," to a lively bossa nova beat. Molly's voice, not always on pitch, was louder than the rest. Monsignor Sullivan, preceded by eight altar boys, promenaded up the aisle. The Mass had begun.

Monsignor Sullivan's homily was about spiritual joy in the face of adversity. At Communion the group sang a ballad to the words, "Lord, make me an instrument of your peace." Next came what Monsignor Sullivan called the kiss of peace. He descended from the altar and went into the congregation, greeting those at the front of the church. They shook hands with those near them, who in turn passed the greeting on to others. The kiss of peace moved through the congregation like ripples on the face of a still lake.

Meanwhile a soloist in the folk group, unaccompanied, intoned a serene melody with the words, "My peace I leave to you, my peace I give to you." After the first verse, one guitar played softly behind her. Then the second guitar joined, playing a different pattern. Two more voices added a counter melody, and the remainder of the group, Molly included, entered singing a third tune, all to the same words. The music, a skein of patterns, filled the chapel.

As Chuck received a handshake from the man beside him, Molly's voice vanished from the musical tapestry. He turned to look at the altar. There she was, where she was supposed to be. She raised her eyes above the heads of the congregation. Her voice reappeared, rasping, unsteady, but determined.

Monsignor Sullivan turned to the people and said, "The Mass is ended. Go in peace."

The guitars struck up a joyous beat resonating with irrepressible good humor, and the group sang a rousing recessional ending with the refrain, "Oh, how great it is to be alive!" After the monsignor and altar boys had passed down the aisle, Chuck got to his feet and milled with the rest of the crowd out of the chapel. He made his way to the rear courtyard where he usually visited Philippe. The monsignor was already there, talking to the parishioners gathered about him. Molly stumbled in, went to Monsignor Sullivan, and blubbered apologies for breaking down during Mass. Ike came in and went to her. She leaned on him.

Chuck put his hand on her arm. "That's no way to celebrate Easter."

She threw her arms around him. "It's my last Mass. I'm leaving Friday, flying out with the first contingent of orphans."

"She decided last night," Ike said. "She'll take care of them en route to Travis Air Force base near San Francisco. President Ford's supposed to meet the plane. But keep it under your hat. No public announcement."

Another woman, an American, was talking to Monsignor Sullivan. She, too, was in tears.

"What's going on?" Chuck said.

"They're moving out American families starting tomorrow," Ike whispered. "On the sly, quiet-like, so's not to stampede the Viets. And the Ambassador's not calling it an evacuation. If anybody asks, it's a redeployment to save dollars for aid to the Vietnamese military."

Chuck was going nonlinear. He'd worked too long without sleep. After church he got Chi Nam to cook him sausage, eggs, and home fries. Then he went upstairs and slept. He awoke at 0400 Monday morning, showered, shaved, dressed, and drove to DAO. In the tank he found Sparky reeling. He hadn't rested since Saturday night, but his toothpick still clung to his lower lip. His breath smelled like a cesspool.

"A lot's happened since last we met," Sparky mumbled. "Was that only a day ago?"

"You're getting soupy," Chuck said. "Go home."

"Can't." His eyelids stretched and blinked. "Da Nang fell yesterday. I Corps is in rout. And the safe haven on the coast where all those people tried to flee from the highlands? Tuy Hoa? It's under enemy fire. A hundred thousand refugees are stranded along Route 7B between Pleiku and the coast. No food, no water, no medicine, nothing. Jesus, Chuck." He ran his hands through his hair. "Did it have to end like this? After 58,000 American military dead, at least a million communist soldiers, and who knows how many million civilians? What the hell have we done?"

"Go home, Sparky," Troiano's voice said. Chuck turned. Troiano stood behind him, the class A uniform replaced by combat fatigues. A .45 was strapped on his hip. "Can't have you going to pieces on me."

Sparky blinked. "Aye, aye, sir." He shambled from the room.

"Chuck," Troiano said, "we're issuing radios to everyone. Walkie-talkies to be carried on your person and a Prick 25 for longer-range comms. Plenty of spare batteries. Pick yours up from the guys in the comms center before you leave. General Weyand will be here for the presentation at 0900 in the conference room. I want you ready to answer questions."

The presentation went smoothly. The briefer was well prepared and cool. The summary and conclusions, presented as Chuck had written them, drew a grave nod from General Smith. Questions from General Weyand, Colonel Carver, and other members of the party were mainstream and predictable. Chuck and the other analysts ticked off the numbers with precision. Neither they nor Troiano made any effort to sugarcoat the ugliness of the rout in I Corps or the debacle in the highlands.

At the end of the session Troiano turned to face Weyand. "We in the field want to be sure that the president understands what's at stake. If the U.S. does not intervene, the Republic of Vietnam will fall within six weeks, probably less."

The general said nothing. The session was over.

By 1700 Chuck was in the bar at the DAO officers' mess to keep his appointment with Carver. The Filipino bartender, jovial and easy-going, mixed drinks with unhurried banter, and the waitresses, all in dark *áo dài* with camellia blossoms in their hair, clustered chattering at the end of the bar, waiting to serve cocktails. Half a dozen patrons lolled on barstools; more loitered around the room at small tables spaced far enough from one another that low-pitched business conversations couldn't be overheard. Show tunes from unseen speakers, so soft as to be almost inaudible, blurred the hum of conversation and the occasional laugh.

Chuck scanned the room. Carver was at a secluded table in the corner, the only patron in uniform. As Chuck approached, a smiling waitress was picking up Carver's empty glass. Carver spotted Chuck and pointed to him as though imitating a pistol shot. Chuck sat and ordered a Coke.

"On the wagon?" Carver said.

"I'm working," Chuck said.

"Manhattan," Carver said to the waitress. "On the rocks this time. A couple of cherries, if you please."

The waitress moved away with the soundless grace unique to Vietnamese women.

"I'm finished for the day," Carver said with a barely detectable slur, "except for what's being called a working reception at the Defense Attaché Residence. The general doesn't want to waste a minute. Things are looking pretty shaky. Did you hear that Tuy Hoa might fall?"

"Yes, sir."

Carver lit a cigarette. "I know we got the official assessment of the situation in today's briefing with Troiano, but come on now, don't you think he's being a little melodramatic? Look at all this." He waved his cigarette at the room. "Life in Saigon hasn't changed since '67 when I was here. Hard to swallow all this dark foreboding shit."

"Forgive me, sir, but I think Colonel Troiano actually underestimated. I believe the country will fall within the month."

Carver chuckled. "Sticking to the party line, huh?" He clapped Chuck on the arm.

The waitress served their drinks from a tray. "Can I bring you anything else, gentlemen?" she said in careful English.

Carver ogled her. "You're about the prettiest thing I've seen this year."

She gave him a polite smile and hurried away.

"Vietnamese women," Carver said. "Like little birds. You ever bedded one, Griffin?"

Chuck bit his tongue.

Carver chortled. "I'll tell you something not for public consumption. The president is going to evacuate orphans. You know why? He found out our guys fathered a bunch of 'em. Little mixed-race, slope-eyed mongrels. And he wants to get them into the States." He shook his head, stubbed out his cigarette. "I wouldn't be surprised if one of those little half-breed bastards looks a lot like me." He poked Chuck and laughed.

"Excuse me, sir," Chuck said, "but the purpose of our getting together—"

"Your son. I was getting to that. Your son died a hero's death, defending his country."

"Combat?"

"Killed in action, as I reported at the time."

Chuck bowed his head. "I need to know what happened. I know there was a fire—"

"Your son's death sheds honor on his family. A sacrifice that a grateful nation—"

"Please, Colonel. How was he killed?"

"Killed on the battlefield, fighting for freedom." Carver's smile looked self-satisfied.

Chuck clenched his fists. "Colonel, can the bullshit. *I want to know how my son died.*"

The smile vanished. Carver bared his teeth. "Big-ass gunjy Marine, right? Balls of brass. Yeah, I checked you out before I left the States. Okay, asshole. You want it gory? I'll give it to you gory." Carver paused long enough to slurp his drink. "A kid named Kerney killed your son. Multiple tracer rounds from his M60 went into cans of gasoline strapped onto the jeep your son was driving. Jeep blew up. At the inquest, Kerney said he thought the VC had penetrated the perimeter and were attacking, killed your kid by mistake. He told me privately that Ben had come on to him for sex. That changed things. The Army's not big on coddling queers. Kerney wasn't indicted."

Chuck closed his eyes.

"'Course, reports of casualties from friendly fire get leaked to the press," Carver said, "and if the homo angle had come to light, that could have hurt Kerney's chances for promotion and made the U.S. Army look bad. So I reported it as a KIA. Honorable shit. You know the drill."

Chuck shuddered.

Carver sneered. "You asked for the fuckin' truth."

"This man, Kerney. I'd like—"

Carver shook his head. "No can do. U.S. Army policy. Can't tell you who he is or how to find him. Shouldn't have mentioned his name."

"What about other men who were witnesses at the inquest?"

"Same policy." Carver tilted back his head, chugalugged his drink. "That's it for me. Still have a reception to go to. Can't show up half swacked."

Chuck defeated the impulse to coldcock Carver. Instead, he got to his feet and left Carver at the table. He walked back to the DAO building in a fog. He took Carver's story apart, piece by piece, and looked for flaws, false assumptions, factual errors. The best he could come up with was that it all could have been the imaginings of a drunk. All but how Ben died. An American soldier had killed him. Burned him to death by exploding gas cans on his jeep.

Suppose everything Carver said was true. Nothing in Ben's life suggested that Ben was a homosexual. Chuck had never seen any signs of it. But what if he was? What if Ben had thought Chuck knew and that his greatest anguish was that his father was ashamed of him? Chuck stumbled, almost fell. There never had been any cause for shame. It wouldn't have mattered whether Ben was straight or queer or anything else. Chuck loved Ben unconditionally.

He saw now that he'd taken Ben's decision not to join the Corps as his son's rejection. All Ben had done was to choose for himself. They would have found a way to reconcile. Chuck's pride would have surrendered to his love. But he never had a chance. Ben's choice had cost him his life. Chuck had struggled to win this war so that Ben did not die for nothing. What a crock. North Vietnamese didn't kill Ben.

Galaxy

APRIL 1975

CHAPTER 15

Tuyet took a reluctant bite of her *bánh mì*. The coarse-grained Vietnamese bread was a poor substitute for croissants or brioche, but she couldn't get to Brodard to buy such delicacies. Caring for the orphans left her no time. Not long ago she would have considered *bánh mì* inedible, but the child she carried required the best nutrition she could provide. The palms of her hands massaged her swelling belly. Within weeks all Saigon would know she was with child. This child would thrive; maybe a son for Chuck who had lost a son. She needed to run away, to bear this child far from the war.

She sipped her coffee. April was beginning, and she had barely seen Chuck since before Tet, hadn't felt his hands on her at all. After their first time together she had told him that one must live in the moment. "If we let ourselves love each other, the future will write itself for us," she'd said. Beautiful words for a beautiful time now faded to ashes. Reports on the radio detailed the collapse of the highlands, the loss of the north. Thanh had taken off from Da Nang moments before the airfield was swamped with hysterical South Vietnamese soldiers trying to escape. Now he slept at JGS and came to the villa only to eat, bathe, and change his bandages and clothing. She begged him to go to the Seventh Day Adventist Hospital and have his wound checked, to no avail.

Thanh. She loved Chuck more than she had thought she could love, but he was not Vietnamese. Thanh was the soul of Vietnam. He *was* Vietnam, her homeland, about to die. She saw him in the distorted faces of the orphans in Gia Dinh, in the frightened refugees along the highway en route to the asylum, and, most of all, in Thu, who was his father incarnate. She, of the royal house of Nguyen, was less of Vietnam than Thanh was. He spoke no French, ate no croissants, had never seen the streets of Paris or the palaces of Monte Carlo. But he knew the taste of Vietnam's soil. He knew how Vietnamese fought and died. He had seen their blood, heard their death cries. He spoke of An Nam, "peace in the south." Tears moistened her eyes. An Nam was no more. And with its passing, Thanh was no more.

Thu's memory of his father would be dim. Thu would become an American, and Thanh's legacy would be lost. How wrong she had been to rear Thu as a Nguyen prince when it was his peasant side that was strong and brave. Starting now she'd work to undo the injustice she'd thrust on Thu. She'd teach him about the greatness of his father. She'd remind him that he, like his father, was Annamese.

And she would emulate Thanh in the days she had left in her homeland. She had already started. At first several times a week, now every day, she went by motorized cyclo out of the city north to the orphan asylum in Gia Dinh to help the sisters feed, bathe, and clothe the growing population of foundlings, so many of whom resembled men like Chuck as much as men like Thanh. Other days she spent at Cité Paul-Marie, where she had run into Molly working in the kitchen and dispensing medicines.

She sensed a change. The sisters were sorting clothes and packing small parcels. Were the children to be moved? Where would they be safe? She pushed away her breakfast dishes. The sun was well above the horizon. Time to put on the gray nursing dress.

Late in the morning, as she washed a toddler, she heard the two sisters working next to her whispering. She caught the phrases "planes to take them there" and "because their fathers are American." She blocked a gasp in her throat. The children were to be taken to America.

When she returned from Gia Dinh around 2100 hours, she found a note left by the Chinese servant from Yen Do. She tore it open. Chuck wrote that he wanted to see her right away. He was working around the clock but could take an hour to meet her at the French military cemetery on Hai Ba Trung, which would afford them a measure of privacy. Could Tuyet be there the next day at 1400? She dispatched Chi Tu by cab with her affirmation.

Wednesday she listened to the radio as she ate her morning rolls. The BBC reported that the North Vietnamese Army had occupied Chu Lai and South Vietnamese forces were abandoning the seaport enclaves at Nha Trang and Cam Ranh Bay. If Mai was following the coastal route north, she would pass through these towns. The route didn't matter. Half of South Vietnam had been lost to the North Vietnamese who were pressing into the remaining provinces north of Saigon. How soon were the orphans to be flown out? Was there enough time?

And what about herself and Thu? She bit into the rough Vietnamese roll and fought back the panic scuttling through her belly. Perhaps if she volunteered to care for the orphans during the flight, she and Thu could leave with them. How soon? She had no word on the timing of the orphans' departure. Salvation for herself, Thu, and her unborn baby . . . and freedom from the daily terror that they might not survive what was coming.

But to abandon Thanh? Was his wound healing? He could read her soul, but he kept himself hidden from her. These days she rarely saw him. Could she once again refuse to leave him? And risk Thu's life? Risk the life of Chuck's baby? She had already lost Thanh. He didn't need her as he once had. Soon she would cease to see him at all as he spent all his time with his troops. Her children must live, no matter what it cost her, no matter how much she wanted to bask in the light from Thanh's spirit. She never should have returned the Pan Am tickets. She must escape.

She hurried through her morning ablutions and went by cab to Cité Paul-Marie. Mother Monique greeted her at the office door and seated herself at the desk. "Madame?"

"I overheard the sisters talking," Tuyet said in French. "The orphans will be flown to the United States."

Monique nodded. "All our children and most of the sisters will go."

"So it is true. Mother, I propose two more people to go on the flight. An adult and a child." Tuyet bit her lip. "Myself and my son."

Weariness clouded Mother Monique's face. "I am overwhelmed with volunteers who wish to leave the country, Madame."

Tuyet tightened. "You know Mister Charles Griffin, of course?"

"A volunteer and benefactor."

"He will personally second my request that my son and I be on a flight out of Saigon."

Mother Monique shook her head. "Madame, I—"

"And so will Miss Molly Hansen, the nurse who has been of such great assistance to you."

Mother Monique put on her spectacles and ruffled the papers on her desk. "Miss Hansen will be on the first airlift, acting as a nurse and guardian, but," she lowered her eyes, "I cannot ignore others who have come before you with a request to flee the country."

Tuyet's blood chilled. "Surely you need specially trained people. I am a nurse—"

"I have an abundance of nurses."

"I can act as an interpreter. As you can see," Tuyet said, using an English sentence memorized years before, "I am competent in French, Vietnamese, and English."

Mother Monique studied the desktop. "I don't see how—"

Tuyet seized Monique's hands. "You know my husband, Pham Ngoc Thanh. You know that except for him, Phat Hoa would have fallen in 1972."

Mother Monique faltered.

"Thanh," Tuyet said, "we cannot save, but his son, Thu . . . Mother, let Thu live."

Monique stared past her and said nothing. When her eyes came to rest on Tuyet's face she took off her glasses. "You could be here at 0900 hours on Friday morning, ready to depart?"

All the way to Hai Ba Trung in the open cyclo, Tuyet reviewed what would have to be done to get ready. The weather in the States was like that in France, much colder than here. They'd dress in the woolens she and Thu wore here in January and February—long pants for him, a full-length skirt for herself. Packing would have to be at the bare minimum—nothing but essentials. What keepsakes? Just photos. Herself with Bao Dai and Tu Cung; the best pictures of Thanh for Thu to cherish. Jewelry? The only things of even paltry value were the sapphires. Worth next to nothing. She'd give them to Chi Hai.

She arrived at the cemetery, paid the driver, and opened her parasol to conceal her face from passers-by. Moving through the stone gateway, she hurried along the walk among the weathered headstones searching for Chuck. She found him at last near the center by the mausoleums. His face was lined with weariness, but he stood straight. A portable radio with an antenna was strapped to his hip. When he saw her, he opened his arms.

"No," she said. "Forgive me, but we cannot touch."

He dropped his hands to his sides. He'd lost more weight. His temples were grayer. He was spare now, distilled by work and grief to his essence. She yearned for the solidity of his body.

He shuffled, restless. "I can't stay, but I wanted to talk to you. You and Thu must leave the country. I'll go with you. I'll break my contract with DAO, curtail my tour, and the three of us can book out together. I'll go straight from here to the Pan Am office. If they won't sell me tickets, I'll bribe them or try another airline, anything that's still flying. I'll see about going out by sea." He squinched his eyes shut and lowered his head. "Tell me you'll go."

Her heart clenched. "I learned that your President Ford has ordered the evacuation of orphans. The first group will leave Friday. I talked to Mother Monique this morning. I will be on the flight as an interpreter with Thu by my side."

He raised his head. "You already . . ." He folded his hands and looked down. "Thank God."

She took his hand.

"We're not supposed to touch," he said in a choked voice.

"Just for a moment."

Their hands embraced. His fingers were rough, warm, reassuring.

"We'll be together," he said, "in the States."

She nodded, unable to speak.

He withdrew his hands. "So little time. I'll come to the airport to say good-bye."

"Thanh sleeps at JGS now. I could come to Yen Do—"

"I won't be there. We're on a twenty-four-hour shift at DAO, but we'll make up for it when we're together again." He shut his eyes. "As God is my witness, I love you, Tuyet. Will you marry me?"

"Yes," she whispered.

He reached for her, but she stepped back.

She fumbled for a handkerchief. "I must be at Cité Paul-Marie at 0900 Friday. From there we go to the airport. I don't know what time the flight leaves."

"I'll be there." He extended his hand, pulled it back.

At home she realized how little time she had. From the chiffonier in her bedroom she selected a canvas bag small enough for her to carry without help. While Thu lay down for his afternoon rest, she and Chi Hai sorted his clothes. One outfit to wear, one to be packed, extra underwear and socks, the sweater her cousin had brought him from Paris. In her own room she found no clothing suitable for the trip. She decided she'd wear the heaviest of her *áo dài* and take along the one pair of slacks she had kept from her student days in France. Would she have her bag with her at all times? If not, what were the chances someone would steal items from it, as they did on domestic Air Vietnam flights? The photos and her money she'd keep in her purse.

Chi Hai watched her anxiously. She would, of course, guess that Madame was preparing to leave the country, and by dinnertime all the servants would know. *Qu'importe?* Thanh would not be home . . . Thanh. He stayed at JGS day and night now. He'd been home yesterday for clothes, a bath, and fresh bandages. Not likely he'd be back before Friday.

She pictured his massive, awkward presence, his mutilated skin, his eyes grown so otherworldly. Her heart hurt. She had injured him in a way no one else could have. He could have taken vengeance, but the worst he had done was to look at her with pain in his eyes. He was a great man, and she was abandoning him. She wouldn't sneak away in shameful cowardice. She was a Nguyen, of the line of Gia Long and Minh Mang. She would go to him and bid him good-bye.

Thursday morning she dressed in her royal blue *áo dài*, wore her star sapphire earrings for the last time, and pinned her hair away from her face. The gardener hailed a cab for her, and she went to JGS. At the gate she showed her ID and requested permission to visit Colonel Pham Ngoc Thanh, RVNAF Marines. After a five-minute wait Thanh's aide-de-camp bowed before her and offered to escort her. They drove in Thanh's jeep to the enclosure near the rear wall. Thanh came into the courtyard, smiling.

"Tuyet." He signaled the aide to help her as she climbed from the jeep. "What a pleasure and surprise." He escorted her to his office and poured boiling water from the tea stove into a pot. "Vien, a pastry for Madame."

She seated herself at the tea table by the window, set down her parasol, and removed her gloves. "Please do not trouble yourself for me."

"Trouble? It is my joy. Thu is well? And Lan?"

She nodded. "We are all in good health. I have come for another reason."

The corporal returned with teacups and a petit four on a saucer.

"The tea will be steeped directly," Thanh said. "How lovely you look today. You are perhaps en route to a gathering?"

"No. I wished to spend a few minutes with you before—"

"The tea." He took her cup and poured. "Do not neglect the sweet. Vien makes a special trip to La Pagode to buy them when we expect an important visitor."

"Thank you, but I'm not hungry. Who were you expecting?"

His eyes saddened. "You."

"How did you—"

He shrugged. "I knew. Have you been to the Cercle Sportif? The weather is ideal for swimming."

"No. My time these days is taken up with the orphans. At Cité Paul-Marie and Gia Dinh. That brings me to the reason for my visit. I have come to tell you—"

He held out the palm of his hand toward her. "Not yet. Give me a few moments of your time first. I have seen so little of you since the tragedies of Pleiku, Hue, and Da Nang."

"It is because of that—"

"Please." He fidgeted, looked away. "Must we hurry?" He closed his eyes. "You must forgive me. Your presence has undone me. Let me cherish you a little longer before you tell me."

He leaned forward, breathed deeply, and settled back into his chair, composed. As he continued, his voice was serene. "President Ford held a press conference a few hours ago. He announced that orphans will be airlifted from Vietnam. Their evacuation is now public information."

He knew she was leaving. Of course. She should have foreseen it.

"I am grateful," he said, "that you came to see me. I only wish you had brought Thu."

She was chagrined. Why hadn't she thought of that? Thu and Thanh would never see one another again. She studied him across the little table. She wanted to reach out to him, to help him, to serve him. How could she leave him?

"You have the bloom of a woman who will bear a child." His smile warmed her. "Life glows in you. Heaven has blessed you."

Her child, Chuck's child. That was why she could leave Thanh. Because her child's well-being was more important than what she wanted.

He nodded as if agreeing with her thoughts. "I have learned that the orphan airlift will begin tomorrow. A C-5A Galaxy, the largest airplane in the world, lands today at Tan Son Nhat. It will leave tomorrow with the first contingent of orphans and caretakers. You have come to tell me that you and Thu will be on the flight."

She lowered her eyes.

"So be it." His body relaxed. "Chance has intervened to offer you escape. The Mother Goddess watches over you."

"Come to the villa tonight and see Thu before he leaves."

He shook his head. "I leave at noon for the coast. Of the 12,000 Marines who were in I Corps, only 4,000 are left. Battalion and company commanders have been killed. I must aid in refitting the survivors and forming a new division."

So this was truly the last time she'd see Thanh.

"Thu will know of your greatness," she said. "I will teach him to be a man of the people, an Annamese, like his father."

He smiled. "Thu will be Thu. He has the power of two traditions in his blood."

She hesitated. "I was a poor wife to you. I am filled with regret. Will you forgive me?"

"Will you forgive me for marrying a princess without seeking her love first? For forcing a woman of royalty into the life of a dirt farmer?"

The peace that engulfed him touched her. "So we part in forgiveness and harmony," she said.

"The balance in our lives is restored. Heaven is pleased." He stood. "You must go now. My men await me." She rose and started toward him, but he lifted the palms of both hands and smiled. "Corporal Vien will drive you home."

Two buses the color of horse droppings took Molly, Tuyet, Thu, a dozen caregivers, and more orphans than Tuyet could count from Cité Paul-Marie out of the city to Tan Son Nhat. The civilian side of the airport was mobbed, but the military side was stark and orderly. The buses carried them past the DAO building to the hangar closest to the runway. Beyond the building the C-5A Galaxy, a silver monster too big to be real, crouched with drooping wings as if ready to spring.

They streamed off the buses into the blinding sunshine and passed through the oversized hangar door into the hot darkness. People sat on olive drab blankets, stretches of canvas and burlap, and the concrete floor. The din of voices was edged with the crying of children. Moving among them with clipboards were airmen in flight suits recording identification data and distributing boarding passes. Mother Monique shuffled from group to group embracing the children.

"What is she doing?" Tuyet asked Molly.

"Saying good-bye. She says she has to stay here to face the North Vietnamese. She's sending all the sisters out."

They found open space near the wall and settled. Molly, in her perennial nurse's scrubs, this time a vivid pink, sat on a low stool, gathered an infant into her arms, and spoke to Angélique and Philippe, who sat at her feet. She motioned to Tuyet to join her and pushed a stool toward her. With Thu clinging to her *áo dài*, Tuyet accepted a baby into her lap, handed to her by a nun.

"I found you." Chuck's voice. He was a silhouette against the glare from outside. He handed Molly half a dozen comic books and a box of chocolates. "For the trip." He turned to Tuyet. She couldn't make out his face, but she felt his hand on her shoulder. He leaned close and rubbed his face against hers. With the baby in her arms, she couldn't embrace him, but she kissed his cheek.

Chuck pulled back, swallowing. "And here is Mister Thu. How you doing, Tuffy? And Angélique and Philippe. Hi, Pipsqueak." He scooped Philippe into his arms. "You ready for your new family?"

Tuyet dutifully translated.

Thu tugged Tuyet's sleeve and said into her ear, "I don't want to go to a new family. I want to stay with you."

Tuyet chuckled. "You will, my hero. With me and with Mister Chuck."

Thu giggled. "Mister Certain."

She laughed. "Yes, Mister Certain."

"Miss Hansen?" An airman stood next to Molly, clipboard in hand. "You have three, and Mrs. Pham has two, including her son, right? And they are . . ." He squatted and examined the nametags hung on strings around each child's neck, matching each to names on his clipboard.

"Miss Hansen, you'll be in the cargo compartment with your three, and Mrs. Pham, you're assigned to the troop compartment with two—the baby you're holding and your son. We'll be boarding soon." He moved on to the next group.

"By the way, Chuck." Molly flipped out a pen and notebook, "I want to give you Huong's address. And here's the map she gave me with the way to her place marked in red. I told her she could come to you or Ike if she needs help. And she's waiting to hear about her husband."

Chuck deposited Philippe on the ground and pocketed the papers. "I'll swing by JGS and ask if Colonel Thanh has had any luck tracking him down."

"Thanh left Saigon yesterday," Tuyet said. "I don't know when he will return."

"Excuse me, sir." The airman was back. "We're clearing the area of personnel not on the manifest. Trying to keep the confusion down to the routine pandemonium."

"Captain Saunders from the embassy will be coming to check on us," Molly said. "Can he get in?"

"Official business? No problem." The airman moved off through the crowd.

"Okay, guys," Chuck said, "guess it's good-bye time." He looked at Molly. "So long, Dragon Lady. I'm going to miss you. Here's hoping you always have plenty of big men, booze, and chocolate."

Molly grinned. "Can't hug you—got too many kids. But thanks for the good wishes. All except the big men part." She reached into her scrub shirt and pulled out a medal on a chain. "I was baptized on Wednesday. My next big man has to put a ring on my finger before he puts his . . ." An uneasy smile crossed her face. She glanced at Tuyet and the children.

"So you did it," Chuck said. "You glad?"

Her face shone. "Happier than I knew I could be."

He hunkered by Angélique and Philippe. "So long, you two. My heart goes with you."

Still stooping, he shook Thu's hand. "So long, buddy. I'll catch up with you wherever you end up." Lastly, he turned to Tuyet. "Write to me and tell me where you are. As soon as I'm out of here, I'll come find you." He took her, baby and all, in his arms and kissed her, then got to his feet, gave them half a salute, and walked into the crowd.

Tuyet watched through her tears until he disappeared into the mass of people.

Ike made his way through the mob. Molly handed Tuyet the infant and told Angélique and Philippe to stay put. She followed Ike through the knots of people until Tuyet could no longer see them. Fifteen minutes later they were back. Molly's face was wet, Ike's locked in a frown. He gave her a perfunctory kiss and left.

Molly hefted herself onto her stool and took the baby. "He said he'd miss me." She wiped her eyes. "First time he ever said anything like that."

Airmen passed out sandwiches, fruit, and chips and instructed everyone to make a final bathroom call. Close to 1500 hours the airmen led the evacuees to buses that carried them almost up to the aircraft's near wing. With Thu clutching her hand and a baby in her arms, Tuyet tilted back her head to look to the top of the six-story-high shining behemoth. Could this monster actually get off the ground?

CHAPTER 16

Chuck trudged from the hangar down the short road to DAO. He wished they'd had a night together before she left, wished they'd been able to say a decent good-bye, wished she weren't going and was thankful she'd soon be gone. He remembered the frightened faces of Philippe, Angélique, and Thu. And Molly getting all sentimental in her shocking pink outfit. He grinned. What a piece of work she was.

Ahead of him lay the gruesome task of chronicling the collapse of the Republic of Vietnam, whether or not his own government wanted to hear it. But the job was turning surreal. Wednesday, Secretary of Defense Schlesinger had said publicly that there was relatively little major fighting in Vietnam. Wasn't anybody reading what Chuck and Sparky and Troiano were writing? Were the Ford administration and Congress so determined not to get involved again that they were pretending there was no war? Or maybe it was lies for public consumption only. The Defense Intelligence Agency, the secretary's own intelligence organ, had just issued a classified estimate, paraphrasing Chuck, that the Republic would last less than thirty days. And the Ambassador, under pressure from every side, looked the other way when employees and dependents, under a variety of pretexts, left the country. Why didn't the story the government was telling the people match the facts?

He had to try again to persuade Thanh to leave as soon as he could. Macintosh had finally transmitted a message of thanks for the ceramic elephant and issued an official invitation to Thanh to visit the United States for consultation. Chuck had forwarded the message to Thanh and his JGS superior. Neither had answered.

The pile of incoming messages on his desktop had grown several inches since he left this morning. He set his jaw and worked his way through the heap. The full impact of losses in the north was emerging. Whole units had disappeared in the fighting. A few stragglers had made it out of the captured territory, but lack of equipment and ammunition—a direct result of Congress' cutoff of U.S. funds—crippled the effort to organize units from the survivors. Major battles were shaping up in the arc of provinces north of Saigon. Most disturbing was accumulating evidence of enemy intent to seize Xuan Loc, the capital of Long Khanh Province, less than forty miles northeast of Saigon—as close to the capital as Baltimore was to Washington. Elements of three North Vietnamese divisions were converging on the town. The first attacks had been repulsed, but more were to come. Chuck posted the location of friendly and enemy units on the Long Khanh map.

Back at his desk, he dialed Thanh's office number and asked for the colonel.

"He travel, you know?" the voice said. "He come back Sunday."

That confirmed it. Thanh was out of pocket until the beginning of the week. Chuck drafted a note to him asking for any word on Huong's husband and reminding him of Macintosh's invitation and dropped it in the mailroom.

A little past 1645, as Chuck began his third cup of coffee that afternoon, Troiano strode into the tank. He went straight to the middle of the room. "Gentlemen, we've just gotten very bad news. The OPERATION BABYLIFT C-5A Galaxy is down. It crash-landed about two miles from the runway."

Dead silence.

"No word on casualties yet. We haven't heard—"

Chuck was out the door, down the corridor, out of the building, and past the tennis courts before Troiano could finish. He threw himself into the jeep, started the engine, and screeched away. He drove straight to the flight line where the C-5A had been parked. Far in the distance past the runway, well beyond the perimeter, he could see smoke in a rice paddy more than a mile—maybe two miles or more—past the fence.

Black objects, scorched, not reflecting the sunlight. One large hulk and smaller chunks surrounded by people running around like ants.

There was no way across the runway and through the paddy, but he could see a road that cut through toward the wreckage coming from the north. He roared away past the hangars, past DAO, out the front gate, onto Vo Tanh, then northward on side streets and back roads, heading toward the blackening sky. The jeep squealed into and out of blind alleys, down dirt tracks, until he found the way in.

White-clad police had cordoned off the road. They were holding back the growing crowd and signaling to vehicles to turn back. He slammed on the brakes, hurtled from the jeep, jammed his way through. A policeman yelled at him, waved him back. Chuck vaulted over the first of the sawhorse barricades. More police were yelping at him. They were on him, dragging him back across the barrier. He tried to fight them off, but now he was on his back, everyone shouting at him. He tensed his muscles to leap up but a sound stopped him. A pistol was cocked close to his ear. The policeman holding it to his temple squatted beside him chattering. Chuck lay stock-still. The policeman stood, waved the pistol. Chuck got carefully to his feet and walked away from the barricades and onlookers to the jeep. He looked over his shoulder at the smoking fuselage in the paddy. Helicopters descended in the distance like late-summer gnats. Ambulances screamed past the roadblocks. Still watching him, the policeman swung the pistol in a circle. Chuck climbed into the jeep with measured deliberation, started it, backed up, turned, and headed in the direction he had come from. He blinked the sweat from his eyes and drove with meticulous care. All he had to do was hold himself together until he got back to DAO. The tank would have the list of casualties as soon as the embassy did.

He parked with uncharacteristic precision, checked to be sure he'd turned off the ignition, set the brake. He walked evenly past the tennis courts, through the entrance, down the corridors. In the tank, work had ceased. Two men were on telephones, four others crowded together around yellow rolls of teletype paper. Chuck tried to read over their shoulders.

"You went to the wreck?" Sparky was behind him.

"Tried to. White mice wouldn't let me through. I saw it. The aircraft was all torn up. Broken into at least four pieces. People all over. Medevac zoomies coming in. Ambulances . . ."

"We're getting reports in. Seems that about twelve minutes after takeoff they'd gotten up to 29,000 feet. They were out over the South China Sea when the locks on the rear loading ramp failed. Rear door flew open. Some of the crew and maybe some of the orphans and caretakers were sucked out. Rudder and elevators and some of the hydraulics quit working. The pilot managed to turn around and head back toward Tan Son Nhat, but he was losing altitude. He knew he couldn't make it, so he touched down in a rice paddy, skidded a thousand feet, went airborne for half a mile, and hit a dike. The aircraft broke up."

"Casualties . . ." Chuck said.

"Lots killed," Sparky said. "Bodies all over the place. No names or numbers yet."

Chuck weaved to his desk and collapsed into his chair, then sat bolt upright. *Ike.* He could get through because he was embassy. Chuck dialed Ike's number. A gunnery sergeant told him that Captain Saunders had gone to Tan Son Nhat on business and hadn't returned.

Sparky was standing next to him. "Hey, look, I know this is . . . can I, you know, do anything?"

"Yeah. You got your radio? Turn on ARS."

Sparky switched on the portable and set it on Chuck's desk. Other analysts gathered around to hear " . . . more than 300 passengers, including 243 orphans, being airlifted to the United States where they were to have been adopted by American families. No casualty figures are yet available. Survivors report that the bottom level of the plane, normally used for cargo but outfitted for this flight to carry passengers, suffered the worst damage. The injured are being transported by ambulance and helicopter to the Seventh Day Adventist Hospital. Eyewitnesses close to the hospital report that the building is mobbed and streets on all sides are clogged with vehicles and pedestrians, hampering the passage of ambulances. Hospital officials have requested that local residents stay away to avoid further crowding of access corridors—"

Chuck leaped to his feet. "The hospital."

Sparky seized his arm. "Don't. You'll never get through."

Chuck yanked himself free and dashed out of the building. Sparky ran behind him and jumped into the jeep's driver's seat ahead of him. "I'll drive."

Two blocks from the hospital traffic was at a standstill. Police had blockaded the street at the next intersection. Chuck bounded from the jeep, darted though the jumble of vehicles, and forced his way through the crowd. At the barrier he found himself face-to-face with Vietnamese soldiers armed with M16s, bayonets fixed. The three closest to him stiffened. One switched off his safety and aimed, the other two leveled their blades toward him.

"Let me through," he cried. "My wife, my baby—"

Hands were on his arms. More soldiers were on both sides of him. They shoved him back into the crowd. He pushed forward, but an arm locked around his neck and dragged him back.

"Goddammit. You want to get shot?" Sparky's voice yelled in his ear.

Chuck lashed and writhed and tried to pry the arm away. The grip on his neck tightened. No air. His vision was dimming. His body turned to rubber . . .

He was on his back. A man was leaning over him and calling his name. They were beside the jeep. Vietnamese of all stripes crowded around. The stench of *nuoc mam* stained the air.

" . . . all right," the voice was saying. "Just lie still. There you go."

The head silhouetted above him was ringed with strawberry blond hair. Sparky. The air, laden with exhaust and dust and the odor of rotting fish, was the sweetest Chuck had ever breathed. The prickling on his skin dissipated.

"Buddy, I'm sorry I had to do that," Sparky said. "Can you sit up?"

Chuck lifted himself with Sparky's help.

"Come on." Sparky loaded him into the jeep and strapped the seat-belt around him. They drove slowly. Chuck shook his head to clear the cobwebs. Word about the casualties might be held at DAO and not released to the public. But he had to get to the villa in case Ike showed up there.

"Sparky," he said, "drop me at the villa and go back to DAO. If anything comes in about the dead and wounded, call me on the radio."

Chuck commandeered the dining room for a comms center. He braced the AN/PRC-25 transceiver—what Troiano called the Prick 25—on the table with Sparky's books and laid the walkie-talkie beside it. Next he stacked spare batteries for both radios in the chairs. He called Purple 1, Troiano's call sign, to do a comms check and to request that Purple 1 let him know if he picked up any news on casualties. Then he set up an hourly schedule with Sparky (Purple 13). Meanwhile, he moved the stereo into the dining room. During the 2000 ARS newscast the announcer interviewed a DAO employee, name withheld, who'd been on the far side of the runway and close to the accident site when the plane went down. He'd been helping with the rescue operation.

"Jesus, you should have seen it," the man said. "Mud and metal all over the place. Bodies. Little kids all mangled and screaming. The ambulances couldn't drive all the way in because the mud was so deep, so we were carrying people out on stretchers. They called in choppers."

After that, no more reports. Maybe the news was being censored, either to avoid panicking the Vietnamese or to keep the VC in the dark.

Chuck found himself thinking the same thoughts again and again and checking his watch even though he'd just looked at it. Past 2200 and no Ike. He asked Chi Nam to fix him a sandwich and brew coffee. While she worked he carried the walkie-talkie upstairs, changed into shorts and a T-shirt, and soaked his face in cold water.

Close to midnight the gate bell sounded. Oanh hastened out. Chuck heard the gate open and close but no conversation. Footsteps came across the courtyard, up the stairs. Ike stood in the doorway, Oanh behind him.

"Ike?" Chuck said.

Ike's arms hung at his sides. His uniform was blotched with mud and blood. In one hand he carried a bruised box of chocolates, in the other three muddy comic books. His eyes were out of focus.

"You all right?" Chuck asked.

Ike didn't move.

"Were you there when it happened?" Chuck said.

Ike nodded.

Chuck went to him. "Tuyet, Thu. Are they—"

"Didn't see them."

"Molly?"

"Molly's dead, Chuck." Ike blinked. "Don't want no food." His voice was dead. "Going to go up and sack out." His eyes dropped to the comic books and candy in his hands. He huffed and shuffled toward the stairs. On the second step, he tottered but recovered and resumed the climb until he was out of sight.

Chi Nam served breakfast at the wicker table on the veranda. Chuck was well into his eggs when he heard the whine of the radio.

Sparky, toothpick in place, lumbered in, slapped his portable on the table, and poured coffee from the carafe. "You look like shit," Sparky said. "Stay home today. Troiano doesn't want you to flame out."

Chuck sucked coffee. "You going in?"

Sparky nodded.

"Then so am I."

" . . . cargo compartment destroyed," the radio said, "killing 141 of the 149 orphans and their caretakers. Three of the 152 in the troop compartment died. Five crew members, three healthcare personnel, and three unidentified adults were also among the dead. Names are being withheld pending notification of next of kin. A USAID spokesman—"

"Turn it off," Chuck snarled.

"We need to hear—"

Chuck seized the radio and smashed it across the edge of the table. Plastic fragments, metal clips, and batteries rattled across the floor tiles. Chi Nam came to the doorway, disappeared, and reappeared with a broom.

Ike plodded to the table. He was in his utilities, freshly bathed and shaved. Dark crescents hung beneath his eyes. He pulled up a chair and lifted the carafe. "Need more coffee."

Chi Nam stopped sweeping, took the carafe, and went into the house.

Chuck pushed away his plate and turned to Sparky. "We need to get a move on."

"They'd have radioed us if they heard anything. Cool it."

Chi Nam brought the carafe and two breakfast plates. Sparky ate in silence while Ike poured coffee.

"How did you manage to get to the wreck?" Chuck said to Ike.

"Forced my way onto the first whirlybird across the runway to the crash site. We didn't separate out the corpses. We just loaded everything that looked human onto stretchers and hauled it out to the ambulances and the choppers. Ambulance guy told me they'd do triage at the other end. The dead ones would be sent to the morgue at the Seventh Day Adventist Hospital."

"I'll go there."

"You can't get in," Sparky said. "The place is a zoo."

Chuck's jaw tightened. "When will they identify the bodies?"

"Probably already started," Ike said. "The embassy will get a list. DAO, too."

Chuck shook his head. "So we don't know who got killed."

Ike put down his fork. "We know some of them. I identified three bodies."

Chuck sucked air. "Who?"

"Molly and the two kids she had with her."

"Jesus, Ike."

"Angélique and Philippe. That's what their nametags said. I didn't recognize them. They were too torn up. Molly was clutching a baby. I couldn't identify it. There were some nuns, too. Couldn't tell which ones."

Chuck's gut tightened as if kicked.

"If it makes you feel any better," Ike said, "they probably didn't feel much. An Air Force guy at the site told me there wasn't no oxygen masks in the cargo compartment. When the door blew out at 29,000 feet, all the air got sucked out, so they would have suffocated before the plane went down."

Sparky's hand was on Chuck's arm. "Let's go to DAO. See what we can find out."

All the way to the tank Chuck remembered the feel of Philippe's tiny body pressed against his chest. *Pee-kwee.* He forced himself to contemplate the unbearable—Philippe suffocating in the airless cargo hold and then crushed by the plane's collision with the earth. Chuck welcomed the grief. No one else would mourn the death of the Amerasian "manglemorph" whose real name nobody knew.

Chuck read official reports, the AP news bulletins, even the transcripts from the propaganda broadcasts of the Liberation News Agency. No new facts, just more nauseating detail about body parts and cadavers being pulled from the mud. He tried to work. North Vietnamese units were closing in. Nothing but time stood between Saigon and defeat.

At 1800 Troiano, his face drained of energy, stopped by Chuck's desk. "Ambassador's office called. Your monthly briefing with him scheduled for Thursday is canceled. I want you and Sparky to head home. You're both under orders to use good judgment about when and how much you work. I don't want any exhaustion cases. If you're too tired to think, stay home and rest."

Ike was already there when they got to the villa. Chuck and Sparky changed clothes and met him on the veranda. When the three of them were settled in the wicker chairs, Chi Nam, all her jolliness gone, brought a tray of cheese and crackers.

"Molly made the best martinis in all of Asia," Sparky said.

"Shut your fuckin' mouth," Ike snapped.

They ate dinner on the veranda. As they were finishing, the gate bell sounded. A moment later Oanh handed Chuck an envelope. He tore it open.

> My dearest Chuck,
>
> I am home—at Thanh's villa. Thu is with me. I need to see you.
>
> Tuyet

Chuck dashed into the house and found Tuyet's servant in black pajamas waiting at the front door. He grabbed her upper arm and rushed her to the jeep. Oanh opened the gate. He butted the jeep, tires shrieking, into the traffic. He sidled through the maze of bicycles and cyclos, whirred around traffic clumps, and sped whenever he found an opening. The jeep lurched to a stop before the gate to Thanh's villa. He jumped to the ground and rang the bell. The bony Vietnamese gardener admitted them to the courtyard. The same woman who had greeted him the last time ushered him into the house, down the hall, and into a bedroom.

Tuyet lay in the bed under a coverlet of silk. Her hair was loose, her face drawn and pale. When she saw him, she struggled to sit up and reached for him. He ran to the bed and enclosed her in his arms. Her body, frail and tiny, pushed against him. He stroked her tangled hair, pulled back, and studied her.

"How bad are you hurt?"

She offered him a weak smile and shook her head. A bruise ran from her temple to her cheekbone on one side. Her face on the other side was bandaged. Both arms bore scratches and contusions.

Chuck caught his breath. "Thu—"

"Broken arm. He will be all right."

He clasped her to him again. "Thank God."

The servant stood close by, hands folded, eyes down. The girl who had ridden with him in the jeep brought a chair, bowed, and left the room. Tuyet spoke to the older servant, who appeared to argue but then bowed and left, closing the door behind her. Chuck sat but kept Tuyet's hand in his.

"Tell me," he said.

"When we board, they separate Molly and me. I say I should be with her, I am her interpreter, but they ignore me. She and her children were put in the cargo compartment. Thu and I are sent to the troop compartment with the baby I carry.

"The baby—"

"Is fine. I cover her and Thu with my body. She is not injured."

He closed his eyes. *Tuyet is alive.*

"The people on the ground send me and Thu to the hospital in a helicopter. He is terrified, but the people there, they are very kind. They put us in the same hallway. Our cots were side by side. I ask about Molly, Angélique, and Philippe. Nobody knows."

Chuck drew back. "Molly . . . was killed."

Tuyet gasped. "Angélique and Philippe?"

"Dead."

Tuyet's eyes closed. She sat very still.

"Why did the hospital release you to come home?"

She lay back against the headboard. "There were too many injured. They told me Thu's arm was set and in a cast and sent us home to make room for others. I knew Chi Tu and Chi Ba would take care of us. Thu and I got through the crowds outside. We had to walk a long time before we found a cyclo to bring us home. After I arrived home, I . . ." She averted her eyes. "I cannot tell you."

Chuck watched her, frozen.

"I bleeded. I could not stop it." She wept. "Our baby. It came out of me. A boy. Dead."

"Oh my God." He closed his mind, held her words away, not wanting to understand.

Sobbing, she kissed his hand. "You forgive me this?"

He took her in his arms.

She shuddered, stiffened, pulled back. "You must go now."

"I'll stay with you."

"No. We already create scandal by being together alone in my bedroom."

"The servant left us," he said.

"I ordered her to leave. I wanted to be with you."

"I'll sleep in another room so—"

"No. Thanh is not here. It would ruin his reputation."

He sighed. "I'll come back in the morning."

"No. We cannot be together here."

"When you are well enough, come to my place."

She nodded. "You go now."

He kissed her and left. He drove through Saigon's streets in the dark. His child was dead. Like Ben and Philippe before him. Angélique. Molly. Heaving, he swerved to the side of the street. He sobbed until there was no weeping left in him. When he could control his hands he drove home.

The sun had been up less than an hour and the air was already tan with pollution. The jeep idled at the traffic circle, impatient in the purple-gray exhaust fumes, as swarms of bicycles rolled past. At last, the policeman stopped the flow and signaled. Sparky eased the jeep forward while Chuck kept watch on bikes and cyclos close enough to drop a grenade. Sunday morning. Was it only a week ago that he'd been at Easter Mass and heard Molly sing? He remembered her yellow dress, her ample chest rising and falling as she belted out folk hymns at the side of the altar. She was so alive in his memory. How could she be dead? He recalled the fear on Angélique's face, the weightlessness of Philippe.

They turned in at the DAO gate. The worst wound was the loss of the child in Tuyet's womb. A boy. He couldn't think about that anymore.

Troiano was in the tank when they went in. He was moving from desk to desk, talking to each analyst.

"You two look dead on arrival," Troiano said as they went to their desks. "Thought I told you to get some rest."

Chuck shrugged.

"Get through the morning take," Troiano said, "then home to bed, the both of you. Be back at 2000 tonight. You're both on night shift. Twelve on, twelve off."

"Yes, sir." Sparky headed to the comms center for the morning take.

He and Chuck sorted and carried stacks to the other analysts and flopped into chairs at their desks to start through the bad news and prepare for the 0800 briefing.

Sparky stepped to Chuck's desk and dropped a teletype sheet in front of him. "Is this the Thanh we know?"

Chuck lifted the paper from his desk. It was a Liberation News Agency dispatch. "The puppet Marine colonel Pham Ngoc Thanh, infamous murderer of dozens at Phat Hoa, was wounded during our courageous forces' attack on Phan Rang airbase. The cowardly enemy escaped by helicopter when our valiant soldiers seized the base."

Chuck dialed Thanh's office.

"We not know, sir," the voice on the other end told him. "The colonel, he not come Saigon yet, you know?"

Chuck hung up.

He and Sparky did what they were told. By 1000 they were at Yen Do, both asleep. Chi Nam woke them at 1800 for dinner. As they ate on the veranda, Sparky pulled a portable radio from his pocket. "A spare,"

he said with a grin. "Never want to be without." He switched it on. The tone was more nasal than its predecessor's.

"It is plain that 'the great offensive,'" an authoritative voice was saying, "is anything but that. What we have had here is a partial collapse of South Vietnamese forces, so that there has been very little major fighting since the battle of Ban Me Thuot, and that was an exception in itself."

Chuck and Sparky gawked at each other.

"That," the ARS reporter said, "was Secretary of Defense Schlesinger speaking today on *Face the Nation*."

Sparky swung his head from side to side as if to fight off a case of the wobblies. "What's that guy smoking?" He sighed. "You can bet we'll be drafting a message for General Smith to send to Washington ticking off the facts."

Chuck didn't answer. They'd be correcting Washington rather than the other way around. Sinister topsy-turvy had become a way of life.

CHAPTER 17

Ike was still at the villa when they got home Monday morning after the briefing. He had cleared off a corner of the dining room table and sat drinking coffee. He was in his blues, his hat beside him on the credenza.

Chuck put down his walkie-talkie next to the hat. "What are you doing here in the middle of the morning?"

Ike raised his head, focused his eyes. "Heading to, uh, CONUS."

"What?" Sparky said. "Going back to the world in the middle of the cave-in?"

"The Ambassador says everything's hunky-dory, not to worry," Ike said.

Chuck sat next to him. "Never mind the official lies. Why are you going to the States?"

"Accompanying Molly's body. I volunteered."

"Not going to look good on your record." Sparky sat on the edge of the table. "Smacks of fleeing under fire."

Ike gave him a weak grin. "Temporary additional duty. I'm supposed to come back after the funeral, but they know damned well ain't nobody here going to finish their tour. Nobody expects I'll make it back before the collapse. So they're going to pack my stuff out . . ." He blinked as if he'd lost his train of thought. "And, um, they're sending a TAD replacement. Name of Riggs."

"You'll be at her funeral?" Chuck said.

"In her hometown in Minnesota." Ike smiled sadly, then raised his head. "Wonder what folks will think? Molly told me they're not partial to blacks."

"Jesus," Chuck said. "When are you leaving?"

"Today. Waiting for the military taxi to take me to Tan Son Nhat."

Chuck drooped. He hadn't banked on Ike not being here. "What's your ETD?"

"Noon," Ike said. "But everything's so fucked up, could be earlier. Or later."

Chuck stood. "Let me get cleaned up and I'll come out and see you off."

"Forget it," Ike said. "I know how to load myself onto a C-141." His fluttering eyelids were the only part of him that moved.

Chuck slept for three hours, then drove north into the mangrove swamps to Thanh's villa. Molly's body and Ike would be airborne by now. Chuck's heart tightened. It hurt to remember Ike's empty face. He'd cared more for Molly than he admitted, even to himself. There'd be no letters. Molly's death had killed something in Ike.

The gardener admitted Chuck to the courtyard, and the jabbering servant urged him up the stairs into the house. She conducted him not to Tuyet's bedroom at the front of the house but to the last bedroom at the rear. When she opened the door for him, he saw Thanh propped up in bed. Tuyet, in a purple-gray apron over a full-length smock of the same color buttoned to the throat, looked up from a bedside table holding gauze, tape, and a basin.

"Mister Griffin." Thanh raised his hand. "You come to see me."

Chuck stifled his surprise. "We received word that the Colonel was wounded."

"The hospitals, they are full. The military doctors wanted to expel some wounded soldiers to make room for me, but I say no. My family can care for me." He glanced at Tuyet. "My wife, she is trained and experienced as a nurse."

The servant brought a chair and pointed to it. Chuck, not allowing himself to look at Tuyet, sat. "How serious are the Colonel's wounds?"

"Shrapnel in the belly, chest, legs. When we have fewer wounded, the doctors will remove it."

"Will the Colonel allow me to see if an American doctor—"

Thanh raised his hand, palm out. "No need, Mister Griffin."

"I will inform Colonel Macintosh."

"Colonel Mac is well? He will come here soon, no?"

"No, sir."

"For the evacuation," Thanh said. "The Marines will come. So Colonel Mac will come." Thanh laughed. "Never mind." He nodded, as if talking to himself. "The U.S., they do not tell us about the evacuation because they don't want to frighten us." His face sobered. "You sent me a note about Sergeant Giuong Minh Phuc of Ranger Group 25. Few of the rangers escaped to the coast after the flight from Pleiku. After the fall of Tuy Hoa, fewer got to Vung Tau." He stopped long enough to take a painful breath. "I dispatched Corporal Vien, my aide, to review the list of survivors. Sergeant Phuc was not among those few."

"So—"

"Phuc is in the hands of the North Vietnamese, or he is dead."

Thanh spoke to Tuyet. She nodded and moved toward the door. Her eyes met Chuck's for a second before she went out and closed the door behind her.

"I ask Tuyet to leave us," Thanh said. "She will make sure that no one hears us. When will the evacuation begin?"

"The Ambassador has not ordered it, sir," Chuck answered.

"Soon, I think. When I can walk enough, I will go to JGS and stay there. I must destroy documents. Tuyet will help me because I am too weak to carry papers outside to be burned." He leaned forward and spoke in a low voice. "When the evacuation begins, please to telephone me. I bring Thu to the old gate between JGS and Tan Son Nhat. It is on an old road, not used now, a few feet off the main road."

"The abandoned road . . ."

"Close by the deserted cemetery," Thanh whispered. "Nobody cares for it now. The gate is sealed, but a person can climb over. You know this place?"

"I'll find it, sir."

"I make rendezvous there with you and bring Thu and hand him over the gate to you and you take him."

Chuck couldn't speak.

"And Tuyet, if she wishes to go. I bring her, too. You take my wife and son and save them."

"Surely she wishes to go with Thu."

"She will decide," Thanh said.

"I remind the Colonel that he is on the U.S. evacuation list. More important, Colonel Macintosh is waiting for an answer to his invitation to the Colonel to visit the U.S."

Thanh nodded impatiently. "Yes, yes." His head fell back on the pillow. "And now, you forgive me, Mister Griffin? You send Chi Ba to me, please?"

Chuck stumbled to his feet and made his way from the room. Tuyet stood gray-faced in the hall.

"He wants Chi Ba," Chuck said.

Tuyet waved her fingers. The servant shuffled into Thanh's room.

Chuck took Tuyet's hands. "Pan Am is still flying."

"They are not selling tickets."

"I could offer the ticket seller something on the side—"

"Thanh is hurt. I cannot abandon him at this moment. I need to wait until he is better."

"You have no more time."

She tried to pull away. "A shard is lodged near his heart. He could die with no warning."

"Tuyet, listen to me. Saigon could be overrun any day now." He lifted her chin and forced her to look at him. "Do you want Thu to be here when the North Vietnamese come?"

She tried to free herself from his grasp. He yanked her closer.

"Do you know what they will do to him?" he went on. "They'll send him to a reeducation site, a nice name for a concentration camp. They'll teach him to hate you and Thanh. He'll be a member of the Ho

Chi Minh Youth League, ready to sacrifice his life for the memory of the great leader."

"*C'en est assez.*"

"Or maybe they'll behead him outright as an example of how the rich should die."

She pried her hands free. "Stop it."

"No. You've got to face it. There's no way to get him out without you. You must leave together. I'll come with you."

"I will go," she breathed, "to save him." She massaged her hands. "To live. To be with you. To bear a child for you. But—" She wrenched her shoulders. "You have seen Thanh. I cannot turn my back to him, walk away, and desert him now. He is my fatherland. My An Nam. My country is dying."

He paused and let his voice turn cold. "You will destroy Thu."

She uttered a low cry, as if he had stabbed her. "I will go."

"When?"

"A week. Two weeks. I don't know."

"More orphans will be evacuated," he said. "You could—"

"No. Some other way."

"Send Thu out with them."

She shuddered. "No."

"If you wait you might not get out."

She bit her lip, said nothing.

"Come to Yen Do," he said.

"I can't leave Thanh alone."

"You risk your life for him."

"He risked his life for many."

"At least get U.S. visas for Thu and you. Tonight I'll ask Troiano for time off tomorrow. I'll go with you. Meet me on Thong Nhat Boulevard at the square in front of the presidential palace at 0830. Will you do that?"

She nodded with a sigh. He left.

In the jeep's acetate map case he found Huong's address in Molly's handwriting and the map Molly had given him. Following the red line marking the route, he drove through the blistering air past Cach Mang toward the outer fringes of the city. Traffic was light, but everywhere the streets were clogged with people on foot, sad-eyed, frightened, restless, on the move.

Huong's address was outside the city limits, beyond the racetrack, past Cay Go in Phu Lam, a shamble of shacks and lean-tos reeking of human waste. In an alley almost too narrow to drive through, teeming with scrawny chickens and naked children, he came to a shanty made of corrugated iron and cardboard. An old man sitting in the dust at the doorway nodded to him after seeing the paper. He creaked to his feet and limped inside.

Huong came out into the sunlight, blinking, a child in her arms. She looked up at him, uneasy, then recognition lit her face. "Mister Griffin, you come here? You come in now, take a load off, have tea, yes?"

He didn't want to have tea. He wanted to finish this ugly business and get some rest. He went in.

The interior was a single room crowded with makeshift furniture. He sat at a rickety table while a toothless old woman served him tea. Huong handed her the baby, shooed her and a scattering of children and chickens out the door, and sat next to him.

"How's it hanging, Mister Griffin, *sir*?"

"I'm fine, thank you. How are you?"

"I good, but not much work now, you know? The way the cookie crumbles." She sipped tea as if waiting for him to begin the conversation. When he said nothing, she put down her cup and clasped her hands. "Miss Tuyet? She is well?"

He nodded.

"And Mister Captain?"

"Captain Saunders has returned to America."

Her smile dimmed. "Oh." She busied herself with rearranging the cups and teapot. "He never tell me about my husband." She gave him an apologetic smile. "You forgive me? I not ask about Miss Molly. She is well?"

His throat closed. *She doesn't know.*

"Miss Molly . . . Miss Molly is dead, Huong. The plane she took to the States crashed." How could he say it like that, straight out, a routine statement of fact?

Huong's polite face cracked. The smile remained as if forgotten. "Oh."

"I'm sorry," he said with crazy calmness. "I thought you knew."

She didn't answer.

"I came here to tell you," he said, "that I have inquired about your husband." She raised her head and looked at him, the smile still in place, the eyes terrified. "We have no word on him. He was not with the men from his unit who made it to Vung Tau from Tuy Hoa."

For a moment she didn't move. She shivered, wrapped her arms around herself, and turned from side to side. Then she folded her hands in her lap and sat very still. "You very good to come and see me. I thank you very much, Mister Griffin, *sir*."

He understood that his visit was over. He rose. "God be with you, Huong."

"Yes, sir, Mister Griffin, *sir*." She was on her feet, looking down over her shoulder so that he couldn't see her face.

He went outside. Inside, her voice rose, nasal, keening. The old woman hurried in. Others gathered around the door.

Curious children surrounded his jeep. Two had crawled into it and were fiddling with the knobs on the dashboard. Adults watched him with undisguised curiosity. He chased the children from the jeep, started it, and threaded his way through the crowded maze of alleys, honking, halting, easing along, until he came to the main street back toward Cholon.

That afternoon he got five hours of sleep. He and Sparky reported in at the tank at 1800 and resumed their grisly work. At 0600 the next morning he headed home, ate, bathed, changed, and went by cab to Thong Nhat Boulevard.

While the rest of Saigon groveled in the heat, the square before Independence Palace radiated well-watered health. White flowers in borders glowed in the sunshine, backed by manicured lawn and sculpted vegetation in vibrant green. Yet even here the growing stench of the city waited for the cleansing of the monsoons.

A cyclo meandered through the traffic and delivered Tuyet. Chuck helped her step from the pavement to the curb and paid the driver. They stood looking at each other, then turned and trudged toward the U.S. embassy.

A whine cut through the clatter of the city traffic. A turbojet engine, getting closer. Chuck looked up in time to see an F5E Tiger fighter dive like a raptor, its attention riveted on the palace. Chuck yelled to Tuyet, but the scream of the plane blocked his voice. The jet swooped low, left behind black smudges, and shrieked upward.

Chuck tackled Tuyet. As the grass met their bodies the air imploded into his ears. The earth beneath them jerked. He looked up. The plane circled and came in for a second dive. Ear-shattering thunder, and the earth jumped again. Antiaircraft guns on the palace grounds spat tracers into the air. He covered his head with his arms, tried to push himself into the earth, then turned to look toward her. She was struggling to her knees, staring at the palace. He grabbed her, forced her down. As a section of the palace collapsed and burst into flames, he threw his body over hers. Gunfire split the air around them.

The plane flew off. Silence. People sprang to their feet and ran in all directions. He was up, dragging her across the square toward Pasteur Street. They were three blocks up Pasteur when the firing erupted again. They fell to the pavement, arms over heads. When the shooting paused, he yanked her up. She struggled for breath, stumbled in her high heels. He caught her as she fell.

She was shaking. "I cannot go more."

He carried her to the Pasteur Institute's low cement wall and sat her between the wrought iron spears rising from its narrow top. Blood darkened the skirt of her underdress.

"Got to get you to a doctor," he said.

"No. I still bleed from the loss of the baby. It is nothing."

"We're not far from Yen Do. I'll take you there."

She shook her head. "I go home."

"Tuyet . . ."

"You please not to worry. I know how to care for myself. You walk with me. We find a cab."

They doddered through the streets. The stunned silence gradually gave way to the tentative sound of the city coming back to life. On a side street they spotted a blue-and-white and flagged it down. Tuyet struggled into it and, ashen faced, gave Chuck half a wave as it sped away.

Chuck lifted his walkie-talkie from his belt. "Purple 1, this is Purple 19. Over."

Nothing. Probably out of range. He'd try again when he got home. He saw no sign of Sparky at the villa. Probably upstairs asleep. He radioed Troiano on the Prick 25, told him what he knew about the attack on the palace, and dragged himself upstairs to bed. As he lay listening to the rumble of traffic outside, he wondered at his grotesque existence. Still no visas for Tuyet and Thu. He pictured the blood spreading on the white of Tuyet's dress. No. Grief was a luxury he could no longer afford.

That night in the tank he read the follow-up reports on the palace bombing: four 500-pound bombs dropped by a renegade Republic of Vietnam pilot who had been trained in the United States. He took off from Bien Hoa and landed in communist-held Phuoc Long Province after the raid. The entire city had been shaken. And now, for the first time, the North Vietnamese had a combat aircraft.

Meanwhile, the North Vietnamese Army was tightening the noose around Xuan Loc. The war was getting closer.

—⎍⎍⎍⎍⎍—

The next morning, when Chuck and Sparky were pulling out of the parking lot en route to the villa, Sparky slammed on the brakes and backed up. "Oops. Forgot my toothpicks."

"Jesus fucking Christ, Oopsie. Okay. Go back and get them. If I'm asleep when you get back, drive gently."

After breakfast, while Sparky slept, Chuck carried empty boxes to Ike's room to get stuff ready for the packers. Ike and Molly were all over the room—chocolate bars stacked neatly on the bureau, black military dress shoes in the corner, Ike's shorts and T-shirts folded on the bed where Oanh had left them after she washed them. The potted palm Molly had bought at Tet was on the windowsill, dead. In the top drawer of the bureau were Molly's nametag from the dispensary, a can of Brasso, four sets of captain's bars, and a cup with a broken handle filled with Vietnamese, Thai, and Hong Kong coins. Beneath the cup he found pick-up slips for dry cleaning and shoe repair. These he pocketed. The remaining drawers were filled with Ike's clothes. A brassiere nestled among the boxer shorts.

Chuck turned to the wardrobe. All Ike's military gear was gone, but a nurse's uniform hung among the civvies. On the deck among the loafers and tennis shoes were a pair of white nurse's shoes, three muddy comic books, and a battered box of chocolates. On the shelf—his heart jumped—sat the tiara. He moved quickly to the desk. The usual stuff. A notice for a magazine subscription renewal, a pack of Wrigley's Spearmint gum, a handful of loose keys. In the bottom drawer he came across snapshots. Molly and Ike in her apartment. In one she was giving the finger to the camera. At the bottom of the stack was a picture of Ike, Sparky, and Chuck at the wicker table on the veranda. Molly must have taken it last summer. Ike was grinning, Sparky was smiling, too, but Chuck was serious. He studied his own face. How young he looked then, less than a year ago.

Better not to send Molly's things to Ike's home. Chuck was sure Ike hadn't told his wife about Molly. He gathered Molly's possessions into a box. He'd find her parents' address and mail them. Nothing else to be done here. He'd leave instructions for the packers to take the things as they were. He glanced around one last time and turned toward the doorway, then remembered that Ike had screwed a hook into the back of the door. He closed it. A set of purple scrubs hung there. He lifted them from the hook and spread them in his hands. They smelled of Molly's perfume. The cloth was warm, as if she had just stepped out of them. He folded them, put them in the box next to the tiara, and left.

Thursday morning Chuck sent Sparky back home without him. Too much was happening. Muscles aching, eyelids like sandpaper, he tracked the probes by the North Vietnamese 341st Division against Xuan Loc. The town had been subjected to an artillery bombardment of four thousand rounds, one of the heaviest in the war, and enemy tanks were in the streets. At 1800 Sparky was back, helping him track hand-to-hand combat that lasted until dark when friendly forces drove the North Vietnamese from the city. Troiano commanded Chuck to go home and rest. Starting Friday he'd be on the day shift. That meant working from before 0700 until long after dark. On the cusp of incoherence, he was afraid to drive. A cab dropped him at Yen Do. He went straight to bed without eating.

As soon as Sparky got home Friday morning, Chuck drove the jeep to DAO. He parked in the assigned spot, then walked back out of the DAO compound and headed south. Near the entrance to Tan Son Nhat he turned east toward the fence separating Tan Son Nhat from JGS and followed the abandoned road to the cemetery Thanh had spoken of. What was left of a cinder-block wall obscured the several dozen crumbling headstones shaded by untended banyans. Standing next to the graveyard, Chuck inspected the story-high barrier to the southeast. Nothing that looked like a gate. He followed the discolored chain link for a dozen feet into a clump of vegetation taller than he was. Here the fence ended abruptly at what once might have been a double-frame gate large enough for a truck to pass through. It was chained in the middle, the links rusted. Both supporting posts had sagged, and the gate frames were sunk in dirt to what looked like more than a foot. Chuck rose on tiptoe and looked across. Overgrown brush obscured the JGS side of the barrier. Satisfied that he had found the rendezvous spot, he walked back to DAO.

In the tank, he read the incoming dispatches. The battle for Xuan Loc raged on. Elements of the North Vietnamese 7th Division had joined the 341st in the battle. Liberation Radio urged the populace to rebel against the South Vietnamese government. Chuck pulled together signals intelligence, prisoner interrogation reports, and aerial photography and concluded that the North Vietnamese had set up a corps headquarters in Phuoc Long Province. It commanded four divisions, two of which were dispatched to the battle for Xuan Loc. Two more divisions were moving toward Saigon.

Then came the word they'd been expecting: Phnom Penh had fallen to the Khmer Rouge, the Cambodian Communists allied with North Vietnam. One more domino down.

Sparky came in before 1800 and helped with the sorting and analysis. By 2000 Chuck was too tired to function. Sparky agreed to get a cab in the morning, so Chuck drove the jeep to Yen Do.

Chi Nam met him at the door. "New person, Mister Tommy, he in back."

Chuck passed through the dining room to the veranda. At the table sat an earnest young Marine officer in jungle utilities—blond, blue-eyed, baby-faced, and ruddy, with captain's bars stitched on his lapels. When he saw Chuck he stood.

"Hi." He extended his hand. "You must be Chuck. I'm Tommy Riggs. Here TAD, standing in for Ike Saunders."

When Chuck shook hands, he felt the Naval Academy ring on Tommy's finger.

"Exchanged a few messages with Ike to get up to speed," Tommy said. "He told me the house drink is martinis, so I mixed some. Can I pour you one?"

They sat. Chuck sampled the martini. Never would have passed the Macintosh test. Tasted like Tommy had added as much vermouth as gin.

Tommy gave him a doubtful smile. "I'll be using Ike's room for the duration."

"All his stuff's in there—"

Tommy shook his head. "The other guy, Sparky? He was here this afternoon when I got in. Said they packed Ike out yesterday. Guess they figure he's not coming back."

"Didn't know the packers would come so soon. I haven't picked up his laundry and shoes yet. I'll have to mail them to him."

Tommy drank, his leg jiggling. "So, you've been here, what, a year?"

"Since seventy-three."

"You know, life here isn't as bad as it's cracked up to be." He swept the villa with his eyes. "Nice place. Guess I could do without those lizards on the walls."

"They're geckos."

Tommy snapped his fingers. "Right. I knew that. Anyway, there's a lot going on. The airport was a zoo. And the street traffic—something else."

"You never served a tour here?"

"Never did. It was mostly over before I got commissioned."

"It's not 'mostly over' now."

"Oh, I know, but you know what I mean, Chuck."

Chuck ground his teeth. Where did this kid, younger than Ben, get off calling him, a major when he retired, by his first name?

A distant rumble stopped the conversation. Tommy sat up. "Shelling? Us or them?"

"Them."

"They have heavy arty?"

"Plenty," Chuck said. "Soviet 152 and 122 howitzers and U.S.-manufactured 155s and 105s captured from the ARVN."

Tommy cocked his head "AR-what?"

"Army of the Republic of Vietnam," Chuck said. "The good guys."

"Wow. Howitzers. I thought the VC were mostly guerrillas."

"U.S. types say VC or Viet Cong to mean the southern guerrillas, and NVA or North Vietnamese Army to mean the regular forces. False distinction. It's all the same crowd, and they've got everything from booby traps to SAMs."

"Damned shame." Tommy shook his head in disgust. "Should never have gotten to this point. We should have kicked ass and taken names."

Sadness descended on Chuck. *And the twits shall inherit the earth.*

The distant thunder started again. Closer now. Louder.

Tommy tipped his head toward the roar. "I'd love to get out and watch some of that. I hear the scrap up at Sue-Anne Lock is going great guns." He sipped. "Embassy duty's not what I was trained for." He grinned, boyish. "But they didn't give me a chance to say no."

"It's pronounced Swuhn Loke." Chuck had taken about as much of this as he could stand. "Let's see how soon Chi Nam will have dinner ready."

In the kitchen, Chi Nam was all business. "You out now. Dinner soon, okay?"

Tommy smiled at her. "You're about the littlest thing I ever saw. What's your name?"

"I Chi Nam."

Tommy sniffed. "Smells wonderful."

Chi Nam paused in mid-hustle. "You like?"

"Mmm. You must be a *fine* cook."

Chi Nam blushed. "You out. I bring. You sit."

Chuck left the villa Saturday morning before Sparky got in. The city was already writhing in the heat. Dust trailed after everything that moved. The canals and gutters that riddled the city had turned black, oozing with clots of human waste. The morning mist, suffused by exhaust and smoke from charcoal fires, hung in the blighted trees and discolored eaves. The ubiquitous orange-and-white banners sagged, some falling into the street. Refugees choked byways and alleys and spilled over the boulevards and parks. Chuck smelled the raw force of incipient panic.

At midmorning he removed unit symbols and grease pencil lines and arrows from the acetate covering the map of Long Khanh Province and sprayed solvent to clean off the dark residue. He wiped it with cheesecloth until the discoloration was gone, but the image of the map beneath was still murky. The acetate was scratched from too many postings. No time to replace it. He pasted fresh unit appliqués and drew arrows to display the current positions of units facing each other.

The North Vietnamese had turned the Xuan Loc battle into a meat grinder. They were willing to sacrifice unit after unit to drive out the South Vietnamese 18th Division and seize the town. Somehow the endless reports of gore and annihilation no longer moved Chuck. Was there such a thing as disaster fatigue?

At lunchtime he stopped at the shoe repair shop on his way to the snack bar. Behind the counter of the miniature shop stood a Vietnamese in khaki shirt and shorts—no doubt once the property of the U.S. Army—and the inevitable clogs. Chuck handed him the green cardboard ticket he'd found in Ike's room and watched him search through shelves. The man was already old, even though he looked like he'd never grown up. He had the face of a young boy, but his hair was graying and his skin was creased.

The man put a brown-wrapped package on the counter. "Five thousand three hundred twenty pee."

Chuck counted out a wad of bills.

"You want give me tip, sir?" the man said, his eyes hungry.

"You're supposed to get a tip?" Chuck said.

"The prices, they go up. Now cost fifteen hundred pee for one bread. And DAO, it set what I can charge. So now I ask customer for tip."

Chuck put another thousand pee on the counter.

"I thank you very much, sir." The cash vanished.

Next Chuck went to the dry cleaners. The clerk was a young girl in shapeless black pajamas. Her ready smile reminded him of Huong. She took his slip and produced two class A Marine uniforms on hangers for his inspection.

"Six thousand five hundred pee, sir."

He reached for his wallet.

"You meet my mamma, sir?" the girl said.

At the end of the counter sat a caricature of an ancient Chinese woman, her white hair smoothed back into a bun. Brocaded pajamas hid her tiny frame. Her face was a map of lines, her cheekbones protruding. She smiled and nodded, her eyes mere slits.

The girl took his money. "My mamma and me, we very afraid." She leaned toward him and whispered. "We Chinese, sir. We work for American. The VC tortures us, kills us. You help us?"

Chuck was jarred. "Look, I just work here. I don't have any planes or boats."

"You American, sir," she said, as if that explained everything.

He slung the uniforms over his arm and escaped to the corridor.

Late in the day he went to Troiano's secretary's desk. "Can I have a minute with the colonel?"

She nodded, sniffled.

"What's the matter?" he said.

"My last day. They're packing me out tomorrow." She blew her nose. "Nonessential personnel. Guess that tells me what I'm worth. Me and most of the analysts in the tank. We'll all be gone in a day or two." She buzzed the intercom. "Sir, Chuck Griffin would like to talk to you." She listened, nodded to Chuck.

He went through the open door. Troiano was at his desk, his face drawn.

"Just a question, sir," Chuck said. "All the locals working in the concessions—the barbers, sales clerks, cooks, launderers. Is there any provision for evacuating them?"

"We'll take as many as we can. U.S. personnel, government of Vietnam officials, and contract hires are higher priority. All depends on what happens at the end, how much warning we have, what kind of seacraft and aircraft are available."

"Excuse my questions, sir, but have those folks been told where to go and what to do when the evac begins?"

Troiano laughed. "Hell, no. We don't even know that ourselves. Shut the door and sit down."

Chuck did.

"The embassy's dragging its feet," Troiano said. "The Ambassador thinks there's going to be some kind of cease-fire to negotiate the formation of a coalition government. But we haven't been idle. Ever hear of the DAO Special Planning Group? Don't let the name fool you. The SPG's the forward evacuation coordinator. It's been quietly working with Marines flying in from ships off the coast to get everything ready. But the Ambassador is doing everything he can to throw obstacles in their path. He won't allow the Marines to wear uniforms, fly in on Marine helicopters, or stay overnight. Because we're expecting mobs outside the gate, the deputy DAO, General Baughn, sent a message to higher-ups requesting additional security guards when the evacuation begins. The Ambassador was furious—ordered Baughn out of the country. So now all the preps are sub rosa. Trouble is, the city is already rolling toward panic. That's going to make it rough."

"So the servants at the houses, the chauffeurs—"

Troiano wilted. "If the Ambassador had faced the facts and started evacuating people other than high-risk Viets, we could have gotten many of them out. As it is . . ." He shook his head.

"What *will* we do, sir?"

"When I find out, I'll tell you."

Communications
Deception

MID-APRIL 1975

CHAPTER 18

An exchange of notes told Chuck that Tuyet was spending her days helping Thanh burn documents at his JGS office. Midmorning on Tuesday, while Troiano was in the tank for an update, Chuck asked his permission to visit Thanh on Wednesday.

"Fair enough," Troiano said, "but I want you armed. What's your choice of weapon?"

"M16, M9 Beretta, and a .38 snub nose. And I need another walkie-talkie for my shavetail housemate. He's assigned to the embassy, but since he lives with us he needs to be on the net."

"You got it. For now, only carry a single handgun on your person and keep the rifle at your desk. Don't want to stampede the Viets. The weapons and radios are locked in the cabinet in my office. Stop by when I get back." Troiano strapped on a holster.

"You're heading out, sir?" Chuck asked.

Troiano gave him a bitter smile. "To see the Ambassador. While I can still get through."

Chuck's ears registered the concussion first. It threw him from the rack and slammed him to the deck. Change and keys flew from the bureau. The walkie-talkie clattered to the floor. He listened through the ringing in his ears. Silence. He crawled to the bedroom window. Sliding up the wall until he was upright, he leaned to the side far enough for one eye to peer through the taped glass. Under the hostile glare of security floodlights the city lay tense but unmoving. Something big had exploded. As he headed down the steps, he heard footsteps behind him.

"What the fuck was that?" Tommy's voice.

In the dining room Chuck cranked up the Prick 25. "Purple 1, this is Purple 19. Over."

"This is Purple 1. Get off the air. Every-fucking-body is calling in. Over."

"What was it? Over."

"Damned if I know. We'll call you if there's anything to lose your dinner over. Sign off. Over."

"Roger and out."

"Who's Purple 1?" asked Tommy behind him.

"That's Sparky. He's covering for Troiano. Since you're living here, you'll have to be on the net. I got you a walkie-talkie." Chuck turned. Tommy was dancing in place in his Jockey shorts, a huge grin on his face. His lip was bleeding. Chuck touched the cut with his index finger, showed the blood to Tommy. "Get something on that. Better use peroxide. Impetigo's making the rounds." The excited smile on Tommy's face turned to revulsion.

Chi Nam scurried in from the back of the house.

"Go back to bed," Chuck said to her. "Whatever it was seems to have passed."

She studied Tommy's bleeding lip. "You hurt. I fix."

"That's okay," Tommy said.

She was into the kitchen and back with a cruet within a minute. She shook it, upended it on her middle finger, and brushed fluid on Tommy's cut. "There now. You be better."

Tommy sucked air. "Ow."

"No, no," she said. "It okay. You hurt now, better. You fixed now."

Tommy laughed. "Didn't think I was going to Nam to get fixed."

"Let's all get some rest," Chuck said. "Tomorrow's almost here."

She nodded and disappeared.

Tommy looked after her. "Nice little woman. So concerned about us. Does she have a family? Husband? Kids?"

"Out in Go Vap. North of the city. Visits them on her day off."

Wednesday morning Chuck learned from a Liberation Radio transcript that the explosion had been the mammoth ammo dump at Bien Hoa, less than eighteen miles northeast of them. Friendly after-action reports confirmed that enemy sappers had penetrated the perimeter. The airbase, the largest still in the hands of the South Vietnamese, had been hit the day before with rockets and artillery, and the runway had been closed for repairs. Meanwhile, the defense of Xuan Loc was over. Withdrawal had begun. The enemy's pincers were closing. He rubbed his eyes, shook his head.

"The Ambassador wants you to brief him."

Chuck looked up, startled. Troiano stood beside his desk. His fatigues were wrinkled and sweat-stained.

"Sir?" Chuck said.

"Tomorrow at 0900. Wants a complete update on the military situation." Troiano laughed. "Guess he didn't believe me yesterday. Maybe he'll listen to you. My guess is that he already knows everything you can tell him, but he has to cover all bets. I'll have my sedan take you. That is, if we can still get through. Streets are jammed with refugees. Fall of Xuan Loc will push even more into the city."

Chuck holstered his Beretta, thrust the .38 snub nose with a box of fifty rounds into his briefcase, and walked through the fusty heat to JGS—it would be faster than driving through the glutted streets. Still no monsoon. The heat and stench forced him to breathe through his mouth.

Thanh's jeep was parked in the dirt courtyard, but the enclosure appeared deserted. Smoke hung in the air. In the hall, the door to Thanh's office stood open. No one inside. Chuck went outside and looked for any sign of life. The sound of voices came from the rear of the house. He followed the gravel walk beneath the palms. Amid the scraggly pines and stunted banyans was a rusted fifty-five-gallon drum spewing flames. Paper was heaped beside the barrel, and behind it were two figures obscured by the conflagration. As Chuck got closer he recognized Thanh. He was in utilities, sitting in a chair, crutches by his side. Feeding the fire was Tuyet in a full-length frock of rough material covered by a gray apron. Her hair was pulled to the back of her head and tied with a strip of gray cloth. A smudge of ash darkened one temple. They were separating documents into single sheets and feeding them into the roaring fire. Both looked up when Chuck came around the corner.

The smile on Thanh's lined face was as merry as always. "Mister Griffin. A pleasure." He struggled to his feet and pointed toward the rear door to the office with one crutch. "I come in with you."

Chuck felt Tuyet's eyes on him as he followed Thanh. Inside, Chuck politely refused Thanh's offer of tea, helped him into a chair at the table by the window, and leaned the crutches against the wall. Smoke from the fire floated through the window.

"I wish to remind the Colonel," Chuck said, "that Colonel Macintosh is expecting a reply to his invitation to go to the States for consultations."

"You and Mac are both kind to me. I thank you."

Chuck shifted. "I didn't see the Colonel's aide when I came in."

Thanh's smile was steady. "I give him leave. I send him to his village. He brings his family to Saigon. They are now at Tan Son Nhat. They will be evacuated."

"The Colonel takes good care of his subordinates, but what about the Colonel himself?"

Thanh waved the words away and sat smiling as if waiting for the next topic.

"I will inform Washington that the Colonel may come later," Chuck said.

"Yes, better that way. Now you will excuse me?"

Chuck stood.

Thanh got to his feet and grappled with the crutches. His face was serene, but the pain showed in his eyes. He nodded to Chuck and hobbled toward the rear door.

Chuck walked through the main entrance to the courtyard. Tuyet hastened around the corner of the house. As she came close, he saw the stress lines around her eyes and mouth. He took the .38 snub nose and the ammunition from his briefcase. "I don't know what will happen at the end, but you must be able to protect yourself and Thu."

She eyed the revolver.

"Please," he said.

Hesitantly, she took the pistol and ammunition and slid them into a pocket in her full skirt.

He sighed. "Thank you. It's loaded and there's no safety switch. Be careful."

"Thanh taught me to fire guns when we lived in Da Nang. I know to be cautious."

"I've got to go."

She stepped toward him, stopped. " 'No war but this.' You remember? I got through the mobs to the Tu Xuong villa. The new owners have moved in. Even from the outside I could tell that the garden has changed. As the fighting comes close to Saigon, the birds have gone away."

Chuck lifted his face to the trees. It was true. No birds. "They were wise. How soon will you and Thu leave?"

"A few days. I must wait for Thanh to recover a little more."

"He's not better?"

She shook her head. "He suffers. Refuses to rest."

He raised her chin and looked into her eyes. "Do you know where the old gate is in the barrier between JGS and Tan Son Nhat? Near an abandoned cemetery?"

"I know the cemetery, just across the fence from JGS. That will be our rendezvous. Thanh told me."

"I'll get you and Thu across the fence and into Tan Son Nhat," Chuck said. "From there we can get you on a plane."

She nodded.

Back in the Intelligence Branch, Chuck went straight to Troiano's office. "Can we speak privately, sir?"

Troiano closed the door. "Your nickel."

"There's a woman. I'm doing everything I can to get her and her son out of the country. I may need the Colonel's help."

"I'll do what I can when the time comes. We'll talk about it then, when we see how things stand. With the Ambassador refusing to call for an evacuation, I don't know what to expect five minutes from now." He squinched his eyes. "You missed my announcement while you were at JGS. Starting tonight, I want all remaining personnel here around the clock. While we can still get through the streets, we'll go home to bathe and change. When we can't, we'll bring toiletries and changes of clothing here. We'll sleep in shifts."

At midafternoon a field dispatch reported that Phan Rang, one of the last of South Vietnam's coastal cities, had fallen.

Close to 2000 hours Chuck finally broke away long enough to go back to the villa. Tommy, mindlessly cheery, sat with him while he ate. Back at DAO, Chuck slunk onto a cot in the hall between the colonel's office and the tank, his Beretta under his pillow, his M16 on the deck beside him, and instantly fell into deep slumber.

Hands rattled him.

"Goddammit, wake up." Sparky was leaning over him, his face rutted. "It's 0600, shithead. Time for you to get your ass on duty."

Chuck got to his feet and made his way to the head. Cool water did nothing to bring his face to life. When he got back to the office, Sparky was already out cold. Chuck threw ice cubes in his first mug of coffee and chugged it. The second cup he gulped while reading the incoming dispatches. Propaganda from Liberation Radio demanded that President Thieu resign as a precondition for cease-fire talks.

Chuck brushed his teeth, shaved, and sponge-bathed in the latrine. Despite his best efforts to look respectable, his face was haggard and his utilities were rumpled and sweaty. He locked his hastily prepared briefing book and the Beretta in his briefcase, chained it to his wrist, took his M16, and at 0800 headed for the embassy in Troiano's chauffeur-driven sedan.

It was stop-and-go all the way into town. The mobs in the streets were thicker, slower to move out of the sedan's way, looking more desperate and menacing than ever. Even following a circuitous route the four-mile trip took more than an hour. Chuck arrived at the Ambassador's office seven minutes late.

"You'll have to wait," an aide in the anteroom told him. "The Ambassador has an unexpected visitor. Have a seat."

Chuck was tense enough that sitting still was a challenge. The minutes edged by.

The door to the Ambassador's office swung open, and a man Chuck recognized but couldn't place emerged followed by the Ambassador.

"Please convey to your government," the Ambassador said as he placed his hand on the man's shoulder, "my gratitude for your help."

The man smiled, almost triumphantly, and strode out.

Chuck placed him then. The Hungarian member of the International Commission of Control and Supervision. Chuck had seen him at the party for Senator Nunn. He stretched his memory. The ICCS. A group established by the United Nations to monitor the so-called peace after the signing of the treaty in 1973. Chuck grimaced. The Ambassador was consulting with a representative of a communist government allied to North Vietnam. It sucked.

The Ambassador spotted Chuck and waved him into his private office.

"My apologies for arriving late, sir." Chuck slid into the chair beside the Ambassador's desk. "The crowds in the streets—"

The Ambassador, all graciousness gone, shook his head. "Let's get on with it."

Chuck opened the briefing book on the desk with the pages facing the Ambassador. He reviewed the status of North Vietnamese forces within striking range. "Sir, the situation is critical. The fall of Xuan

Loc removed the last barrier to the North Vietnamese approach to Saigon. We know from signals intelligence that sixteen to eighteen North Vietnamese divisions now surround us, poised to invade Saigon. An intercepted message early this morning sent by an unidentified North Vietnamese unit two kilometers north of Tan Son Nhat told a subordinate to await the order to attack."

The Ambassador glanced at his watch.

"Our best estimate," Chuck went on, "is that the enemy won't be completely ready to move against us for another two to three days. But the North Vietnamese are in no hurry. The South Vietnamese military is crumbling fast. We expect that when the attack begins, we'll be hit first with rockets and mortars, then artillery as enemy troops enter the city."

The Ambassador gave him a patient smile. "Anything else?"

Chuck's mouth opened in surprise. "Sir?"

The Ambassador stood. "If there's nothing more, I need to get on to other matters."

Chuck stumbled to his feet. He took a deep breath and calmed himself. "Forgive me, sir, but we have little time left to get U.S. citizens and vulnerable South Vietnamese out of the country before it falls to the North Vietnamese."

The Ambassador came from behind his desk and rested his hand on Chuck's back as if to urge him toward the office door. "Thank you, Mister Griffin. I'll handle it from here."

Despite the pressure from the Ambassador's hand, Chuck didn't move. "Mr. Ambassador, to save lives, I plead with you to order the evacuation immediately. Even if we start now—"

The Ambassador put his arm around Chuck and edged him toward the door. "Son," he said as they moved away from the desk, "when you're older, you'll understand these things better." The Ambassador smiled, showed Chuck out, and closed the door behind him. The Ambassador's aide was by his side immediately. "Thank you, Mister Griffin." He gestured toward the exit.

The base of his spine tingling, Chuck allowed himself to be escorted into the hallway. For a moment he stood panting, then, on impulse, turned and hurried to the office of the CIA chief of station. The secretary took him immediately into the chief's private office.

"Forgive, the interruption, sir," Chuck panted. "I just briefed the Ambassador on the military situation and urged him to call for an evacuation. He cut me short."

The chief smiled up from his desk. "He's a busy man."

Chuck's desperation got the better of his sense of protocol. "Sir, we gotta get people out of here."

The chief laughed. He opened a manila folder on his desk and handed Chuck a message printout. It was from the Ambassador to the president and secretary of state, dated that morning. It declared that the North Vietnamese were using communications deception to mislead the Allied intercept effort. They were trying to frighten the Republic of Vietnam into negotiations by transmitting false data.

Chuck's mouth dropped open. He read the message again to be sure he got it right. "What evidence do you have," he said to the chief, "what evidence does the Ambassador have, of communications deception?"

The chief laughed. "Tell you what. I'll bet you a bottle of champagne, vintage and chateau of your choice, that a year from now you and I will both still be in Saigon, at our desks, following our usual routine."

The man was serious. Chuck blinked, then turned and faltered from the room.

Responding to the signals from the base of his spine, Chuck ensconced himself in the sedan's passenger seat to the right of the driver rather than sitting in the back on the return trip to Tan Son Nhat. His hand grasped the Beretta hidden inside the briefcase. They'd gone less than a mile before refugees filled the street and blockaded the sedan. As the crowd surrounded the car, the din grew louder. The faces outside the car windows were savage. Fists thumped on the sides and trunk.

The terrified driver tried to move forward, but the screaming mob swamped the sedan, preventing all movement.

Chuck sat straight and with a calmness that surprised him drew the Beretta into the open. He aimed it through the windshield and drew his lips away from his teeth. The thugs directly in front of the sedan drew back, startled. "Drive through," Chuck growled at the chauffeur. "*Now.*"

The car crept forward, gaining speed. After twenty feet it was up to ten miles per hour. Chuck kept the Beretta on display for the rest of the trip.

As soon as he was back in the Intelligence Branch door, he went straight to Troiano's office.

"Sorry to bother the Colonel, sir," Chuck said, "but I'd like to give the Colonel a quick recap of my visit to the embassy." He ran through his meeting with the Ambassador and his exchange with the chief of station. "They don't believe what we're reporting to them, sir. They won't call for an evacuation."

"Sit down, Chuck."

Chuck did as he was told.

Troiano's tired face leaned toward the desktop. His eyes closed, opened, fixed on Chuck. "The Ambassador cannot even contemplate that the communist flag will ever fly over South Vietnam. To him the prospect is unthinkable. It cannot happen. The Hungarian member of the ICCS has done what he can to reinforce the Ambassador's conviction. He told the Ambassador that the North Vietnamese have no intention of attacking Saigon. That they want to form a coalition government with all the patriotic forces in the south and rule jointly."

"But, sir," Chuck said, "the intelligence of a forthcoming attack is overwhelming—"

"Not to the Ambassador and his immediate subordinates. They're waiting for the North Vietnamese to sue for peace so that negotiations can begin."

"Why in the name of God would they do that when the conquest of South Vietnam is within their grasp?"

Troiano shook his head. "I agree. They won't negotiate. They'll attack. Meanwhile, the Ambassador has persuaded Secretary of State Kissinger and the president that there's no need to evacuate anybody."

〰〰〰

More grim news from the front flooded in Friday morning. When he returned from the dinner and cleanup run to the villa Chuck learned that Phan Thiet, the last of the coastal enclaves in the latitudes north of Saigon, had fallen. Unable to focus and desperate for sleep, he and his two closest friends, the Beretta and the M16, bedded down early.

Explosions jarred him awake. Not too far away. He staggered into the tank and checked with Sparky. No info yet. He stumbled to the cot, collapsed, and forgot he was alive.

After Sparky was back from Yen Do and asleep Saturday morning, Chuck was making coffee when ARS reported the location of last night's shelling: Phu Lam, where Huong lived, less than five miles southwest of them, had been hit with 122-mm rockets. He remembered Huong, the old woman, the chickens, and especially the children.

〰〰〰

When Chuck came back from his cleanup at the villa Sunday morning, he brought rolls Chi Nam had baked. He prepared himself for the grind through the mountains of incoming traffic, but for the first time he could remember the total take was less than an inch high. Nearly all the classified message traffic was code-word signal intelligence reports that had originated in the States. The rest was the usual screed from the Liberation News Agency and news reports from the wire services. What was going on? The Republic of Vietnam, its northern provinces ripped away, lay quivering. The North Vietnamese watched and waited like a cat toying with a wounded bird. With little to post or report, Chuck, on Troiano's orders, drafted a cable to Washington, info General Smith, updating the estimate he'd given General Weyand. In it he listed the sixteen North Vietnamese divisions known to be positioned and the two believed to be close by for a three-pronged attack against Saigon.

He flipped on Sparky's portable to get the latest ARS reporting on the war. He heard news about Hollywood films and debates in Congress followed by songs from Dionne Warwick and Al Martino. Nothing about Vietnam. Toward noon, word arrived that the embassy had commanded ARS to cease all reporting about the war. Troiano speculated that the Ambassador was afraid of panic.

The eerie calm prevailed. Analyses from stateside agencies surmised that the North Vietnamese were regrouping, but the embassy responded that the North Vietnamese were waiting for President Thieu to step down so that they could begin negotiations with the United States and South Vietnam. Monday afternoon the embassy announced that President Thieu had left office and was fleeing the country. Troiano told Chuck that Thieu was flying with his family to exile in Taiwan.

The sitzkrieg continued into Tuesday. Chuck had become inured to the routine of disaster, the endless repetition of gruesome details as the Republic disintegrated, but the uncanny quiet unnerved him. He knew now what was going on. Unhampered by threats, external or internal, the North Vietnamese could take the time to do a thorough preparation for the coup de grâce. Almost as an afterthought, a dispatch from the field reported that the North Vietnamese had completed the occupation of Xuan Loc.

As Chuck refilled his mug—he'd lost track of how much coffee he'd had that morning—Troiano stood beside him. "What's your sense of when the downtime will end?"

Chuck rubbed his eyes. "From the signals intelligence, I'd guestimate two or three days until they get their ducks in a row. But once they get rolling, it'll be over fast. The Republic's in collapse, the military's near panic. The populace will go nuts as the North Vietnamese get close."

Troiano nodded. "Our biggest worry at the end won't be the bad guys but the friendlies. I'm having deadbolts put on the doors to the outside corridor. Every person entering has to be identified by someone inside." He grunted. "My guess is that we'll be out of here by the first of May, with or without the Ambassador's blessing. You?"

"Thirty days in April, sir," Chuck said, "and today's the twenty-second. Yeah, give or take a day or two."

After lunch Troiano was back. "Telephone for you."

Chuck picked up the receiver at his desk.

"Chuck." Tuyet's voice. "You are all right?"

"What about you?"

"Thanh grows worse. I took him to the doctor this morning. The shrapnel must come out, but the doctors have no time to do it. He suffers from swelling caused by infection, and he smells bad. So the doctor, he gave him antibiotics, but he is not better."

"Where are you?" he asked.

"Thanh stays at JGS. I come every day to help him." Silence, then she said, "I know we cannot meet, but I wanted to hear your voice. It is okay that I telephoned?"

"Of course."

"I must go," she said. "I burn documents alone now."

"God be with you all."

"*Et cum spiritu tuo.* And with you."

Chuck hung up. What could he do? For the first time in memory, he prayed.

The Associated Press reported on a speech President Ford had given at Tulane University on Wednesday. He had spoken of the war in the past tense, as if Saigon had already fallen. Vietnam was the "war that is finished." Chuck scratched his head. *If it's finished, what the fuck am*

I doing here with nothing but a Beretta to defend myself against eighteen North Vietnamese divisions?

Another wire service dispatch announced that the Pan Am clipper *Unity*, a Boeing 747 filled to capacity, had taken off from Tan Son Nhat on Thursday. It was the last commercial flight scheduled from Saigon.

Late Friday morning Chuck went to the snack bar, miraculously still operating, for a sandwich. As he headed back to the office, he tripped on empty boxes and scrap paper littering the corridors. The floors hadn't been waxed. A fluorescent tube in an overhead fixture was burnt out. Pentagon East was turning into a shambles. Walking toward him were two well-built young men with crew cuts. One wore a faded chambray shirt and jeans, the other tennis shorts and a ragged T-shirt.

"Man," one said, "it was fan-fuckin'-tastic."

The other snorted. "I'd have pushed his gunjy skull through the goddamn bulkhead."

When they came abreast of Chuck their grins disappeared. They straightened up and fell into cadence, as if marching. *Marines*. Chuck knew all the Marines in-country, but he didn't recognize these two. What the hell was going on?

At the Intelligence Branch he entered the code, but the door didn't budge. The deadbolts. He rang the bell. Troiano admitted him.

"I just saw Marines in mufti in the hall," Chuck said. "What's the skinny?"

"Ever hear of OPERATION FREQUENT WIND?"

"Sounds like a bad joke."

Troiano didn't smile. "It's the cover name of the emergency evacuation. The president hasn't ordered it, but CINCPAC, the Seventh Fleet, and the Marines are getting everything lined up. It'll come soon. Either over the objections of the Ambassador or maybe without his knowledge. I just got the word from the SPG. The *Oklahoma City* and Seventh Fleet are in the South China Sea, far enough out that they can't be seen from land. Every day Air America choppers bring the Marines ashore for planning and preparation. Every night they go back to the fleet. We have fixed-wing aircraft leaving every half hour filled with people we want to get out."

Chuck squinted. "Why are the snuffs in mufti?"

"The Ambassador insisted on it. Their presence in-country is a violation of the cease-fire agreement with the North Vietnamese. Pretend you didn't see them."

"Like we pretend we don't see the North Vietnamese ready to invade Saigon?"

"Exactly," Troiano said. "The war's over. The president said so."

"In that case I'm going to go home and get some sleep."

"Right. Pick up the incoming at the comms center on your way back to your desk."

Nothing of moment in the new mail. The battlefield was dormant.

Sparky came in from the hall, only half awake. "Go back to sleep," Chuck said. "You're not due to relieve me until 1800."

"Got to get cleaned up and make a PX run. Got the word last night that they're selling everything half-price starting today."

"The PX is still operating? What have they got that you need?"

Sparky grinned. "TEAC tape recorders, Wharfedale speakers, Minolta cameras—"

"What are you going to do with all that junk?"

Sparky searched his desk for a toothpick, found one. "Take it back to the world. They're packing our stuff out ASAP if not sooner. By Sunday for sure. I'll have enough booze to last until I'm eighty."

Chuck hesitated. "If they're packing us out, where are we supposed to clean up and eat?"

"Here. Where else?"

CHAPTER 19

It started Saturday morning. Reports swamped the comms center. Long Binh was under attack and Ba Ria had fallen. North Vietnamese shelling of Bien Hoa was low thunder that shook the floor. The final assault was under way. To get around the Ambassador's edict that no one was to be evacuated, Troiano sent most of the remaining personnel out of the country by air on trumped-up "temporary duty" missions. The Intelligence Branch, the comms center, and the tank were now manned by five people—two comms techs who'd volunteered to stay to the end, Chuck, Sparky, and Troiano. "We're just here to turn off the lights when the Ambassador gives us permission to leave," Troiano told Chuck. They adopted the eight-sixteen rule (eight hours of sleep, sixteen hours of work on rotating shifts) so that two people could man the tank at all times. Sparky made a food run, found out that the snack bar was deserted.

At midmorning, while Troiano was on watch, Chuck and Sparky, armed, drove together through the throngs of refugees to Yen Do to pack enough clothes and toiletries for three days into getaway bags and filled plastic bags with extra socks and underwear. While there, they paid Chi Nam and Oanh triple wages in U.S. dollars and gave them all the food in the house. Then they loaded two suitcases with half a dozen bars of soap and all the bar snacks that would fit.

By the time they headed back to DAO, the crowds in the streets, a mix of ragged soldiers and panicky civilians, were blocking traffic and choking the byways. Back in the Intelligence Branch, they helped Troiano shove his desk into the tank and moved the cots and suitcases into his office. They pushed the three desks they'd be working at to the center of the room and moved all the rest into rows to form barriers in case the room was penetrated.

"Give me the keys to the jeep," Troiano said. "All vehicle keys are to be handed over to the SPG guys so they can clear the parking lot for helos."

"What if we need to go somewhere?" Sparky said.

"None of us is going anywhere from now on," Troiano said, "except by chopper."

By that afternoon the eight-sixteen rule was already breaking down. Too much to do. Chuck and Sparky took turns sorting the incoming cables and passed the most urgent to Troiano, who briefed his boss, General Smith, in Smith's office on the second floor. As if by habit, Chuck and Sparky posted positions of friendly and enemy forces on the wall maps and sent hourly situation summaries to the embassy, General Smith, and Washington. They started through the file cabinets, shredding everything until one of their three shredders conked out. Piles of burn bags filled with mangled ribbons of paper all but blocked the door to the external corridor. Sparky and Chuck alternated carrying the bags to the incinerator in the corner of the parking lot, burning them, and stirring the ashes to be certain that nothing legible was left. Sparky, who'd done the night shift, was near the end of his usefulness. Troiano sent him into the "dormitory"—his office—to get some rest. By 2000 hours Troiano was getting flaky. Chuck respectfully suggested he, too, retire.

Left alone with the piles of incoming, Chuck pushed all thoughts of Tuyet away. He couldn't handle it and still keep going. He read and sorted, munched on crackers and olives. He had to stay rational until midnight, when he'd wake Sparky to relieve him. Fighting roiled just north of them, and the North Vietnamese had begun an offensive in Long An and Hau Nghia Provinces on Saigon's western flank. News reports from Phnom Penh told of public beheadings of former Cambodian government officials. The Intel Branch had been put on comms distribution for SPG traffic. The Special Planning Group, code-named ALAMO, had quietly activated the forward evacuation operations center, even though the Ambassador still hadn't approved it.

The bell at the door to the exterior corridor startled Chuck. He yanked the Beretta from the holster and went to the entrance hall. Through the peephole he saw a middle-aged American man in an oversized Hawaiian shirt of iridescent orange and gold overlaid with neon blue palm trees. Beneath it were cut-offs and bare legs ending with feet in flip-flops. The face was somewhere in Chuck's memory, but it belonged to a different context. Chuck's weary brain struggled to make the image slide into the right frame of reference. Then it kicked in. *Macintosh*. He disengaged the deadbolt and opened the door two inches. Macintosh raised his hand in an open-palm wave accompanied by a silly grin.

"Hi, Griffin. May I come in?"

Chuck looked past the colonel into the empty corridor, opened the door enough for Macintosh to sidle in, then closed it behind him and bolted it.

"You look like shit," Macintosh said. "You should be taking better care of yourself. There's a war on, you know." Macintosh lifted his hands and turned in place. "Like my outfit? It's all the rage in the islands. Ambassador won't let the advance evac personnel dress in uniform."

Chuck stammered.

Macintosh's face turned serious. "Where can we talk?"

"This way, sir." Chuck led him toward the tank. "I'll wake Colonel Troiano."

"Don't. If he's as burned out as you look, he needs his rest."

As they entered the tank, Macintosh surveyed the room. Dirty coffee cups and empty soft drink cans littered the desktops, and candy bar wrappers, potato chip bags, and used paper towels lay in random disarray across the deck. "This place has seen better days."

"My apologies, sir," Chuck said. "We're down to a skeleton crew. The only food we have is bar snacks. Haven't had time—"

Macintosh's grin returned. "I'm not in the proper uniform for a class A inspection. Got coffee?"

Chuck stumbled to the coffee maker. "Not very fresh, sir."

"Make mine black."

Chuck drew two cups.

Macintosh took the chair by Chuck's desk and lifted a fistful of shirt. "I'm here incognito. We're preparing the evacuation, and I'm the ground security officer—the guy in charge on land. The order could come any time if the president countermands the Ambassador. I sky in at night via Air America chopper from the *Hancock*—no Marine birds authorized by the Ambassador. We're doing recon. What's going on?"

"The Communists' final thrust began this morning, sir. Bien Hoa and Long Binh will fall momentarily—"

"I know the military situation. What are the friendlies doing?"

"The roads are jammed with refugees and lots of uniformed ARVN," Chuck said. "Unshaven, slovenly, spoiling for a fight to get airlifted out. I'm guessing they're deserters."

"They're getting mighty thick outside the DAO fence. How'd they get into Tan Son Nhat?"

"Military discipline is failing, sir. The gate guards may have left their posts."

Macintosh nodded. "Signs of panic?"

"I can feel it bubbling up, sir. It happened in Hue and Da Nang and on Route 7B after Pleiku was abandoned. My sense is that Saigon will make all those look like maypole dances. I hope the fence around the DAO compound will hold."

"The DAO evac team reinforced it, and my troops rigged petroleum barrels around the perimeter. They've been wired so that they can be exploded if the North Vietnamese penetrate the fence. How about the embassy?"

Chuck hesitated. "If it were up to me, Colonel, I'd post armed Marines there to hold back the mobs."

"How are the U.S. types holding up?"

"We're hangin' in. Biggest problem is exhaustion."

"No signs of panic among the Americans?"

"None that I've seen, sir, but I'm a poor source. Spending all my time here. The Colonel might want to chopper down to the embassy and take a look—"

"No can do. The Ambassador wouldn't hear of it. Besides, I have an embassy expert with me on the *Hancock*. Ike Saunders. He's been promoted, by the way."

"Ike's a major?" Chuck broke into a smile. "I'll be damned. He and I will have to celebrate after the duration. Hope he doesn't expect me to call him 'sir.'"

Macintosh turned serious. "How's Thanh doing?"

"Wounds are getting the better of him, sir."

"Still at JGS?"

"Yes, sir."

Macintosh shook his head. "That's going to make getting him out dicey."

"I've arranged a rendezvous point for him, his wife, and his child. I believe he will send them out without him. He'll stay to face the North Vietnamese alone."

Macintosh lowered his eyes. His face took on a sadness Chuck had never seen there before. "My old friend." He shook his head, blinked, and stood. "Tell Troiano I'll be by sometime tomorrow to get his take on the situation. And as for you, trooper," he gave Chuck a playful slug in the belly, "get some sleep."

Sparky woke Chuck at 0600 Sunday morning. When Chuck was fully conscious he stood before Troiano's desk and waited for the colonel, who had been working with Sparky since midnight, to look up from the stack of incoming reports. Troiano lifted his head.

"I had a brief visit last night," Chuck said. "Colonel Macintosh was in the building. He'll be by sometime today to speak with the Colonel."

Troiano squeezed his eyelids with his thumb and index finger. "Chuck, I'd appreciate it if you'd drop the Marine-speak. I won't be offended if you address me as 'you.' If Macintosh shows up while I'm asleep, wake me. Meanwhile, it's your turn to take out the burn bags."

Chuck strapped on his Beretta and carried burn bags through the outside corridor. He sidestepped abandoned furniture and empty cartons, kicked his way through tin cans and broken glass. The proud MACV building, so recently gleaming in vanilla plastic, aluminum, and shiny linoleum, was shabby. Abraded by war. *Just like me.*

In the parking lot, while the bags burned, he caught the buzz of voices. Outside the compound, held back by the reinforced chain-link fence two stories high, people swarmed, scraggly, unkempt, lupine, fifteen deep up against the interlocking metal links. Most were men in tattered uniforms, blouses open against the heat of the sun, bare chests emaciated, hollow eyes following Chuck's every move. Several called to him. One whistled. Chuck breathed through his mouth to block the stench of unwashed bodies.

A woman forced her way through the crowd. She stood back from the fence, kissed a bundle in her hands, and handed it to a man. He used both arms to heave it upward. A foot short of the top, it bounced off the fence. The man caught it when it fell and tried again. As it sailed through the air, it emitted a cry. It was a baby. Its blanket snagged on the barbed wire at the top of the fence. It swung once and unwrapped. The baby fell and splattered on the pavement. The woman shrieked and fell to her knees beside it. The mob closed around the woman and the infant.

Back in the tank, Chuck leaned on Troiano's desk. "A Vietnamese woman just tried to throw her baby over the fence into the compound. It got caught on the fence and fell to the ground."

Troiano nodded. "Same thing's happening at the embassy. They want to save their children from the Communists. The panic is spreading. Take a look at this."

An embassy cable, date time group of an hour ago:

Looting has started in Saigon. Boutiques on Tu Do Street have been vandalized, display windows smashed. Shoe stores on Le Thanh Ton, the street of shoes, report that hooligans, referred to as "cowboys," and renegade soldiers are forcing shopkeepers to give up their goods. Merchants specializing in televisions and stereos have been stripped of their wares.

Chuck handed the cable back to Troiano. "And so it begins. The end of An Nam."

Troiano's bloodshot eyes looked up at Chuck.

"An Nam, sir," he explained. "The old name for Vietnam. It means 'peace in the south.'"

After a lunch of pickles and Vienna sausages Chuck fought off drowsiness. He couldn't remember when he was supposed to take a break. He was reading a dispatch from the U.S. Defense Intelligence Agency estimating that the Republic wouldn't last another week when his elbow slipped off the desktop. He shook his head, blinked, and tried again. A deep rumble from beneath the floor snapped him awake. "Jesus," he said, jumping to his feet. "Rockets." The room was shuddering.

"Sounds close." Troiano stood.

They waited. Silence.

"If it was rockets, there'll be more," Chuck said.

The floor trembled again.

Troiano edged away from his desk. "Not too close."

"Maybe four, five miles away."

Chuck leaned on his desk, palms flat. "I'm going nonlinear. I'll go get cleaned up. Maybe that will get my brain back in gear."

He snapped up soap and a towel from Troiano's office, strapped on his Beretta, and lurched to the external corridor. In the head, he stripped and washed himself with paper towels. His stomach was going into spasms. He stumbled into a stall and emptied his bowels with a whoosh. God. What a time to get dysentery. As he sat, eyes shut, drifting off into a dream, he stretched his palm over his forehead. Fever? He reeled back to the Intelligence Branch. Troiano admitted him.

At his desk Chuck dialed Thanh's office.

"*Allô,*" Tuyet said.

"How's Thanh holding up?"

"No different. We can't get out to get to a doctor. Outside the JGS gate, mobs are trying to get in. Inside, soldiers are looting."

"You have food?"

"We brought food last night," she said. "Lan, Thu, and the servants, we are all here now. The North Vietnamese are getting close."

Chuck exhaled forcefully. "Take Thu and go to the abandoned gate by the cemetery. I'll meet you there, get you into Tan Son Nhat."

"I cannot. The renegades and looters, they take hostages."

Chuck closed his eyes and tried to make his brain work. "Okay. We'll hold off." He shook his head hard to clear the brain fog. "Look, if I can't make it to the gate when the time comes, I'll send someone else. He'll look for you and tell you he's there for me. Start thinking of ways to get to the gate. We have to do this."

He hung up. He had to get himself into working shape. In the utility closet he found the first aid kit. Inside were bandages, tape, iodine. At the bottom of the box he uncovered Kaopectate and aspirin. Dumping six pills into the palm of his hand, he tossed them into his mouth and washed them down with three mouthfuls of the liquid cement. The room swayed as he made his way back to his desk. *Not operating on all cylinders here.* He tried to force his brain to function, but he was slipping into waking dreams, symptoms he knew from combat: he'd reached the point of overload; he'd lost the capacity to react to threat. He might collapse. Or maybe he'd get caught in the onslaught and not make it to the gate to meet Tuyet. He had to have a backup plan. He'd ask Sparky to go in his place if anything happened. But Sparky was foundering with exhaustion, too. He looked across at Troiano.

"Sir?"

Troiano looked up.

"A request for the Colonel, sir. If I become incapacitated or get sidetracked, will the Colonel ensure that two people are evacuated?"

"The woman you've been telephoning? Who is she?"

"Colonel Thanh's wife. Thanh may choose to stay and face the North Vietnamese, but his wife and son must escape."

Troiano nodded. "They're on the approved evacuation list along with Thanh. All they have to do is get inside the base."

"That's the problem, sir. They're in the JGS compound, waiting for the renegades to calm down so they can make a break."

"The streets are mobbed, Chuck."

"The plan is for them to come over the fence at the old gate between JGS and Tan Son Nhat. It's rusted shut, but you can climb over it."

"I don't know where that is."

"Does the Colonel know the abandoned cemetery, just off the main road by the entrance, maybe half a mile from here? The fence there is all overgrown. The vegetation hides the old gate. If anything happens and I can't get there to meet her and her son when the time comes, will the Colonel go in my place? Get them onto the base and evacuated?"

Troiano studied him. "I'll do my best."

"Forgive me, sir, but that's not good enough. They'll be prime captives for the North Vietnamese. She's a member of the royal family, married to one of the staunchest foes of the North. Torture and death for them is a certainty if they don't escape. I need the Colonel to promise as an officer that he'll save them."

Troiano took a deep breath. "You have my promise."

Chuck held out his hand. "Shake on it, sir?"

They shook hands.

They woke Chuck at midnight. Groggy, he put on his holster with the Beretta and made his way to the head. The wastepaper cans were overflowing, and one mirror was cracked. He pissed, washed his hands, and reached for paper towels. The dispenser was empty. Stepping through heaps of used towels and toilet paper rolls, he went to a stall. No toilet paper. Down the corridor was the latrine supply closet. Its door had been broken open. Chuck took as many rolls of toilet paper and packages of towels as he could carry. At the Intelligence Branch entrance he kicked the door.

The peephole flickered, and Sparky, pistol in hand, opened the door. "You've lost your childhood belief in doorbells?"

"Hands full. Here. Stack them by the door. Each time you go to the head, stop by the supply closet and grab some more."

"Chuck, we're not opening a latrine supply shop."

"Just do it, Sparky. We don't know how long we'll be here."

Irrational? Maybe. But better than being forced to use teletype paper to wipe his ass. He tossed down another handful of aspirin and breakfasted on cocktail onions and anchovies washed down by Canadian Club Margarita mix. Before Sparky took a rest break, Chuck went by the supply closet and copped another load of towels and toilet paper and settled down to read the latest disaster reports.

Once Sparky was asleep, Chuck collected the stack of new incoming dispatches from the comms center. They now got just a single copy of each to cut down on the amount of paper they had to destroy. He flipped through the pile, marking each page with his initials—when all three men had initialed, the paper was shredded—and put aside items of immediate importance for the colonel to look at first. Cu Chi had fallen and Go Vap, a suburb of Saigon where Chi Nam's family lived, was under siege. Chuck yawned and rolled paper into the typewriter to draft the hourly report.

Troiano came in from the room that used to be his office looking ghostly. "I'm off to the head."

"Recommend you take toilet paper and paper towels with you, sir."

Troiano grinned. "You called me 'you.'"

When the colonel was back, he read the take at the desk opposite Chuck and gulped down olives and mixed cocktail nuts. The building shuddered. They looked at each other.

"Rockets," Troiano said. "Close."

"Could be Go Vap."

They went back to their reading.

Before noon the embassy reported that Duong Van Minh, a neutralist, had assumed the presidency of the Republic and had appealed to the North Vietnamese to negotiate. No response from the North Vietnamese. An AP dispatch datelined Saint-Tropez reported welcoming ceremonies held by Vietnamese expatriates to honor the arrival of General Tran van Tri, formerly the commander of II Corps in South Vietnam.

Chuck was too tired to care. His stomach cramps and diarrhea were constant, and he was running a fever. He was eating aspirin like candy. His stomach was acid personified. After a head run he left the colonel and Sparky shredding what he hoped was the last of the classified files and collapsed onto a cot.

They woke him before sunset in time to do a quick recon of the parking lot. Dopey, he carried toilet paper with him, and on the way stopped at the head to empty his guts. All liquid. He cursed, scrubbed himself clean, and went outside into the late afternoon sun. As he scanned the thickening crowd outside the fence, his mind started to function. His eyes cleared. He felt god-awful, but the horizon was level and stayed in place. He headed inside. He stopped at the latrine again, this time to piss.

While he stood at the urinal, the wall lurched toward him, as if to swat him down, and then snapped back into place. The floor jumped with a deafening crack. A truck must have hit the outside wall and damn near knocked it down. The driver must have been drunk. Enraged, he zipped his pants and made for the side door to give the driver holy hell. He unlocked the door and stepped out into the rays of the dying sun onto the concrete between the west side of the building and the chain-link fence. No trucks, not even any cars. The area had been barricaded with sandbags so that no vehicles could crash through. He looked both ways. Sandbags to the end of the building in both directions. What was the source of the concussion?

His ears picked up the whine of turbojets. He shaded his eyes and scanned across the road to the military airport. The glare of the sun low in the sky half-blinded him, but he was able to see smoke rising from the runway. To the northwest, above the sun, five aircraft circled. He squinted. A-37 Dragonflies. Why were they circling? One of the planes, flashing in the sun, released a bomb. It fell toward the runway, its target obscured by palm trees. The earth jerked. His ears rang and he fell to his knees. The planes circled again, getting ready for another bombing run. He bolted into the building and down the corridor. At the Intelligence Branch door he banged and rang the bell. When Sparky opened it a crack, Chuck forced his way in. "They're bombing the runway."

Sparky returned his pistol to his holster. "Shook a light fixture loose in here."

Chuck scudded past the door to Troiano's office, through the hall, and into the tank. The coffee maker was on its side. Thin brown liquid lay in puddles beside it, streaming over edges of the table and dripping to the deck. Paper, pens, coffee mugs were sprinkled across the room. His desk chair lay on its side.

Troiano, the telephone receiver to his ear, looked up. "He just came in." He leaned toward Chuck. "You okay?"

"Somebody's bombing the airfield, sir. Five A-37s. Looked like they were hitting the middle of the runway."

The rattle of antiaircraft fire was getting louder.

"Chuck Griffin was out there when it happened," Troiano said into the phone. "Says it's five A-37s. Could be the North Vietnamese using aircraft captured in Da Nang. Yes, sir. As soon as I hear." He hung up. "Check the comms center, see if anything's in."

Sparky strode away. Chuck picked up the phone and dialed Thanh's office. Tuyet answered.

"Where is the attack?" she asked.

"On the runway. What's happening there?"

"Soldiers fire big guns into the air," she said. "Little guns, too."

"I can hear it. How's Thanh?"

"He grows sicker. Sometimes he talks, does not make sense, you know? He asked me to help him put on the robe Colonel Mac gave him, the one from Japan. He tries to sit on the floor, legs tucked under him, but the pain is too much."

"Thu must be frightened."

She sighed. "He cried when the explosions started. Lan tries to comfort him."

"Take Thu and meet me at the gate."

"I cannot. The soldiers, they are outside our courtyard walls shooting."

"Call me as soon as you think you can make it." He hung up.

Sparky had emptied a package of paper towels onto the table next to the dented coffee maker and was mopping. "We're going to have to start carrying our trash out along with the classified waste. Not much bare floor left."

Chuck helped clean up. Adrenaline flooded his veins. *This is it. The end.*

Troiano came from the comms center. "The A-37s were from Da Nang. Best guess is that the pilots are Republic of Vietnam defectors."

"And the small arms fire?" Sparky asked.

"Some of it's friendlies getting off their jollies, but we're receiving enemy fire, too. Probing attacks. Up to the west, far side of the runway."

"Jesus," Sparky said. "They're that close?"

Troiano's eyebrows went up. "You're surprised?"

No one slept that night. The moment a new scrap of information arrived in the comms center, the three of them read it and shredded it. They sent out the last of their hourly summaries, stating that they would resume when conditions permitted. By 0400 on 29 April the trickle of incoming reports from the field had dried up.

"Bien Hoa and Long Binh must be in North Vietnamese hands," Troiano said, "but there ain't nobody out there to tell us about it."

"How're we going to know what's happening, sir?" Chuck asked.

"The Marines and ALAMO will keep us up-to-date on their operations. Other than that, we'll have to depend on Liberation News Agency, cables from the embassy, and out-of-country communications intercept. That's all we have left."

Sparky was picking up cans, jars, and bags of food from the deck and restoring them to an unused desk in the corner. "Anybody want to share a jar of marmalade? Top came off."

"We could do our own visual reconnaissance, sir," Chuck said to Troiano.

"There's pretzels," Sparky said. "They go good with mustard." He peered at a jar. "Pickle relish, cocktail sauce. Let's see . . . we'll be out of coffee in another day. Maybe we should start rationing."

"With your permission, sir," Chuck said to Troiano, "I'll go out to the parking lot and take a look around."

"Do it," Troiano said. "And I'll settle your scuzzy partner in for a little rest."

Chuck checked the Beretta, loaded the M16, slung it over his shoulder. "I'll take the walkie-talkie."

"The freq was reset. Guys came in from ops while you were asleep. We're now part of the DAO-wide net. We're Tampa and ALAMO is Des Moines."

Troiano followed Chuck to the outer door and bolted it behind him. In the dirty corridor, Chuck stopped and listened. Silence, then a spatter of small arms fire, far away. He moved toward the northern entrance. As he turned the corner, three Marines in full combat gear thudded toward him. His heart leaped. Macintosh's troops had come out in the open. Their faces beneath the helmets were unlined, child-like, serious.

"Sir," one of them mumbled as they passed.

He nodded and kept going. Their boots clumped away from him. *The Marines have landed.* He wished he were still one of them. Out the door into the parking lot. The air smelled of dust and smoke. Utter darkness. The security lights had been doused. If the building were lit with hundreds of floodlights it would be a target flirting with the attacker. For the first time, he was glad he worked in a windowless office. Above him a few blurry stars glowed uncertainly. To the west, over the runway, a rusty glow—fires were still burning. Aircraft must have been hit. An occasional burst of automatic weapons fire. No other sounds. Dark shapes huddled outside the fence, silhouetted against the orange glimmer.

As he closed on the north end of the compound he heard muffled voices, many of them. The Vietnamese chatter was nasal, almost wheedling, but beneath it was a deeper, more solid sound. American males speaking. At closer range he could distinguish the expected hover of Vietnamese outside the closed vehicle gate and the tall Americans inside.

The tallest swung toward him. "Halt! Who goes there?"

"Chuck Griffin, DAO Intel," Chuck said in a loud voice.

"Advance and be recognized."

As Chuck approached, the Marine shined a flashlight in his face.

"How many of you on guard?" Chuck asked.

"Two on each gate, sir," the voice snapped back.

"You part of the force from the fleet?"

"Yes, sir."

"As you were."

Chuck moved away into the darkness, threading his way through the vehicles parked crazily in the open space around the building. At the pedestrian gate on the east side of the complex another Marine challenged him. He identified himself.

"Curfew in effect, sir," the guard said. "No nonoperational personnel permitted in the zone."

Chuck entered the building and walked the full length, exiting again on the western side, as he had earlier when the bombing started, and moved toward the west pedestrian gate. Again he was challenged.

This time he heard a rifle cock. He froze, spoke loudly to identify himself. The Marine told him to return to the building.

Troiano, pistol drawn, let him in. Chuck told him about the scene outside.

"Okay, we know where the enemy is," Troiano said. "We can see him. We can hear him. We could probably smell him if we could get the friendlies out of the way. So—" He waved at the wall boards. "These come down."

He'd already started. The I Corps maps at the end of the room were gone. Shreds of acetate and the remnants of maps covered the floor.

"Use the box cutter," Troiano said, "and feed any paper larger than your hand into the shredder. You work on III and IV Corps while I finish II Corps. When the sliding panels are stripped, we sweep everything into the corner."

Chuck let his eyes wander around the bay. Empty now. Hollow. The wall Troiano had been working on reminded him of peeling wallpaper in a ghetto row house. The deck was coffee stained, cluttered with jar lids, corn chip bags, and spent felt-tip markers. Waste baskets overflowed. *Sic transit gloria mundi.* And so, too, passes the glory of Chuck. And of Ben.

Operation
Frequent Wind

29 APRIL 1975

CHAPTER 20

The blast toppled Chuck to the deck. Troiano, on his hands and knees, was yelling, but Chuck couldn't make out the words. The room shifted again. The coffeemaker lifted into the air, bounced, tumbled to the floor. The telephone landed beside it. The room lurched from a third concussion. A hanging light fixture on the ceiling jumped and swung, one of its posts broken. Dust from the ceiling powdered Chuck's neck. He and Troiano both crawled under desks.

Sparky lunged in from the hall. Another blast knocked his feet out from under him. As he hit the deck, the room jumped again. He snaked under a desk.

All quiet. Chuck could hear the other two breathing.

"Anybody hurt?" Troiano said.

"Not that I can tell, sir," Sparky said.

"Rockets," Chuck said. "Hit inside the compound, maybe even the building."

The slamming erupted again. Chuck's typewriter rose and smashed back onto the desktop. Loose paper floated like snow.

Minutes passed. No more explosions. They eased out into the open and stood. Disarray had spread across the room. Troiano sent Sparky out to reconnoiter. While he was gone, Chuck retrieved a fresh crop of cables from the comms center. The first ALAMO report on the attack said that a rocket had impacted under the wing of a taxiing C-130 and destroyed it. Two others took off immediately. Further evac by fixed-wing aircraft was postponed indefinitely. From now on, they'd sky out by zoomie or not at all. Chuck turned to shred the report, but his shredder was on its side. He righted it and fed the paper into it. No response. He moved to Troiano's shredder. It still worked.

Sparky was back. "A rocket hit the gym. Another set the general's quarters on fire. Another one hit near the north gate. Two Marines killed."

"Christ," Chuck breathed. "I just talked to those guys."

Troiano scanned the chaos around them. "Let's police up the area. We can't work in this mess."

Why bother? Military discipline and orderliness. Right. The skipper was going nonlinear. While Troiano and Sparky swept, Chuck surveyed the scattered pieces of the coffeemaker. Tidiness might not matter, but caffeine did. He reassembled the appliance and plugged it in. It worked. He cleaned the wet grounds from the desk and floor, mopped up the spilt coffee, and went to the head for water to make a fresh brew, but this time he positioned the coffeemaker on the floor lodged between two desks.

The room had regained some semblance of order when the bombardment started again. They hunkered under desks and watched the room toss and tilt into anarchy that rearranged itself with each new detonation. During lulls they checked to be sure the comms guys were all right. They learned from incoming dispatches that the North Vietnamese had seized a bridge in Cholon, a couple of miles to the south. After an hour of intermittent explosions they left their haven under the desks and resumed something like normal operations, hampered by the bouncing floor and flying paper. New bulletins told them that Phu Lam as well as Tan Son Nhat was being shelled, and rockets were falling randomly in Saigon. Despite the shelling, Air America helicopters were lifting off from the DAO compound carrying evacuees to the Seventh Fleet. Some three thousand people, mostly Vietnamese, had assembled by the gym and pool awaiting evacuation. South Vietnamese military personnel demanding evacuation had occupied the Air America compound across the road.

By 0800 hours the shelling had ceased. The three of them looked at one another.

"You suppose they're out of rockets?" Sparky said.

Troiano grunted. "Probably just moving in for more accurate targeting."

"Based on everything we know," Chuck said, "they're already close enough for pinpoint accuracy. They could rain rockets on us and the embassy. Besides, by now they've moved their arty to within a few clicks of us. They could blow us off the map."

"They don't want to," Troiano said. "They've already beaten us. Now all they have to do is harass us until we give up and go home."

"But, sir," Sparky said, "with nearly all reporting from the friendlies gone, we don't know where they are or what they're doing."

Chuck picked up his M16. "With the Colonel's permission, I'll take a run outside and see what's going on."

"Do it."

Chuck exited the building to the north. The crater where the north pedestrian gate had stood was blocked with barbed wire. The mob of stragglers outside the fence had dispersed, probably because of the rockets, but now they were gathering again. Chuck turned toward the parking lot and stopped dead. ALAMO guys, including several Chuck knew, were cramming cars into the eastern side of the building by driving them into one another so that they formed a compacted mass. As Chuck watched, the drivers turned their attention to the half dozen cars still in the parking lot, all of them large sedans except for Chuck's jeep. These they used as ramming devices, crushing the heap of cars more tightly together. Now they turned the mangled sedans on the tennis courts. Again and again they backed their vehicles almost to the compound fence and burned rubber to smash into the poles holding the fence around the courts until they tore out of the pavement. Next they used the cars as battering rams, flattening the nets and court fencing against the building. They left their cars idling while they gathered mangled wire, misshapen chunks of metal, and lumps of torn pavement and added them to the packed debris next to the wall. Lastly, they ground the remaining vehicles into the jumble of mashed automobiles. The area between the perimeter fence and the wall of the building was now clear. *Of course.* The small Air America UH-1 helicopters had been able to get into and out of the parking lot one at a time without hitting cars or the tennis courts, but the much larger Marine CH-53s, the birds to be used for the evac, needed more unobstructed space.

The *whup-whup-whup* of eggbeaters echoed across the compound. Air America slicks came sailing in from the east and descended gingerly into the parking lot. A convoy of buses drew up outside the eastern pedestrian gate. Marine guards kept the thugs at bay while the certified passengers streamed into the compound and toward the waiting birds. Chuck dashed back inside the building. In the corridor he nearly collided with a stepladder. The man on top of it was running cable along the ceiling. Another ladder was at the far end of the building. Chuck hurried back to the Intelligence Branch.

"Air America zoomies are in the compound."

Troiano nodded. "They've been at it for hours. They're getting as many out as they can on the little Hueys. When FREQUENT WIND Phase IV—evac by military chopper—is declared, Marine CH-53s will come in from the fleet and ferry people out."

"Big mothers," Sparky said. "Can carry more than fifty gunjies."

"ALAMO guys have cleared the parking lot," Chuck said, "and taken down the tennis courts. Plenty of room for the CH-53s. What's the holdup on Phase IV?"

"I understand the Ambassador is still hoping for negotiations."

Sparky grunted. "Jesus H. Christ. That asshole is going to get us all killed."

Chuck set the safety on the M16 and laid it on his desk. "What're the chances we could get a slick into JGS?"

"Zero to none. A zoomie going in there would be mobbed before it set down."

Sparky took another load of burn bags to the incinerator. He was back in fifteen minutes. "What's with the wiring? I saw guys running cable in the corridors."

"When we leave, we destroy the building," Troiano said. "We'll set a delayed fuse. Last man out pulls the pin and runs like hell." He dropped into a chair. "Look, guys, we don't know how long it'll be before they get us out of here, and we can't keep going on adrenaline alone. So we'll take two-hour breaks. One sleeps while two keep watch. Chuck, you're first. Eat something and go rest."

"May I make a call first, sir?"

"Make it fast."

Chuck phoned Thanh's office. No answer. He tried again. He let the phone ring fifteen times. Nothing.

"Sparky, will you keep calling for me? Try every fifteen minutes. Talk to Tuyet. Find out if she and Thu can make it to the old gate. If she's going to try, wake me."

Against his will, Chuck stretched out on a cot in Troiano's office. He was asleep instantly. In his dreams, searing visions of Ben burning to death collided with scenes of Tuyet and Thu bayoneted by North Vietnamese.

—613613—

The sound of fixed-wing aircraft flat-hatting over the building woke him. He sat up and looked at his watch: 1230 hours. He tumbled into the tank.

Sparky looked up. "I got through to the lady. Nothing's changed. I didn't wake you because there was nothing to tell you. She said not to telephone. She'll call you as soon as she can get through. Meanwhile, they're not answering the phone."

Chuck slumped at his desk.

"You hear the planes?" Sparky said with a smile. "FREQUENT WIND Phase IV has been declared. President or somebody countermanded the Ambassador. That's the air cap. All services participating."

"Sir," Chuck said to Troiano, "I don't know who's supposed to rest next, but I respectfully suggest it be you."

Troiano stood. "Two hours. Wake me at 1430."

Armed, Chuck went to the head. The dysentery was back with a vengeance. He was sweating. Was he feverish? Could be the pre-monsoon heat. He washed thoroughly but didn't bother to shave.

Back in the tank, he changed clothes and took a handful of aspirin and a swig of Kaopectate. Sparky took out the last of the burn bags. The file cabinets were finally empty. From now on it would be only what they received from the comms center, and that operation was due to shut down as soon as the Marine evac helicopters arrived.

Sparky filled Chuck in on the new procedures Troiano had ordered. Only command messages and reports of unexpected developments were to be kept for the colonel. Everything else was to be destroyed as soon as Sparky and Chuck had both seen it. Together they read of the Republic's dying gasps as Hau Nghia fell, Tan Uyen was overrun, and the enemy main force moved south of Long Binh toward Saigon. They shredded the reports.

At 1430 they woke Troiano and brought him up-to-date. A little after 1500 Chuck sealed the burn bag with everything shredded up to that point and carried it to the parking lot to be burned. As he was stirring the ashes, two slicks landed on what had once been the tennis courts. He headed back into the building and glanced at the choppers, then stopped. These weren't Air America craft. These birds bore Marine Corps markings. The lead whirlies of the Marine evacuation force had arrived.

By the time he got back to the tank, Troiano had already given orders to the communicators to close up shop and destroy the communications and crypto gear. Chuck, Sparky, and Troiano started close-down procedures. They cleared their desks of all papers and started through the drawers.

Chuck ransacked his desk. All the drawers save one were empty. In the bottom left was the Ben file. Ben. Tears clouded Chuck's vision. Ben killed for nothing. And the war he fought in was now lost. Shame? Ben's couldn't have been any worse than Chuck's at this moment. He put the contents into a manila envelope, sealed it, and placed it on the desktop to be stowed in his getaway bag.

He drummed his fingers on the telephone. Tuyet had told him not to call. He lifted the receiver and dialed Thanh's number. It rang twenty times. He hung up.

Troiano was giving the filing cabinets a last check, opening and slamming the drawers. "We'll wait here until we're called to the staging area. Sparky, go take a look outside. See if the CH-53s are in yet."

Sparky took his rifle and left. Troiano unplugged the coffee maker. "Still some hot java." He drew two mugs, passed one to Chuck. "Down as much as you can. You'll need to be clearheaded for the evac."

But Chuck wasn't clearheaded. He was sliding into a dream state. He yearned to lie down. His intestines were complaining, and his neck ached. He gave his head a fast shake and got to his feet. "Sir, I can't leave without Tuyet and Thu."

"Chuck, you'll go when you're ordered out."

"Colonel, I respectfully request that you do all you can to delay my departure until I can get them out." He could hear the rasp in his own voice. "I . . . won't leave without them, sir."

The doorbell rang. Troiano drew his pistol and left the room. A moment later he and Sparky trudged in.

"They're landing and taking off like clockwork," Sparky said happily. "Fifty-five people at a shot. The ALAMO guy told me they're on a ninety-minute turn-around between here and the Seventh Fleet. He said we have tankers, radio-relay aircraft, and electronic countermeasure planes all over the place."

"How soon will they be taking us?" Chuck said.

"Damned if I know. They're bringing busloads of people in, some from the gym-pool area, some from outside the base. It's going to take awhile."

They waited. The three of them alternated doing recon runs to the parking lot. When his turn came, Chuck verified that the crowd was reassembling outside the fence. Clouds were gathering. The monsoon rains were finally here. *Jesus.* The last thing he needed was for the evacuation site to be socked in, preventing helicopter flights. He checked his watch. Almost 1800. Almost sunset. The moment he was back in the door, he asked if Tuyet had called. Troiano and Sparky shook their heads.

They sat in silence. The phone didn't ring.

Chuck was sinking again. He forced himself to his feet and paced. He had to keep his mind clear. He knelt at the cold coffeemaker, put his cup under the spout, and pressed the handle. The floor quaked. Coffeemaker, cup, rifle, and walkie-talkie flew through the air. Chuck landed on the deck with a thud, Troiano and Sparky beside him. Shifting light from the swinging fixture kicked his nausea up a notch.

"That wasn't no rockets," Sparky whispered.

"Arty," Troiano said. "Under the desks. Quick."

Chuck crawled on hands and knees. The room shifted again. Knocked flat, he shimmied under the desk.

"Not hitting the building," Troiano said, "but not a mile away. Chuck, as soon as there's a letup, go find out how soon they're going to get us out of here."

After three minutes passed without a blast, Chuck was on his feet, M16 in hand. Out the door, down the corridor at a dead run, out the door into the parking lot. Warm rain beat his face. In the twilight a CH-53 lifted off before him and another swiftly descended in its place. Two others were hurriedly loading passengers. Another took to the air and was replaced. The parking lot jumped, and a flash came at him from the northwest. They were shelling the airfield. He ran to a Marine in flight gear holding a clipboard.

"How much longer?"

"We'll be out by 2000 if the weather don't fuck us up and the shelling don't get no closer."

Chuck sprinted back into the building. Halfway down the corridor, a blast sent him sprawling, but he was on his feet in seconds.

"We'll be in the air by 2000 unless fubar sets in," he told Troiano.

"Now 1830. Be prepared to go the instant we get the call."

The walkie-talkie crackled. "Tampa, this is Des Moines. Over."

Troiano snatched the radio. "Tampa here, over."

"We got renegades in the building, Tampa. South Vietnamese air force officers. The Marines have taken over the ops spaces. We're moving everybody else to the Logistics Branch. All personnel from that office are already evacuated, so we have plenty of room. Bring your weapons and get down there on the double. Lock the door when you leave so they can't hole up in your area. Over."

"Roger, Des Moines. Over and out."

The floor shook. Sparky took his getaway bag, and Troiano picked up his suitcase and the last remaining burn bag. Both checked their weapons.

"Sparky," Troiano said, "tell the comms center guys to meet us in the hallway. We're moving out."

"Sir," Chuck shouted, "I need to make one more call before we pull out."

Troiano grimaced at his watch.

Chuck dialed Thanh's number. Three rings, four.

"*Allô.*" Tuyet's voice.

"You answered—"

"I guessed it was you."

"The evacuation is getting close to the end," Chuck said. "*You must come now.*"

"Too dangerous. Lots of soldiers outside. They are shooting."

Chuck fought to control his shaking. "All right. Do this. Dress in a pair of Thanh's utilities. Cut off your hair and wear a cap. Strip the insignias off just in case. Bring Thu and meet me at the old gate."

"They will see us."

"Meet me at 1900. That's almost thirty minutes from now. By then it will be completely dark. In the rain no one will see you."

"Yes, okay. I will be there." She sounded distant. "Chuck, we never know what will happen. You always remember that I love you. Good-bye."

He fell back in his chair with a sigh. "She'll be there at 1900."

"Meanwhile," Troiano said, "we've got to clear out of here. Get your stuff."

The three of them moved toward the corridor exit. The door to the comms center opened and the two communicators, overnight bags in hand, followed them.

Chuck stopped short. "Goddammit." He'd left the envelope with the Ben file. "Go on, I forgot something. Take the M16. You might need it."

Troiano, Sparky, and the comms guys filed out the door. Chuck closed and bolted it, ran back to his desk, and jammed the envelope into his getaway bag. The doorbell rang. Sparky must have forgotten something, probably his toothpicks. Chuck waited to hear the apologetic "Oops." He went to the door and from habit drew his Beretta. He looked through the peephole. No one. The coast was clear. What had caused the bell to ring? He opened the door a crack and looked out. Nothing visible.

The door flew open and bashed him hard. Three Vietnamese men in Republic of Vietnam Air Force officer's uniforms burst through the door. One kneed him in the groin. Another clubbed the back of the head with a pistol grip. He staggered backward and fell. They stood over him. Two pistols and a carbine were pointed at his face.

"You up," the biggest one said.

As Chuck got to his feet, the smallest of them picked up his Beretta and slid it into his belt.

"Telephone," the big one said.

Chuck limped to the tank. Blood drizzled down his neck. They followed.

The big one pointed to the telephone on his desk. "You call."

"Who?" Chuck said.

"You call. We want leave here. You get helicopter. Or not, we shoot you."

"I don't have any helicopters," Chuck said.

"You call!" He waved his pistol at the telephone.

Chuck picked up the receiver. The Marines. He dialed the number for the Operations Division.

"Lance Corporal Larson, sir."

"This is Chuck Griffin. I'm in the Intelligence Branch office. Three South Vietnamese air force officers are here with me. Do you copy?"

"Run that past me again?"

"The three VNAF officers here with me want to be evacuated. They say they're going to shoot me if they don't get their way."

Chuck could almost feel the news sinking in.

"Do they have weapons trained on you now?" the voice on the other end said.

"Yes."

"What the fuck . . . tell them . . . tell them I will have to call you back after I inform my superiors of their request. You got that?"

Chuck clamped his teeth. This was no time to hew to chain-of-command protocol. "Yes."

"You think that will hold them for a minute?"

"Maybe," Chuck said.

"Any other ideas?"

"No."

Chuck hung up. "The man who answered will inform his superior of your request and call back immediately. Do you understand?"

The one in charge spoke in a low voice to the others. All three pulled up chairs. Chuck listened to the breathing, his own and theirs. When the phone rang, he jumped.

"Yes?"

"I reached Colonel Macintosh. He's on his way in from the staging area by the gym. As soon as he gets here, he'll call you. You understand?"

"Yes."

"Everything all right so far?"

"No, it's very fucked up, but I'm still alive."

Chuck hung up. "The American Marine colonel named Macintosh is en route to the operations branch. He will telephone me with instructions."

The officer nodded impatiently. He conversed with the others in sour tones. The smallest one seemed to be disagreeing. He nodded toward Chuck, waved his carbine at him. The big one snapped at him. They all turned toward Chuck and sat in silence.

Sweat slithered down Chuck's spine. The blood on the back of his head was coagulating. When he raised his wrist to check his watch, all three gun barrels followed his motion. Nearly 1900. Why was it taking Macintosh so long to get in from the gym? Chuck ached to rub the sweat from his eyes but didn't dare. The moments ticked more slowly. Tuyet and Thu would be waiting.

The phone rang.

"Griffin," Macintosh said, "what's going on?"

Chuck told him.

"Where precisely are you in the room?"

"Just about dead center."

"Could we break into the room and surprise them?"

Chuck calculated. The door wasn't bolted, but the rescue squad would have to come through the entry hall and past the comms center and Troiano's office before they got to the tank. "I doubt it, sir."

"Can they hear what you're saying?"

"Yes, sir."

"Uh-huh." Macintosh paused. "Hang up. Tell them I will not negotiate with them while they are armed. If they will give you their weapons and come out into the corridor with their hands up, I'll personally talk to them and see what we can work out. Get their answer, then call me back."

Chuck swallowed. "Yes, sir." He hung up. Speaking as distinctly as he could, he relayed Macintosh's message.

The leader translated. Their faces darkened. They argued among themselves in undertones, their teeth glinting in the half-light.

The leader turned to Chuck. "No. You send helicopter or we shoot you."

Chuck dialed. "The officers turn down your offer, sir. They get a zoomie or I'm dead."

"Tell them," Macintosh snarled, "that they have no choice. They must do what I say or I'll send the U.S. Marines in there with orders to shoot to kill." He paused. "What'll they do when you tell them that? You think they might really shoot you?"

"I think that's possible, sir."

"I don't. They know they wouldn't have a chance of getting out of there alive if they killed you. Tell them what I said. I'll hold the line."

Chuck held the receiver at his side and opened his mouth to speak. The leader leaped from his chair, snagged the receiver, and put it back in the cradle. The phone rang again.

"What happened, Griffin?"

"They don't wish to talk with the phone line open, sir."

"God *damn!* Hang up, talk to them, and call me back. If I don't hear from you in three minutes, I'll call. If you don't answer personally, I'll instantly fill that room with Marines, guns blazing. You tell them that."

Chuck hung up and repeated Macintosh's words slowly and clearly. "Do you understand?"

They held a heated discussion among themselves in whispers. Chuck's sweat seeped from his armpits. His neck itched where the blood had dried. He risked a look at his watch: 1910. *Tuyet . . .*

The phone rang.

"You okay, Griffin?"

"So far, sir. The officers are discussing what you said."

"They now have two minutes."

The three officers wrangled on. Surely more than two minutes had passed. Chuck glanced down the hall toward the entrance and cocked his ears. How soon would the corridor door fly open to a barrage of firing M16s? He gauged how long it would take him to hit the deck.

"Okay you," the big officer said. "We do." He handed Chuck his pistol. Chuck stripped it of its ammunition and set it on his desk behind him. He took the second officer's pistol and emptied it. The man with the carbine surrendered it and returned Chuck's Beretta. Chuck holstered the Beretta and trained the carbine on the three officers. He telephoned Macintosh, told him the outcome, and said that they would come to the corridor door in sixty seconds. Enunciating carefully, he asked the colonel to meet him there with armed Marines, weapons aimed and ready to fire. If Chuck and the officers did not appear at the doorway in two minutes, the Marines were to smash down the door and charge in with orders to kill all in sight. Macintosh agreed. "Nice job, Griffin."

"Thank you, sir."

Chuck hung up and waved the carbine at the officers. They raised their hands, palms facing him. "To the door," he said. "*Now.*"

The little one snarled, but the big one pushed him toward the door. The three moved past Troiano's office and the door to the comms center. Chuck followed. At the exit to the corridor they stopped, hands still in the air, and turned to Chuck.

"Open the door *slowly*," Chuck said.

The middle-sized one pulled the door open. The corridor was filled with Marines in full combat gear, M16s trained on the entrance. The little one dove for cover.

"On your feet, asshole," Chuck screamed. The Marines tensed. The big officer hoisted the little guy to his feet. The three trundled into the hall. Six Marines immediately frisked them for weapons. Macintosh, pistol in hand, shoved the officers, one at a time, down the corridor.

Chuck looked at his watch. Almost 1920. He'd missed the rendezvous with Tuyet. Troiano had promised to meet her if Chuck couldn't. The ground jarred. The bombardment had begun again. He shouldered his getaway bag and the carbine, ran to the Logistics Branch, and rang the bell. A Marine opened the door.

"Colonel Troiano?" Chuck said.

"They've all moved to the LZ in the parking lot."

Chuck raced through the corridors and out of the building. Rain splashed across his face. Smoke clogged the air. The low cloud cover flickered orange from fires still burning to the west, but the floodlights in the compound blazed away as if there were no shelling. Three orderly groups of people were lined up for embarkation. One CH-53 was rising into the air. A second was loading. Chuck rushed to the first line of passengers already climbing into the helicopter, looked from face to face. No Troiano. On to the second line, waiting to board.

Halfway through the line he yelled, "Colonel Troiano here?"

A man in the line pointed toward the airborne chopper receding into the dark. "Up there."

Chuck jerked. "He already booked on out? Did he have anyone with him?"

The pavement shook.

"He went out before he was scheduled," the man said, "because he had some Vietnamese with him."

Chuck took him by the shoulders. "Who?"

"A woman in Marine utilities way too big for her. Her hair was cut real short. And a little kid. Tiny little thing. Wrapped in an army blanket—"

Chuck fell to his knees. "They made it." He was bawling like a little kid.

A hand grasped his shoulder. Macintosh. "Get your ass on a chopper, Griffin. *Now.*"

Chuck wiped the tears from his eyes and weaved his way to the last group being formed into a line by two Marines.

"You'll have to surrender the carbine, sir," one said.

Chuck handed it to him.

"Name, sir?"

Chuck tried to speak. He had no voice. He tried again. The words came out as a croak. "Charles Griffin."

The Marine checked his clipboard. "You were supposed to go out with the group several ahead of this one."

"I was stuck in a room with South Vietnamese officers."

The Marine smiled. "Oh, you're that guy. Good work, sir."

Chuck was sagging. When the earth shook, he reeled. Dizziness was drowning him. He tilted back his head and sucked in the moist air. It tasted of dust, ashes, and hot pavement. He let the rain wash over him. He remembered Thanh sitting in the rain. *The Heaven weeps. An Nam no more. An Nam was. You listen to her weep now.* Chuck prayed. *May the Mother Goddess watch over Thanh.*

Hands helped him climb on board. He settled near a window, and the bird lifted him into the air over the stricken city dotted by fires.

Lights burned here and there as if the residents had forgotten they were under siege. Flashes from weapons made the face of the earth sparkle in the darkness, but the roar of the helicopter drowned their sound. Tracers rose toward him. They were shooting at him, but his tilted consciousness went on marveling at the glittering lights, like those little lights Ben so loved as a child. Ben. *Oh, Jesus.* The city retreated into nothingness behind him. His heart contracted. Panic rose in his belly, the mindless terror of something urgent overlooked, left behind, forgotten. Nausea flooded him.

CHAPTER 21

He tried to sit forward and discovered that he was strapped in. The deafening roar of rotor engines filled his ears. Where was he? Total darkness. No, a dashboard was gleaming maybe ten feet from him. The dials and gauges were a jumble of meaningless green lights, numbers, lines, spaces. He and a lot of other people were flying. The pressure in his head made him wonder if they were upside down. How could the pilot tell? He couldn't get his brain to cooperate. He shook his head, forced his eyes open, slapped himself to keep awake. Memory clicked in a piece at a time. He was en route to the Seventh Fleet in the South China Sea. He hadn't been airborne long. Had he blacked out?

Now they were descending toward moving lights, thousands of them, everywhere. The CH-53 paused, resumed its downward motion. Bigger lights came up around them. The helicopter rested gently on the deck, its pitch and yaw replaced by the solidity of the ship. The engines stopped. Silence crashed into his ears. The doors opened. Chuck loosened the straps, tried to stand, nearly tipped over. Hands helped him restore his balance. As he stepped onto the deck, rain cascaded over him and flashbulbs blinded him.

"Your weapon, sir," a voice said.

He unstrapped the Beretta and held it out. Someone took it.

"Welcome aboard the *Midway*," the voice said.

He was herded below deck with the others. His consciousness was fading again. He couldn't distinguish what he was seeing with his eyes from the kaleidoscopic images of Ben flitting through his brain. He went through some kind of processing—papers, questions, signing his name.

Now he was standing. "I need to find . . ." His voice faded in his own ears. He shook himself. Somebody with a clipboard was close to him. "Please." He forced his voice and lips to work against their will. "Please . . ."

"Sir?" a voice said.

"I need to find someone. Please. Okay?"

"I don't understand."

"Some people, goddammit." He looked around. He was in a ship's compartment. "A Vietnamese woman. Tuyet. And Thu, her son. And Colonel Troiano and Sparky Groton. Are they here?"

"Sir, we don't know who's aboard right now. We've taken on more than 3,500 evacuees."

"Got to find her." He stumbled into the passageway, looking left and right, stopped a passing sailor. "I need to find someone. She was evacuated just before me."

"Sir, she might have been taken to a different ship," the sailor said. "The whole fleet's here."

Chuck wandered until he was on a deck. Bits and snips of light flickered uncertainly over the ocean's surface like specks of moonlight, but no moon was in the sky. The deck was wet from recent rain. The ships of the fleet he could see clearly. But there, away from the ships— no, sometimes in between them—were fragments of light, some like candles, others like dying flashlights. Little boats. Thousands of them. He watched them, hypnotized. Who were they? Why were they there? He closed his eyes. He could still see them. They were swirling now. He felt himself sinking . . .

"Help me lift him," someone said far off. "Did he hit his head when he fell?"

"Don't think so. Just sort of slid down in a heap."

"Let's get him into a bunk. Grab his bag."

He felt himself being carried. He tried to protest. "Tuyet . . . where's Tuyet?"

But the men carrying him ignored him.

Lights—little flecks of them, playful, zesty—swam and fluttered and hovered and vanished. They were stars on a black sky swimming over a black ocean. Ben's little lights. They smiled as they flew about, streaked themselves into lines and circles, then merged and disappeared. He couldn't hear them, but he knew they were singing sweet songs about breathing clean air. They told him to let go. He could grieve later, but now all he had to do was rest. No more searching. She was safe. The last shred of awareness blanked out as if someone had switched off the sweet lights.

Absolute quiet. Then a deep vibration, very far away. He smelled canvas. He opened his eyes. Black. He shifted his vision and saw red—dark red, almost black. He moved his head. A red light was mounted on the bulkhead. It was quivering. He realized he was shivering. His body tightened against the cold. He focused his eyes. Stacks of hanging berths, like so many rough-hewn hammocks, some with inert forms in them. He gave full attention to his ears. Breathing. People were sleeping near him. Beneath it the low-pitched vibration.

His head throbbed. His stomach ached. His memory stirred. Tuyet. He climbed from the berth and managed to get to his feet, but it hurt. Standing unsteadily, he felt about him in the dark. His fingers told him about cold metal and canvas. He tottered past towers of berths, located an opening leading to a passageway. More red lights. The head was directly opposite. He went in, found a commode, and emptied himself. Dysentery. His watch told him it was 1015. The morning of 30 April? He returned to his berth. His getaway bag was on the deck under it. Back in the head, he opened the bag. The Ben file fell out. For the first time in days he brushed his teeth. Then into the shower. Only when warm water rolled down his back did the shaking stop. He dressed again in the same clothes, the only clothes he had. Last of all, he slid the Ben file back into his bag, left it under the berth, and headed for the upper decks.

After several false leads and stopping sailors to ask for directions, he located the flight deck. The sky to the east was brilliant with sunshine. Boats covered the ocean surface as far as he could see, some interspersed among the ships of the Seventh Fleet, others disappearing into the west. Sampans, junks, fishing vessels, commercial craft, tugs, even what looked like large rowboats, each overloaded with Vietnamese waving and calling to the ships. Two helicopters with South Vietnamese air force markings appeared out of the sky. They hovered not more than twenty feet above the water and dropped into the ocean. Their pilots swam away from them as they sank. Both were rescued and brought on board.

He headed belowdecks and meandered until he came upon the wardroom. Inside, he found an empty table and sat. Silverware, china, even a lighted votive candle. When a mess attendant brought him coffee, he asked for bacon and eggs and Kaopectate. He looked from face to face. No sign of Tuyet, Thu, Sparky, or Troiano. At other tables were Navy officers in fresh uniforms, two men in green hospital scrubs, and a collection of evacuees, American and Vietnamese, all ragged and scarred with weariness.

"You look like you came back from the dead to haunt us."

Chuck turned. Tommy Riggs stood next to him. His utilities were stained with grease and sweat, his cheeks tarred with stubble. His face was a crosshatch of fatigue. His eyes darted. "Can I sit down?" He dropped into a chair, set down his coffee mug. With his face in his hands, he asked Chuck, "How're you doin'?"

"Not too good. You?"

"Lousy."

"When did you get here?"

"I don't know." Tommy gave his head a loose shake. "Maybe three, four hours ago. Maybe more."

"Where were you?"

"Embassy."

"Jesus. How was it?"

Tommy raised his head. "It was bad, Chuck." He averted his eyes. "We had to leave a bunch behind."

"A bunch of who?"

"Vietnamese. We'd been evacuating them by chopper for more than a day. Then we got orders to clear out. We locked the doors to the stairway up to the roof, but the ones left behind guessed what we were doing and broke through. We had to use tear gas to hold them off while we got on the chopper and took off. We just flew away and left them there. More than four hundred of them." Tommy drank his coffee, his eyes looking through Chuck. His voice dropped, as if he were talking to himself. "Chi Nam was there. I got her and her kids into the embassy. Then left 'em there." He laughed shortly to himself.

Raised voices caught Chuck's attention. Against the far bulkhead, some thirty feet away, a group had gathered. Three American women, a male civilian, and two sailors were knotted together in front of a row of chairs.

"We can't get him to stop crying," one of the women said.

Through the mêlée of voices came a piping cry. The sound raised an image in Chuck's mind—a tiny child in his arms in the pool at Tu Xuong. It was Thu's voice. Chuck pushed his way through. Sitting on the middle chair, all but hidden in an Army field jacket with the name TROIANO stitched on it, was Thu, his arm in a cast and sling. Chuck lifted the miniature brown chin with his finger. "Tuffy?"

Thu's eyes widened. "Ông Chuck. Bo-di." His good arm came out of the jacket and reached for Chuck.

Chuck gathered him into his arms and hugged him close. "Yeah, it's Chuck. I'm here, buddy. Don't be afraid. It's okay now."

Thu grasped Chuck's shirt in a tight fist.

"Poor little thing," he heard one of the women say. "Scared to death."

"Have any of you seen his mother?" Chuck's eyes moved from face to face. "She's here somewhere."

"No, sir," a sailor said. "There's an Army colonel and a civilian with him. We've been watching the little guy since midnight so they both could get some sleep."

"Colonel Troiano and Sparky Groton?"

"I don't know, sir. They're bunked out around here somewhere."

"They had a Vietnamese woman with them," one of the women said. "Hair cut real short. Wearing a uniform."

"That's her," Chuck cried. "Where is she?"

The woman shrugged.

An alarm sounded in Chuck's head. Would Tuyet leave Thu in the care of strangers? He sat in the chair, put Thu on his knee, and looked into his eyes. "Thu, where is your mother?"

Thu eyed him gravely. "Chuck. *Bo-dì. À ghên.*"

"No, Thu." How could he communicate? "*Mère.*" He pointed to Thu and repeated, "*Ta mère.*"

Thu's face puckered. "*Ma mère.*" He reached inside the field jacket and pulled out a crumpled envelope.

"You made it."

Chuck looked up. Troiano and Sparky stood next to him, beaming.

"When we left," Troiano said, "we had no way of knowing if you'd get out."

Chuck handed Thu to one of the women and grasped Troiano by the shoulder. "Where's Tuyet? I've looked everywhere."

"*Mist-tah Go-rì-phân,*" a woman's voice said.

Chuck looked over his shoulder. Lan stood close by, her hands clasped beneath her chin. She wore oversized Marine utilities stripped of insignias. Her hair was cropped.

Chuck stared at her in horror. "Where's Tuyet?" He grasped Troiano by the lapels. "Where's Tuyet?"

"She's not here," Troiano said.

"What do you mean?"

"She's still in Saigon."

Chuck let go of him.

"I telephoned her," Troiano said. "Told her I'd be coming in your place. But when I got there, she wouldn't come. She sent her niece, Lan, in her place. She handed her son over the barricade. I asked her why. She said she had to stay. She said her boy had a letter for you."

The envelope was still in Thu's hand. Chuck's legs buckled. Sparky's hands caught him under one armpit, Troiano's under the other. They lowered him into the chair. Troiano sat next to him, took the envelope from Thu, and closed Chuck's fingers around it. Chuck glared at it. He tried to open it. His hands wouldn't cooperate. Troiano lifted the envelope from Chuck's grasp, opened it, and pulled out a single sheet of onionskin paper. Chuck unfolded it and read.

My most beloved Chuck,

You always forgave me the lies I told you. I have deceived you one last time. I hope you will still forgive me.

Thanh and I, we wait now. The VC will come soon. Maybe by morning. The soldiers here are very frightened. They panic. But we do not.

I wanted to be with you. I wanted to marry you and bear you a son. That was my dream, and I wanted to live my dream, but I cannot.

I am writing this because I want you to understand even if you don't forgive me. You always loved me enough to understand. Love me enough now.

Sometimes being happy is not as important as doing what is right. I know I must stay here. "No war but this," we said. My war. My people. My Thanh. My An Nam. My peace in the south.

I give you my son, Thu. He is the last of the Annamese. You take care of him for his father and mother, and you love him for us.

I weep now, hurting you again. I love you.

Tuyet

Chuck was on his feet, yelling. "I have to go back." He forced his way toward the passageway. "A helicopter—"

Troiano caught him from behind. "They've stopped flying. You can't—"

Chuck wheeled and slugged Troiano. Sparky sprang at him, pushed him against the bulkhead. Lan screamed. Sailors were all over him. They forced his arms behind his back.

Chuck's voice went raw. "She's still there. I have to . . ."

A shape in green scrubs forced its way through. A hand unsheathed a hypodermic.

"Colonel Troiano?" a distant voice said. "He's coming around. You want to come on down?" A telephone receiver being hung up. Chuck's stomach rolled, and he had a special kind of headache associated with the smell of medicinal alcohol. He opened his eyes, then slammed them shut. The light stung his eyeballs. He forced the lids open. He lay on a gurney in a compartment that was all chrome and the pale green of sickly places. The ship's engines reverberated at a great distance. He didn't want to think or know. He slid off the edge into unconsciousness.

Troiano was sitting next to him, smiling. "How do you feel?"

Chuck's brain ordered his lips to speak, but nothing happened.

"Thu's been asking for you."

The pain started in his belly and spread. He tried to weep but couldn't.

"You want some soup?"

Troiano cranked the gurney and raised Chuck to a sitting position. He pressed a mug into Chuck's hands. Chuck tried to lift it to his lips and failed. Troiano helped him. The soup tasted warm, soothing. Again Chuck tried to speak. His voice responded with gurgling noises, and his lips were out of practice. One more try.

"Wha . . . day?"

"Thursday, 1 May. Dinnertime."

Chuck shook his head. The motion hurt. "How did I . . ."

"They sedated you. Do you think you could eat something?"

An orderly brought him a hamburger patty and vegetables. Troiano helped him eat and then cranked the gurney down. "I'll see you in the morning," Troiano said. "Get some sleep."

—⊟⊔⊟⊔—

When Chuck awoke, Troiano was again by his side.

"Where's the ship heading?" Chuck asked.

"Subic Bay eventually, but we're sailing in circles for the moment. I don't know why."

A hulking Navy officer in scrubs with a stethoscope and a nametag that read COMMANDER HOLLOWAY interrupted them. He examined Chuck and asked him questions. "Take it easy for at least a week," he said afterward in a southern drawl. "You been through more than a man's supposed to."

"Tell him the diagnosis," Troiano said.

"Exhaustion, scalp lacerations, amoebic dysentery, severe shock, emotional trauma, pneumonia brought on by inadequate diet, muscle fatigue, and sleep deprivation. Chuck, if you promise to eat three full meals a day and sleep twelve hours each night, I'll release you and let you move to a berthing compartment, but . . ." Holloway handed Chuck a vial, "take these three times a day and check back with me every day until I tell you not to." He glanced at Troiano. "I think he's ready."

Troiano pulled his chair close to the gurney. "I discussed it with the commander, and we decided to tell you instead of waiting. We don't want you to get the word somewhere else."

The base of Chuck's spine tingled. He sat straight. "What?"

"Tuyet's dead, Chuck."

It was a sledgehammer to his chest.

"We found out from Liberation Radio. It's moved into Saigon— they're calling it Ho Chi Minh City now. So you'll know all of it, I'll read a translation of their broadcast from 0600 this morning."

He took a paper from his breast pocket, unfolded it, and read.

> The running dogs of the imperialists are now all either
> dead or captured. Yesterday our valiant troops seized
> the so-called Joint General Staff of the puppet army
> almost without resistance. Only one of the puppet
> officers, the infamous Colonel Pham Ngoc Thanh, the
> notorious butcher of Phat Hoa, tried to fight us. Our
> forces quickly overcame him and his wife, hiding in
> his office. Unable to face the strict justice of the people
> after we captured him, his wife produced a snub-nose
> .38 pistol, the weapon of cowards, and killed the col-
> onel and herself before our troops could stop her. Her
> treachery is typical of the running dogs . . .

Troiano took a deep breath. "It goes on, but that's the important part."

Tuyet dead. Like Molly. And Philippe, Angélique, Thanh. And Ben. He'd known it before Troiano told him.

"I'll stay with him," he heard Troiano say.

Lunch came and went. So did dinner. Chuck ate nothing.

Holloway scolded him. "You keep this up and I won't release you from sick bay."

Troiano came in at 1730. "I went to check on Thu. He's in bad shape. They can't get him to eat. He keeps saying two words, something like egg-hen or egg-end."

"Could it be 'again'?" Chuck said.

"Nobody can tell. The Vietnamese woman we asked says it's not Vietnamese. She says he keeps asking for Mister Certain."

Chuck didn't answer.

"That's you, isn't it?" Troiano said.

Chuck looked away.

"He's lost everything, Chuck."

Chuck closed his eyes.

Troiano sighed and nodded. "I'm getting claustrophobia. Sick-rooms give me the willies. Are you ready to go out for a walk?"

"No."

"Do it anyway. You have to start living again."

"No."

Troiano stood. "Come on, Chuck, on your feet."

Chuck got up, washed his face, and let Troiano lead him to the flight deck. They walked slowly in the horizontal rays of the setting sun. The Vietnamese boats were fewer. The smallest ones had disappeared. All the boats, even the largest, were gradually falling behind, unable to keep up with the ship.

"Refugees?" Chuck said.

Troiano nodded. "Thousands of them. Trying to escape the North Vietnamese."

"Why don't we take them aboard?"

"Every ship of the fleet is already overloaded. We've taken on as many as we can."

Chuck watched the boats. "What will happen to them?"

"They'll have to sail back."

"They're too far out. They won't make it."

Troiano shook his head and sat on a bench facing west into the fading light. He motioned to Chuck to join him. Chuck remembered gazing through the open window of Thanh's office at the dying sun. He asked himself again, as he had at the beginning, *do all memories have to hurt?*

His eyes came to rest on the row of benches facing them. Evacuees sat talking, watching the sun and sea, laughing occasionally. Out of place was an olive drab object huddled at the feet of one of the women. An Army field jacket. It was moving.

"Colonel," Chuck said, "is that Thu?"

Troiano nodded.

The jacket weaved and shuddered.

"He keeps asking for you," Troiano said.

"It hurts too much."

"Do what you have to do," Troiano said. "Whatever it takes."

He couldn't do it. It was too much. But he *had* to. Against his will, Chuck stood. He walked to the benches and knelt beside the field jacket. "Tuffy?"

The hood of the jacket fell back. Thu's face turned to him. The eyes were Tuyet's, but the face was Thanh's.

"Chuck?" Thu said. "*À ghên? Bo-dì?*"

"Buddy." Chuck swept Thu into his arms.

Thu contoured himself against Chuck's chest. Chuck pulled him close. He felt his heart breaking. His tears dripped from his chin and wet Thu's hair.

AUTHOR'S NOTE

I wrote *Last of the Annamese* to find peace. I returned from Vietnam in May 1975 an emotional wreck after living through the fall of Saigon and escaping under fire after the North Vietnamese were already in the streets of the city. I had pneumonia and ear damage (caused by the shelling of Tan Son Nhat, where I was trapped) and suffered all the symptoms of post-traumatic stress injury—flashbacks, nightmares, irrational rage, panic attacks. Because I held top secret code-word-plus clearances, I couldn't seek psychological help; I'd have lost my job. So I turned to helping others and to writing. The result was a series of stories about Vietnam and my novels, *Friendly Casualties* and *The Trion Syndrome*. But there was more to get off my chest. I needed to tell of the horrors of the final collapse; hence *Last of the Annamese.*

I was in Vietnam on and off for thirteen years. Most of that time I provided covert intelligence support to Army and Marine combat units throughout Vietnam. My cover was as a soldier or Marine in the unit I was working with so that the enemy wouldn't realize there was a spy in their midst. But unlike my protagonist, Chuck Griffin, I was a civilian employee of the National Security Agency.

In *Annamese* and elsewhere I have tried to report accurately the historical events when and where they occurred. Declassifications over the years, and particularly in 2015, allow me to recount in this book some events I could previously not speak of. But the characters in the novel are fictional. Granted, some bear a resemblance to their real-life counterparts. Faithfulness to reporting events as they actually happened required that my characters sometimes duplicated the actions of real people, including myself, during the fall.

Last of the Annamese had its origin in a short story I wrote after returning to the United States from Bien Hoa in 1968. The story, called "Trip Wires," is one of many in my novel-in-stories, *Friendly Casualties*. It tells how Ben Griffin actually died. As a father myself, I cringed at the prospect of learning someday that my son had died while serving in the military. I imagined what I would have done in Ben's father's place. That gave rise to *Last of the Annamese*.

I have found an imperfect peace thanks to my writing and public speaking about Vietnam and my volunteer work with the homeless and the dying. But as another Vietnam veteran explained to me, memories of war never fade. My job is to come to terms with them, to learn to live with them, to channel my despair into my writing and my work to help others, not into my living. I've learned that compassion heals. Maybe in the process of telling Vietnam stories I can express for others what they cannot express for themselves. Maybe I help them to heal, too.

GLOSSARY OF ACRONYMS AND SLANG

Alamo Code name for the Special Planning Group, the innocuous title given to an ad hoc unit set up within DAO to act as the forward command post and coordinator for Operation Frequent Wind, the evacuation of U.S. personnel and foreign nationals from Vietnam at the end of the Vietnam War

amah A nanny

APO Army/Air Force Post Office. An APO address designates a unit that will receive U.S. mail for personnel assigned to that unit.

ARS American Radio Service, a broadcast service of the U.S. government

arty Military slang for "artillery"

ARVN Army of the Republic of Vietnam (South Vietnam)

ASAP As soon as possible

ASAP if not sooner In short order, immediately

bulkhead Marine and Navy term for "wall"

blue-and-white A Saigon taxi, usually a small Renault, always painted blue and white

CINCPAC Commander in Chief, Pacific, the U.S. joint military command responsible for all military operations in the Pacific and Far East

CONUS Continental United States

cyclo Pronounced *see-clo,* a pedicab. The term came from the French slang *cyclo* and was adapted into Vietnamese as *xích lô.* A motorized cyclo (*xích lô máy*) has the pedals and bicycle chain replaced with a small gasoline engine.

DAO Defense Attaché Office, subordinate to the U.S. embassy in Saigon. DAO replaced the Military Assistance Command, Vietnam

(MACV) and was housed in "Pentagon East," the large building that had served as MACV headquarters, located within the military base at Tan Son Nhat airport on the northern edge of Saigon.

deck Marine and Navy term for "floor"

DEROS Date eligible for return from overseas—the last day of an assignment outside CONUS; sometimes used interchangeably with PCOD

ETD Estimated time of departure

Frequent Wind Code name for the evacuation of U.S. personnel and foreign nationals at the end of the Vietnam War

gunji A term used by the military to refer only to Marines. As an adjective, it means "tough and ferocious." As a noun, it mean "Marine," especially one good in combat.

gyrene Slang for "Marine"; a portmanteau composed of "GI" and "Marine."

Intel Branch The Intelligence Branch of DAO, which replaced J2 MACV as the principal intelligence organ of the U.S. government in Vietnam after the 1973 cease-fire. Its mission was to assemble, analyze, and report all-source intelligence findings to CINCPAC and Washington.

jarhead Literally, a mule; slang term for "Marine"

JCS Joint Chiefs of Staff, the supreme command of the U.S. military, headquartered in the Pentagon

JGS Joint General Staff, the Republic of Vietnam (South Vietnam) senior military command, located adjacent to the U.S. military base at Tan Son Nhat

KIA Killed in action

Montagnard The tribes ethnically distinct from the Vietnamese that live in the Vietnam highlands along the Laotian and Cambodian borders

mustang An officer promoted from the enlisted ranks, usually as a result of a battlefield commission

mufti Civilian clothes

Noforn Classification meaning "Not Releasable to Foreign Nationals," a caveat that restricts information distribution to U.S. officials only

nonlinear Adjective used by U.S. intelligence personnel meaning "irrational"

Nung A Montagnard tribe characterized by fierceness, kinked hair, and brawny physiognomy

NVA Acronym for North Vietnamese Army, a term used by U.S. personnel. The North Vietnamese called their military force the People's Army of Vietnam, abbreviated as PAVN.

Pacific Command Same as CINCPAC

PCOD Pussy cutoff date, used by the military to mean the date of departure. *See DEROS.*

RA all the way RA in a soldier's serial number stands for Regular Army, indicating that the soldier was not drafted but enlisted. "RA all the way" means gung-ho, extremely devoted. The term is applied only to Army personnel.

real world The United States

RVNAF Republic of Vietnam (South Vietnam) Armed Forces

slick A small, unarmed helicopter

snuff A young Marine

SPG Special Planning Group, the forward command post and coordinator for Frequent Wind

splib A black Marine

TAD Temporary additional duty, a term applied to a trip or mission of short duration as opposed to a permanent assignment

Tet The Vietnamese lunar new year. In 1975 it was celebrated on 11 February.

twix A message sent by electronic means

VC Viet Cong, Vietnamese for "Vietnamese Communist." Often used by U.S. personnel to refer to indigenous communist forces in South

Vietnam or to designate local forces as opposed to regular forces (NVA), a distinction not used by the Vietnamese. The VC and the NVA were interchangeable, both commanded by Hanoi.

Viet Minh The name by which the Vietnamese Communists were known during the French Indochina War. Viet Minh is an abbreviation for Viet Nam Doc Lap Dong Minh Hoi, or League for the Independence of Vietnam.

VIP Very important person, usually a visitor

world The United States

ABOUT THE AUTHOR

Tom Glenn's prize-winning seventeen short stories and four novels draw from his experiences during the thirteen years he shuttled between the United States and Vietnam on covert intelligence assignments before escaping under fire when Saigon fell. Comfortable in Vietnamese, Chinese, and French, he writes and speaks frequently on war and Vietnam.